MAKING A STO

Making a Stone of the Heart

A NOVEL

Cynthia Flood

KEY PORTER BOOKS

National Library of Canada Cataloguing in Publication Data

Flood, Cynthia, 1940-
    Making a stone of the heart

ISBN 1-55263-452-3

    I. Title.

PS8561.L64M33 2002   C813'.54   C2002-900066-1
PR9199.3.F5642M33 2002

The Canada Council | Le Conseil des Arts
for the arts | du Canada
since 1957 | depuis 1957

ONTARIO ARTS COUNCIL
CONSEIL DES ARTS DE L'ONTARIO

The publisher gratefully acknowledges the support of the Canada Council for
the Arts and the Ontario Arts Council for its publishing activities.

We acknowledge the financial support of the Government of Canada through
the Book Publishing Industry Development Program (BPIDP) for our publishing
activities.

Key Porter Books Limited
70 The Esplanade
Toronto, Ontario
Canada   M5E 1R2
www.keyporter.com

Design: Peter Maher
Electronic Formatting: Heidi Palfrey

"Who" by J. Kern/O. Harbach/O. Hammerstein III, Universal-Polygram
International Publishing, Inc. (ASCAP) 100%.

Printed and bound in Canada

02 03 04 05 06 07 6 5 4 3 2 1

To SDM
with gratitude

Contents

Too long a sacrifice
Can make a stone of the heart.
W. B. YEATS, "EASTER 1916"

Departures and Arrivals

O W E N

July 1997—Owen, Looking at the River

After Thursday 14 March 1996, Owen Jones speaks no word. Although the staff of the Bella Coola Valley Long Term Care Facility dutifully attempt geriatric counselling and speech therapy, in time and with gratitude they understand that the old curmudgeon has shut up.

On that March 14 Cheryl Preston comes to the Home, as she does regularly to get her Work Experience credits so she can graduate from Sir Alexander Mackenzie Senior Secondary; she reads aloud to non-bedriddens who still have their wits about them. These include Great-Uncle Owen. Cheryl hates him, also Bella Coola and all her fellow students who think driving drunk to Williams Lake is cool.

The old man won't wear his dentures or his hearing aid, and because for decades he's cupped his hand round his right ear it sticks forward. Like Popeye's, his bristly chin shoves out. Bloodshot gummy eyes squint under hairy brows. Unpredictable as a snake's, his tongue spits out *goddam fuckn asshole jerkface* and *piss ass sissy* and *fuckn suckn pricky dicky cocksucker*, on and on until Indian Tom yells at him, or an orderly wheels him away. Only with the stray cats that hang about the Home's kitchen is Owen gentle. When on warm days the residents sit out on the terrace, the animals always find his lap.

Cheryl starts on the *Coast Mountain News*, reads letters, obits, reading on through the residents' steady commentary and reactions.

What kind of goddamn fool couldn't make a go of good land?

And what the hell do you know about it?

Well, that's a mercy after what she suffered, with the chemo and then her girl gone, way down in Vancouver. Those drugs....

Him and me started out together. I was there when he lost his fingers. That's right. On the same crew.

She's just saying that 'cause her son's on the School Board. It don't amount to anything.

Cheryl reads from *TV Guide*, the soaps and the stars' divorce settlements and contract battles, and the *Province* sports and "Dear Abby" and "Rex Morgan" and the weather.

Will it never stop raining?

Winter innit, asshole?

That isn't what the Weather Channel said.

Almost spring, I'd say. Equinox the twenty-first.

La-di-da fuckn Equinox is it then?

Some residents subscribe to papers from their past lives elsewhere—*Times-Colonist, Daily Townsman, Alaska Highway Daily News, Kelowna Courier*. Everyone enjoys Cheryl's reading of these obits; she picks out people with funny names or of great age.

From the *Gulf Islands Driftwood* she reads, "Bracegirdle, Alice (Morgan). Born 1900."

Imagine that for a name! Laughingstock you'd be.

It's Welsh. Welsh wish wash walsh splash splish dish dash. Same as me, Owen Jones, that's how I know ho ho.

Shut up, Owen.

Shut up yourself, Tom.

Born 1900—well, she had a good run!

"Dearest mother of Alison Barrett (Dale) of New Westminster and Henry (Joon-Mi) of Ganges."

Now that's nice, mother and daughter, Alice and Alison.

No one calls a boy Henry now. You never hear that name.

Married a stinkn Chink, did he?

"Loving grandmother of Marilyn, Brenda, David, Mark; dear great-grandmother of Jason, Deborah, Joshua, Caleb, Kristy, Byron, Shannon, Chelsea."

Why do they call children after places, now?

Been reading the bloody Bible if you ask me.

Nobody did, Owen.

Nobody asked you for your Jesus-loving opinion, Tom.

"Funeral at 11 a.m."

A good time. You can serve a nice buffet lunch, after.

Except you'd be dead! Ha ha, you're dead in the head, bonehead, already dead.

"Donations to...."

Don't catch me giving money where people tell me. I'll do what I bloody well choose. Don't you forget that, you, Cheryl!

Don't interrupt her!

Be surprised if you'd got a penny to your name, Owen Jones.

S'lot about me'd surprise you, Indian Tom. Anyways I didn't live all my life off the feds like some people. And I never had no cushy union job either, to sit on my fat white pension on my fat white ass like a lot of other people in this place.

Owen, you never worked a minute there wasn't someone keeping after you with a whip. Never. King of the freeloaders, you were.

You two! Keep quiet and let the girl read!

Shove a candy in Owen's mouth. That'll shut him up.

Indian Tom gets up and leaves the reading area, walking with a heavy, offended gait.

Cheryl picks up the *Province* again. "A really old one here too...where is she...here. 'Dow, Dora (Cowan). Born 25 August 1900 in Vancouver, died 6 March 1996 in the Vancouver Hospital.'"

Just two days older'n my sister that died last year!

Joo say Dora? Dora Dow?

The Vancouver General it always was. Why don't they call it the General any more?

"Dear wife of the late Edward Dow."

There's another name you never hear nowadays. Eddy—there were always Eddies and Neddies, at school.

Dora Dow? That's the name?

"Dear mother of John (Joyce), Mary (William Cornish), and predeceased by Carole in 1934. Grandmother of six, great-grandmother of thirteen."

Oh, that's sad, a daughter dead. What, I wonder?

John, Mary. Plain jane names, eh?

"Service at 1 p.m., Monday 12 March 1996, at St. David's, Kamloops at Franklin. Interment to follow in Mountain View Cemetery. No flowers."

Doesn't anybody like to get flowers, these days? Funeral bouquets—lovely, they used to be. Arum lilies.

Read those goddamn kids' names again. Fuckn read 'em I said!

With sarcastic clarity, Cheryl reads, "Johnnnnn. Mare-eee. And Carole—she died in 1934." She glares at Owen. "Dora Dow was Dora Cowan. Then Dora Cowan married Edward Dow. Dora had John. Dora had Mary. Dora had Carole. Who died in 1934. Got it?"

The goddamn bitch.

Friend of yours, Owen?

From the old days?

Ladyfriend, Owen?

The bitch. Fuckn bitch. Shit. Goddamn. Goddamn.

Mister Owen Jones! Some of us get awfully tired of your profanity, don't we, girls?

Don't you know any other words?

"Shall I read it again, Uncle Owen? About Dora Cowan and Edward Dow and John and Mary and Carole?"

Shuddup. That bitch. Owen puts his hands up to his head and boxes his own ears. *I beat her though! She's dead before me. I got nothin' more to say.* He lowers his fists.

On Owen's small old face, a red blotching spreads. His bulging plaid shirt heaves. His hands leave his wheelchair's armrests and clamp each other. He turns his head away. Through the streaming plate-glass windows of the lounge and across the terrace to the grey rush of the Bella Coola River, he stares.

Eventually Cheryl slings on her black leather jacket and goes home for lunch. Chowder and crusty homemade bread. Again.

Elizabeth Preston sees her daughter's red eyes. "What?"

Cheryl tells. "And then he wouldn't say a word, Mum. Everyone tried. Nothing. I got Indian Tom to come back—not even to him."

"*Dora*. Over the years Owen's said *Dora* sometimes. When he's very drunk." Mrs. Preston makes a face. "Your dad and I, we've talked about it. Prayed for Owen. So old, so alone. So angry. And he's made such a mess of his life."

Back at school, Cheryl goes to what is termed the library—as if, she thinks, as if a real library could exist in this dump of a town where everyone searches the Internet for porn and Nazis and paintings of the Virgin Mary that weep gelatin tears.

For a Lit Twelve assignment on connotation, she is *doing* the Venus of Willendorf—a stone sculpture of the kind termed *an upper palaeolithic human figurine* by the *Shorter Oxford*. Cheryl loathes the Venus. *Fat little slob. Those awful V-breasts hanging down, pointing down. Stone bag. Hag of stone.* She turns pages, makes notes. *Fatties.* Not once does it occur to Cheryl that real women she's known all her life, white and Nuxalk alike, who sing in the choir with her mother and work at the grocery and in the local motels and for DFO and Parks and on the fishboats, stand as sisters to that antique shape. *Stone cellulite. Horrible.* Surreptitiously, Cheryl feels her own sleek thighs. *Stone women. Pears. Turnips. With stone babies inside, ugh.* She guts the reference books and then goes on-line, collecting enough material to ensure another A, another kilometre on the Cheryl Preston construction project: her own Road, one-way, out of the Bella Coola Valley.

At the Home, Owen says nothing.

Cat got your tongue?

It's certainly nice not to have to hear all that swearing, isn't it, girls?

D'you suppose he'll ever say anything again?

Only a few days into Owen's long silence, Indian Tom comes looking for him, flapping a newspaper. "One of them babies, Owen, right down there in Vancouver! They did an autopsy and *took it out.* Sixty years inside her. Sixty!" Owen stares at the river. "A stone child, they call it." Indian Tom takes off his glasses and prepares to read. "Now, *listen,* Owen. This woman, she had three kids. This stone child, it'd have been the fourth. 'Her son'—now he'd be getting up there himself, eh? In his sixties anyway. An *old* son, Owen!— 'Her son told the doctors that she had become pregnant at the age of thirty-two, developed abdominal pain and then recovered. Her menstrual periods resumed.' How's about that, Owen? Bleeding still!"

Owen turns his wheelchair so his back is towards Indian Tom.

"Hey, now, not so fast!" Indian Tom goes round the chair, squats (which hurts his knees horribly) so as to be on Owen's level, and tries to make eye contact. "You *like* this stuff, remember? All these years you've wanted one of these things? Well, *listen.* 'A large abdominal mass.' For sixty years, inside her, Owen. She had to know it was there, right? She *kept* it! Don't you want to read about your litho, lithopede, whatever? It's *here,* Owen." Tom crackles the newspaper at his friend, who snatches it and throws the *Province* clean across the room.

Tom gets up and limps away.

For his arthritis Owen now swallows his aspirin dry, and if his stomach complains no one knows. For days he refuses to eat.

Meanwhile Indian Tom checks the Vancouver papers for any follow-up on that story, hoping to try again to interest Owen, but the press's attention is seduced by another Sasquatch sighting in Oregon.

The staff, seeing that Owen's withdrawn and self-harming behaviour is not whimsical, hold meetings and strategize. All their designs fail. By September, his malnourishment is obvious.

Then the young locum attending at the Home grabs hold of the old man's collar as he sits motionless in the dining room, yanks him up out of his wheelchair, and shakes him so hard a button bursts off Owen's shirt. "You old *idiot!*" the doctor shouts in his whiskery face. "You're not dying on me, you hear? You know what force feeding is? Don't think I won't do it, 'cause I will!" She drops him.

Perhaps something Owen recognizes shines in Dr. Kimberley Kineson's exasperated eyes, for when he gets his breath back he silently takes up his spoon.

In October Tom brings another clipping, datelined Rio de Janeiro: *Fetus removed after 22 years.* "They call it a mummy, Owen—a mummy in a mum! Betcha you'd have liked that for your show, eh? Eh?" Owen stares. His fingers do not move to take the square of newsprint.

Now the staff note that Owen sits still always and never tries to get up and use his walker. His hands are often still, though formerly he'd flexed his fingers constantly and squeezed his plastic ball. When a cat jumps on his lap now, Owen strokes it briefly and then just holds the purring animal to him.

"It's like he wants to *stop*," says an orderly, standing right next to Owen and speaking in his normal voice.

"And not to move," agrees a nurse. "Turning to stone."

Indian Tom tries one more time, with a clipping headlined *Baby that grew outside uterus born healthy*. "Look, Owen!" Tom glares and reads aloud. "From Montreal. The doc said, 'One of these miracles.' The mum said, 'I would have to call it a strange thing.' Strange! And how! Eh, Owen? Eh? Eh?" Owen will not touch the clipping. Indian Tom leans back with an exhausted sigh.

Dr. Kimberley Kineson, attending the high school's production of *Grease*, chats with Elaine Gold, the school's librarian. They start with the dearth of datable men in Bella Coola but soon are theorizing that small, isolated places produce more eccentrics than cities do. Simultaneously the women ask each other, "Do you know Owen Jones?"

"He's so *tough!*" exclaims the doctor. "He's wretched, he hates to be alive—but the old buzzard just won't give us the satisfaction of taking his own life. He could let the brakes go and roll into the river, easy, but no. He's sticking it out, but not *here* with us. In his head. Of course he won't tell."

"You're still at the fascination stage," says Elaine. "Libraries always attract weirdos, but he's truly disgusting. Obsessed with the grotesque, Mr. Jones." She gives details.

Next day in her borrowed office Kimberley searches the Internet for *lithopedion*, one of Elaine's details. "Weird," she mutters, "weirder, weirdest." An archaeological dig in

Texas has produced, from a burial site, six vertebrae and an ilium of a 3,100-year-old specimen. The article, titled "The Autopsy of Time," is illustrated. She stares at the photos. Logging off, Kimberley looks out the window to contemplate the forested mountains and old earth.

When Dr. Grainger returns to the coastal rains from his Mexican holiday and hears how *that woman doctor you hired* shook Owen up, he watches Mr. Jones. Doctoring up and down the Coast for decades, Dr. Grainger has seen many working men wear out their bodies. Logging, fishing, breaking trail, mining, trucking, building—these jobs exhaust unreplenishable reserves in the flesh. Instead of getting old, such men simply "lose interest in the whole proposition," as Grainger puts it, the way dying animals do. Yet in Owen's hunched body and his refusal to make eye contact the doctor sees more than life-fatigue.

"His heart's broken, I think," old Dr. Grainger tells the staff, finally. "Let him be." They still see to it, though, that Owen gets his aspirin, and from time to time they massage his hands with oil or fetch him a frolicking kitten.

Stiffer and stiffer, silent as an idol, Owen gets pushed about from dining room to day room, TV to sing-song, program to program, participating in none. Is he even watching?

Cat still got your tongue, eh, Owen?

I never thought I'd miss his yammer yammer.

No, never thought I'd see the day.

When Owen is alone for any length of time or has his wheelchair placed so that his back is to the group, tears fall steadily down the wrinkled channels of his cheeks. He uses no tissues. Irritated by the salt, his skin develops two reddish trails. Sometimes one of the staff, passing, mops at the old man's face or wipes his nose. In the mornings the side of Owen's head is wet, and his pillowcase.

"Does his noise at night bother you, Indian Tom?"

"Owen don't bother me. He don't bother me at all. He never did."

One of the LPNs puts his pillow to dry by the heating element each day. Owen takes in less and less food, although he sits calmly at table and drinks the water poured for him.

When Indian Tom dies just after New Year's in 1997, an orderly and an LPN empty the locker by his bedside and set out his few things for the family to take. Laboriously Owen Jones wheels himself into the ward, to watch. In the heap on Tom's bed lies a leather wallet, much worn, with a braided trim. The orderly flips it open. "Nada." The LPN ticks her checklist.

A movement makes the two look round to see Owen's face breaking up in silent laughter. All his wrinkles fold themselves into new folds while his toothless mouth opens to its widest possible. Bending over in his chair, he slaps his hands on to his face and then leans back again. Back and forth, back and forth, the gums huge behind the distorted knobby fingers....

Crazy, he is.

First foul-mouthed and now nuts.

In 1997, Canada Day on the mid-Coast is hot, thundery. The Home staff are run off their feet getting the residents out onto the terrace for fireworks and cake and opalescent apple juice, but soon lightning zigs across the sky and they have to herd everyone inside again. The cats skitter off. In the lounge the orderly finds Owen Jones alone, in his wheelchair, warm but dead.

⊰⌘⊱

To clean Uncle Owen's cabin, Elizabeth Preston takes a shovel, rubber gloves, disinfectants, bags, newspapers.

Planks, laid on brackets attached to the studs, hold the old man's "show." Elizabeth tips each shelf so everything slides down onto piled newspapers—those stupid lumps of stone with other stones stuck inside them, the pathetic things Uncle Owen called *fossils*, the boxes and bottles with their nasty contents all crunching or splintering or sloshing. Wrapped in thick newsprint, this conglomerate gets stuffed in trash bags.

One bottle holds a paper. Uncle Owen's holograph will, in greasy ballpoint, leaves to Cheryl Preston "all I have, but she has to finish university first."

Mrs. Preston works till the cabin is bare. Uncle Owen's coffee pot with the black insides, his oil lamps and sticky propane stove, his *Amazing Facts* and *Ripley's*, his drawersful of photocopied magazine articles, his dreadful pisspot— she throws them all in the back of the pickup and slams the tailgate shut. The keys she drops in the farmhouse mailbox, though no one there cares any more, for the farmer is dead and his widow too sad and fat to bother with any tenant's leavings.

First to the dump, then the Credit Union.

⊰⌘⊱

I'd never have dreamed I'd miss him.

What a character.

Remember how Owen put words together? Those lists, like? God, he could be funny.

It's not everyone can do that.

In October the high school students as usual visit the Home with their tape recorders; because so many old folks die off in winter, the Social Studies teachers like the kids to finish their oral history projects before Christmas.

You didn't know him? Well, you missed something.

Sure did. What a tongue on that man.

Although some male residents can recite verbatim Owen's word-chains, they are of a generation that does not use offensive or obscene language in front of schoolgirls. They look away from the bewildered students, look through the streaming lounge windows at the grey river with its snowy banks, and snort with laughter.

16 September 1902—A Dream of the Princeton Hotel

Lying on the grass outside the old livery stable, David Jones figured he could go downtown and be set up by nightfall: check the notice boards, have a drink along Cordova, Carrall, Pender, Hastings, meet informed people till a job appeared—some donkey operation seeking end-of-season help to get the logs off.

Once signed on, he'd step over to the Union Steamships and book himself on to the *Cassiar*—tonight! So soon? Well. Perhaps Thursday. At the stern he'd stand, his heart thudding with the engine as Vancouver's lights sparkled against the big blackness and dwindled while the *Cassiar* chugged up the Coast.

There, up the coast, the September air would be resonant of sawn wood and hot metal; it hummed with insects.

Sunlight swirled with sawdust, glittered off resin and off dewdrops on the spider webs strung everywhere. Sun slid down the towers of green. Green, green, sun, green.... Back in a grey Welsh colliery town spread like a crust above the mines, David's father and uncles and brothers spent their dark days.

Up the Coast, David's body would ache from working, a good ache as his twenty-year-old limbs rediscovered their skills. At the camp's cookstove his tin plate would be heaped with beans, stew, cornbread. Always someone on the crew had a banjo or an accordion or, like David, a fine tenor voice for "Oh, Susannah" and "Vancouver Town" and "On the Banks of the Wabash" and "At Britain's Side Whate'er Betide." The men sang for hours without ever the same song twice.

Likely he'd have six weeks, before the rains. Then David could winter in Victoria; palm trees and cactus grew there, some said, though Ellen laughed scornfully. Surely in that mild climate he'd avoid his usual crushing chest colds?

And ... standing "at Britain's side" was all very well, but this country was only the top of North America. South lay Seattle, Portland, San Francisco. Beyond even that avatar glowed Mexico. No colds there! *Aztec*, a man said in a bar. Gold lumps tumbled along the streets, pearls too, some said. Ellen got angry. *Latin America, Latin America.* Smiling at the cadence, David closed his eyes. Another ugly cry came from the loft of the livery stable. He sat up and swore.

How much longer must he endure this? Except for the noise of birth above him, the lane was quiet. The traffic on Powell was a block away, while on Alexander the American

Can punch press sang a muted song. Yet even by thinking *Mexico Mexico Mexico*, he couldn't shut out Ellen's friend Patricia chatting up there with the midwife (bad), the clink and splash of a tin basin (worse), and these awful groans of Ellen's (worst).

This morning when she grimaced in pain, Ellen's eyes had bulged like a gargoyle's on the church at home. *Ugly as her belly.* For months now David had feared she'd split open. She told him to touch it. Finally he got drunk enough. A hard drum with a goblin inside, her belly was. *Names*—she wanted to talk about names for the thing! "David, listen! You'll have a *son*. Do you like the name Owen?" Ellen's breasts seeped. They got dark and ugly. "Or Rhys, or Evan? Dylan? Ivor? Don't you care?"

Another cry sounded. David cursed his empty pockets. Yes, he'd learned from personal experience all the lyrics to "The City of Sighs and Tears"... but after this new job he would get when he went downtown, very soon, later today probably, everything would be completely different. Six weeks' work, well paid! No, David Jones would not again get blown away by bars, sporting houses, vaudeville, burlesque, slots, punchboards.

Those sounds...he could escape them by walking over to the Princeton Hotel. Someone would stand him a drink. But if the baby came while he was gone? Rages like Ellen's David had not witnessed since Wales, at home with his mother. Ellen even resembled Mum—big eyes, slight frame, little gripping hands.

Why this baby, anyway? It was beyond him. He had always gone off outside Ellen, even the first frenzied time.

Pulling out, his brothers and father and uncles always declared, was the way to stay clear of a baby or anything like that. Might Ellen have been with someone else? She'd jumped into bed with him quick enough—but when David hinted a doubt, Ellen's nails nearly tore off his earlobe. For days he couldn't hear a thing.

I will marry you, Ellen—how on earth did she get him to say that? David couldn't get the history straight. Tiny Ellen stood beside him in the bar, the smell of her red hair filling his nostrils. There was fighting there, too, but mostly all the world was singing in the New Year with "Men of Harlech" and "The Maple Leaf Forever" and "The British Grenadiers" and "The Dominion Song" and "God Save the Queen." The roll of money in David's pocket shrank and shrank into the dawn of 1902. *I will marry you.* The words rose in his throat like a song, up into the air.

But he hadn't had enough women to get married! The girl back in Wales did not count; she and David weren't naked or in bed. Nor did the girl working the docks in Montreal or those in Vancouver's sporting houses, because he paid for them. So really Ellen was his first. Not nearly enough! He'd married her, yes, so she'd have no shame, but surely she couldn't expect him to *stay* with her? What could he do for a baby? Disgusting. Early that morning, egg-white had dribbled down Ellen's legs. *My good summer shoes, they're ruined!* Now this once-lovely girl grunted like a team hauling up a steep grade.

The afternoon was turning to the dark gold syrupy look of summer's slide to autumn. By the stable door, asters and goldenrod and sharp-smelling tansy bloomed.

At the Princeton Hotel, so close, David could drink and borrow. Then, responsibly, he would come back to the loft and see—*it*. And then off! Yes, best defer the job hunt. Wednesday lay clear before him; before noon, only the few sober would be downtown at business. He'd have a job then and the *Cassiar* ticket in hand. Tonight and Wednesday night were therefore free. Twice, he could wake up in a strange bed in a room with an unknown view! Right now some woman stood dusting her nakedness with sweet talc. For him, though she didn't know that yet. The puff patted the tuft between her legs. David groaned. He loved to be beneath, to lie back with his eyes full of breasts, his willy upright in ecstasy and his face stroked by long fragrant hair.

Laughing, he rolled up his jacket under his head. The tweed felt soft. He bent his legs and tucked his hands between his thighs. A few ants still bustled about, their thoraxes shining like blackberry nodules. On the hard-packed earth, they heaved themselves over twigs. David smiled at their toil and slept.

Dora

7 March 1996—Dora, Undergoing the Autopsy of Time
Dr. Randhawa lifts off the covering.

She sees an old white woman, one day dead. Dora Cowan Dow.

On throat and arms the skin is coarse, tanned; like the discarded sheath of a snake, it's cross-hatched. The fingers are bare.

Dr. Randhawa lifts the covering further.

Down the sides of the chest hang the breasts. The draping effect is accentuated by the body block that raises the old torso. The nipples are blurred, soft-looking.

Pale as yogurt, the rounded belly with the peculiar hardness all down its centre is sprinkled with a nutmeg of moles.

Sun, rain: past childhood, that belly-skin hardly ever felt either golden warmth or falling water. In the green bower, though, among tangled blackberry and salal and on the grass circles flattened by the sleeping deer, sun and shadow flickered over that skin.

What else has touched it?

Thousands of times, rays from bedside lamp, bathroom bulb.

Very few hands besides her own.

Drawers knickers bloomers teddies combinations underpants panties briefs covered that pale smoothness. And petticoats girdles garter-belts slips half-slips bras camisoles. Cotton cotton cotton. Flannelette rayon nylon spandex polyester. Once or twice, embroidered lacy silk. Light pink bright pink white white white black yellow blue peach, and, from granddaughter Tessa, Day-Glo orange. Flowered checked striped polka-dotted. Held on held in held up through nine decades by drawstrings buttons dome-fasteners hooks-and-eyes yards and yards of elastic that gradually puckered and loosened and *went*.

Hundreds of times that underwear soaked up the whitish exudations leading up to each month's release and then the first trickles of menstrual blood. Underwear accepted sweat, urine, feces, semen, the liquid stains of sexual arousal and vaginal infections, of pregnancies and childbirths and mid-month breakthrough bleeding, of menopause, of female great old age.

Boiled and bleached and torn into squares, cotton underwear eventually swabbed tubs and drains and floors and cupboards, soaked up spilled brine and pork fat and jam. (For shame's sake, though, some pairs never saw such use but got rolled up tightly at the bottom of the waste-pail where no one could ever ever see their terrible stains. Direct to the dump, they went.)

And over that supple field of Dora's skin spread more than ninety years of creams ointments scents oils lanolines glycerines milks lotions washes gels foams salves salts soaps.

Now, in the autopsy room at the Vancouver Hospital, Dr. Randhawa observes that from the right upper abdomen down to the pelvis, the inert white flesh mounds up. Not obesity, this, although a looseness in the old flesh suggests that earlier in life this woman may have been *a little on the plump side*, Dr. Randhawa thinks.

Carefully the doctor weighs and measures, presses hard with her thin fingers all over the mound. Dr. Randhawa marks up her printed diagram. She writes at length on her checklist; she turns the page over, to write more. Her expression is concentrated.

In the fluorescence of the autopsy room where light bounces off metal trays, the porcelain table, the doctor's instruments, the old woman's stretch marks glint like silver stitching.

Brought to the hospital by her elderly son, John Dow, this aged patient was, according to her chart, disoriented and unintelligible. *Marasmus senilis, pneumonia.*

An old naked woman. Dr. Randhawa does not know about the patient's appearance on arrival at Emergency: a tent-dress like a green crazy-quilt, dotted with angular bright buttons, flows over fine wool trousers lined with silk.

"Tailor-made," sigh the nurses. They finger the invisible zipper and the brilliant green patches.

The patient's elderly daughter, Mary Cornish, rages at her brother. "You brought Mum here in this rig-out? She looks like the balloon in *Wizard of Oz!*"

John Dow's mouth moves soundlessly. He points at Tessa.

"I might have known it! One of your crazy designs."

"Grandma loves this outfit," sobs Mary's daughter.

"Your grandma looks like a fool. Just because you took sewing in *college*, Miss High-and-Mighty!"

Some days pass, punctuated by the simple nursing care required as all body systems in their due order shut down.

Dora dies.

With her dies Gladys Smith, in whom for decades Dora buried disguised hid covered and clothed herself. A pseudonym. Nom de plume—no, Dora wasn't a writer. A false front that was real.

Also with her dies Annette LeClerc. This girl for a few of Dora's young years met her desperate need to be unrecognizable. Dora put on Annette, buttoned her up, and wore her.

The watchers leave the hospital and drive east by north through the early-morning city to Dora's street. The air is damp and fresh, the leaves of the tall oak trees glossy. There's a smell of raw lumber; down the block, two more of the small post-war stucco houses have disappeared, and framing-in has begun on the much bigger Vancouver Specials to replace them. Dora's cottage is at the very back of her lot, tiny, almost hidden.

"An autopsy? Disgusting." In her mother's kitchen, Mary slams about, making coffee. "John, why on earth did you agree? What'll they find, cutting Mum up?" She bangs mugs on to a tray. "Nothing's done right unless I do it. You don't even know where her will is. Tessa, get some spoons. Hazel, see if that milk's sour. John, turn up the heat. This place is freezing."

Mary's husband, Bill Cornish, does it all and even finds a package of cookies. He gets everyone to sit in the living room; facing north, it is darkened by the big oaks on the street.

Red-haired Hazel Morgan sips, nibbles, puzzles in the uneasy silence of the mourning. Suddenly she catches her breath. "I bet I know where Aunty Dora's put her will!"

Mary Cornish rises, crosses the room, and slaps Hazel three times across the face. "*You're* not her daughter! She's not your *real* aunt! You can't know that!"

Hazel's nosebleed won't stop. Bill wants to take her to the drugstore, but she drives there alone and then lies down on the back seat of her car with the plastic ice pouch tucked behind her head, just under that odd bony ridge near the base of her skull. No one else in the Morgan family has that ridge.

Rain pats on the car roof, yet the day isn't dull. Time passes quietly. North over Burrard Inlet rises a pale rainbow. Hazel smiles, wiping her eyes sadly. *In the sewing machine.* She checks the tissue tucked in her nostril; less blood, now. Back at Dora's house, she will whisper *in the sewing machine* to Bill. Then in her undramatic manner she will face Mary and say, "All my life I've loved your mum, and my mum was her best friend."

In the Vancouver Hospital, the autopsy proceeds. Briskly Dr. Randhawa caps her fountain pen, sets down her papers, and swabs the torso with Providine. White flesh gets iodine-red stripes. Taking up her scalpel, the doctor makes the Y-incision; its arms curve under the breasts so the letter is actually more V-like, a giant red V. Dora's body opens up like a book.

When the doctor has read the text before her and made copious annotations, when Dora has been closed and veiled and rolled away, Dr. Randhawa calls for the stuttering son, John Dow.

Later she briefs Dora's geriatric social worker, who will need to talk to John as well. "Mr. Dow does not have a speech defect," Dr. Randhawa explains to this colleague. "It is not that simple. The man's speechless. You'll have to take hold and pull out whatever information you can about his mother. *Pull it out.*"

The social worker has a long interview with John Dow and then vomits in the women's washroom.

A few hours after the autopsy Dr. Randhawa must confer with the hospital's public relations staff, for already someone has talked to the press. *Some eager nincompoop.* At least this chatterbox has held back the name, although, as the PR man assures the doctor, that nod to privacy won't last longer than a snowball in hell if the story takes off. Certainly no one from the family, called back to the hospital to be informed, can face the media. The son's dumbstruck at the clarification of the vague strange story he once heard from his father, long ago. The grown-up grandchildren are bewildered or embarrassed, except for Tessa. She cries and smiles and says, "Grandma was never like anyone else." The daughter is furious.

The PR man and Dr. Randhawa, exuding slickness and expertise respectively, meet the press. To seem less official and more maternal, or perhaps sisterly, the doctor does not wear her white coat. On TV, the complex gold embroidery on her red sari looks spectacular. Dr. Randhawa strikes a scientific note, gentled by human interest. With authority she offers explanations and statistics, answers the gabbled questions. The conference goes well, but when it's over the doctor sighs, imagining the leads and headlines. The prurient, the crazy, the millennium fanatics, the misogynists— all, aroused by Dora's story (though with any luck they will not know her name), will hop skip jump to their phones and faxes and computers and writing paper.

Dr. Randhawa rejoins the family in the conference room. Astounding, this old daughter's rage. When she's not raving about "that hypocrite Hazel," Mary Cornish screams at her bald stoop-shouldered brother, "You knew! You knew! And Mum's will! Ridiculous. Why should Tessa get a house of her own, free?" Angrily she paces the room. She's heavy, the daughter, and though not tall she takes up space. Ramrod stiff she stands, with her fury pulsing out to suffuse the room with a poisoned heat. Staff and family alike move away from Mary Cornish.

As Dr. Randhawa fills a paper cup with ice water in hopes of assisting Mrs. Cornish to calm herself even a little, she says to a nurse, "She is beside herself." *A curious phrase, that. Hysteria, hysterical. Unreasonable, neurotic. An impossible woman! Imagine having to endure such a child. To carry her weight in your life. For so long.*

1900—A Difficult Tenant

Mrs. Findlay, a boarding-house keeper, aimed to progress from boarders to tenants: to be a landlady.

Soon Vancouver's streetcars would leap east again, to the city limits. Cambridge, Oxford—such street names would attract English immigrants, but to get a double lot for under two hundred, she must buy soon. Build on one half, rent, and save to build on the other: that was Mrs. Findlay's plan. Eventually she'd sell her boarding-house and retire to the slopes above Wall Street, by then a fine neighbourhood.

At present, though, her reality was 850 Powell and a pair of prospective tenants on the doorstep: Charlie and Betty Cowan.

Through many years as a boarding-house keeper in Toronto and Vancouver, Mrs. Findlay had learned to see immigrants as coming in three varieties.

No-goods tippy-toed down her dawn-dark steps before the milkman's horse was heard, with *her* rent money in their pockets, or walked out at noon with valuables under winter coats. Mrs. Findlay learned. Now she rarely got stiffed. She took no boarder darker than an Italian, absolutely no Irish, and never a woman alone, even if British. All about Mrs. Findlay's house, the Japanese rented; none knocked at 850. Americans of any colour she did not care for. *Try Mrs. Nicholls, on Alexander Street.*

A new boarder she watched as once she watched Mr. Findlay, for signs. Did the man get work quickly? Arrange for laundry and lunches? Receive letters with plausible return addresses? *An all-righter*, then. Many such departed soon for more permanent housing, pleasantly confirming her estimate of them.

The third kind of man she termed *it depends*. With journeyman's papers, a strong wife, or a job with someone from home, this unpromising material might prosper. However, as Mrs. Findlay put it to Mrs. Nicholls, *There's no floor to put your feet on.* If the wife didn't like the raincoast or the relatives put on airs, such weak men collapsed. Failing, they mumbled *could* and *might*. Instead of job hunting, they hung about and offered to do her yard work, which meant to reminisce about Bideford or York. On the porch, they chatted with others of their ilk. (*Tsk!* Mrs. Findlay brought her good wicker chairs indoors, except on Sundays.) Such men took *naps*.

How long till such a man ran out of money? She made bets with herself and laughed as she told Mrs. Nicholls. Winning, she filled an olive-and-dart glass with salmon-berry wine. Losing, she put her dollar fine in the bank, while the boarders ate rutabagas and mutton instead of spring lamb with mint.

Now this amiable, full-bellied Charlie Cowan, with his snappish wife and his boy—Mrs. Findlay saw how he might sidle up, full of her good beef and Yorkshire, to ask for "a private word" and assure her of payment in full, oh very very soon....*Lazy*. He had Findlay's easy manner of the once-handsome. "I'm a clerk." He said *clark*, still. Well. Clerks added tone. Loggers, fishermen, miners abounded but gave a house a transient feel. Better boarders worked at coal yards or hotels or retail concerns like Stark's Glasgow House or the Cheapside Grocery.

A weak agreeable man, a cross woman to keep him up to the mark, a child who must be fed....*There's more to running a house than some would think*, Mrs. Findlay and Mrs. Nicholls agreed.

More included *things*. Mrs. Findlay's own room was stuffed with *my insurance*. Back in Toronto, she'd made a *no-good* leave her his new Empire typewriter. It sold for fifty dollars. Amazing! After that she noted what lodgers brought in. Violins, new corsets, books (even *old* books, her husband taught her) meant cash at auction or the pawn-broker's. On moving West, alone—*Mr. Findlay's habits of life*, she told Mrs. Nicholls, *were not conducive to profit*—she let some rooms unfurnished. More saleables! At Scott's Auction Rooms and at Rankin's, Mrs. Findlay studied the values of the Coast.

Looking at Mrs. Cowan, Mrs. Findlay wondered *Why wear pearls to traipse about getting lodgings?* The woman's look held the answer. *You're selling, I'm buying. I wear pearls, you don't.*

"Snobbery," Mrs. Findlay advised Mrs. Nicholls. "We can always use snobbery." The pearls looked of tolerable quality.

Mrs. Cowan was expecting, the boarding-house keeper saw. *Better than pearls! That'll keep his fine nose at the grindstone.* So Mrs. Findlay offered her best double-room let, across the front with a bay window. It faced the English Fish Curing Company, but beyond was pretty Deadman's Island, a name the Cowans need not learn from her. "See the mountains!" The Lions helpfully glistened white as meringue against the blue.

The Cowans moved in.

Easy indolent Charlie got on with the Union Steamships, a going concern if ever there was one.

Mrs. Cowan liked good furniture. With her landlady she spent several visits "looking through" Mrs. Findlay's collection of whatnots and hassocks, cross-stitched chairs, mirrors, a dear perfume table. This boarder was knowledgeable. Admiringly she stroked a bird's-eye maple table. *A housemaid back in England,* Mrs. Findlay guessed.

For several days in June, Mrs. Cowan stayed unseen in their rooms. Her husband, apologetic, took trays up and down.

Nonsense! On the third day, Mrs. Findlay rapped on the Cowans' door after the man hurried away to work. (At least he was going; unspecified *biliousness* or *a general offness* sometimes kept Charlie Cowan at home.)

"Your laundry, Mrs. Cowan? The Chinaman'll be here directly and he hasn't a word of English. I can't ask him to wait."

Bundled linen was squeezed through, allowing a glimpse. *Such a shiner!* Mr. Findlay looked so more than once, after discussions with his wife. The room reeked of Norway Pine Cough Syrup; that was familiar too.

Next to this image of a purple-ringed eye the boarding-house keeper set another: Cowan in the back lane, behind a mock orange along with Mercer and Wylie, respectively teller and clerk at the Bank of Montreal and the Hudson's Bay. Nice clean working men these two lodgers were, and regular payers, though probably not one bit better than they should be in their relation to each other, or so Mrs. Findlay surmised. Cowan was opening a bottle.

Quite soon after this the Cowans said casually, "We're thinking about moving to Mount Pleasant later in the year. A house, perhaps." *Are you now?* Mrs. Findlay was amused. *But that doesn't suit me.* She relished controlling that soft lazy man, his lips wet with drink.

Mrs. Findlay now bought a double lot in the 2100-block of Cambridge, halfway up a prickly slope studded with snags. *But just wait till the sidewalks go in!* At meals, Mrs. Findlay smiled on whiny Alan Cowan and gave him spoonfuls of condensed milk. Weekly she exhumed Charlie Cowan's bottles from the grave under the mock orange, to check the rate of consumption. She waited, calmly, for something she could use on Mrs. Cowan.

One summer morning the boarding-house keeper set off for Vancouver Hardware to inspect ice boxes, meat safes, lavatories, washstands. Her house was a year away, but Mrs. Findlay could never bring herself to buy things quickly. At Westminster, she realized she'd left her watch at home. Delia, who "helped out," might help herself....

Turning her key in 850, Mrs. Findlay heard what she later described to Mrs. Nicholls as *a skittering noise.* In her landlady's own room stood Mrs. Cowan. She held an elegant and very portable cherrywood table with a piecrust edge. *Behind a standing full-length mirror that little table was. I mightn't have missed it for months. Oh, such cringing and crying!*

After Mr. Cowan grasped that Mrs. Findlay would not inform Union Steamships of his incorrigible drunkenness, and after Mrs. Cowan understood that neither the police nor her husband would be told of her thievery, the three held *a little colloquy* over tea and soft ginger biscuits.

Alan burrowed under his mother's arm. Mrs. Findlay said *Peekaboo!* Mrs. Cowan did not wear her pearls.

Yes. The Cowans would live, so happily, on Powell until they took the first floor on Cambridge—the address sounded so well! Modern. Nothing shabby, stained. "In England, people like you would never have such a place to live." Mrs. Findlay smiled. Downstairs, she filled and refilled her dainty glass, enjoying the rosy wine. *First prize at the fair!* When had she last felt so resoundingly pleased with herself? *I'll just give her that bird's-eye table she likes so much. Sweeten her up.*

Of course Mrs. Findlay did no such thing—but she sold it to the Cowans for barely more than they would have paid downtown and promised to keep an eye out for matching chairs.

Busy with the late summer's turnover of boarders, Mrs. Findlay hardly noticed the pacing upstairs as the parents "walked" the newborn. A girl. Dora.

One October day the Cowans went to Wiegand's to look at baby buggies. When they returned, buggyless—Mrs. Findlay could have told them they'd find prices there too steep—the boarding-house keeper was just putting on her heavy cloak. At the throat shone a large diamanté button.

Charlie Cowan's breath smelled of Norway Pine.

Elizabeth Cowan looked like the "Before" pictures in testimonials for Milburn's Nerve Pills or Dr. Pierce's Favourite Prescription. Pale, stoop-shouldered, the new mother held her baby like a dead fish.

Bored Alan tugged at his mother.

"Do be careful, child! You'll tear my shawl! I didn't bring it all the way from England to be ruined by a careless boy. Stop whining, Alan! Charlie, get him upstairs. I'm so tired."

"Nose out of joint, I see. May I hold the baby?" Sweetly Mrs. Findlay pressed the small warmth to her gabardine bosom. On her arms, the baby lay rigid.

The deep frill on Dora's muslin bonnet suggested that a bald doll lay at the bottom of a well. Dora's bonnet strings were wet, her neck red with rash. Whiteheads dotted the plush cheeks. From lips to chin ran a crust of dried milk. Her eyes were half-open.

"So greedy and troublesome," complained the mother. "Always at me and at me, so I can't get any rest. See how fat she is."

"There's a pretty girl!" The baby looked at Mrs. Findlay's sparkling button. *Of all the plain poor mites I ever saw!*

Then the landlady jabbed in her hat pin and set off to take another hard look at those meat safes.

JONATHAN

1967—Jonathan, Sighting the Quarry

"You won't get well just feeling sorry for yourself." Dr. Smyth's last patient of the morning lies sullen on her hospital bed. "Got to move those bowels, literally. Run 'em around the block. *Brisk up!*" So Hilda said, decades ago, to whiny children.

Out of the stuffy room at last, patients seen, rounds done, head aching. A cup of milk at the tiny coffee room, a word at the nurses' station. Scribble, sign, sign. Go. Down the corridor—go!

"Goodness, he's tired." Nurse Elphinstone watches the tall figure recede.

"Usually I don't notice his limp." Nurse Tetley. "I wonder will he make it all the way to the park, today?"

Too big for their britches! Aunt Julie's phrase, that. He could go right back to those two women and say *I heard you*. He could…Better to take coat and cap and gloves and warm red scarf from the doctors' lounge. Yes, better! Go now! Swing the door. Down down down the turning stairs, seven six five four three two Main. In Jonathan's head sound voices from old committees that met and met and met in the era of the building's construction. *First Floor? or Main? First! No, Main!* And the numerals above the elevators— *Arabic? or Roman?* His own voice sounds, quoting Miss Lawrence from grade six: "Roman is for important numbers." Such arguments, votes, resentments. All long past.

Out gratefully on to the snowy sidewalk of Twelfth Avenue. Knees—a little wobbly. Left thigh—a major tremor there, but Dr. Lee's latest prosthesis does its work, holds him up.

Snow! When did that begin?

Vancouver's soft snow scribes the air delicately. Between passing cars, this veil on the black shining street lasts only a minute. Snow floats about the doctor's aching head and on the young skirted conifers on Willow Street. In his leather hand Dr. Jonathan Smyth catches three flakes—blobs really, not the geometrics of colder weather. As he does every working day, he heads south towards Queen Elizabeth Park, to keep himself going in the face of his failures. This morning he thinks of the hoarfrost's glitter in Saskatoon forty years before. Each single twig was glazed on the caragana hedge by his boarding house; blinding bright wind blew against him en route to the School of Medical Sciences. Windchill. Frostbite. Toes off, ears chipped like teacups, a baby abandoned and found just too late.

Too late. That's what I was, for her.

Adjusting his tweed cap, Dr. Smyth crosses Fourteenth and turns east. His head hurts. He's sick of it. If he takes time to greet the Conservatory toucans and ride the Cambie bus downtown and stop at the Dairy Lunch on Granville for a glass of milk, he may be late at the office for his afternoon patients. Whatsername, his receptionist, will scold. What *is* her name? Her face is never the one he wants to see. Once, though, on that very Cambie bus, he almost saw *that* face. *Almost saw…silly. Scatterbrain, rattlebrain,* Aunt Julie always said so.

As he nears Cambie, the wind pushes into the small of his back. His coat flaps.

In autumn, on the child Jonathan's way to school—two hundred and thirty-seven steps walking, one hundred and eighty-two running—the wind pushes his back so he can run right up the Sasamat hill. Yellow leaves spin. *Shooooof* goes the wind. When the leaves fall, Locarno Beach appears before his bedroom's window seat where he looks at the stars—though he never really learns them. *Tsk! Lazy!* Or he reads. *Nose in a book,* Aunt Julie sniffs. *Milksop.* Up the stairs waft the smells of Hilda's raspberry jam, her roast chicken and rosemary, her gingersnaps.

Without a glance, Jonathan passes his current home, the Huntley Manor apartment block. On its glass door, the gilded script runs uphill below a leaping antlered deer. Mrs. Hanover, polishing the brass doorknob, sees the doctor smile. She tells Mr. Hanover so at supper, before word comes.

Past the Park Theatre, currently showing a ballet version of *A Midsummer Night's Dream.* A young woman sweeps the pavement by the box office. *Anaemic. And—rickets? Surely not.* Not in British Columbia now—but in the 1920s, the '30s—oh my! Childish bent limbs. Pinched-face mothers. This woman stoops gracefully to fill her dustpan with squashed cigarettes.

Smoking. I've not wanted to, all morning. A wavelet of nausea ripples through at the idea of a cigarette (not that Jonathan Smyth, M.D., would ever smoke in the street). That first prickling shudder in the lungs! *Midsummer. Rattlebrain. Headache.*

Summer dream: In the long-ago garden in the house on Sasamat stands a bust of a woman, on a plinth by the weeping birch. Jonathan dislikes the whiteness of the head, which looks soft but is hard. Even in summer, it exudes a cold dew. Repeatedly he has to wipe his hands. Jonathan has no memory of his mother. He and his older brothers, Richard and Geoffrey, never speak of the bust.

Aunt Julie screams at the gardener when an orb spider uses a curl on the bust's right temple to anchor a web stretching way up into the birch tree, flexing and bellying in the breeze. "Full of dead flies! For days the horrid creature must have been on her." Dew pearls on the line tremble and reflect light.

Rattlebrain! Dr. Smyth is now at Twenty-fourth. In a mirror by a barber shop he sees his own face. Sixty-five. So like Uncle George! *Basset-hound*, the boys name their uncle. Jonathan sees his own droopy jowls, his smoker's skin—but somehow he'd been that skinny boy running up Sasamat hill! Lips deeply runnelled, brow scored, hair a metal brush. Uncle George didn't have as big a head, of course.

On long-ago summer evenings at the house on Sasamat, white-clothed garden tables stand covered with platters of cold meat, salmon mayonnaise, tomato aspic, potato salad with watercress, the mustard pot with its liner of cobalt glass, the striped jar of hellish horseradish. Hilda calls, "Water's boiling!" In the corn patch, mint and rosemary fill the boys' nostrils as they pick the cobs. Bees bumble in the red bean flowers, squash lurk in spiralling foliage, heavy tomatoes ripen on crutches the gardener's rigged up.

Sometimes on those childhood Sundays, Jonathan's aunt Julie declares, "We'll take a turn in the garden now." As aunt and nephew tour the orchard and lawns and herbaceous borders, she reviews his sins of omission and commission. Surprisingly well-informed, she is. The "turn" culminates at the marble bust, where she takes Jonathan's hand. (One awful time, his fingernails are dirty.) Aunt Julie then always says the same thing. "Your mother's life ended when yours began, boy. Never forget that." Then he can get away, go to Hilda, peel apples or stir a cooling custard so it won't get a skin. He loves the milky custard.

Once Jonathan tries to pre-empt his aunt. As they reach the bust, he says, "Her life ended when mine began. Can I go now?"

She shoves her face into his. "How dare you, boy?"

"You always tell me never to forget. I don't."

She pales. (Jonathan has seen this amazing phenomenon in Geoffrey, who threw up at the sight of custard skin hanging off a spoon, and in Richard when he broke his ankle falling from his pony.) Aunt Julie's mouth opens. A yell? No, a whisper.

"That is my sister." Her hand touches the marble curls. "She's dead because of you. Whom do you suppose I'd rather have alive? Your father has no wife, your brothers have no mother, because of *your big head*." Three times her knuckles resonate on Jonathan's skull. He wants never never to see his aunt again.

Dr. Smyth's big head aches. Weather makes headaches worse, or so he fancies, though perhaps only the gloom of raincoast winter makes it seem so. Still to come are the darkest rains of December, January, February, March—all those, before a watery sun returns. Now snow flows like smoke. The flakes' aerial pathways are dizzying.

All these new shops on Cambie, plate-glass windows and sheets of mirror—selling what? To whom? Everything in the city is changing. But—*Brisk up!* Jonathan is warmer, not as stiff, moves well on his leg-and-two-thirds. Only eight blocks to the park now.

On the sidewalk across Cambie marches the kind of elderly man the doctor admires. See him step out smartly in his cap and bright red scarf, tall and sure and purposeful! Jonathan has never been effectively purposeful.

The girl on the stolen bicycle that day—oh, such desperate purpose! She knew exactly where she was headed.

The north slope of Queen Elizabeth Park is wet and green under streaked white. On a pond at the hill's base float four mallards, one female and three males, their iridescence dull in the winter light. Around the quivering water only a hatband's width of ice has formed, thin as egg membrane, pliable. Bright orange maple leaves lie drowned. Dr. Smyth's head aches. *I've never headed anywhere.* With pleasure he takes off his glove to feel the sharp furled buds, chartreuse, of the rhododendrons.

Cutting diagonally up the quiet hillside, his feet tamp the snow into black muddy prints, the left ones deeper. Halfway, he pauses for the delight of watching snow fall into the quarry's stone bowl. The flakes tumble in loose fluttering strings past the new specimen trees and the Centennial cherries, past the firs self-planted a century ago. The quarry's granite against the ambient white shows as ashes-of-roses. Such a colour! Aunt Julie's velvet evening coat: Jonathan remembers its satin lining.

He remembers a girl's face, mutinous and dour. He stands still at the edge of the quarry.

A green striped dress on English Bay. *That face—there she is, at last!*

On Spanish Banks lie salmon eggs, gritty with sand.

A harbour seal shoots up False Creek.

These images take seven seconds to succeed one another. Then the ache inside Dr. Smyth's skull blows up.

In the early afternoon, the temperature rises. Soft rain falls to wash away the snow, so the doctor's footprints vanish. The quarry turns grey again.

Later, when the rain lets up, a walker—the woman from the Park Theatre, in fact—comes by, heading home. She likes how the sober conifers are glancingly lit as their branches move in the wind and the cloud cover breaks, reforms, breaks. The quarry is a Corot: in this restrained palette, dusk veils the rock. To focus the viewer's eye, near the bottom of the composition there's even the painter's signature red streak. She focuses.

❧☙

"They said an aneurysm." Nurse Tetley.

"Gone in a flash. Gone for ever." Nurse Elphinstone.

"And just about to retire, too. So sad, isn't it?"

"But to die alone! As if he were homeless. As if no one cared." In vain Nurse Elphinstone wipes her eyes. "I know there were those nieces, but that's not what I mean."

Nurse Tetley puts her warm plump arm around her long-time colleague's shoulders and squeezes. "He never knew how you felt, did he?"

"Never. Jonathan never saw."

1902—Dreaming of a Grand View

The handsome house of Arthur and Amelia Smyth, parents of Richard and Geoffrey, stood at 1272 Davie Street, high above English Bay.

Westward, the whale-shapes of the Gulf Islands bulked up blue at the terminus of the glittering path laid down by the sun, or else their silver-grey masses floated in silver. Was that a curve of cloud or was it a forest? Amelia loved not being sure. Further south ranged the Olympics, white-glazed. South and east, on winter evenings Mount Baker hung like a dreamed mountain, suspended from a vault of clear cold rose. But Arthur Smyth wanted to move to newly fashionable Grandview, the site of a coming real estate boom, big profits guaranteed.... Secretly, he'd already bought a double lot there, high on another hill; when the baby girl was born, he'd surprise his beautiful Amelia.

Now in his master bedroom, in his mahogany bed with his wife, Arthur frowned. They'd spent a pleasant time this morning looking at sample birth announcements he'd brought home from Smyth, Stationer, but now it was eleven o'clock. Arthur heaved himself up, pushed aside the fat pillows, and shouted, "Hilda! Hilda!"

She was on her knees in the bathroom, scrubbing tiles. Hearing the call and the *ting-ting!* of Mrs. Smyth's bell, Hilda started and banged her head hard on the rim of the claw-footed tub. The soup, the clear soup at eleven! *I forgot. Again.*

This mansion bulged with things to learn and remember. Sinkbrush crumbbrush windowbrush banisterbrush shoebrush bottlebrush silverbrush stovebrush...and that was only one *thing*. The names for different sorts of plates glasses cups bowls knives staggered Hilda, let alone what these people ate and drank. And the carpets. And the little boys' clothes. *I can never be a good maid, never.*

Cook agreed. How she glared, when Hilda forgot to remove the salt cellars from the dining table before carrying in the ice pudding! *I'll give notice.* Back to the dairy farm at Eburne she'd creep...to her mother, who without ever having met Cook agreed completely with her estimate of Hilda's abilities and potential. Mother would cuff her jaws till her gums bled, pinch her arms purple, shout shout shout....She scurried down to the kitchen.

Cook was out, at a New Year's Day service at St. Paul's. *I forgot.* Nowhere could Hilda find the clear soup she'd seen Cook pour, steaming, into Mrs. Smyth's ivy-patterned cup. Daily Hilda took the tray—"Careful! Such a clumsy!"—up to the bedroom with the amazing glass tulips in the window. What to do? If she could produce no soup....At the thought of Mr. Smyth's anger, Cook's, her mother's, Hilda gasped. Taller than all of them, she'd have to look down into their infuriated eyes.

In the ice box stood a crock packed with fat. She sniffed: Christmas turkey. Never having touched any food in this house except at Cook's command, Hilda hesitated before she reached for a spoon. Yes. Under the grease gleamed the jelly. Heated, the stock was richly fragrant. She tasted. *Salt.* Among the bunched herbs in the pantry she found sage.

"What a wonderful smell!" Mrs. Smyth smiled at her young trembling maid. "What has Cook invented for me?"

"You're late, girl. This won't do. We keep no Chinamen here, just so we can employ good white girls, but they must be *good*."

"Arthur, Arthur! Hilda has brought my lovely soup and hasn't spilled a drop. Now do let me drink it in peace."

Back in the kitchen, Hilda smoothed the surface of the fat, set all away—but later on Mrs. Smyth praised Cook for the delicious novelty of her morning soup.

"Girl, are you blind?" Cook threw open a cupboard; there waited a regiment of Belle's Real Turtle Soup, tinned. That night Hilda cried even harder than usual before she slept.

Next day Mrs. Smyth sipped the Belle's, sighed. "Take the slipper chair, Hilda. There. Now—you made me that fine soup?"

The maid nodded.

"Don't cry! It's the first thing that's tasted *good* since this baby started. So Hilda, from now on you're to do some plain cooking. The boys' meals, to begin with. Would you like that?"

God bless Mrs. Smyth, Hilda prayed with every aching stroke as she polished tables, ironed the boys' collars to a glistening rigidity, sugar-starched doilies, feather-dusted banisters, rubbed stove blacking on the Royal Alexandra Range until Cook exclaimed, "Oh, do let up, girl! You're in my way."

Rubbing, Hilda pictured the old life. Her mother frowned out the grimy kitchen windows that overlooked the silty Fraser near the Great Midden; her mother's hard fingers gripped the wash bowl, scummy from the men's hands. *God bless*. Again Hilda hurried down the spidery basement stairs to sweep the fruit cellar and to wipe its whitewashed shelves, heavy with preserves.

The pregnancy continued difficult, or perhaps Mrs. Smyth was simply tired; Richard was six, Geoffrey four, and eavesdropping Hilda learned that two babies had been "lost" since the latter.

Mrs. Smyth oiled her finger, slipped off her wedding ring. "It hurts." Her ankles swelled. Dr. Bristoll prescribed bed rest.

"Strengthening food, he says." Cook peered at a list the doctor had left "for the little mama."

Daily, eggs and cream came from the Avalon ranch; Hilda learned custards and mayonnaise. Mr. Smyth himself went to Billingsgate for fish—Hilda poached, grilled, glazed in aspic—and to the butcher for Saltspring lamb and well-hung beef; Hilda roasted, braised, stuffed, and made frills for crown-rib bones.

A hired nurse now attended Mrs. Smyth. Ethel would also assist at the birth, although modern young mothers in the Smyths' milieu took private hospital rooms for their deliveries.

"Our daughter will be born *at home*," declared Mr. Smyth, "where a baby ought to be born, and where her beautiful mother can get the best care money can buy." He kissed Amelia.

"How does he know it's a girl?" Hilda asked Ethel.

"He just wants a girl. And she's carrying low."

"A boy would be carried high?"

Ethel only shrugged. She was annoyed at having to eat with the help, a sixteen-year-old at that and raw off the farm. She cleaned her plate of chowder, though, rubbing up the fishy cream with a thick cut of home-baked bread. They didn't skimp, here.

Hilda, taking up to her mistress the reddest strawberries from the garden and a pitcher of double-rich custard, tried to see this "carrying low," but the mother-to-be in spite of the June warmth was layered with shawls. Her face looked drawn.

For a treat, Arthur Smyth rode with his two little boys by streetcar out to see the Grandview property. On the ride, Geoffrey felt a little queasy.

"Someday we'll build a special house for Mummy and live *here*," the father announced, waving his arms expansively towards the prospect of False Creek's forget-me-not blue and the beehive burners oozing smoke on Granville Island. Shouting, Richard galloped round the property; he was a wild Indian, a bear, an eagle.

Just as the Dominion Day fireworks on the beach at English Bay ended, Amelia Smyth went into labour. Dr. Bristoll came immediately. In May he'd diagnosed mild pre-eclampsia in this "little mama." Urinalysis hinted at diabetes. The baby's head, though presenting normally, felt large. Because giving patients information led only to time-wasting talk, Dr. Bristoll had kept these disquiets to himself and did so now as he settled in for the night. The husband interpreted the doctor's presence as a tribute to the stature of Smyth, Stationer among the city's merchants. Ethel was affronted.

When the second stage of labour began, at dawn, Amelia Smyth was already near exhaustion.

"She has no reserves," said Dr. Bristoll. "Forceps."

Hearing her mistress's cries, Hilda was glad that Richard and Geoffrey had been bundled off to Haro Street, home of their aunt Julie. The maid prayed, crouching in the front hall where visitors left their calling cards. One floor above, her master sat stolidly in an armchair outside the bedroom door.

After the bloody rush of the baby's arrival, after palpating the loose belly-flesh to encourage the uterus to contract, after stitching the great tear and arranging the pads, Dr. Bristoll saw that his patient slept. He straightened his aching back and called to Ethel for soap and scalding water. He scrubbed hard under his fingernails.

"Another fine boy, Smyth."

"But his *head*." The father still shook.

"Within normal range. I'll stop in this evening."

By then the household was calm. Fresh linen—not from the Chinese laundry, but boiled at home and sundried—lay on the bed. Amelia's nightdress had a pretty ribboned front that undid for nursing. Cook and Hilda spent all day confecting delicate treats for their mistress, who picked at them, and solid food for their daughterless master, who devoured all.

Richard and Geoffrey, resentfully hand in hand with Aunt Julie, were marched over to meet ... *not* their sister. The bruises at the baby's temples alarmed the boys, as did his unfocused eyes. Intuitively, neither said anything but obediently kissed the baby's cheek. Off his skin came a gamy niff.... Once, when the brothers drove out to Eburne with their father to collect Hilda, they were taken out to the barn to see the newborn calf, pat its damp coat and feel the swirls of fur on its knobby head. Going home, the city boys smelled their fingers and wiped them on their knee-pants, wiped them again. Neither now spoke of this.

After tea with Hilda, the boys went away again to Haro Street with Aunt Julie. While she "just stepped down to see about dinner"—this meant badgering Wong in his kitchen till the cook compressed his lips to invisibility—the brothers punched and scuffled and bit each other until they both cried.

The hired nurse greeted Dr. Bristoll with a full report but knew that the medical man was not listening to her. "And the appetite is low," she finished. He simply pulled back the bedclothes. The discharges were normal, the uterus contracting appropriately. Fingers and ankles were far less swollen. At her wound, no infection appeared; it was Dr. Bristoll's pride never to have lost a *little mama* to puerperal fever.

"Jonathan," Mrs. Smyth said, smiling fatuously as little mamas were wont to do, even with fourth or fifth children. "For my brother. We lost him at Mafeking. Jonathan doesn't seem hungry."

"I'm very pleased with you both," Dr. Bristoll declared, seeing no reason to state that the baby was obviously tired.

Relieved, everyone at 1272 Davie went to bed early.

Amelia woke at midnight, happy because her breasts ached now. She loved Jonathan; the summer night was warm; the moonlight would be shining on the wrinkled bay. "See the world!"

Carrying her baby, Amelia went barefoot to the window. She kissed his head. "Look, sweetheart! Your papa wants us to move, but you'll never see a grander view than this. The ocean, the stars! You'll know them all, when you grow up." The infant's gaze veered about the heavens. He clasped his mother's finger.

Humming to her son, Amelia gazed at sky and sea till her feet grew cold as stone. Her legs wobbled; she nearly collapsed on to her bed.

Did Ethel's resentment stop her ears? Displaced, ignored, unheard except by that hayseed girl, the nurse was deaf to Amelia's footsteps and whisperings and later to the fretful murmurs of the hemorrhaging woman.

What awakened all the household, except unconscious Amelia, was Jonathan's wail. He'd discovered hunger.

"I'll put that Grandview lot up for sale," wept the widower. "I'll never set foot there again."

The merchant kept his word. He also made a fine profit when the sale went through at the height of the Grandview boom, just before the CPR bought the Shaughnessy lands.

Under the Care Of

February 1996—Mary Cornish Summons Her Brother, John Dow

You have to come to Vancouver now.

Yes, you do. Mum's dying.

I don't care how busy you are. *You're the son.* For once in your life you have to do something with this situation here.

Scouting? At almost seventy? Don't make me laugh. Your precious Scouting'll keep. She's going, I tell you.

What do you have to do? You have to get in your car. Drive to Swartz Bay. Board that ferry. Drive to Vancouver.

What have *I* got to complain about? The daily. The usual. Shop. Cook. Drive. For years. Clean. Pay bills. Do the government stuff, pension, taxes. Bill just did her eaves-troughs—those huge oak trees! Dangerous on that ladder, at his age. Never a word of thanks, but when *you* phone, it makes her day.

She wouldn't care if I wasn't there for a week. If I wasn't there, period.

Five minutes a day on the phone wouldn't cost you more than pennies. She'd be so happy! She loves *you*, John.

No, she doesn't. Not like you and not like Caddy.

Don't want to hear that? Too bad. Mum loved Caddy. If she could, she'd have picked me for the polio. And *you* were the son. You *are*.

Don't call me Maddy!

Don't you remember how Mum always sent me over to Aunty Marjo's to get me out of her sight? Always held your right hand and Caddy's left, so I had to walk alone? She even made Dad buy Garden Drive, just because Caddy was coming.

Yes, she did.

It does matter. It does so.

I don't care what you think of me, John Dow, not even if you call me *Maddy*, 'cause you're just a mama's boy who ran away. I didn't run. I stayed. I did what had to be done.

No. *You* listen. It's your turn, mama's boy. Mama's dying, and she keeps trying to talk to you.

December 1995—Mary Does Not Do the Bath
If Dora in her mid-nineties got dizzy from fatigue or from company, a cold dew filmed her forehead. Hands and feet were cold, almost always.

At her back door she might feel squashy. When she sat and looked, shit was pasted to her underpants, with more mushed up in her bottom. To wipe off all the brown took lots of paper and flushes. Getting the underpants off, past the Naturalizers Mary bought or the blue runners Dora liked, wasn't easy. Once Hazel Morgan found some brown on the rim of the bathtub. "How'd you get it there!" A laughing riddle that was, for both of them. But—all her life Dora had done *that* just before breakfast. Perfectly regular. Now, any time, it seemed. "Funny how things go," said Hazel, wiping the tub. Yes, funny. And rinsing the garment out was like baby diapers, nothing to it. Mary snatched the dirty underpants away, though. "You always make things worse."

Pee came out, too, when Dora didn't mean it. Mary said, "You smell bad." She brought pads like Kotex, but these had no neat white belt, no clever clasp. Instead, flaps stuck to Dora's pubic hair. She cried. "Tsk!" Mary yanked down Dora's underpants—right in the living room, by the window!—to adjust the pad.

Dora's eyes leaked constantly, but at night she woke with a dry mouth. Getting water from the bedside table often meant spills. Mary brought a baby's cup, tightly lidded, with a spout. In the dark, Dora sipped coolness. Caddy had a cup like that, didn't she? But back then there wasn't plastic. Was there? Dora fingered the three-sided spout.

Three, always three: the yellow umbrella. The child's whisper (warm breath on Dora's cheek). The hard chest of the dressmaker's dummy.

She tried to hide her toenails. Those hard dark yellow crusts! Dora strained to reach them, with her sharpest scissors, and stabbed her foot. Now Mary used fierce steel nippers.

Mary said, "You're shorter because your bones are eaten away." They lay close under the skin now, for Dora weighed less than she had in eighty years. At night she fingered down from rib to rib. Dora's granddaughter Tessa after a skiing accident had a metal pin embedded in her shoulder; Dora had felt the young sewn skin. Steely her own bones must be, studs of hard cold in the house of her body.

What had been soft in Dora's body was hard, dry was wet, thick was thin, flesh gone to air, breath to cough, sleep slept by waking and turning, voice like silence but silence louder than voice. Sunshine chilled and rain reached to the bone even when Dora sat dry in her house looking out through the dripping trees.

She saw the yellow umbrella, felt the warm breath, embraced the dummy.

Nothing tasted right. Hazel drove to a U-Pick in Richmond for strawberries. Oh how red! Years ago, Dora scrambled down the Wall Street slopes for blackberries, soapberries, salmonberries. Pink as Caddy's party dress, those salmonberries were. In August, along all the lanes in the East End, berry bushes still hung thick, but now the fruit was just pulp in Dora's mouth, faintly sweet, the salmonberry's little cup hairily dry and the blackberry dissolving to pointy seeds that stuck in her teeth.

All Dora's life she was *fat fatso plump fat heavy bulging Dora Dora Two-By-Four fat Dora Cow-Cow Women's Sizes fat Half-Sizes Chubette Above Average big-bottomed buxom chunky chubby fat fat fat.* Now she was sticks and string. Only the torso curved still.

"You don't eat enough." With no warning, Mary poked her mother hard in the tummy. Inches from that jab lay the child with its closed eyes, calcified long ago and hard inside her skin. Dora's brain, though, flowed loose and soft like mercury or eggwhite or liquefied pearl. The stone baby's father was *him*, she hoped. Or *him*, she feared. And *he* tried to help. Owen, Ned, Jonathan: often she knew their names, but never the baby's.

Lying awake, Dora felt her body the way another woman would page through familiar poetry. She stroked her arms, she touched her loose throat skin and her knobbed clavicle. Over the breasts her hands slipped, down to the dry open lips with their soft hair. At last Dora's fingers rested on her torso, studying the quality of the baby's hardness. She couldn't make a dent. Unlike all the other things under that skin, all her organs, the stone child didn't feel. There wasn't any *give*.

"None!" Dora whispered proudly into the dark tiny house.

Once a week, Hazel Morgan came in love to give Dora a bath.

Hazel switched on the space heater, and when the room was toasty she helped Aunty Dora to sit on the old backless chair.

As the hot water gushed out, she slipped the chenille dressing gown off the old woman's shoulders. When one elbow abruptly bent at an awkward angle, the trembling began, so Hazel loosed the difficult sleeve and waited, stroking her shoulder, till calm came back.

"Time to lean now," Hazel said. Aunty Dora held on to the sink while Hazel pulled the flannelette nightgown up to expose the flat buttocks. "Down. Rest a bit." Hazel checked the water. Once on request she'd added "more hot" till Aunty got out of the tub wearing scarlet pantyhose. The canvas bath-seat was secure. Hazel waggled the shower tube to get rid of any chilly water.

"One." Lifting the nightgown up and over, Hazel laid the rosebuds on the laundry hamper. "Two." Hazel grasped Aunty Dora under the elbows. Old hands gripped her upper arms. "Up." Aunty Dora shook but did not stagger. Face to face, the two laughed, and Dora looked at herself in the mirror, grinning. "Three!" The old woman got the grab-bar. She lifted a foot and with Hazel's guiding hands at her waist stood in warm water.

With a great sigh of pleasure, Aunty Dora sat and closed her eyes. Her shoulders relaxed. Her palms turned up. Her toes flexed. Like a preening bird she turned her head and stretched every warm wet limb. Hazel knelt. Turning on the tumbling flow again, she depressed the shower valve. As if in worship the old woman turned her face up to meet the spray; her lips opened and smiled. At the front of the seat, yellow pooled and trickled over the edge; Hazel steered the spray there to rinse the urine away.

When the hot water flowed over Aunty Dora's hair, its silver darkened. Tendrils curled by her ears. Water flowed across the shoulders, bent, narrow, and down the spine, knobs unremarkable except in their age: for ninety-four years they'd knobbled their way down to the sculpted white crack. To receive the blessing of the shower, the old woman lifted each foot in turn—hot wet needles against the sole, between the crumpled toes.

Aunty Dora's breaths slowed, deepened. She leaned back to expose her trunk fully. Few hairs stood in the armpits.

The soft-nippled breasts, draped long and thin over the belly, formed an inverted V. Past torso and stomach this V met the right-way-up V of the old thighs. A puff of hair still veiled the vulva. Now the puff was flattened, darkened by water. She spread her legs and Hazel held the stream on her centre till Aunty Dora tensed all over and then let go.

Soap now, soap and laughter, for grandchildren and great-grandchildren gave so many Christmas and birthday soaps that every week the two women picked a new one from the drawer full of jasmine sandalwood lavender musk rose coconut pine lily-of-the-valley violet mint lime apple-blossom peony gardenia grapefruit mimosa.

There was no Pears' soap, because once, when a grand-child presented the dark ovals, Grandma burst into tears. "Caddy!" she sobbed and wouldn't stop for the longest time.

That night Dora lay awake and endlessly rotated those three images: the strong chest of Flora the dressmaker's dummy; a wet yellow umbrella, twirling, dropping; a child's fretful whisper.

Today Hazel lathered up the washcloth with magnolia and handed it over. She herself shampooed the old scalp till that sweet essential smell of clean fine hair filled her nostrils.

Early on Hazel had tried to get Aunty Dora out and dried quickly, but suddenly the old bowels moved and everything turned to shamed whimpering. Since then Hazel went slowly. She draped Aunty Dora with towels hot from the radiator and knelt to rub feet, shins, thighs. Hazel lifted each breast, nuzzled the towel into the folds between belly and thighs, moved lightly across Aunty Dora's torso. Early on, she'd sensed the resistance underneath and lifted her hand. Aunty Dora took the younger woman's fingers and pressed them into the hardness. Hazel leaned close. The two women spoke to each other. In pearl-drop strings, tears slid down.

As gifts, flowered nightgowns also appeared abundantly. Tonight's was sprigged with violets. The women left the warm steamy bathroom and murmured their way along the hall. "Surely it isn't always this cold?" Past the dining ell they went, where Flora the dressmaker's dummy presided, matronly, over the covered Singer. Here also the button jar winked its myriad colours on the maple dining table, unused because Dora now ate all her simple meals in the kitchen.

In Dora's bedroom, the hair dryer whirred. Hazel held the strips of old hair to the blast and they separated into their strands, ready to be combed, brushed, smoothed. Neither woman spoke. The house was quiet. Hazel reached for the hand mirror and showed Aunty Dora her old smiling face with its smooth frame of hair, and then she began brushing again. Gently gently, softly softly—the only sounds were of those ever-slower ever-smaller movements of hands on the scanty hair, fine silver hair, hair exuding its insubstantial yet persistent fragrance on to the tines, the bristles, the caring fingers.

Hazel bent for the goodnight kiss and felt the old fingers come up into her own red curly hair, greying now. Affectionately, Aunty Dora rubbed the ridge at the back of the younger woman's head, just above the skull's base.

Then Hazel tiptoed across the room to set the comb and brush on the dresser, by the old Toby jug, and before she reached the bedroom door the old woman was asleep.

After two years of this weekly ritual, when Dora began to deteriorate rapidly, Hazel arranged for an official assignment as her community-care nurse. From then on, she came to the house on Eton Street twice weekly.

1995—*Owen Is Taken into Care*

Nurse Rose went through the minimum necessary paperwork as fast as she could, her face screwed up, and then fastened a name-bracelet around Owen's grimy wrist.

"Get him in there." Dramatically, she pointed towards the men's bathroom. "Lice—check for those, first thing. Scabies, whatever. Scrub him! *Hot* water. Shampoo."

Owen grinned at her.

"And for God's sake brush his teeth. *Scrape* them. They're green. You're a disgusting old man, you know that?"

Owen grinned again, as the orderlies took hold.

Late on that summer afternoon the ambulance had headed east from Bella Coola, with a party of four: Elizabeth and Russ Preston, an RCMP constable, and an orderly from the Home, who drove.

At the farm gate the vehicle turned in, lurching over ruts. No rain had fallen for days; the air smelled of cottonwoods, pine, and the sun-warmed rot of spawning fish. As the expedition got out of the vehicle, feral cats skulked about, jumping over leaves and deer droppings.

"But where's Ginger?" Elizabeth looked about.

The cedar cabin that Owen Jones had rented for years stood on a scenic stretch of the Bella Coola River. For many,

who helped! *And* your mum was in a Home. People got *paid* to look after her.

So Aunty Marjo got abused at Seton Villa? Well, she wouldn't be the first. The staff—why should they care? They get their cheques, don't they? In those Homes they feed them worse than dogs. God preserve me from ending my days in one of those! Canned, frozen, steam-table mush. Not that Mum would mind. She never cooked, never cared about food. My poor dad.

Well, if the staff didn't abuse her, then who did?

Emotional neglect? Ridiculous! Maybe you reproach your-self for how you dealt with your mum. I certainly don't. I've done everything necessary for mine. More. Far more. *And* held my tongue. Most people wouldn't. If Mum's lonely in her old age, that's her lookout.

Yes, Aunty Marjo was Mum's best friend. Yes, you came after the war and the rest of us were so much older. So what?

A big girl? I'm *not fat*, Hazel.

So I was Mum's *big girl*. Why was that an excuse for Mum to dote on a baby who wasn't even hers? For neglect-ing her own grown daughter? Mum *favoured* you. She taught *you* sewing and smocking.

Don't try to kid me, Hazel. Face it, when I was a kid, your mum *put up with me* out of pity. Aunty Marjo knew what home was like for me, so she let me hang around your place. She called me *Daughter Number Three*, remember that? Third place. That was me.

I am not my mother's Number One.

It doesn't matter, Hazel, if you forgot to count Caddy. Doesn't matter that she's been dead fifty years and more. To

Mum, Caddy was *perfect.* So at best I'd be Daughter Number Two. I could even be Three.

I don't want to explain.

Mum does *not* appreciate me or what I do for her. That word's not in her dictionary. The bath alone … what a job! Heaving pushing shoving, she gets all mad, won't let me wash her, can't wash herself. Wears me out. Wears me down. I'm not young. No one thinks, no one remembers I have a business to run. John certainly doesn't. *Your cooking,* they call it, him and his snobby Joyce.

A chartered accountant and a teacher—of course they look down on me! He's older. He's the son. He hears secrets I never do. He says not, but John knows where her will is. Mum talks to him. Then him to Joyce. Then her to me, if she's drunk enough, sometimes. She told me about the abortion.

Why so shocked, Hazel? You trained before they changed the law, so you must have seen some botched jobs. Or can't you picture your dear Aunty Dora with the knitting needle?

Way back. The thirties.

How would I know did she use slippery elm or what? Whatever, *Mum did it herself.* Late. And made Dad bury it. On Wall, down by the tracks. That's the worst—*Dad* had to. Poor Dad. Sweet man, sour woman. By the end, she made him a bitter man.

Yes, those bushes at the foot of Cambridge.

I should confirm it with John? Joyce'd never tell me another thing—and I don't need to confirm. That story's Mum, through and through and through. *If the kid doesn't suit you, get rid of it.*

That's what I mean, exactly. Mum threw me away.

Which is why I'm going to be *on your case*, Hazel, now that you're getting paid to do home care for her. After all I've gone through, I'm entitled. I've *earned* whatever she's got to leave. D'you hear me? I won't be done out of what's mine.

Of course I didn't care, before! Why should I care if you wanted to spend your spare time washing an old woman? But to get *paid* for it, paid money...well, that's always different, Hazel.

Spring 1992—Mary Complains to the Geriatric Social Worker
I've all my own housework to do first *and* I've got a business to run, but around ten the bridge rush hour's over. You're too young to remember the ferries over the inlet. That was a good system, so of course they stopped it.

First I help Mum dress. Properly. What I've had to do! She'd be out all hours, roaming the alleys in some rig-out you'd think she was a witch. Long crazy tents sewn every which way. Oh, I tried. Got those nice fleece outfits, pastels, wash so easy. And the Bay had caftans—decent looking at least—but *no*. But since Mum's knees went, things have been easier for me. She has to stay home. Now Dad was *always* easy. I kept him looking sharp, a good crease in the pants, collar set just right. With him it was a pleasure. So sweet-tempered! He'd listen to his music and tap his hand on his knee, hours at a time, his dish of allsorts and his Bible handy, picking out the pink ones first—oh my. With Dad, even with the diapers and all, at the end, I didn't mind.

Then I make coffee for Mum—not that she drinks much. Waste! I've never liked coffee. I listen to her. Dad saw the bright side, but if I had a nickel for every time Mum complains—oh my! And I pick up. Mail, papers, her sweaters lying about. I ask does she want anything, Safeway London Drugs Seven-Eleven? It's her pee. I buy those maxis that stick right to the crotch. I check has she been to the toilet. I get her soup hot, put the thermos by her window. No, she doesn't *do* anything—just looks out. It's funny, she can see my house here in North Van but I can't see hers. Those trees on Eton are something awful. Often I'm not home till one or two. By then the day feels *gone*. Not that she cares.

Dad loved all my food, especially desserts. What a sweet tooth that man had! Mum won't touch my soup. We make all our own stocks, I've had recipes in the *Sun* nine times, won again and again at the PNE—but *no. Too rich*. What a joke, rich! Did I dream I'd be working at my age? First it's Habitant pea with ham she wants and nothing else will do, so I haul out to Superstore for a case on sale—but then it's tomato bisque. Bill hasn't a stomach for canned soup. Guess who eats all that Habitant? Never was my favourite.

In the late afternoon I get back to Mum's before the home care leaves. To check. Oh, they're some help I suppose. They run a wash through. Tidy. Get the phone. Go over her bits of mail. Company, I guess. They get her supper. But with the taxes we pay you have to ask yourself, *Is this all?*

Her bath! They won't do it. Not a one of them. They run scared, those home care girls, when Mum says *I don't want to*. See, Mum won't cooperate. She won't tell us where her will is. She won't spend on maintenance 'cause she says the place'll just go to a developer for the lot. A fine thing, getting her way so easily! Life's sure not been like that for me, or Dad either.

Her health concerns? That's a laugh. *Fifty-four years since I was last in a doctor's office, not counting with my kids.* That's what Mum always says. So lucky! I couldn't go a month without a doctor. Gallstones, arthritis, sinus, asthma, allergies—you name it, I've got it. *And* the irritable bowel. Crohn's, they said. Wrong, of course—surprise? And I've got a grandnephew on Ritalin and a granddaughter on Prozac and a grandson they want to give that growth hormone to. You have to ask yourself, what's happening to the world? Mum's *fine*.

I don't like Bill driving in the rain at night, the bridge deck reflects so . . . but we have to check her. Is she cosy in bed, has she got her water, is her radio on, are all the doors locked?

My brother's on the Island. He phones her once a month. *If* we're lucky.

My kids—they're *good*. They take Mum out. Tessa got tickets for Tina Turner at the Coliseum, can you believe it? But Mum doesn't like crowds, never did. Now Dad—he loved to be with a gang, the PNE and Nat Bailey and hockey games. Loved his union days. Not Mum. A loner, always.

They're good, my kids, yes, but they've got their own lives, their own kids, even Tessa now—and *they don't do the daily!* They don't wake up knowing they'll make three trips over the Second Narrows and get no thanks. They don't get the silent treatment. I tell them, *It's not anything like caring for your sweet grampa.* And no way they'd give Grandma a bath.

I'm past it, I tell you. I'm sixty-plus.

Why shouldn't I be bitter? Mum's never loved me, not since the day I was born, and now who's left to do the work? And what in heck do we pay all these taxes for?

Dependent

December 1987—Marjo, Dora's Oldest Friend, in the Nursing Home

Nothing but nonsense coming out of Mrs. Morgan now.

Nothing.

Not a word.

No. Get that wretched blue rag off Mrs. M. and throw it out.

Yes, out.

September 1987—Marjo Has a Few Words Still
blue
no no no no no
ow ow ow
ugh
dark
gaga
blue blue blue

June 1987—Marjo Puts Words in Pairs
vile bile
cut gums
door slams
phlegm, hem hem!
dark air
witch bitch
nurse curse
oh God no
bad girl bad girl bad girl
red head

February 1987—Fragmenting
grey, grey, end of the day
pain in the shin bones
over the inlet, blue thunder
Javex—pew! pew!
bitter first, the cough syrup, then sweet
sweet canning peaches, round and rosy
bright bright
brightest and best of the sons of the morning

bruise
my eye!
my clock! jumpy-jump ring
pressure-cooker ding ding
that nurse and her visitor, ha ha
ha ha, pew! pew! on the rag
skin on the milk, wrinkly skin

Winter 1986—Marjo's Syntax Intact Still
here they keep the lights on all the time
did you ever?
clocks don't tell time
I want to go home, oh God, why can't I, why?
I declare, there's no one here
not a soul to talk to
they changed where the toilet is, I can't find it, I have to
go I have to go I have to go
I go
they get mad, they laugh
all the time they change the rules
it's their fault, I declare
all my life I've had someone to talk to
with the lights on how can I sleep?
broad daylight
how can I go back to bed like a good girl, good as gold?
when I was bad, there was no bed
I want to go home, I want someone to talk to
they don't even knock
I'm Hazel or *I'm Mike*, they say it and say it
but Mike died, I know that, God

they're mean, it's not funny
that black nurse is really mean
Dora never ever comes
I hate her
I declare I'll hurt her, I'll tell
always the lights are on
that awful wrinkly woman hides behind
the washroom door but
I see her wrinkles in the mirror, I see her
she doesn't fool me, I know what she did, bad bad bad
no, none of them fool me
so mean
why would I want to talk to that nasty woman?
Dear God where is my good blue dress?
I ask them and ask them
all the time the rules change
and Dora never comes
I hurt her hate her
I want to hate her
She's never done anything for me, never never never
I want to go home
this robe is stained
this robe smells
worn for weeks and not washed—
I declare, did you ever?
it's not mine
it must be that woman's, the ugly bitch in the mirror
she was bad
the peaches were sweet and spicy
that nurse is black

I've told them I don't like black
told them, God, told them
I declare—I never wear
beige
where are my good gold earrings?
where is everyone? Sarah Luella Laura Sally Isabel Dorothy
Marion Gwen Jo Freda Alice Marjorie Peg Betty
Pamela Toni—
and Gladys? and Annette, after all these years?
where did everybody go?
what do they all say?
what can they tell me about how to live, here?

1980s—Owen's Three Rules

I've got my rules, son, you know that, Owen said firmly to Jerry, *but I'll go over them again. You got to learn how to live.*

Don't pay any more than you have to. Number One. Not a cent more. Bargain, haggle, jew, I don't care, I never cared, but I only pay what I have to. So when you get to Bella Coola, Jerry, you talk to that bitch on the farm, first thing, about the rent.

The forty acres on which Owen's cabin stood formed one of the original allotments for the Norwegian settlers arriving from Minnesota in 1895. Three generations of Eriksens farmed it. Then in the 1960s came hippies with money from California and Toronto, draft dodgers, drug addicts, back-to-the-landers.... *Who are these people?* the Valley asked. They bought rich earth and for a season or two scandalized the neighbours. All but a few moved on then, to the Slocan's sunny valley or to Grand Forks, or back to Bay Street. Those who remained got down to work with animals, wood, water, machinery, fish; they became solid Valley citizens. Loudly as the locals, they groused about taxes and prices.

A pair of these newer farmers, having no use now for the riverside shack that once offered seclusion for drugs and sex, rented it to Owen Jones. Perhaps they felt a nostalgic solidarity with the old man who proudly owned nothing but gun and fishing rod and frying pan and a couple of moose racks...but the general Valley assessment was that Owen Jones had *ended up after fifty years without a damn thing to show for it. Serve him right!*

Many times Owen talked to Jerry about Bella Coola. *This Valley—you got to picture this place, Jerry. Pig-fat farmers everywhere. Mad for money, mad for more. Hear them talk. If you were here you'd get after them for me, help your old man. I keep asking them, "You heard something I haven't, about the feds pumping up the pension?" I've never been late with the rent, Jerry. You make that point to her. Not by a damned day! You tell her. The only other place to go is the Home, see. You can't let that happen to me, Jerry. Not the Home. I'd rather the river.*

And that bitch has the nerve to tell me I drink too much. Jerry, in the seventies that acidhead cuntbag went round town so stoned she could hardly walk. Whole place laughed at her. But I fixed her wagon. She used to come out to the cabin, see, come out to rat a rat tat rant at me...but now she leaves me alone, mostly. Seems Pig-bitch don't like the way I smell. I don't smell well, ha ha, I smell like hell, you tell her, Jerry. I told her, 'Your shit don't smell no better'n mine.' Yes I did. And I bet her she couldn't hold hers the way I can. 'I've gone a solid week without,' I said. 'I've lasted till my shit was so hard I had to pull it out of myself with my own two hands.' That took care of her but good. But she's at me about raising the rent, Jerry.

Owen, don't own and don't owe. That's my second rule.

Goes nice with my name, see? If you owe, then they own part of you. And the other…if you haven't got anything, they can't take it away! So simple. Joke's on them. Nothing to take.

Many times, so many times Owen got wearily off a fishboat or a road crew, or off shift at a logging camp, or off a ladder or a truck or a float, or out of a ditch, a culvert, a bog. He went to sign out, sign off. There'd be a shack with a girl at a table, or some guy going about the work site with a clipboard and a smeary ballpoint pen. As he wrote his name, Owen Jones listened for the girl, the guy, to say the words he wanted so to hear: *Kid from Vancouver stopped by, looking for you. No, didn't get his name.*

How often had Owen waited thus for someone to speak up?

Good-looking kid. Left a phone number, where'd I put it? Here, Owen. He says to call him. The words resonated in his mind.

Often in the early fifties, when The Road out of the Bella Coola Valley was under construction and Jerry was nearing eighteen, almost grown, Owen imagined how he could go south to kidnap his son.

Boat's quicker of course, and warm, but there's too many people know you. Nosy. Want to talk. "Whurya going? Whaffor? How long? Whurya stayin at, down there in the Big Smoke? With folks?" All that yammer. Being in a boat gets them going. But the other way's a long haul, oh jeez a long one till Williams Lake. Hitch. If you're deaf they'll just drive clear through to Vancouver, leave you alone and not yammer at you. Or you can hop the train. Get a car to yourself, with luck. Cold. Noisy. But it gets you to the station, free!

Always a good laugh, that. Then I'd hike north on Main and along the waterfront, my dogs all tired and tuckered out by then, to Cedar Cove—and there you'd be, Jerry! On that hill. I'd see you. I'd give our secret whistle. "Dad's here!"

When at the age of seventy-five Owen moved into the cabin on the banks of the Bella Coola, he had what Cheryl Preston called "a view to die for." Tall cottonwoods and second-growth Douglas fir of a good height framed the green flow. Here the river was broad, laced with swirls of deep currents, fretted with foam; the water ran floury with glacial till. On the opposite bank stretched away fields, and beyond them reared up jags of rock and glacier and sky.

What Owen liked was to sit with Ginger in his lap and watch the Bella Coola run. Best of all was when the Native kids came down in their boats.

When I was a kid we went all over Burrard Inlet on rafts, Jerry. You ever done that, rafting? Fun. I did it at Snauq too, with the Siwashes there, Indian Tom a couple of times, but it wasn't like here. No no! Here the water's high, Jerry, running fast, those kids in a rowboat, forty miles an hour, no motor, of course no lifejackets, are you kidding? And standing up! Yes boy, I said standing up. Nine or ten, those kids, and they steer with sticks and those boats do just what they want. They're laughing, Jerry! Laughing!

When the kids disappeared down the bend in the river, Owen sighed and went back inside. The arthritis didn't like it if he stayed out in the cool damp air.

On the shelves, Owen arranged his bottles: the stones, the string, the shrapnel, the surprisingly long splinters of glass. His face wrinkled up with contempt as he set his hearing aid alongside. *Damn doctors. Ruined my life, they have.*

Back in 1918, if that butcher'd only done the job right on that god-damn girl. If she hadn't bled like that.... He wrenched out his false teeth. *Damn dentists, too.* The dentures went on the shelf. *My whole life could have been different, without that bloody bleed of hers. I could've had Jerry.* Where was Ginger? Just coming in the door, too. *And had Dora, for that matter.*

Simple, isn't it, Jerry? Don't owe and don't own.

And the last rule: Stay on your lonesome, so you don't let them drag you down. Ginger's gotta find his own food. Scraps I'll give him, sure, but I'm not spending money on that canned kitty catty crap.

I didn't let your mum drag me down. Well, I never got back to her, did I? So she couldn't. And I never told, Jerry. Not anyone. Not Indian Tom. Not Mrs. Major. Ginger I did tell. He kept it to himself, guaranteed.

In Jerry's early years, Owen wondered what the boy looked like. *Hope you're not as short as me. Probably not. Better food, likely.* Did Jerry's hair tuft up like his own? If there'd been a resemblance, how'd she handled that? He wondered whether Dora might have snuck in *David* or something else Welsh, *wish Welsh,* as a middle name for their son. *Whether whither weather rather.* Did the husband have a clue? *Damn dumb ox he looked like to me, the one sighting I got.*

Maybe that seems hard to you, Jerry-boy, that I never got in touch with your mum again. But it had to be that way. Had to. See, I know what happens when a person's stuck, the way my mum was. I lived that. Better I wasn't there, Jerry. Believe me.

He wondered when she'd told the boy. *Dora wouldn't tell a little kid. No, she's smarter than that, your mum. She'd pick a good time. You'd be fifteen, sixteen maybe, pissed off at Pop and ready to run.* Owen saw Jerry's eyebrows go up, eyes go wide, at the moment of realization: another father! A *real* father and a *real* life were waiting for him to find them....

So it's me who has to wait for you. But you better finish school first, you hear? Later Owen told his son, *Finish university. Get your ticket,* he insisted. *Get youself a good job.*

As background to the scene of *Jerry finds his father* was Owen's wondering *how?*

She'd tell you my name, of course. Jones—there's Joneses all over, sure, but not many Owens. A long ways you'll go before you'll meet an Owen. That'll help you, Jerry, finding me. And Dora'll know the kind of place you should look.

Look for an Owen who sings, Jerry. Who makes those word-chains—I've never met anyone else can do that. People talk about that kind of thing. They remember what makes them laugh, even if they can't remember the chains. Gives me a chuckle, that does, when they try to repeat. They can't, Jerry, not for love or money—not that either's on offer! It's a gift. That's all.

Owen wondered if Jerry had kids. Or rules. If he was doctor lawyer merchant chief. If Jerry's hands really were smooth and well-kept, as they appeared on his birthdays. If Jerry even lived in Vancouver. If he held a cat purring to his chest when he went to sleep. *And do you sing, Jerry? Hell, I don't even know that. Or if I'm a fuckn grandfather. Hell, could be great-grandfather, Jerry, depending on when you got going!*

And now I can't get to the city, see, even if I wanted to, Jerry. It's beyond me now. You have to come here.

Repeatedly, Owen tried to make it clear to Jerry about staying unentangled.

Watch out for Christers, Jerry! Your mum wouldn't have gone that way, but your pop sure looked stupid enough to get religion. Make up your own mind. Probably you did already, years ago. Not so young as you were, are you?

See, those Prestons got their claws into me. Chance, that's all it was. Nothing you can do about chance, Jerry. Nothing, believe me. There's been Prestons in Bella Coola always, la-di-da nice people, I didn't know them or want to. But…I knew Lizzie Preston's aunt, Mrs. Major.

Lady, her name was. In Quesnel—she kept a cathouse there. When I went to war I left an envelope with her, for you. Well, addressed to your mum. Sealed and signed, wax and all. So you'd have what there was, if I got killed. My son.

Killed? No. Close, though. Yes, your dad came close to dying then.

The Canadian fight for Hill 76 had made mincemeat of Owen's eardrums. A steep slope caved in underfoot, killing seven men, but Owen was only flung high into the air and fell among rocks and mud clods to land prone on an upturned pump, just like the one by the Powell Street livery stable at Wall, near the green room of salal and berry bushes. His and Dora's room.

The sound of the stableboy priming that pump: through the bombardment, Owen clearly heard the gurgling wheeze. It was the last noise that reached him for weeks. He couldn't smell anything, either, and his guts hurt horribly.

During Owen's leave, an English doctor said his busted ears and wonky smeller would recover, with rest and quiet. Because Owen was deaf, the medical man wrote this recommendation on his prescription pad. "Rest?" Owen laughed harder than he'd done in weeks.

With Indian Tom that night, he was still laughing as they drank what the English called beer and ogled the buck-toothed dowdy English girls in Piccadilly. Their summer didn't seem to tan these girls; they stayed fish-belly white. Back in the green room, Dora's skin had been honey and almonds, honey and cream. Did Jerry have that skin? Dora had smiled, laughed, unbuttoned her blouse.

We never even got to lie down in a bed.

Jerry, do you have kids?

After the war, not long after, Lady died. By God she looked awful at the end! Just bones. So at her wake, there's her sister. Mildred Marks. She marked me! She could smell a sinner, Jerry, 'cause she was all over me like butter on bread before even we got into "Abide With Me" and "Shall We Gather at the River." An inheritance, I was. From Lady to bloody Mildred.

For thirty years then I went on working. Well, you know I did. All over! Is there any dump in the Cariboo or all across the Chilcotin or in this goddamn valley or up and down this whole jeezly coast I haven't busted my ass in? But Mildred always caught up with me. Jesus postcards. Phone calls. Bloody Christer things to read—make a cat puke. She wouldn't let up, Jerry! I was her duty, see. Watch out for that!

When that sister died, I thought—"I'm clear!" But back in Bella Coola, double-damn me if Mildred's daughter Elizabeth wasn't on shift. Another bleeding Christer, and this time with a goody-goody husband, Russ Preston. Fuss fuss fuss. "You don't eat right, Uncle Owen. This isn't a good place for you to live, Uncle Owen. See my little girl Cheryl. Isn't she cute? I'm doing this for your own good, Uncle Owen."

For your own good....I tell you, boy, at my age those are words you don't want to hear.

Owen's belief that the Prestons believed he had money gave him strength to endure their *bloody snooping. They think I've got money socked away and all they got to do is hold on and I'll leave it to them. "We know you haven't anyone else to care for you,*

Uncle Owen, so we do it gladly, don't we, Russ?" I'll gladly them, Jerry! I tell you, it's the only thing makes me wish there was a hereafter, so's I could watch Russ and Lizzie get the picture. And the only way I can stomach it when they come visit is watching that little girl of theirs sass her mother. It's a pleasure, I tell you. Good as anything on TV.

When you come here, Jerry, don't tell them I've got nothing to leave. Just in case. I'll never tell.

I never tell much. I've never told, about you. Not anyone.

Most people run off at the mouth. Not just women, either. On a crew, on a boat, walk into a bar, what'll you hear? Yak yak yammer yak. People yakking about every dumb thing's ever happened to them. The stuff pours out like shit. They can't hold it in. Well, I can. I've held shit in for a week sooner'n squat where I didn't choose to. Like stones it comes out, but that's my business. I do my own.

September 1986—Marjo, Chatting Up the Nurse

No no no, I don't need to wear those yet! A little accident, I had. It could happen to anyone—get busy, working away, and simply forget to go!

I *know* the toilet's right there, nurse. I just.... For a moment, I didn't remember.

My friend Dora, she comes every week, yes nurse, you've seen her, Dora says it's bad that I don't remember. I say remembering can be even worse. What do you think?

Sit with me a little, nurse? Watch the Expo fireworks? Ever so pretty, I declare! There, isn't that a lovely view?

Caddy died in 1934 but Dora went on and on about her. At her eighty-fifth birthday! We all stared at that blazing cake. What could we say? We just sat tight, wondering *when can we start talking again?* What did Dora do that for? And looking like a witch in her black tent. I wore my good blue.

Why Dora, my friend, her birthday party! Whatever did you think? No, I haven't told you about it before. How could I, nurse? It was just last week while you were away in Mexico.

But I don't *want* to come inside! The fireworks aren't over. I won't wear those diapers.

Do look at my shoes, nurse! Dora says slingbacks are too young but I say two-tone blue is pretty. What do you think?

Now if I talked about another dead child of Dora's... well! *Poke your granny right there*, I could say to her grandchildren. *Poke her. Hard as a rock, isn't she? Guess what's inside.* Now that'd be a birthday they wouldn't forget! Can you guess, nurse?

Please don't go! Mr. and Mrs. Whatsit next door have each other to talk to, all the time. Can't they wait five minutes for their pills? I declare I haven't told you half the story, nurse! Not even half.

I said *no*, nurse. You can leave those diapers here if you like, but you can't make me wear them.

1984—*Marjo, Reminiscing with Her Friends*

On the dark balcony outside my room here, the coloured lights on the Inlet look so pretty—white and yellow on the bridge and up the mountains in North Van, red and green on all the boats, orange at the Wheat Pool.

Look, Luella.

Look, Gwen.

Look, Dorothy. Strings of light across the inky water.

When the kids were little, if one bulb went on the Christmas tree the whole string went. Remember unscrewing every light, trying a new bulb in every socket till you found the bum one?

Mike used to say *It's a red one, every time.*

Look at the strings of light, Jo.

Indigo.

Like a necklace, I declare.

Diamonds are a girl's best friend, Marilyn's arm in the long pink satin glove. Remember, girls? There used to be good movies.

Ned gave Dora an Add-A-Pearl necklace. Now—when was that? Every birthday and Christmas and anniversary, another pearl came. Years, for years. Very sweet, that man could be. What happened to those pearls? Does Mary have the necklace now? I must ask Dora.

What happened at breakfast today was the milk for the Cream of Wheat. *The milk's off,* I told that girl. *It's not just on the turn,* I said, *it's off. Smell it yourself, Miss Smarty-Pants.*

Marjorie doesn't like PineSol. Makes her eyes water. But you can't tell them that. *Stick it up your nose!* They use it everywhere here. PineSol, Lysol, Javex—the place reeks.

Freda says her friend on Seven got Big C of the nose and they cut it off... *before it fell off,* ha ha!

A lot of us have bits off. Breasts moles eyes. A lung. A kidney. A slice off the colon. *Two for tea, tea for two, You for me, me for you.* Freaks, we are, eh Luella? Such a pretty dress she wore, who? *No No Nanette.* Sweetheart neckline for a sweetheart. Good movies then, but now there's all coloured on TV, Chinese next door. Did you ever, girls?

What do they do with the cut-off bits, the cut-out bits? I wondered, always.

What happened to Dora's Add-A-Pearl? I'll ask. She might not tell. I've never told about Ned and me.

At first a necklace like that looks skimpy, but the years fill it up quick. Add up, Peg! Add up, Betty! We *can* add, too. Not like our grandchildren that can't do two plus two without a calculator. *Tea for two.* Peaches with Ned. Not just sugar. Onions too, ginger, cardamom, cloves.

In the harbour the coloured lights are so pretty, yes, strings of light on the dark water. Mike and me, we'd go up the Inlet in the dark, on our boat, all the way to Port Moody. Dancing at that hotel—what was it called? With Dora, with Ned, with all the others when all of us were young. And come home again in the middle of the night. All the way, we'd sing.

At Christmas the kids went right round the tree till they found the bum one. *Always the green.* That's a long time ago. Indigo. *Oh, Dad you always say that.* Blue's always been for me.

Dora could wear any colour, though she didn't think so. Dora's skin when we were young—oh my! Long ago. Dora never knew how pretty she was.

I still wear make-up, girls, and earrings. I declare, in a place like this a woman has to watch herself. Eh, Pamela? We mustn't let go, mustn't get those awful whiskers. Dentures. Leaks. And we mustn't mustn't mustn't wear beige! It's bad enough on men—rinsed out in dishwater. Rinso. Long ago.

Some people here don't even get dressed any more. If you see them in their nighties all day, that means they're going soon. *Whiter than white.* I remember that. *You'll wonder where the yellow went, When you brush your teeth with Pepsodent!*

Yellow lights in the harbour, Alice. A necklace of coloured light. I wonder where it went? I'll ask Dora. She might not tell. I've never told. With Dora, you can never tell. When they were courting, Dora and I called Ned *the sugarman* behind his back. Her sugar heart. But her sweetheart, he turned bitter.

The whole string went dead.

Some were bum years all right! Bad, very very bad I've been, sometimes, once. But our Christmas trees were always real. In the lobby here they have a fake one. Colour's wrong, smell's wrong.

Cheaper, Dora says. *She would!* I declare, that woman's so tight she squeaks. Years ago when I saw those red velvet dresses in Mackenzie's on Hastings, I was thrilled. Dark red's no good on me or Hazel, but Mary? Perfect! She'd be twenty-two or so then, I s'pose, with that dark brown hair. So I grabbed the store phone right then and there and dialled Garden Drive.

Mary wasn't home.

"Mary doesn't need anything like that," Dora said.

Did you ever? I said, "Dora, I just think Mary'd *like* it."

The dress came in dark green, too, so I got it for Hazel. To her, I've always given more presents than I did to the others. Clothes, money, trips. Oh, partly we just plain had more money, by the time she came along. With the first three, Mike and me were scrambling to pay the bills. But mostly I give Hazel more in order to make up. I wasn't the same kind of mother, for her.

The only person Dora gives money to is her granddaughter Tessa. Just to spite Mary, I sometimes think, but no, that's not all true. Dora does love that girl! Who loves her too. What did Tessa say? "Grandma's so much fun you can strike sparks off her."

We have our fun here too, eh girls? Our canasta and our bingo and our parties. Come Christmas, I send out my cards just the way I always did. And there's my picture in the *Legion* newsletter: "Our lovely redhead's lively still: Marjo Morgan on the dance floor (Mike, Seaforth Highlanders, 1901–1963)." The library comes round, the hair stylist, that little girl who does massage. And the sing-song man.

From my window I've a view of the Inlet and the mountains, much better than ever at home. I can see where we used to take the boat.

The lights lie on the water like a necklace. Whatever happened to Dora's?

So much happened to Dora. She was even other people sometimes, Mademoiselle Annette LeClerc and Miss Gladys Smith and Mrs. Smith too. She was herself.

We've been friends for almost eighty years. Friendship— it's a wonderful thing.

1914—Dora Cowan and Marjo McEwan Walk Home from School
"Remember Joanie fainting, right in front of Mr. Wooster?"

"And Elsie screaming in the girls' room when she saw blood on her knickers and thought she was dying?"

"And Jessie saying three weeks running she couldn't swing Indian clubs 'cause she was *on her time*, and Miss Eakins sent a note home to her mother? 'I'm so concerned!'"

"Remember Olive Burton's mum hung her rags *on the line?* To bleach?"

"Alan *saw*," Dora recalls in a whisper. "And Owen Jones too." Briefly, the girls are subdued. Trembling sighs issue from them as they find handkerchiefs, wipe their eyes, turn off Wall up Cambridge towards home.

Now Dora's voice is back to normal. "Marjo, how do you tell when your visitor's coming?"

"Easy! Count the days."

"I can tell without counting."

"I draw a star on my calendar, pale so no one but me can see...." Marjo stared. "What d'you mean? Everyone counts."

Dora's right arm is held to her nose. "Ordinary. Tomorrow, maybe. A day or two before, my skin smells like copper."

"Can you tell when other girls have it?" A well-loved topic, this.

"Josie in Domestic today—you saw her feel herself? Acorn saw, too."

Explosive giggles, as the girls take the roles of teacher and class.

"When do we add salt to vegetables as we cook them, girls?"

"To vegetables that grow above ground, Miss Acorn."

"To what classes of vegetables do we not add salt, girls?"

"To vegetables that grow underground, Miss Acorn."

"And how may we prepare veal?"

"Jellied, Miss Acorn."

"Good, Elsie! And?"

"Stuffed fillet, Miss Acorn."

"Good, Luella! And?"

"Stewed knuckle, Miss Acorn."

"Good, Annie! An economical dish. But we don't serve

lamb and pork and veal one after another, do we? Always remember—"

Here the dialogue shatters as the two girls shout, "The wholesomeness of beef, girls! Beef roast in between!" They collapse on each other, laughing.

Marjo recovers first. "I hate veal. Anyway, Josie for sure, today." She ticks off on her fingers. "And May. Perhaps Annie."

"Patty's easy—she never washes."

"Olive told me Miss Acorn talked to Patty about being 'fresh and dainty.' Did you ever!"

"Josie told me Miss Acorn told Patty to tell her mother to buy those Hartmann towels. *From Eaton's.* Imagine—*buying* them?"

"Josie told *me* Patty likes your brother."

"Alan?"

"He *is* good-looking. Lots of girls like him."

Dora's nose wrinkles. "Helen waddles." She imitates, and the girls laugh so hard they stop walking. "She should fold her rag thick but *narrow*. I can't *bear* that bulge. And if I leaked and a boy knew, I would die."

"Awful! Remember when Jenny leaked and Mr. Merritt told her to come to the blackboard and she begged not to and he made her and she dripped red on the aisle and Owen Jones laughed and she cried and cried?"

Breathless at the horror, the girls sway up the slope until they see Mrs. Cowan and Mrs. McEwan ahead. At once their gait smooths to sedateness.

"What about teachers? Acorn? Eakins? Old Hollander?"

"But they're almost dead!" Riotous giggles as the girls arrive incoherent and stumbling at their mothers.

Next morning Mrs. Cowan arrives without knocking in Dora's room. "Don't be silly, child, there's nothing of you I haven't seen. I'll help you with your binder. It's not tight enough. Yesterday you were wobbling something awful when you came up the hill with Marjo. Where do you get these big...? Not from *my* family." Mrs. Cowan's lips thinned.

"Mum, that hurts!"

"No, it doesn't."

The girl wriggles. "They get all sweaty underneath."

"Dora Cowan! *Perspire* is what a young lady says. You eat too much. A girl has to watch herself, Dora. You're so hippy. Look!" Mrs. Cowan smacks her daughter's naked thigh. "Marjo has a lovely figure. *She* doesn't take second helps. Don't you care? You've quite a pretty face, Dora. Such a pity. And why on earth are you wearing that grey dress Miss Dearing gave you? Again?"

Dora silently buttons the dress. Her mother watches. Unaware, Mrs. Cowan's hand slides up to her neck; she is wont to finger and finger her pearl necklace.

"Is it at the pawnshop again, Mum?"

"Don't take that sarcastic tone with me, miss!" But Mrs. Cowan's hand falls, limp. She sighs. "Your father always calls them *the pearls I gave you*, but Granny Cowan sent them."

"Wasn't she poor?"

"She was a saver. Charlie Cowan could never save a penny." Abruptly Mrs. Cowan straightens up. "Such a dull colour, Dora! Don't you want to look cheerful and bright like Marjo?"

At fourteen, Dora's adult body, designed at conception and complete while still housed in Mrs. Cowan's womb, with hundreds of eggs, has declared itself. Slightly taller than her mother, Dora has sloping shoulders; breasts not girlish rosebuds but full-bloom peonies; a trim waist; hips flaring to robust thighs. With horror she stands on the scale while her mother fiddles with the weights. "Nine stone, Dora! *Far* too much for a girl your age." Every single stone Dora feels, dense, weighing her down.

Dora has slim calves and ankles and small high-arched feet but discounts any compliments on these or on her skin and her abundant soft hair. Even the minister at All Saints, Mr. Nurse, has smiled at Dora, quoting Corinthians: "If a woman have long hair, it is a glory to her." Then he blushes and looks away. Flustered, Dora wants only not to be there, not to hear that.

As she walks to school with Marjo in hot early September, Dora's breasts are sore under that binder. She's belted herself so severely that her stomach bulges. Her pelvis aches, her arms exude metallic odour, her thighs rub. Sweat at first reduces the friction, then pools at all tight or hairy places.

"Am I wet at the back?"

In spite of Marjo's reassurance, Dora scurries across the schoolyard where boys are at play, Owen Jones quick and shouting among them. She is a head taller than he and feels like an elephant. To Marjo she has said nothing of this. Dora heads for the girls' washroom.

Mrs. Hollander that day drills her class for the city-wide spelling bee, enjoying herself as they warm up with easy homonyms—*plum plumb, mantel mantle, boarder border, canvas canvass*—and the not-quites, *allusion illusion, centurion cente-*

narian, moral morale. Marjo gets the old team *principal principle* and so allows Mrs. Hollander the old joke about Mr. Everett: "Our pal, isn't he?" *Utter* and *udder* are next. "Dora?"

As she rises to spell, her binder slips. Instinctively Dora clutches at her breasts.

Owen's crowing glee sounds first in the mirth of thirty.

Mrs. Hollander can rap with her pointer all she likes; the roaring laughter won't stop. Furious, Marjo protests, but not even her golden popularity can protect Dora now, Dora the quiet, Dora the usually unnoticed. Dora runs. Squeals of "Utters! Udders!" and calls of "Can you utter udders?" explode. Girls and boys fall about the classroom, pounding their desks.

Without raising her hand for permission, Marjo leaves the class and goes to her weeping friend in the girls' washroom.

This private weeping, though, is Dora's last of the schoolday, even though laughter continues in every lesson. Arithmetic, Geography—snickers, sputters, snorts, even hiccups. Art, Social Studies. All through, Dora denies her desire to cry. She holds tight the muscles of eyes, jaw, shoulders until her head and neck are stiff as stone.

By three o'clock the mockery's pretty well spent, and only a few murmurs strike Dora as she leaves for home. Steadily, not looking at anyone, she walks across the schoolyard. Owen stands apart from the other boys, clearly waiting for her. His expression is serious, even sad. She does not glance but goes on.

Her house is quiet. In her room, Dora pushes a chair under the doorknob, takes off her green gingham waist, unties the hateful binder. With a cloth dipped in water she refreshes her hot skin. No tears fall, although they are packed tight up there behind the dam of her eyes. She lies down on her bed and pulls the counterpane over her face—but in the dimness there's Owen's face right up against hers. He's laughing. Quickly Dora uncovers. She tries to cry. She can't. She sits up on the edge of her bed.

The afternoon goes on. What can she do? Homework is impossible. *Elsie Dinsmore* is much too sad.

Then come footsteps outside. Miss Dearing, coming home. Tap tap tap. The dressmaker moves around upstairs, flushes her toilet, boils her kettle. Faintly there sounds the hiss of water hitting tea. Now Miss Dearing is working the treadle of her machine, *rum*-rum, *rum*-rum. Soothed by the rhythm, Dora lies down again, first taking her doll Flora from the shelf. *Rum*-rum. She holds Flora close, tells all the pain. Abundant tears fall. *Rum*. Then Dora sleeps till Mrs. Cowan, cross as two sticks, shouts at her daughter to set the table for supper right *now*.

Her father flaps the newspaper at his family. "A day to remember."

No one responds.

"Does no one in this house care that we've won a great battle? *Marne*—don't you see this headline?"

"I see a girl who's not cleaning her plate. I'll have you know, miss, that cooking takes time *and* effort. Most girls would be grateful."

"Betty, must you badger her?" Charlie Cowan glares. "Give your mind to what's important! We are a nation, a proud nation, at war." He sips his beer, glances smiling at his son. "And if this war lasts long enough, we'll have our very own soldier."

Alan blushes, gobbles.

"I won't stand for it, Charlie! Do you hear me? I won't stand for that kind of awful talk about our boy!"

While washing up, Dora tucks a wooden spoon into her pocket. Later she slips out to the side yard, where the strawberry arbutus and the hydrangeas grow. In the clayey soil she digs a hole for the binder. Tomorrow her angry mother will rummage in her work-basket for another cloth to strap her daughter tight—but at least this one lies buried.

Next day as they walk to school, solicitous Marjo pats Dora's arm and asks repeatedly, "How do you feel, Dora? Do you feel all right now?"

Dora can't answer. Her friend is too close, Marjo the slight and slim with small breasts so beautifully shaped. Dora can't tell her. She is too near.

"*Tsk!*" Annoyed, Marjo moves away a little from Dora till they turn south on Victoria and see Owen Jones going up the hill ahead, towards school. The girls slow their pace.

Dora tries a safe topic. "Marjo, how d'you suppose Mr. Hubble holds on to Miss Eakins when they kiss?" A love affair between the principal and the gym teacher has long been supposed, believed, vividly described.

"With that awful arm-thing of his? I don't know!"

Laughing, the girls imitate Mr. Hubble's nervous sleeve-patting.

"He really likes her."

"I saw them touching, remember? Outside his office? I told you first."

"No, you didn't. I told you."

"Did too!"

"Didn't."

Sour looks, raised voices.

"Liar! You always lie."

"I only play with you because Mum makes me. She's sorry for you."

They stop walking. Backs are turned. Arms are folded.

"My mum says your mum's stingy as a Jew."

"Your mum keeps a dirty house. Even for Irish she's a disgrace, my mum says."

Glares, hissing, spittle.

"Too bad you're *fat*. You can't ever borrow my new blue sateen dress."

"It makes you look like a scarecrow, Marjo. Olive and Jessie and Annie and Peg all said so. They all laughed at you."

Gasps, deep breaths, red faces.

"You don't know what everyone at school calls *you* now, Dora. And not just the girls, either." Marjo jumps about in triumph. "Dora Cowan Cow-Cow. *Cow-Cow, that's you!*"

Birthdays

1982—Mary, to Her Seventeen-Year-Old Daughter Tessa

You little bitch you little slut where've you been don't you realize your father and me've been half-crazy with worry aren't you ashamed up and down the alleys in the dark one boy after another little slut and you look like a hooker boobs falling out of your dress letting boys paw at you no shame aren't you ashamed and as for sleeping on your grandma's back porch I don't believe it for a minute no no no your grandma took you in I know her for all I know you met her out in the alleys too crazy old bitch roaming around like a bear at the garbage dump all the way over to the PNE grounds she hangs around by the roller coaster might as well be a wild animal might as well be an addict disgraceful in those crazy rig-outs tents and boiler suits looks like a fool looks like a beggar such behaviour when I think of what my poor father put up with I'd like to lock her in her house and throw away the key hard as stone Mum is hard as stone she wore him down wore him out and as for you Tessa you're lying lying lying your damn grandma took you in and you slept cosy in her spare room don't lie and don't you dare call me *Maddy Mum* or I'll slap your face so hard you'll spin into next year Miss High-and-Mighty I know you I know your grandma two of a kind selfish and hard the pair of you no feelings for anyone else she'll pee herself laughing at me over this I know her Tessa you get up those stairs this minute and don't come out of your room until I say so and before you leave this house again you'll name those boys and your father'll phone their parents and between us we'll put a stop to this d'you hear me we'll put a stop to it I'll call the City I'll call the police they'll board up that crazy old garage or stable or whatever it is down by the Princeton that abandoned place disgusting screwing and smoking a fine place for girls your age to be hanging out and don't think for one minute I don't know who showed you that place because I do *she* did *she* did *she* did as bad as you she is who knows maybe Mum's done some screwing there herself I wouldn't put anything past her my poor dad poor dad and if I smell smoke on you one more time there'll be more trouble Tessa I don't care if Grandma lets you smoke at her house it's a filthy habit I don't care what your grandma does I know her there's nothing that woman could do would surprise me I've seen it all seen her smirking at herself in the mirror heard her laughing her head off at nothing at all anyhow you get one thing clear through your head Tessa Cornish no daughter of mine's going to lie on her back in a filthy shed screwing anything that walks in the door with his pants open shut up Bill shut up Bill Tessa needs to hear what she is a dirty slut look at her Bill our dear little girl seventeen today and no underpants on

1978—Marjo, Attending Mary's Fiftieth Birthday Party
Dora's so hard on Mary! Spiteful. In Dora's eyes, Mary can't do anything right. Not in fifty years, I'm thinking as I ring Mary's doorbell. Today she looks nice. A real party dress, that. Dark red suits her. And she's had a good perm, this time.

"Hi, Aunty Marjo." Then right away, "I wish Dad was here."

"Ned always liked your pretty hair," I say, patting her perm. Mary gives her funny shy smile then. She won't meet your eyes, but her mouth curls. Sweet. Look at that grey in her hair, though. Dyeing's so easy now, it's fun, everyone does it—but Mary's Dora all over again! They make things hard for themselves, those two. They won't enjoy what they've got. Or can't.

A *child's* fiftieth! I can't get used to it, I declare.

It's Mary's first birthday without her father, but everyone else is here for her. Mary's husband, Bill. Mary's kids: Bill Jr., Alan, Vicky, Tessa. Good lookers the lot of them, specially Tessa. Lots of Mary's friends. And Mary's mother. Not Mary's brother, because unless Joyce makes him John Dow won't come anywhere near his mum, and Joyce wouldn't lift a finger for Mary.

I wish Mike were alive so I could sit with him.

Dora and I share a settee. Two grandmothers. Two widows. No, a divorcee isn't a widow when her ex-husband dies, is she? Something happens, though. There just isn't a word for it.

Dora's wearing a plain tent. Not black or grey, either—sage green. You couldn't call it festive, but there's no blackberry stains, no rents, no patches, no buttons sewn on at random. I declare, it's hard to believe how smart Dora could look way back when she was being Mademoiselle Annette in that dress shop. So well turned out! And the same when she was at Spencer's, being Gladys. The latest, the very thing—that's what Dora wore. Now the best to be said is that she's presentable. And present, today. Maybe that's her birthday present to her daughter?

When Bill puts his arm round Mary and gives the toast, she really smiles. Her smiling children stand round her. When you think what Mary had to deal with in her own childhood.... She's done it well. Hasn't passed the bad on to the next generation. People take photos. Dora sips her rye, I sip my rum and Coke.

"Mary's all bothered about Tessa," Dora says, sourly.

Tessa: mid-teens, sullen, boy-crazy of course. She's growing too fast to be pretty just now, but she will be. Her skin's as lovely as her grandmother's. She's got taste, too. That's a smart hairdo. Perfect earrings. Right now she's shoving a tray of Cheese Dreams under people's noses as if she'd rather hit them.

Dora says, "Mary's obsessed about teenage pregnancy."

Obsessed! I can't believe my ears.

Doesn't Dora remember obsession? The fear, the praying. Half our Domestic Science class lay awake at night, I'm sure. *Help me, help me. In the morning please let there be blood on my nightie, please.* A miracle! Like in elementary school—*Please can school burn down before the arithmetic test?*—but worse. *Please let me be wrong. Let it be I've just counted days wrong.*

Tessa comes out of the kitchen. It's Angels on Horseback this time, and she brings the platter over to me and her grandma.

"Hello, Tessa dear," but I don't get a response. She can't do that yet, I guess. "Don't these look tasty! Did you make them?"

"No." She shoves the plate at Dora. "Hi, Gran."

"I hate cooked oysters. Why does your mother make these?"

"Because they look horrible. Slimy *and* burnt." And Tessa's off again before I can say *What a pretty dress.*

I shake my head. "Dora, why must you be so hard on Mary?"

No answer. No surprise. How many years have I known Dora? More than seventy.

"Dora, didn't you worry when Mary was young? I know I did, with Maureen and Hazel."

No answer.

Back in high school, we thought we'd worried so hard our insides had got paralyzed so our visitor couldn't come. *Please let something happen, please.* But if time went on and on and no blood came, the *something* to pray for was miscarriage.

And then Dora gives me such a mean smile! "About Mary, there was no reason to worry." So spiteful!

I look away, at Mary, by the fireplace. In her red dress. With her husband. She's putting on the earrings he's given her for her birthday: garnets, with gold. Thank God for Bill. If he hadn't seen past all young Mary's grumpiness and sourness and flying-off-the-handle, where would Maddy be now? Thank God some young men have good sense.

"Dora Dow, you *are* in one of your nasty moods!"

In Domestic Science, we *prayed* for pain. *Is that a cramp?* We held our breath. *Oh let it get worse. Let it hurt really really badly so the thing comes out.*

The pain *did* turn out to be dreadful. I fell down on the street. I fell off the bicycle. My clothes were ruined—my best georgette blouse my mother made. I wore it that awful day, specially, to make me feel better. Dora got me home. All that long way she pulled me, safe to the end. I was a big burden but she never let me go. I can't forget it, so I've never told. Not her, not anybody, though it's been a hard secret to keep.

Yes, we prayed. *Let it come out of me. Please, so I can hide it where no one will ever find out.* The terror of anyone else knowing was worse than the pain, I declare. Worse even than when we realized we weren't dreading or hoping any more, but *knowing* what was inside us. Not our visitor.

In my life I had that happen twice.

One was cut out.

One came out.

The first time, my father found out. Her father found out. My mother. Her mother. The doctor that Dad got to come to our house. The minister. That bad doctor who did it knew too, of course. And his horrid nurse. And all those other girls, waiting in that room with the dishes. I lay in my bed and counted. Downstairs, Mum was in tears. She was mending my blouse. I counted at least twenty people who knew what I'd done, twenty at least, plus *him*. What did that bad doctor do with what he took out of me? I never found out.

The second time, no one knew but me. Maybe Mike suspected, but he's dead. And Ned's dead. I don't think anyone else knows—but with Dora you never know.

I try again. "Such good food, Dora!" I say. "What a spread!" For her birthday party Mary's done seafood, buffet style. There's always plenty to eat at Mary's house. Tomatoes stuffed with crab in mayonnaise. A big chafing dish full of shrimp and lobster and buttered noodles in cream sauce. Avocado salad with Green Goddess dressing—a nip of anchovy, there. It's all wonderful. Mary makes it all *look* good, too. That's a gift.

When she was little I said to them, "Mary cooks *well*," said so again and again when she was in her teens. Of course Dora didn't listen. Ned did. An old-fashioned man, he was, and he couldn't see what I saw, a *career* for Mary, but he listened. He loved her. Thank goodness Mary had that sweetness in her life.

"Rich," Dora says. "Mary's food is always too rich." She scrapes away the sauce and dressing till her food's bare. Did you ever?

Dessert. Whipped white ripples across the cake—now that, by the looks of it, comes from one of those Italian pastry shops on the Drive. Dora pushes away all the cream.

Bill Jr. gives the second toast, to "our grampa, Mum's dad, who died last year." Mary gets teary. Bill brings Kleenex. I clap, everyone claps except Dora; she just happens to be putting her plate down. There's *Ned Ned Ned* sounding all over the room, but on our settee we're silent.

Dora and I don't speak of what's inside her, either. We're the only ones here in this room who could—but since Hazel I've not said a word. Dora never says a word.

What happened to Dora—well, back there in Domestic Science none of us girls dreamed of such a thing. Not in our wildest! What a miracle a stone baby would have been for us! Because, even if you get big as a house, if nothing actually comes out of your body, no one can prove anything. Oh, people can snicker and whisper all they want, but they can't *know*. Nothing to dispose of, no blood on your dress, no *thing*.

A girl in trouble. Everyone called it that then, you don't hear it so much now. But if that trouble *turned to stone*—why, for a girl I declare it'd be a dream come true.

As Mary opens her presents I think about how many of her birthday parties I've been to. The first dozen, for sure—baby, toddler, little girl. Dolls, dresses, toys. I made the cakes too, and later I taught Mary to bake them. Always over at our house, she was, learning right along with Maureen. How Mike used to tease Mary! Not hard, mind, the way he teased our kids. You couldn't, with Mary—she'd cry. He'd joke, "Really you're a Morgan, my girl. Maureen, Mick, Murray, Mary. . . . You *belong* here!" Then he'd give her one of his big hugs. She bloomed.

Today she's pleased with the silk scarf I've brought, and with her other gifts—jewellery, a sweater with sequins, perfume, crystal ornaments, a nylon housecoat are all heaped up around her chair. Her cheeks are pink. She picks up another box and reads the card. "From Mother." I'm relieved. The package is even wrapped decently and tied with ribbon. Last year Dora's present was just some bank calendar, rolled up in newspaper.

Out of the tissue Mary pulls an old mirror, oval, small, framed in carved wood, polished.

"How pretty," all the grown-ups murmur.

The grandchildren ask, "Is that a real antique?"

Mary is tearful, smiling. She holds and holds the mirror, won't hand it to anyone. "Mum, *Mum.* Thank you. You know I've always loved this little mirror."

"For heaven's sake," says Dora, "I don't want it. You might as well have it now as later."

A dreadful second of silence ... and then *Happy Birthday to You!* Tessa almost shouts the words and glares round to make everybody join in. Gratefully we sing. *Happy Birthday Dear Mary....* She *is* dear, though difficult. There's no getting away from that. *Maddy*, John used to call her when they were kids, teasing, and she did get so mad! Not hard to see where the mad comes from, either.

As the song winds on, I check for Dora's voice. She is not singing. That is the *last straw!*

Ned had a fine tenor voice. Sweet. We sang with him in our boat, going up to Port Moody. *Who—who stole my heart away—who?*

When the song and the clapping end, Bill Jr. comes round with more drinks for us. To get up my nerve, I take a big swallow of my rum and Coke, and then I say to Dora, "Mary's missing Ned today. I declare it'd sure be nice for her to have one parent at her party who loves her *and says so.*" I get up. Alone on the settee—that's where I leave Dora. For sure no one else will endure *that cranky old lady*, except maybe nice Bill. Too bad! Off I go to the buffet for more dessert.

Tessa's there. She's eating leftovers with her fingers and stacking up dirty plates with as much clatter as she can make.

"Not so loud, dear," and Mary touches her daughter's arm, just barely touches. The face Tessa makes! You'd think she'd spooned up a mouthful of vomit, I declare. Poor Mary moves away.

Yes, poor Mary.

Poor Dora...and here she comes. With a little grin she slips Tessa some rolled-up bills. The girl blushes. Doesn't speak, glowers a bit, still mad about Grandma not singing *Happy Birthday* to Mum...but then Tessa slides the packet down where her cleavage will be when she gets some.

When you're young, it's hard to say no to money. Poor Tessa.

Poor me.

Poor Hazel—we've never been close.

But really, poor Dora. What chance did she have, the way things were back then?

1910—The Way Things Were for Dora, Back Then

"Dora, do you know how a man makes a baby?"

"Men can't have babies, Marjo."

"I know and you don't! I know and you don't!"

Doll in hand, Dora begins to walk away.

"Wait up, I'll tell!" Marjo follows. "So horrid, you can't imagine." She holds up her doll. "Maggie's the husband. She has a thing here," wiggling a finger between the pantaletted legs.

Dangler is Dora's name for the pale wobble glimpsed on Alan's bath night, the hairy lump under her father's pyjamas. "I know *that*."

Marjo shoves her doll against Dora's. "He goes to the toidy inside her, but Flora hasn't got a hole so I can't get his thing in right."

"Who said?" Dora snatches her child back.

"My mum. She said it was time I knew."

Dora's stopped by that, for a second. "What hole?"

"I told you it was horrid."

The girls sit down again on Marjo's porch.

School is out. They do not talk about the whipping they witnessed today in the gymnasium.

Marjo kisses Maggie, who's better dressed than her sister-dolls Meg, Margie, Peggy, Madge.

All Dora's dolls have rhyming names: Laura, Cora, Nora, Flora, Thora. Alan sneeringly suggests Moira. Dora tells him and tells him, "It doesn't rhyme. Can't you hear?"

Flora is the oldest and Dora's favourite. She is short and square-ish, made of wood and therefore good to hit with, but not easy to dress, being so stiff. Nonetheless she holds the place of honour on Dora's pillow. Flora is sturdier than china Nora or cloth Laura with her flabby fat legs or Cora in her real silk dress. If Flora gets left out overnight it does not matter, as the yellow paint of her hair and the blue of her eyes mostly wore off long ago. She comes from Granny Cowan in England, does Flora, with a little rhyme:

Goodness gracious
Gracious goodness
Dora's doll is
Made of woodness!

The girls look about Cambridge Street. In the sunlight eagles scream, gulls miaow. On the CPR tracks the freights shunt and gasp. The moist spring air moves softly, full of salt, earth, cedar. Underneath those strong smells blow woodsmoke, stew meat, tar, fishpaste, sawdust—and horses, for down the block two grunting animals have been hauling boulders at yet another new house site. The basement's in, so the girls can imagine the shelves of pickles, canned salmon, jam. Bang bang of nails, ruzz ruzz of saws, on and on. Next door, Olive Burton's mother plants radishes and sings "Down by the salley gardens." A black cat licks his bum-hole. The girls grimace.

Alan and a friend appear, snicker, make faces. Marjo would make even worse faces back, but Dora does not want to. The two rise and go into Marjo's house.

In pails of seawater in the kitchen are oysters and clams. Marjo claps. "Chowder for supper, good!"

Different from Dora's home. Dora's English mother, raised inland, distrusts shellfish. "I'll eat things I can see when I buy them, thank you."

"Maybe you'll find a pearl." Dora gazes into the salty sparkle.

"Dad says there's black pearls."

"Alan says there's pearls where the Indians ate. On the beach below Wall, where the slope's full of shells."

Marjo heads upstairs. "Mum! Mum!" This too is different. The McEwans live in the whole house, not just on one floor.

Kneeling before a bureau, Mrs. McEwan sorts out tiny smocked nightgowns, jackets with minute satin bows, knitted boots. Different again. Resentfully, Mrs. Cowan darns. When Dora play-sews with Miss Dearing the dressmaker and makes a whole doll dress almost by herself, Mrs. Cowan scolds. "You don't want to be an old maid sewing for your living! Or like Granny Cowan back home, either, God forbid, traipsing from house to house to sew and living on other people's scraps. No, I'll see that you'll marry a *good* provider."

Mrs. McEwan wears a wrapper flowered in blue. Smiling, she agrees to come down and provide sticky buns; slowly she gets up. The wrapper opens. Such titties! Like big eyes. And such a tummy! Is she sick? Curly dark hair bushes out between slim thighs. Dora blinks. Blue roses hide everything.

Going home, Dora takes her doll into the sideyard between the Cowans' house and Mrs. Findlay's. Here strawberry arbutus and hydrangeas provide cover. Here lies buried treasure: pennies flattened on the railway tracks; green glass, shards of willow-ware; china beads and buttons in tins saying *Doan's Kidney Pills*.

Once Marjo buries a doll. Lost for weeks, she's only found by accident; Mrs. McEwan kills the mildew on poor smelly Meg, who reeks of carbolic ever after. Worse is the buried blueing. When Mrs. Cowan angrily misses it, Dora and Marjo dig wildly, scrabble up the crumbly cubes and ruin their waists. Worst of all is the pearl ring (Alan says it's only pretend), a parental birthday present, buried and lost. For two months, Dora holds that terrible secret. Then Alan, to spite his sister, asks at supper, "Where's your ring?" A whipping follows.

Under the front porch is good too. In this shadowy low-ceilinged hideaway, supple children crawl and curl and giggle silently. Beer and whisky bottles stick out of the soil. They hold dead insects, still smell of hops or rye. Charlie Cowan is too lazy to walk downhill and throw them into the tangled blackberry bushes on Wall, but this is not mentioned between the girls.

Here, once, Dora finds an oval mirror, framed in polished wood. She stares, trying to remember where she has seen this pretty thing. Of course ... in Mrs. Findlay's over-furnished parlour. Later, that mirror lies in Dora's mother's bureau drawer. Then there's the brass candlestick. "Such a quaint curly handle!" Mrs. Cowan exclaims, at the land-lady's again, daughter in tow, to pay the rent. Not long after, there's fresh digging under the porch; Dora notes the can-dlestick's arrival. And sometimes on the maple table a knife or spoon appears that's quite unlike the Cowans' rough cut-lery. Neither the father nor the brother notices, but Dora's mother handles these utensils lovingly.

Dora sits down and pulls up her dress, to hate her thighs. White and plump, they brush together. "You wad-dle," Alan sneers.

Once, a rash develops. Laughing, Mrs. Cowan offers Calvert's Prickly Heat Soap.

"But that's for babies!"

"Lather it up well. Get rid of that nastiness on you."

Mrs. Cowan finds a paste used in the nappy years and tries to smear it on her daughter's thighs. Dora won't let her. She applies it privately, pressing her sticky fingers into flesh that gives way like porridge under a spoon. The ointment does soothe; this is almost worse than if it had not.

Under the porch now, contemplating her flesh, Dora remembers last summer.

One night, hearing her mother sigh, Dora peers out at her; the Cowans' bedrooms all open off the parlour. Mrs. Cowan's pink mull nightdress is blotched with damp and hangs darkly transparent, showing the swell of stomach and rump. Wearily she shuffles to the bathroom. Mr. Cowan's snores resume.

Mum's wet herself. Disgusting, yet according to Marjo's information, *that was Daddy's piss. But Mum didn't have a baby. Marjo must be wrong.*

Now Dora throws Flora away from her, down on the dirt.

Dora's arm brushes her chest, where two awful points burn. Marjo *says* they do not really stick out. Not much.

Mrs. Cowan frowns. "Goodness, Dora, busty already? I wasn't till I was fourteen. Girls aren't, in England.... This country's so different. Well. If you go on like this, I shall have to put a binder on you."

A soft spring rain begins, the sun still shines, leaves glisten.

Dora hears someone coming up the front walk; her father's tipsy steps resound on the porch. She picks up Flora and moves back along the sideyard to a spot by the open kitchen window.

"Coming home in that state ... should be ashamed. Now don't you dare set your lunch pail on my good table! The children kick it and ink it and carve it, you put your boots on it, no one ever sets a hot dish on a towel...."

Mrs. Cowan's mournful tone evokes a good house-keeper's despair, but Dora knows that, by the standards of Miss Acorn's Domestic Science classroom at Macdonald School, her mother is incompetent. She does not scald dishtowels daily, nor each week ream out the icebox drain-pipe with wire wrapped in cloth, nor use carbolic in her refuse pail. Once Dora quotes Miss Acorn: "Every cellar needs an annual whitewashing with lime." Her mother's laugh is harsh. "Who in this family would do anything as useful as that, Dora?"

Dora's father settles into a chair. A boot falls. "What matters a table today, Betty? The King is dead. His subjects grieve." Thump—the other boot. "Mind you, Edward wasn't the man his mum was. Not a patch on the old Queen."

A pillowy sigh—Mrs. Cowan sits beside him. Dora turns up her nose.

"A wonderful lady she was, Charlie."

"Wonderful. Hard on him, waiting so long." A jaw-cracking yawn. "Sixty, when she popped off at last. A lad of sixty, you might say."

"Popped off! To speak so of your Queen? After all she went through. Albert, all those children." Mrs. Cowan's chair squeaks as she rises.

"A boy of sixty," Mr. Cowan repeats. "An old child."

Water trickles. A stove-lifter clanks. "Charlie!"

Dora winces.

"Can't you remember that this stove needs fuel? I don't ask much, only"—Mrs. Cowan's voice begins to shake—"a little help with the heavy work. I can't carry up those great loads of sawdust! And with Alan it's always *later, Mum, later.* Charlie, if you had any feeling for me...."

Another chair-scraping. "I'll get the damned stuff! Just don't nag."

"*Any* feeling ... you'd not stay so long drinking...." A sob.

"*Don't nag!* On this day of all days I've a right to a drink after work."

Footsteps down to the cellar. Up again. A match strikes. Kettle meets stove. Dora knows what's next.

Just in time, she emerges from the wet bushes to mimic—unseen—her mother, who stands on the porch in her bibbed apron, feet apart and arms akimbo, and cries to all Cambridge Street, "Do-o-o-ra!"

"Right here, Mum."

"And where've you been all afternoon? That rain, and me with washing to bring in? At Marjo's, I'll be bound. Again! Is your name Dora McEwan? Stand up straight, for pity's sake. You're hunching again. And your waist's all wet."

Without having to be reminded, Dora places her shoes on her particular corner of the pink chenille mat.

"You're *our* daughter." Mrs. Cowan's voice quivers. "And those McEwans have no reason to look down on us. None! Remember that next time you're lazing over there while I'm working my fingers to the bone. Now get busy, Dora."

The maple table is heaped with laundry at one end and at the other lies a muddle of schoolbooks, scribblers, pencils.

"That's *my* homework! Why'd you let Alan mess my things up?"

"The boy's in high school. He needs space to do his lessons." Back turned, Mrs. Cowan addresses the stove.

Stiff, wordless, Dora sets the table. This week's tablecloth pictures Niagara Falls; Dora puts the best view of the Falls at her own place, near the radiator. If there's tension at table, she always reaches for the round petalled radiator knob. It fits her palm firmly, like a stone. Holding on helps her through. The Toby jug, full of milk for herself and Alan, goes at his place.

Dora sniffs: leftover mutton stew. She will peel the stringy meat away, try to hide the fat under potato to avoid the chorus of *Waste not, want not*. If she fails, hours may pass while she sits alone at the table, silent, rigid, refusing to *clean her plate*. Eventually, her mother will want help or her father will want a fresh glass. "Oh Dora, for heaven's sake, get up."

Full of beer, tonight Charlie Cowan eats sparingly. A critique of this sin of omission will come later, he is well aware. He may even have to reveal that he has not, *still* not been able to retrieve Betty's pearls from the pawnshop. But now the father focuses on his son. "What's twelve times eight, Alan?"

Dora knows.

"Daddy, you asked that already!" Alan pauses. "Ninety-six."

"I'll ask as often as I please, young fellow-me-lad! Twelve times nine."

Dora knows.

"One hundred and six. No, no, wait! I do know! One hundred and eight." Alan looks at his mother. "Can't I just eat supper?"

"Which, Alan? Shouldn't a high school boy know, Betty?"

Mrs. Cowan eats mashed turnip. Dora chivvies fat about her plate: their father's anger is nowhere near the point where she must help Alan.

"Four times eight, then."

"That's baby, Daddy! Thirty-two."

"Eleven times thirteen."

Dora knows.

"But the tables only go to twelve! Mum, can't I even eat?"

"Don't call for your mummy, Alan. You're her gorgeous boy and she'll forgive you anything, but you're dealing with your father now. What's the answer?"

Silence.

"One hundred and forty-three," sullenly.

Mrs. Cowan turns to Dora. "What happened at school today?"

"Nothing."

A public whipping.

In front of two hundred children, a boy gets strapped.

Owen Jones has stolen from petty cash, but Mr. Everett, king of the school, explains that the whipping is also for *habitual truancy* and *rudeness to teachers*. Owen does not cry.

When the punishment is over, he laughs up at Mr. Everett.

"*Sauce!*" A second whipping.

The gymnasium is quiet, even with all the breathing rows of children, quiet except for the *zing!* of leather rising in the air and the *zot!* as the strap bites Owen's flesh. Those nearest the boy, like Dora, can also hear his gasps and the principal's grunts of effort.

Again, it's over. Owen manages a grin. The principal grabs him by the shoulders and slings the boy across the floor. He lands face-down by Dora's feet. His legs and the polished floorboards are streaked with blood. The weals are purple, plum, maroon. Biting his lip so as not to cry, Owen hauls himself up. He stands absolutely straight. His and Dora's eyes meet. He limps to the gym door and slams it behind him so hard the wall quivers.

Miss Hector says, "*Tsk!*" Gently she opens the door and motions to the children to begin marching out. A small nasty smile adorns her face, the same she wore when she managed to get Owen left back for a year, because of absenteeism.

Repeatedly during the rest of the afternoon Dora has thought of Owen's skin, the smooth tanned skin slashed raw.

"Nothing?" Mrs. Cowan pouts.

"Nothing."

"Have you done all your lessons?"

Dora nods. Easy arithmetic can wait till morning. Among the shrubs or under the porch, before knocking on Marjo's door, she'll pleasurably work fractions without an interrupting call to stir a pudding, wring sheets, sweep.

"Nothing to say for yourself?" Mrs. Cowan sighs. "Well. You're not the girl I was. Might as well speak to a stone. Was it dolls, with Marjo?"

"Dolls," Alan mutters. Dora gives him a look. He begins gobbling.

"Well, what's new over there at Marjo's?"

"They're having chowder for supper. Clams and oysters." Mrs. Cowan sniffs.

"Marjo," opines Charlie Cowan, "is pretty. Slim as a wand, light as a feather. A pearl of a girl!" Failing to prevent a belch, he turns on his son. "Seven times eighteen, Alan!"

"Enough." Mrs. Cowan speaks through clenched teeth. "Clear now, Dora. Why must you always be *told* to do things? And bring the pudding."

"Your prune whip and cream! Our late great King could not eat better."

Alan's shoulders relax.

"No cream." Mrs. Cowan spoons out glutinous brown. "Cream costs money. Someday you'll have to choose for good and all, Charlie. Beer or cream?"

Someday, not now. Charlie Cowan settles in for his evening nap. Instead of counting sheep, he tries unsuccessfully to calculate whether the pearls are presently on their fourteenth or fifteenth visit to the three golden balls on Abbott Street, and soon he snores.

Wiping the table, Dora sees Alan slip out into the spring night.

Now Dora deals with the laundry, under her mother's direction. She sprinkles and folds, sorting through her hateful bulky bloomers, the camisoles that scarcely squeeze over her chest, her parents' sheets, the thin tea towels and cleaning rags. Spitting on an iron yields no sizzle; Dora sets it on the stove and turns to her mother, who is darning her husband's socks.

"Mum. At the McEwans' I saw baby clothes."

Mrs. Cowan's needle stops. And starts again. "I'd heard there might be a little stranger coming over there."

"Mrs. McEwan is fat."

"You are a little girl." Her mother's needle trembles. "Too young to talk about such things."

"I want to know." Dora spits on the iron again and repeats her words, adding, "Marjo's mum told *her*."

"Get on with your work, Dora. I wish you didn't have so much to do, but unless and until *he* stops his drinking we'll never be able to get help."

"I *like* ironing," Dora snaps.

"No you don't! You won't be a housemaid, if I can help it."

"*Why* won't you tell me?" Dora's look is stony.

Red-faced, Mrs. Cowan gets up and takes her mending basket into the snore-filled parlour.

(This is the last time Dora tries truly to talk with her mother about something important. Dora's own daughter Mary is far more persistent, trying and trying and trying yet again to get through, well on into her own middle years.)

For an hour, Dora lifts irons off the stove and slides them over sheets and tablecloths, towels and bedspreads. Stiff creases succumb to the iron's point as it searches every seam; they surrender completely to the hot metal hand that feels so insistently over the breadths. Relaxed, smooth, pliable, the fabrics pour over the ironing board. Dora plays with and fondles them, drapes them so they swoop in graceful panels down to the floor, flow down as if blue-flowered, as if veiling slender thighs, as if tumbling with roses.

"Where's your brother, Dora?" comes Mrs. Cowan's querulous tone. "Why doesn't he ever want to stay home with his family of an evening? Why won't he do his lessons? For pity's sake, Charlie, wake up and take an interest!"

"Don't fuss, Betty. The King is dead. Long live the King!"

In bed, Dora holds Flora tight and tells all about her day.

He bled.

He didn't cry. The principal couldn't make him cry.

Flora, I wanted to hold Owen's hand.

Silently the doll listens to the whole story, every word.

I wanted to help him up off the floor. Oh, how his legs looked, where he was whipped!

Dora never mentions the King.

1976—Mary Cornish, Middle-aged, Complains to Her Mother, Dora
I *am* going, Mum. In just a minute. I'm out here in the rain, aren't I? Do I look as if I'm still inside your house?

I don't care if my hair gets flattened. It's flat anyway. With your weird clothes you're a fine one to talk about how I look. Anyway, I don't care how I look.

What I want to know is what does one person need with a dining-room table that seats six? One person *alone.*

Don't shut your door on me, Mum! It's not cold, and you're perfectly dry, up there on the porch.

That table has a leaf, even, to seat eight. You don't do Christmas any more, Mum. You never have people over. What do you need it for?

I know it's *your* table. I don't want to *take it away.* Only to borrow it, use it, while my kids are mostly still at home.

I don't *want* just any table. If I did, I'd go to Sears and not be here in the rain begging for yours.

Not *give! Lend* your table. Our family table. It would mean a lot to me and my kids.

No, I don't want you to die so I can have it!

If John asked for that table for him and Joyce and their kids, he'd have it in a minute. It's not fair, Mum.

Yes, he would.

He would too.

I sound like a child? I *am* your child.

I've heard it a hundred times! Mrs. Findlay stole that table and you wished and wished for it back and it has your initials and Alan's. But *you got it back,* Mum! Years ago. Why can't Bill and me just *use* it for a few years? In our house there's lots of things from his family and hardly anything from mine.

Yes, Dad's in our house. And I'm *glad.* Not many kids these days can say *My grampa lives with us.* It's good for all of us.

What did you say? What did you just say?

I don't believe this.

No. *You* listen, Mum. I'll spell it out. You won't come into our house unless Dad's out, and you mean not just downstairs in his own suite, no, right off the property. And now even your *furniture* can't set foot in the same place with him! I spelled it right, didn't I, Mum? I always spelled well, not that you cared. John was never as good as me.

A poor old man sits down to his supper. He's sweet and dear but he hardly knows where he is or who he is, so Bill and me put him to bed and take him to the toilet. We dress him, like a baby. Yes we do! And we're glad to! But if Ned Dow was to pick up his spoon or butter his bread on that table of yours, he'd *spoil* it?

I've stood here long enough. Rain's coming through my coat.

When'll I come again? Well, Mum, maybe I'll start waiting as long as John between visits. When did my brother last put his precious legs under your precious table? A year ago, was it? Eighteen months? Or maybe I'll play John's trick. I'll say I'm coming and then cancel at the last minute. That's a favourite of John's, isn't it, Mum? See how you like that!

I don't want to say anything else to you, Mum.

Then we're even, eh? Mum and daughter, even steven. But you're alone in this house. You've got no man for company, and in my house I've got two.

You've never had any man, Mum. Not for real. Not for keeps.

Owen Celebrates a Birthday

Sitting in the dark cave of a pub or a hotel bar on the chosen date in January, Owen proposed his toast. *To Jerry Jones!*

If on the birthday Owen drank and mused long enough (the time spent mattered more than the amount of beer), and

if he sat alone so he could concentrate and not get sidelined
into word-chaining to amuse some fuckn cunt who wanted
him to pick up her tab in exchange for a quick in-and-out in
the parking lot, if he remained solitary at his table and completely focused on Jerry—then Owen's body, so taut and tight
and small, began to grow. Owen expanded into a larger man.

The beginnings of this birthday sensation were as
unmistakable as the beginnings of orgasm: from then on,
no choice but to rush through to the end. Owen's flesh softened and warmed and opened out. His muscles and nerves
relaxed until he leaned back royally in his chair, like the big
man he now was, and let his legs fall open and dropped his
big solid hand to lie loose and confident on the table
instead of clutching his glass. The bar's noise went off
somewhere, as if he'd turned a radio way down. The other
drinkers in the bar got smaller and further away so space
opened up in front of Owen, and there in tranquil proces-
sion the minutes passed until the vision began. Then Owen
saw at his table not the harsh light shining down from
above the bar, not the ugly stained terry cloth punctured
with cigarette burn holes, but his son.

Jerry-baby came to him. So did Jerry-little boy in his
hockey gear. So did Jerry-teenager, cocky and sexy. So did
serious handsome hard-working Jerry-young man.

At each of these visions of his son, Owen took a good
long look. He searched the child, the boy, the man for his
own features and gestures. Sometimes he looked for
Dora's. Almost, Owen could touch Jerry-grown-up. He
could just about stroke that hair, put his hand to that hand
so like his own but unscarred, unarthritic, the nails unbro-

ken. All Owen's own skin grew even warmer at the nearness of that flesh.

By now Owen felt every part of himself supple and living. He was big, proud, strong. Drops of sweat he'd wiped off his forehead glistened on his fingers. All through his body the blood hummed and resonated.

This was the birthday feeling.

About this experience, although Owen made Jerry his confidant in relation to almost everything in his life, the father kept silent. There was no reason for the boy to know; Jerry understood that his father wished him a happy birthday and needn't learn that Owen had never found a way to prevent what happened next.

Right when the birthday feeling was largest and strongest, the stone inside Owen began to melt.

All year that stone stayed hard. For weeks, months even, he'd not think of it at all. Even if he woke at night from sleeping rough somewhere or from being broke and out of work, woke up and found his mind moving towards the stone, Owen could pull back. *Easy!* Easy, that is, three hundred and sixty-four days over the year. On the birthday, Owen could not escape; there was nowhere to go. Unpreventably, the long musing and the visioning and the feeling melted the stone till painfully it exploded its hot essence to shoot, flow, sear through every cell of Owen's body and force its way up until it was seething just under the surface of his skin, everywhere, all over him from his anguished scalp to the hard calluses on his feet. This pain, so great, had to get outside of him. Owen tried and tried to prevent that, but every time, in all those fuckn bars around the whole fuckn province, he had to struggle up on to his shaky legs. He had to shove on whatever wet shabby coat was then his winter wear and stumble out the door of the hotel to the alley or a deserted bus stop or the black rainy corner of a Safeway parking lot. There Owen leaned up against something, a fence a mailbox a pickup a dumpster. He cried.

In the early years of the birthday Owen moaned for his son so loudly that passing herds of teenagers mocked him. Several times he got a poke in the ribs from a cop trolling the midnight lanes of whatever town Owen was in. With age, perhaps beginning when he got back from the war, he learned quiet crying, but it was no less painful. Either way, his lungs' meat got shredded off the bone by the razor of his sobbing breaths, his throat and nose and sinuses reamed out till raw.

Jerry's birthday party always ended the same way. All wept out, empty, wretched, Owen lay in bed alone. Inside him, he could tell, the stone of love was beginning to re-form. *No, no need for you to hear about all that. Concretion with a hard nucleus it's called, but you don't need to learn the words.* Owen turned on his side in the fetal position, scrunched up his pillow again. One more image had to come. He waited it out: Dora in her grey blouse, kneeling on the grass, laughing, her hair all tumbling down. *That was the day you began, Jerry. I have to go right back to the beginning and see that. Then you go on. I go on.*

Owen went on knowing nothing of Dora's life since that day in 1935, and then he'd learned nothing of her life since 1918. He didn't have a clue about her losses and her brief joys, her struggles to live, her dead, the costumes she wore with the pretty names—Annette, Gladys.

I go on.

When he'd lain still a while, the cat got up on the bed, found the corner behind Owen's knees and began to purr. *Bitter. Butter. Sunny fanny skinny.* Slowly, words began to chain. He closed his eyes, moved his lips. *Sunny fanny skinny funny nanny finny bonny bunny spinny span spun....That was a long one, eh Jerry?* Soon Owen was not murmuring any more, just hearing the words. Gently as windchimes, the first bars of "Men of Harlech" sounded. The cat's purrs faded. At last Owen slept.

The day following the birthday, always, Owen woke with the worst possible hangover, no matter how moderately he had drunk. He told Jerry, laughing (but did not tell the cause), *Not that I want you drinkin your life away and thinkin it's funny, Jerry boy. Seen enough of that, I have. Drink drank drunk, stink stank stunk, and that's the truth.*

Then Owen got up for work, if he had work just then. For the next few days he felt rotten. No pep. He couldn't even get angry.

Until the crisis of the birthday began to fall away into the past and agony diminished to ache, Owen talked to Jerry a lot, more than at any other time of year. Aging, the father found that with each year his recovery time stretched out further, into February, even into March. The oolichan could be running, even, and Owen shipping out again.

Sometimes Owen thought of telling Mrs. Major about Jerry.

More often he thought about telling Indian Tom, solid kind Tom, Tom who was dearer to him than any other man, but he never did (and never said a word about *dear*, either).

A rule prohibited Owen's telling anyone of Jerry, though he couldn't articulate it as he could his other commandments.

This routine of celebrating Jerry's birthday and remembering Dora and imagining a whole life he'd chosen not to live went on for almost six decades of Owen's life.

The venue altered as he aged. For years in the cabin by the green Bella Coola he drank himself silly on the day, and at last, after his capture and incarceration in the Home, he raised a glass of tap water alone. Always alone.

1912—Golden Rule Days

Alone as always, heading west and so away from school and home, Owen passed a little shed he'd *done* a fortnight before, all caved in and blackened and smelling of fire. Peering in through criss-crossed burned boards, he saw diggings at one corner of the crumpled structure, the earth flung up in a heap. He smiled. Some animal was moving into the scorched wreck. He moved on.

Near Commercial Drive there still lay, had lain for several weeks now, a pile of dumped household rubbish—goods abandoned, or perhaps seized in an eviction, Owen thought. He'd checked through all of it right away, chosen the best for his collection and then tried to *do* the pile, but a night of heavy rainfall worked against him. Since then, much had been taken and the rest stirred about by the scavengers into a tangle of bedsprings, splintered cupboards, plates broken like biscuits, stained linens, torn sleeveless coats. Owen kicked at a few bits of china and moved on, stepping around the horse dung and dead rats in the alley. He smiled because he was free, not in school.

~~❧~~

"Owen, doesn't your mother make you wash? Burnt cork on your hands. Your collar black, your neck worse. You live in a *city*, Owen Jones, not a wilderness. Seventy thousand! And the savages gone, thank goodness, with their drink and lice and idleness. Vancouver's no place for beasts now, nor is Macdonald School. Isn't that so, children?" Miss Hector smiled at her pupils.

Familiar giggling. Owen headed for the door, home, lunch.

He walked north on Victoria, down towards the waterfront, through light rain pearled by sunlight. He fingered his matches in one pocket, penknife in the other as he looked towards the North Shore; striated brightness and cloud stretched along the mountainsides. Owen kicked stones and chanted, "*Kick* Miss Hector down the *hill, kick* her till she *yells* like *hell*." A fat dog trotting across the cobbles presented a new target and yelped off tail-between-legs. Two women shouted disapproval. The boy leapt downhill, laughing and word-chaining. "*Black blacker crack cracker stack stacker quack quacker lack lacquer—now, that's funny!*" At the firehall all was still, even the horses dozed. *Pity!* Owen reached *his* alley, between Pandora and Triumph. "*Clapper pepper dipper copper supper, a-e-i-o-u!*" There stood *his* stable.

To Owen's regret, horses no longer lived there. As a small child he'd pestered Ellen—"Tell about the animals!"—till she slapped his jaws. Almost ten now, sometimes still he rode off to sleep on a jingling beast bounding up the slope to the east and over the City line. But now the Columbia Brewery stabled its Clydesdales on Wall; only the smell of horse endured, in the dusky space below Ellen and Owen's loft. There Owen's collection of found and stolen treasures was stored. People from the nearby cabins tried to squat in the lower part of the stables, but the owners nailed the double doors closed, which pleased the boy. Now Owen took the outside staircase three steps at a time. *"Tipper tapper snapper puppy puppy-dog...."*

Ellen was just getting up. Behind a grubby sheet hung across a corner of the loft, she splashed water in the tin basin.

"Don't talk, Owen. I've a terrible head and what I'm to do with these teeth I don't know. The pain's awful. That oil of cloves Patricia gave me's no good."

Ellen's rippling red hair flew out from behind the sheet as she did her hundred vehement strokes.

The breadbox held leftovers from the all-night café where Ellen worked—loaf ends, staling rolls. Owen took a hunch of brown bread. He found only a rind of cheese, but chewing the waxy stuff coated his mouth with tasty oil. No milk. The blue metal coffeepot sloshed when shaken.

"Don't drink it all, Owen," said his mother. Fabric rustled as she put her clothes on. "I've got to have something in my stomach. And no sneaking for sugar. There isn't any."

The boy sweetened the dark stuff heavily, though the sugar sack was indeed thin; quietly he folded it back into Ellen's hiding place under the windowsill. An even quieter search of her purse produced nothing. Owen stuffed his pockets with hard rolls.

"Going now, Mum."

"You come right home after school. No hanging about where you oughtn't. I want you in your bed before I go to work."

Owen went out into his afternoon.

At Macdonald School, Miss Hector's glittering spectacles waited. And Miss Hector's smell of talc, an acid lilac where Ellen's was sweet rose. And Miss Hector's cold hand tightly braceleting his wrist.

Smello hollow fellow yellow hello.

Those stupid arithmetic problems! Long long minutes squeezed out as Owen waited and waited for the others to finish. *Find the cost of 1,460 yards of flannel at $.75 per yard....* $1,095. Who would buy so much? Stupid. *Calculate the cost of Axminster carpet to cover a floor 16' by 16', the carpet being 27" wide and $1.80 per yard. (Allow 1 1/4 yd. for matching the pattern)....* $92.55, but what fool bought runners for a room?

In the whole class, only that dumb girl Dora was often as quick as he. Sometimes when they worked sums at their desks she looked over when she was done, to see who'd finished first. Once he smiled. Next day Dora called to him in the playground, but he wouldn't look at her. Owen was wise to that, to that and a lot more. In fact, if it wasn't for him being so smart, he and Dora wouldn't be in the same class even, but he'd skipped grades. Twice. That fact stuck like a stone in Miss Hector's wrinkly throat, Owen knew, and laughed to think of it.

Girls at school, including that fat Dora, sang *Owen's a dirty boy* on passing him in the halls; they feigned horror at his ragged kneepants and scabbed shins. *Find the number of tons of ice used, and the cost of icing per mile, for ice at $16 1/20 per car from Vancouver to Calgary (642 miles)....* Flannel. Carpet. Ice. Owen sighed. *Ice. And slice mice dice lice rice twice.*

He veered west.

Keeping to the alleys paralleling Triumph and Pandora and Franklin, Owen chewed his dry rolls as he went.

He looked sharp. Early carrots in an unfenced vegetable patch he found, and then a hard-boiled egg that lay inexplicably in the dust with a rank tomcat sniffing at it. Owen was about to kick the animal, but it sidled past him, purring, so close that its plumy tail brushed his shins. That soft touch! Soft as feathers. Owen laughed and hunkered down to stroke the dusty ginger fur. The cat's ribs were right *there*, hard under his fingers. *Just like mine.* Yellow matter clotted its eyes. Owen rubbed the cat vigorously behind its ears and took the egg.

In the next block he found an unopened box of cigars—*La Preferencia*. Sometimes Ellen's men liked to smoke. In the loft, the odour he hated hung for days, but Owen wedged the box into his pocket and moved on, masticating the pasty eggyolk.

Now he was on unfamiliar ground, nearing Chinatown. *Chinky chinky Chinaman...chink chunk...that's all...and clink clank, link lank, rink rank, think thank...sink sank sunk, three!...but some there's only one, wink...I can't get any with e.* He crossed Hastings. A shopkeeper shook a corn broom at him. On Keefer a housewife scrubbing her doorstep shouted, "Whose boy are you?" She threw her bucket of dirty water his way.

Westering on Pender towards Carl, Owen came to a school and sought the water fountain. On the playground he didn't hear much English. That was different from home; around Victoria Drive and Highlands, foreigners kept quiet. Drinking thirstily, he sensed boys behind him and straightened up to find he was taller than two of the three. All were weedy. Owen stuck out his tongue, to begin a scuffle. Too late: a teacher with a bell appeared and raised her arm.

Into the building with the press of children went Owen and shortly stood in a classroom just like his own. A black-board displayed the same numerals and alphabets. *Dumb damn damn dumb.* The map and globe were the same, and the pictures: King George, Queen Mary, a deer with big antlers, a shepherdess. But far more pupils than at Macdonald were crowded in, poor-looking Chinks and Japs, a few English, the odd Siwash, some boys who were as tall as grownups. And the teacher was a *man.*

Mr. Hugesson didn't take attendance. He didn't snap out names from the register like curses. He only asked, "What's your name, boy?"

"Owen Jones." After a moment he added, "Sir."

The teacher smiled and pencilled a little note.

The class did not calculate flannel or spell picky tricky word-pairs like *gait gate* and *their there* and *pearl purl*—some dumb girl always got that one—nor read aloud sentence by dull sentence all round the room. They sang.

"Men of Harlech," first; Owen had known this tune since smallest childhood, from one of his father's unpre-dictable and always-too-short visits to the loft. Then they sang "D'Ye Ken John Peel." And "The British Grenadier," "The Keeper Did a-Shooting Go," "Hedge Roses," and next a song Owen had never heard.

Three sailors were sailing upon the wide ocean
But where they were sailing they none of them knew
They simply went sailing where'er the wind blew
Where'er, where'er the wind blew

Owen sang. Mr. Hugesson walked among the rows, bending to hear a child more clearly, stopping the class to model a phrase. He listened closely to Owen. Before moving on, the teacher looked and smiled at him. It was like getting caught lighting matches, yet Owen was relieved too, and not afraid, and warm.

Now Geography. Owen sighed. Rivers.... *Morang's Modern Geography* had some murky photos of Niagara and Lake Huron and the confluence of the Allegheny and Monongahela, but Miss Hector only talked about the Thames, jab jab jabbing her pointer at little pink England. Owen imagined the canvas map rolling up in flames.

Mr. Hugesson chalked on the board something like a huge distorted hand, pointing left. He made a small mark on it and turned to the class. "New Brighton Hotel—am I warm or cold?"

"Cold!" the children cried. The teacher moved his chalk. "Warmer! Hot! No no, cold, go back! Hot again! There!" Finally Mr. Hugesson made a precise dot and all the children clapped.

"Lulu Island?" His chalk waved along the board.

"Cold, cold! Go down, go down, Mr. Hugesson!"

"Down? South? Someone had better come and show me."

"Me! Me! Me! Me!"

Laughing, Mr. Hugesson pointed to the biggest weedy boy from the schoolyard, who went eagerly forward; this never happened at Macdonald, where the foreign kids sat silent at the back. "Lulu Island is *here*." In the moment of that boy's pointing, the shapes on the board made sense. Owen recognized a map of where he lived.

Then the class found Point Grey and Brockton Oval and Eburne and Electric Avenue, their own Strathcona School, the Union Steamship dock and the CPR Station and Hollyburn and Port Moody and New Westminster, the Avalon ranch. *Delta, flood plain, sediment, dyke, bog, marsh, estuary*: the words grew meaning. They found the Arms of the Fraser, the Musqueam shore where Simon Fraser came, the False Creek flats and the Asthma Flats and Snauq and the big reservoir.

Snauq: Owen longed to see the Squamish village under Burrard Bridge. Its name resonated with everything that Miss Hector loathed.

Next, Mr. Hugesson sketched the northeastern sector of their own city, and the children chalked wavering lines that were their own streets. They put dots by their homes on Gore and Hawks, Heatley and Carl. For the first time ever, Owen stepped voluntarily to the blackboard, where he made the easternmost mark as the bell rang. Uniquely, Owen was sorry to hear it.

They came to an island and landed upon it
They ate some bananas and knocked down a nut
Then cut down the nut tree and built a log hut
And built, and built a log hut.

Leaving the strange school, Owen saw Mr. Hugesson with books and newspapers tucked comfortably under his arm. What were they? Rarely had Owen felt interest in paper, except for its being so burnable.

And built, and built a log hut.

On his way back Owen found no food and no opportunity to steal from various corner stores.

Trouble waited at home. He'd left the lid of the bread-box loose; Ellen hadn't noticed before leaving for her own afternoon activities. Mice. Also she was still fussing about a stewpot he'd scorched at least a week earlier.

"My one good pot," Ellen muttered, slapping at the table with a rag. "Burn break smash drop! You'd ruin every stick we have if I didn't stop you, Owen."

He paid no attention; there was milk. He swallowed and swallowed till he had to gasp. With a huge satisfied sigh he set the bottle down hard at the table's edge. It slipped off.

"Now look what you've done!"

Gurgly giggly gaggly googly.

Owen squatted. Of the pint, perhaps a teacupful remained. Ellen slapped her son's ears.

"I didn't mean to, Mum!"

"What does that matter, stupid?" she cried. She bent to pick up the bottle. It cracked top to bottom and released the last of its contents. "Not even milk for my tea!" Kneeling, Ellen cried.

The fluid puddled over the gritty linoleum, made floating islands out of dustballs, boats of burnt matches; Owen saw how the milk stretched out white skinny fingers and then soaked into the jute where the lino was worn through.

"Can't you get more, Mum? On tick?"

"How'm I going to get more when the Jap's cut me off? I've no money. None. It's all your fault. Why was I ever ever ever made to raise this child alone, with never any help? At least wipe up that mess." Ellen threw the rag over and lit a cigarette. "David, the dirty bastard. Why isn't it ever him gets killed in the woods? Dozens die every year. You'd think surely something could fall on his head."

Owen sopped up the milk.

He got out the box of cigars and handed it over to his mother. Ellen slit the paper seal with her fingernail; together, mother and son inspected the brown cylinders, touched the crisp silky wrappers, and smelled the tobacco.

"Maybe I can do something with these." Ellen got behind the sheet to fling on stockings and a rumpled dress. She set her combs in her red hair, pinched her cheeks and put salve on her lips. "Wait here. I'm going to the Princeton."

In an hour she was back, loaded with groceries. The salty smell about her soon vanished under the fragrance of the fried fish, potatoes, onions, and eggs that she cooked. Their supper made pyramids on their plates. When Owen was full, he licked his, all over. Ellen laughed at her son and he laughed back. The two sucked gobs of toffee until Ellen's teeth hurt and she gave hers to Owen. They drank strong milky tea. When his mother set the fat new Rogers sugar sack in its place, Owen carefully did not look.

"Mum," he said, scraping crusted fish off the frying pan, "I want a cat."

Ellen sighed. "The boy that broke the milk wants a cat! Give me that pan." Wearily she piled up dirty plates. "A cat? I can hardly feed us, Owen. How I've managed to keep you I don't know." She paused to lick a spoon. "Well, I do know, but I don't want to think about it. Now off to bed with you, so's you're settled before I have to leave for work."

From a cupboard, Owen brought two horse blankets to the chesterfield and then went down to the outhouse in the yard. Returning, he took off his boots and kneepants and curled under the covers to watch his mother twist up her shining auburn hair and button her uniform.

To put on her coat and hat, Ellen stood before the big piece of mirror Owen's father had propped up near the door.

"Mum, when's Daddy coming home?"

Ellen laughed. *That's her nasty laugh.* "How would I know when the logger's coming to Vancouver to get drunk? I'm only his wife." She perched by her son. "Kiss?"

Owen turned away.

Ellen shook his shoulder. "Look at me, stupid boy." Her face worked. Her tone told exactly what was coming, word for word. He shut his eyes. She shook him harder. "You can't shut your ears, Owen. You haven't *got* a father, boy. I'm who you've got. Only me. That's all. And if there's only one thing your mum ever gets into your head, it's *don't get stuck like me, Owen Jones.*" She let go.

"Daddy has money," Owen said obstinately.

"Not for us! For girls and beer and punchcards, yes. Maybe if your daddy didn't have to cross Dupont to reach the Number Twenty, he might save some pennies for us. Might...but *might* doesn't buy a thing, Owen."

The door closed.

Click click click. Down the outside stairs Ellen went. By the side of the stable she made soft blurred noises as she stepped along the boards laid lengthwise where the mud hardly ever dried up. Once on the dirt of the alley itself, she became soundless. *Sound sinned sunned sand send—all five vowels!* Faint rain tapped on the stable roof.

Owen got up. He reached the window in time to see Ellen's skirt twitch round the corner on to Victoria, but not until the Number Twenty sailed singing westward did Owen put on his boots and pants again. He refilled his match box; his supply was hidden under the chesterfield. On each packet a red lion roared, "Scratch me! and I'm your match."

Where was Mr. Hugesson now? Perhaps reading one of his books.

Owen considered whether he might go to explore Snauq tonight, at last, and so make this day even more unusual and memorable. But—if he was not home and asleep by the time Ellen returned, she would be very angry. When angry, his mother was something to see. Of late, though, Owen had dared to think he was now so big and strong that his mother could not whip him.

He sang as he ran down the alley.

But after a while they returned to the ocean
They hoisted a sail and went floating away
And where they are now I really can't say
I really, really can't say

੭੭੭੭

1916

Brown air floated in swirling currents eastward from the beehive burners to the tidal flats of False Creek and up the hill to Britannia High School.

Principal Hubble approved, admired this view. Modifying Horace Greeley, he urged his students, "Go west, young men, and grow up with this city!" Ruining the effect he sought, he then patted the withered arm hanging in his sleeve and added, "I wish I were your age and could do just that."

To grasp Vancouver's amazing opportunities, Principal Hubble knew, a boy must assume a certain attitude, eschew certain behaviours. Observing the youth now seated before him, Hubble sighed.

"We think, Owen," he summed up, "that is, Mr. Everett at Macdonald and I think that you can do far better at your studies. Capable of matriculating, Owen! Yes, and that's why your principal wanted us to have this little talk."

The boy maintained an attentive expression.

"You know, Owen, many boys here on the East Side simply lack the capacity for such success, though in other walks of life they may do well."

The boy seemed to await his next words.

"Owen, remember the parable of the talents? Good! Then you know what I mean. You could matriculate—if you don't bury your talents. Ha ha." Mr. Hubble smiled at the absurd notion of burying. His serious tone resumed. "I'm not only speaking, Owen, of advantages accruing later on in life, but of next summer. This foolish war will be over, all back to normal, and...camp! On Gambier Island. Boys and girls from all over the city, who've studied hard and earned a fortnight of happy island life. Swimming, hiking, woodworking, leatherwork, boating! A worthy goal to work towards, this winter?"

The boy watched the man.

Wasn't this silence far too long? Wasn't this youth at the very borders of rudeness, straddling them even? But how so? This Owen Jones sat still, wide-eyed. He was neat, though grimy of neck. His hair sprouted into tufts above his ears. His brows twisted up. Those pale eyes looked so out of place, somehow, in that little-boy scruff of a head.

"We'll meet again soon." Abruptly, Mr. Hubble ended the interview.

Singing down the Victoria hill towards home, Owen could not imagine why he might either meet Mr. Hubble or see the inside of his school, indeed of any school, ever again.

This moment had been coming towards him for a long time; now it was here, and gone, and walking ahead of him was that girl, that Dora with her long feathery hair. He liked pulling it, or trying to—for a fatty, Dora was very quick on her feet.

There was a jolly miller once, Lived on the River Dee

She was with her pretty friend, an odd name, Owen could not think of it.

No lark more blithe than he

And a lovely figure. At school, all the boys went for this one with her lively laugh. Owen saw why, but the fat girl, always in Whatsername's shadow, drew him. She hunched over, walking; she must be big, there, under her green waist. Owen's palms tingled.

The two girls ambled, chattered, giggled down the hill. Repeatedly they came close to whisper and then flung apart, gasping with shrill laughter.

Nobody, no! Not I

Owen caught up and slid an arm about each waist; the girls cried out and shook him off and giggled, which pleased him mightily.

Owen showed Dora and Marjo just how Principal Hubble gabbled and babbled about the good children's camp on Gambier Island.

"He pats his dead arm, so!" Owen took pretty Marjo's hand.

She snatched it away. "But Owen, doesn't Gambier sound like a lot of fun?"

Owen sniffed. "No stores. No streetcars. Nowhere to go at night. No way to get my hands on any money. Stupid!"

"But...."

"*I'm not stupid.* I know better places, girls. Dupont Street, Alexander, Snauq—now there's fun! Not for young ladies, though. Ta!" Abruptly Owen turned off.

There was a jolly miller once
Lived on the River Dee
He worked and sang from morn till night
No lark more blithe than he
For this the burden of his song
Forever used to be
I care for nobody! No, not I
And nobody cares for me

The girls looked after the singing boy.

1977—Richard Smyth, Retired Stockbroker, Reads His Brother Jonathan's Papers

Louise Smyth stood in the doorway of the study, tapping her foot in that wifely way. "I wouldn't waste a minute on those."

"They're Jon's work, Louise. I've kept these papers because he was my brother."

"Indeed. Who left all his money to the War Amps and not a penny to the nieces he *said* he loved. Yes, I know it's wrong to bear grudges against the dead. Do as you like. Dear. But remember, only essentials go with us when we move, and you've not looked at Jon's papers in the ten years since he died." Louise tapped away down the hall.

What next?

Richard opened another carton; he'd already gone through the late 1920s and the early '30s. Jonathan's messy typing was at odds with the heavy cream laid stock, smartly engraved. *Of course, Dad gave this to him. Good old Smyth, Stationer.* Richard rubbed the paper between finger and thumb. *No one makes letterhead of that quality now.* He continued reading.

Evidently Richard's little brother, Dr. Jonathan Smyth, had enquired about employment at a tuberculosis hospital in Hong Kong. In a children's clinic in Barbados. In Brisbane at a centre for cancer treatments. *To work his way round the Empire—was that the idea? But Jon never left Vancouver!* And here was another packet of letters, this lot from Belfast—a little hospital in a district described by a Dr. Kieran McDiarmid as "truly desperately poor." *Why didn't Jon go? The foot?* No, because in March 1935 there were letters from Trinidad. Sick children, again. *Why?*

Richard considered the 1930s. The old ones in the family were failing then, but all three brothers had carried that burden, and after 1936 when Arthur died much of it lifted; Julie and George were institutionalized by then. *Jon couldn't have felt bound to remain in Terminal City.* Sighing, Richard thought of Geoffrey, who always used that term for Vancouver, with heavy sarcasm.

Another carton held an envelope labelled "Med School." This might be worth keeping. Kimberley Kineson, daughter of Amelia, Richard's own youngest, showed a strong interest in medicine. Might this family material encourage her? But not much was there.

Pencil sketches showed a cat, asleep—"Arlette" underneath, in Jon's distinctive hand—and a fat black-gowned professor who bent to reveal an empty head.

A handwritten essay, thick with statistical appendices, documented stillbirths, maternal deaths, and other obstetrical disasters in Saskatchewan's hospitals for the decade following the Great War. On its last page was a big scrawled *A-plus* beside "NATURE!" and an illegible signature.

A third drawing showed a fish slit down her middle with eggs pouring out.

Jon did talk about ob-gyn. And about epidemiology. And being a baby doctor. But he never did specialize.

The next box held files with typed labels. Richard murmured the names: *Cspd—Suppliers. Ctee: Vanc Block. Ctee: Stats, VGH—Minutes. Ctee: Design, VGH—Minutes. Ctee: Maint, VGH—Minutes. Refs—Cardio, Derma, Eye-Ear, Psych, Ortho. Ctee: Ward X—Minutes.* He opened a file or two. The typed labels looked old in spite of their even impress and perfect spacing. *That girl in Jon's office for a while—not long—in the thirties—what did he call her? His supergirl.*

Jonathan's own handwriting appeared on a separate folder: *King.* From it, Richard withdrew a carbon copy on flimsy paper.

October 12, 1954

Mr. Gordon King, MD, OBE, FRCS (Eng), FRCOG
Professor of Obstetrics and Gynaecology
The University of Hong Kong

Dear Dr. King:

I write to express my admiration of the excellent address you delivered at last year's meeting of the American Association of Obstetricians, Gynaecologists and Abdominal Surgeons; I have this minute finished reading your remarks as published in the AJOG.

To my regret, attending the gathering at Hot Springs, Virginia, was not possible for me. I had anticipated the pleasure of hearing your address, and had also hoped that we might, in the press of the programme of convention activities, find a moment or two to discuss topics of mutual interest.

For a number of years now, I have been engaged in a process similar to your own of studying, in depth, a series of cases involving advanced extra-uterine pregnancy.

My own grouping is not as substantial as yours—only four to date, and of these one must be regarded as uncertain as to outcome, for reasons too complex to explain here. However, several of the cases might interest you, bearing as they do on your remarks about the frequently abnormal presentation of the child and the advisability of complete removal, when possible, of the placenta.

Enclosed please find a few photographs that I trust will be of interest, and some explanatory Notes. Should you be so inclined, I would be happy to engage with you in discussion and analysis of these and other cases, both of yours and of mine.

May I conclude by saying that I found the example with which you rounded off your address (the little girl born in September 1946 and now at school), very affecting. That on being taken from the peritoneal cavity "the child cried well" was most satisfying to read. Would that all such cases ended so!

My thanks again for your most informative and stimulating remarks, and I look forward to hearing from you at your convenience.

Sincerely,

Jonathan Smyth, MD

Bewildered, Richard looked through the file but found no Notes.

From their rusted paper clip, he separated three photos. One showed a murky spinal column; near its base rested a whitish *thing* like a punched-in soccer ball. In the second appeared a dark globe, its surface runnelled. Spigot-like protrusions were labelled *Left Tube, Cervix, Right Tube* and *Right Ovary*. The third, like a museum-case display, presented a madly tidy arrangement of minute bones. Richard counted seventy-three. On the back Jon had written *No right tibia. Passed per rectum.*

Behind the photographs was an article from *The Lancet* of May 30, 1936, by Dr. Loh Guan Lye of the General Hospital in Singapore, titled "Lithopaedion in a Centenarian." Here was another murky image—but also explanatory text. With the hair rising on his nape, Richard read of a full-term fetus lodged within its mother's body for six decades. And behind that in the file was Dr. King's own speech, which began with a review of the literature on lithopedions. Richard scanned through the Spaniard doctor Albucasis (936–1013), the *Gynaecorium* of 1597, Campbell's 1840 *Memoir on Extra-Uterine Gestation.*...

The retired stockbroker closed the folder.

His familiar gooseneck lamp bent over the rippling amber of the oak; for more than half a century, those patterns locked in the wood had given him pleasure. *What in hell was Jon up to? Why didn't he go to that conference?* Richard imagined his lanky brother sitting opposite, drinking his everlasting damn glass of milk. *Myself, I could do with a whisky right now. What on earth were you up to, my little brother?* The light shone on Jonathan's handwriting as Richard picked up the bundled files again.

Jonathan had given four of them Roman numerals. *Why Roman?* Softly, Richard read the names: *I, Mrs. Hawrylko, Sask; II, Mrs. Schwarz, Mtl; III, Mrs. Ogilvy, Van.*...

Louise's brisk high heels (over the decades they had dinted all the floors in this house with innumerable small circles that gave the effect of beaten metal) approached Richard's study. Over top of the Roman-numbered files he slid *Income Taxes, 1956.*

"Are you talking to yourself again, Richard?"

"You were quite right, dear. There's little worth keeping."

Tap tap, away again.

IV. "Mrs. Smith." Horrified, Richard removed this from the pile. *Quotation marks? Good God, is this some hidden wife? Why didn't Jon leave her anything?*

Yellow foolscap whispered in the file. Topmost was a list, all cross-hatched and scribbled round with addresses and numbers and fragments—*None* and *No record* and *Will notify if....*

> *Morgue*
> *St. P emerg and mat*
> *St. V ditto, St. J ditto*
> *pharmacists???*
> *that butcher in Burnaby*
> *Vanc nursing homes—Mrs A make list*
> *Valley hosps ditto*
> *newsp?*
> *N and West V?*

On the second sheet Jonathan had drafted, double-spaced:

> *Pregnant woman, age 38, approx. 26 weeks gestation, 5' 5", grey eyes, brown hair, moderately obese. In condition of medical emergency of which she may be unaware....*
> *Please immediately notify*
> *Please immediately transport to nearest*
> *Please summon medical assistance*
> *Please telephone*
> *Please*

Richard realized that he did not know how long he had been staring at this page.

He was just rousing himself and thinking that Aunt Julie's old term for Jonathan, *milksop*, had never seemed more unjustified, when Louise came briskly down the hall yet again, this time with a definite frown. "My dear, must I at the age of seventy-five move our entire household unassisted?"

Richard gave his wife the crooked smile she always loved. "At the age of eighty-one I'll help you, my dear."

He did not read the last page. He would take this strange folder to the new apartment, along with his mother's bust.

Louise had refused always to let him set Amelia in their garden here at the house on Mackenzie. "So morbid, Richard!" His pale pretty mother therefore had lain wrapped and boxed in their attic all these years. Yes, to False Creek his secret marble Amelia would move. One day, Richard supposed, someone else—perhaps his granddaughter Kimberley, the doctor?—would find the head with its graceful curls and wonder who she was.

He went downstairs to sort books with Louise. Of a thousand, they were to take only three hundred.

Never Tell

1965—Ned Dow to His Son, John

A wise son maketh a glad father. I need you to listen to the old sugarman, son. And fill my glass.

Dora said, "I'll destroy the house so you can't sell it." *Destroy.* Cat's business, horse buns—she'd smear 'em on the floors. Cut the curtains to shreds—she *made* them! Every window, every stitch. Take my hatchet to the furniture, take my good needle-nose pliers. "I'll scar the stove and fridge top to bottom," your mother said. Broken glass in the bathtub, bacon grease down the drains. Tear my chicken wire out, let coons and pigeons in the attic. Pour salt over my raised beds. She swore! She'd empty all her canning on the lawn. Soap the windows. Who'd even *look* at the house, let alone make an offer? The price'd drop like a stone.

Your mother said she'd paint *Ned Dow Cheated Me* across the front porch, unless I gave her half of the sale price. Half!

Get that bottle. No, I'm not drinking too much. *Destroy*, she said. Hear that, John.

Twenty-seven years I lived in that house. John, you haven't bought yet. You don't know how things wear out, weatherstripping, grout, fuses, gaskets, pipes. Clogged S-bends. Clogged gutters and filters and ducts. Torn screens. Mildew. Mould. Things eat a place—termites, carpenter ants, wasps. Wood rot. Oh, a house keeps you on your toes, John, keeps you dancing! But after twenty-seven years the sugarman couldn't dance any more. Fill my glass. Upkeep— it's like pushing a stone up a hill. A big stone.

Getting that chicken wire under the eaves, I nearly broke a leg. Your mother's sewing shelves—I built them *and* Caddy's room *and* the jam cupboard *and* the garden shed. I rebuilt the cellar stairs. The drain tile! Three feet six inches I dug that trench, right round the house, every single weekend of the summer of '49. My back's not been the same since. All seized up, stiff as a board. My whole body went into that house, John.

I painted it. Top to bottom. When I bought it, and in '39 when war was coming, and in '52 for Mary and Bill's wedding. On the ladder, hour after hour. Alone. Yes, you were some help, John, that last time.

Half, she wanted! Her crazy argument—it's like this.

When we met, I'd some savings from B.C. Sugar. She had money put by, too. At Spencer's your mother made a good wage for a girl, and she's not a spender, never was, I'll say that still. Garden Drive cost nineteen hundred and fifty dollars. Three hundred down and a twenty-five-year mortgage. Oh, John, a house is a big thing! *And if a house be divided against itself, that house cannot stand.*

Let me just change chairs, here. The sugarman can't sit one way for too long. That's better. Put my glass nearer.

Pretty soon you were on the way. Of course your mother quit working, and that was the end of her putting any money into the place. *The end!*

I don't care what she's said. Her dressmaking? Pin money. For all her fuss, it never amounted to more than that.

Right through the Depression, I paid. Foreclosures right and left, all through the '30s, but *the sugarman paid!* Your father paid. *And* through the war. *And* after, right up till '51 when I burned that mortgage in my own back yard and danced round the bonfire with your sister. Yelled like wild Indians, Mary and me.

Half the sale price! "I deserve it." She said that. *Deserve.*

Teasing? Oh, John, our teasing days were long gone. No. For your mother, I hadn't been the sugarman in a long long time—but I couldn't believe she meant it. So I laughed.

Without me and what I did, you couldn't have done what you did. She kept saying that. I laughed again, and then...oh my. Hammer and tongs! *A brawling woman in a wide house....*

Like a fool I said *The same's true for you.* You know what I *meant.* Without the roof over her head and the clothes on her back and the food in her belly that *I put there,* Dora Dow couldn't have lived a day of her married life. *I made her living. That's* what I meant. Husbands do that for wives. Because we love them.

But she said, *Exactly. It's our house.* John, everyone says that ... and no one means it. The house is the man's, because wives don't pay. Simple. It's that simple.

Your mother didn't work thirty-five years shovelling sugar. She didn't get muscle-bound. She didn't ruin her back so she can't hardly turn her head. I might as well be a plank! The sugarman's got no *give*, John! *A good union job.* You won't have to do work like that, thank heaven. Now pour me some more and listen.

It wasn't your mum spent the better part of twenty years fighting for a union. It wasn't her came home after the war and saw those young guys win, those twerps who'd never done *anything*! They got the union in at B.C. Sugar as though there was nothing to it. All those years we struggled—they didn't know, didn't care. Thought it was easy and we were fools. Your mum didn't go through that, John. She didn't go to war. She hasn't got arthritis. She never gets colds. She doesn't even wear glasses.

Garden Drive was *mine*.

In '53 when the offer for six thousand five came in, the realtor said, "You won't get a better one. No more sugar than that, Mr. Dow." So I took it.

Your mother has her dressmaking, her typing. Easy work, clean, at home! And in a few years, the government pension. She's only got herself to keep, nothing new to buy—I don't need all the furniture. A woman alone—why does she *need* a house, anyway? *Need* money? It's a mystery, John. Fill my glass.

You're taking her side?

And what does Joyce have to say—not that it's her business?

Son, if your wife takes that attitude then I'd suggest you watch your back in any financial dealings you might have with her. Be careful, John! And get that bottle over here.

I said, *fill my glass*. And *listen*. Your mother robbed me. That's the truth, and here's my only son calling me a liar.

Well, she *should* have been happy! She had a husband in steady work, a nice house, good kids, friends ... Marjo, always Marjo. But she wanted to *work*. Even when you were small! For the life of me I couldn't understand it. Over at B.C. Sugar I'd dance myself round the floor and wonder *Is this the girl I married?*

The sugarman put a stop to all that nonsense about her working. Yes, I did. Husbands have to put a stop. You'll learn.

Remember your wagon? Your ice skates? Your baseball uniform? You never *wanted*, did you, John? Never felt skint? *But if any provide not for his own, and specially for those of his own house, he hath denied the faith, and is worse than an infidel.* I *was* a good provider. Nothing she says can take truth away.

I was *robbed*. All that work and no wife! Bags she wore— when she was so pretty. Full of sin. Full of filth. No repentance. She hardened her heart, hardened it to a stone.

John, what I have to tell you is this: someone else has to *try* with your mother, when I'm gone. Get her to ask forgiveness.

No, I'm fit as a fiddle! The old sugarman's stiff, but he's still dancing. You never know, though. *In the midst of life we are in death.* The point is, your mother's in danger of her soul— *and* she robbed me. She was hard, John! So hard to me.

Angry? Yes. My besetting sin. *He that is slow to anger is better than the mighty; and he that ruleth his spirit than he that taketh a city*. Bear with me, son. I'll change chairs again, sit quiet a minute. Then I'll go on again and tell you.

In our wedding pictures, isn't she sweet? Sweet for the sugarman, so plump and pretty. Look at her dress—see that frilly hem? My sonsy girl! So light on her feet when we went dancing up the water there. *Who stole my heart away— who?* You wouldn't know that song, John, but I swear your mother looked all set to raise a family. God knows I wanted that. I tried my best. Not that I've been a perfect husband. He knows that too. *Be merciful to me a sinner.* Fill my glass again, John. This is hard to tell.

I *am* telling! You're as bad as your sister. Mary's always at me, *Don't get off track, Dad, don't ramble, get on with it.*

After Caddy.... Yes, you *do* remember your sister. *You do so.* You have to.

John, what I'm trying to say is this. *There was going to be another baby.*

Never. It wasn't born.

There was no miscarriage.

A shocker, eh? Yes, it's a shocker.

I've prayed to understand. If I knew why she did what she did.... *The earth shall be full of the knowledge of the Lord, as the waters cover the sea.* Perhaps He knows.

Son, what could the sugarman do?

What's a drink for, except to get you through? Son, I don't *enjoy* telling you this about your mother.

Reverend Simpson at All Saints was clear, when I couldn't bear it any longer and told him. *A terrible sin,* he said when I went to him. *Against God's will.* He said I mustn't be with, you know, *with* your mother until she made herself right with God.

She never would.

We were never together again.

She never gave my sorrow a thought, John. It was my child too, wasn't it? Wasn't it the sugarman's baby too?

I prayed for your mother. Over Caddy, she lost her wits for a while—did you know that? *Father, forgive her, for she knows not what she does....*I thought the grief might make her act so. Or she might be coming into her change, early. Or upset about this and that between us—but as God is my witness I wasn't a bad husband! I provided. *The union between man and woman....* Oh John, the sugarman paid his union dues.

God *is* my witness, John. I've repented all my sins, and *there's* the difference.

Fill my glass.

Yes, bitter. *And I find more bitter than death the woman, whose heart is snares and nets, and her hands as bands.* Much more. I was away at war over three whole years. Whenever I wrote, I asked her. "Have you done it yet?" I'd have forgiven. I'd have forgotten. We could have started fresh. But—home the hero comes, John, to a wife with a stone for a heart! I'm the bitterman, now.

In September '45, it was like seeing her for the first time ever. So pretty, so soft! Even in that bag she wore, soft and sweet. My good sonsy girl, smelling like every flower in my garden. I held her. "Have you repented?" I asked. "Is the sin still in you?" She pushed me away, John. Pushed away her husband!

The bottle. Give it. I don't care if Mary and Bill know.

Your mother may *claim* it was her idea for us to divorce and sell the house, but John, a woman who did what she did will say anything. She can't be trusted. She doesn't know remorse. Your mother is *full of hard sin*—remember that.

No, *I* saw we had to part, when Mary got married and we were left alone in the house. The bitterman knew that was the end.

Nowadays it's hard to imagine how divorce was, only ten years back. Shaming. To be hidden. For her to say she'd paint that on my house! *Ned Dow Cheated Me.* "For everyone and his dog to see," she said, when I'm the one was cheated.

Who stole my heart away—who? Who hadn't a wife for seventeen years and then got divorced? Who lost a child and a child and a wife? All the sugarman wanted was a family, a safe warm place to be at night, someone to hold. Was that so hard?

And who's living in a basement suite, down with Mary's laundry and her storage apples and her freezer full of soup? *Not your mother!* Oh no. Bitterman, bitterman.... Yes, she's snug in her *own* house, that *you* helped her to buy.

Don't deny it, John. The sugarman can still read, still add! The ad gave the asking price. Your mother got three thousand two hundred and fifty dollars out of me, but that wasn't enough for her to buy! Where'd she get the rest, if it wasn't you?

Don't be stupid, son. Mary wouldn't give her mother a penny if she was dying.

Every wise woman buildeth her house; but the foolish plucketh it down with her hands. A fool! There's comfort. Everything a woman could want, Dora had, but she threw us all away. She only kept a stone.

Of course this is a nice basement suite! I built it, didn't I? Yes, Bill helped. *And* I have people round me. *She's* got no one.

Your sister's good to me, John. One thing's for sure—the sugarman's never eaten so well! Things weren't easy for Mary, you know, growing up how she did. You called her *Maddy*, John, but truly that wasn't fair. Not easy for a girl, with your mother the way she was. And when Marjo's little Hazel came along, after the war, it was hard for Mary to see how your mother took to her. But Bill's a kind man. She has this good house. Her kids. Friends. Her catering—now *there's* a woman's business brings in more than pin money! Mary *hires* people.

Your sister keeps very busy. Little Mary doesn't often have time to spend with her old sugarman! So I'm alone a lot, here in the basement. I try not to be a burden. I help in the yard. Run errands. Mind the kids. Of course Mary and Bill know if I had the money that's mine *by rights*, I'd pay more rent...but they still say thank you, every month.

The bottle's almost finished. There—that's their car, in the driveway. The mouthwash, John—on the bathroom shelf.

Husbands, love your wives, and be not bitter against them—I tell you, son, I do my level best, but that teaching's way beyond me. I can't get there.

1964—An Anniversary for Marjo

Mike's been dead two years now. I loved him like my life. Him and me, we *were* a life.

The hardest thing to bear is that part of me's *glad*. There's no more danger he'll ever know. Unless, in heaven, he knows everything. Then he'll understand. He understood so much about me; he could know that too. But there, not here. Never here.

Seventeen years of worrying, I lived.

If I spoke without thinking. *If* Hazel's looks changed as she grew. *If* she put her hair up or had it cut really close and that funny ridge on her head showed. With little girls, the mum decides about the hairdos, but after thirteen.... Oh how I worried!

Or *if* Hazel were to sit beside him. It could happen so easily! A barbecue. A picnic. At New Brighton Pool, every-one with wet hair slick over our heads.

If I talked in my sleep.

If I wrote ... but I never wrote anything down.

If if if. ...

Seventeen years of *if!*

Thank God I kept silent. I still do, I always will, but at least the man I told everything, everything but that, isn't here.

And Mike loved Hazel so much. His last, his little one, his sweetest Valentine. It's often the way.

I've loved her too. I have. Of course I have.

1964—*Jonathan, with a File and a Fish*

On Valentine's Day Jonathan rode the Number Fifteen bus northbound on Cambie, sitting at the back. He was heading to his office, to meet his afternoon patients. At Broadway, among those crowding aboard he saw Gladys Smith.

Jonathan's heart walloped his chest wall. *No. I see someone who looks like her.* Over the years he'd thought this a hundred times, two hundred, five hundred. *It's not her real name, any-way. And that was almost three decades ago.*

The head of this woman, who might at the extreme edge of possibility be Gladys, worked its way along the choked aisle, appearing and disappearing. *Yes, she's about the right height. But that hair's too dark. No. No. Of course not her.*

Emerging, the woman and her companion, evidently a friend, took the bench seat nearest him. Sweat broke on Jonathan's forehead. He gazed down and rearranged his foot. *Is this woman Gladys's daughter? Her name was…what?* As the bus heaved up to the bridge, Jonathan's mind blundered about. *Rattlepate. Milksop. Not the girl who died, her name was odd. The other, the older, she was ordinary….*

This woman's hair was dull, not amber, her eyes brown, not grey. Her thick fingers would never flicker over a keyboard. *Gladys didn't slouch.* The skin was perfection; the shape wasn't—not a pear or a seal, just dumpy. The hair, though this woman's was abruptly cut, sprang forth thickly. The brow was like, the lips, the nose. Gladys had worn a plain gold band, but this woman's was decorative, with a matching engagement ring.

The woman sighed. "Well, we've had a long trip for nothing."

"Let's stop off at Woodward's." In her friend's voice, Jonathan recognized the tone of one who's heard quite enough of a familiar theme. "See if the Food Floor's got any cream cakes pretty as yours. Let's, Mary!"

Mary. Jonathan's heart walloped again.

Mary's frown lines contracted as she examined her transfer. "We haven't got time to stop. Too bad. Always the way, isn't it?"

"Sure we have! Just a peek, for fun." The friend grinned. "When you were a kid, didn't you ride all over town on one transfer?"

Mary's answering smile was so exactly Gladys's that Jonathan almost got whiplash turning his head away.

Out the window streaked with rain, the grey pocked water slopped below the Connaught Bridge.

"We'd fold the transfer so." Mary demonstrated. The smile stopped. "But all over—no. Boys did. John would boast he'd got clear to UBC and back. Mum just smiled, but when I did it on the Number Twenty she and Dad got mad. *What were you thinking of, cheating old Merry?*" Mary pouted down at her shoes. Her feet were bigger than Gladys's.

John, Mary. Plain as you can get. The boy stuttered. Gladys worried. That's how we met. So simple. She reached out her arm to help me. But when she needed help, where was I?

The companion looked sympathetic. "Your Mum favoured your brother when you were young?"

Oh, say her name! Please say her name!

"She still does. John John John, that's all I ever hear."

Jonathan imagined leaning over.... *"Excuse me, Mrs. Grumpy, but would you kindly tell me your mother's real name?"* Silently he got off, at Granville. His knees trembled so he had to limp over to the bench in the bus shelter. *I don't need to ask. I know what I need to.* He sat down hard on the bench. *"She still does." That's what her daughter said.*

Two of Jonathan's patients that day were babies he'd delivered, now grown and bringing in babies of their own. These newborns felt charged with meaning, their flesh made more substantial by the past. As Jonathan held and peered and smiled, he heard *She still does*, again and again.

By half-past five his office was drained of people. Jonathan dug out Gladys Smith's old file; he frowned, puzzling out his own gnomic scribblings and abbreviations. That address was clearly impossible, because the street ran only for a few blocks. He'd checked on a city map, later, far too late. And no letter followed the phone number to indicate a party line—another clue, if only he'd had the wit to see it, if only he'd known his city. *Her mask. Her disguise.*

Taking out his pen, he reached for yellow foolscap and wrote *XIV II MCMLXIV* across the top. He whispered, "It's an important date, Miss Lawrence," and in the middle of the page inscribed *Found. OK.* He underlined this repeatedly.

As the day turned darker and darker in the west, Jonathan sat at his desk in his consulting room where all that happened—and she ran away. He stared out at the rain. His invisible foot was bothering him; still after thirty years the aching came, if he got upset or overtired. Finally he took off Dr. Lee's latest, most splendid prosthesis and rubbed his stump. Sometimes, attention from his own fingers comforted the phantom. Then he fitted himself together once more, reached for his cane.

"Damn! I've left it on the bus *again*. Well...I won't go home just yet." He limped to the tiny kitchen area beyond the reception room and from the mini-fridge got a carton of milk. Then Jonathan took the file marked *King* and the others stored with it—files of letters letters letters, photos, clippings, Gestetnered sheets, dittos, handwritten drafts and one good copy of a manuscript—and returned to his desk.

She still does.

Nothing would be published now.

As long as Jonathan had still thought, feared, felt that Gladys must be dead but hoped she wasn't, he went on with his research, more desultorily over time but never abandoning the work. He read all the obituaries in all the local papers, daily. He made it his business to learn of unusual abdominal surgeries performed in Lower Mainland hospitals. For years he subscribed to clipping services and corresponded with unknown doctors in Asia, Europe, Africa, New York, Leamington, Prince George, and so Jonathan's understanding of extra-uterine pregnancy grew enormously. He knew that if he could be assigned to rewrite the entire entry in *Williams' Obstetrics*, the improvement would be major. Drawings and diagrams he prepared, in large numbers—"Exquisite!" Dr. King wrote. "You could have been a first-rate medical illustrator." Enthusiastically the American doctor wrote on Jonathan's behalf to the editors of the *New England Journal of Medicine* and comparable publications.

But Jonathan couldn't face the annual general meetings of the American Associations of Obstetricians, Gynaecologists, and Abdominal Surgeons. He couldn't go. He got *a cold foot. One's enough!* He couldn't leave the city where she might be or even hand over his manuscript to a typist. And even if he could get so far as having the thing typed properly, the idea of hiding the typescript in a manila envelope and posting it off to some Journal of This or Proceedings of That was intolerable.

If his work were published, Jonathan knew, it would guarantee that Gladys, whoever she might have been, was known dead. And with that thought were easily born its twins and triplets: *I should have phoned the ambulance myself. I shouldn't have told her the baby was dead. If I'd called the police, right then, they'd have found her. All wrong. I did it all wrong. Too big for my britches. Thought I could save her, save everything—and did nothing. Same as always.*

Now, the words that Mary-woman said as the bus groaned along its route—*She still does*—made his manuscript irrelevant. *Even more irrelevant,* Jonathan corrected himself sharply.

She's carried it for almost thirty years. Jonathan wondered how much the fetus had shrunk, since death. Had both it *and* the membranes calcified? A stone baby: twice unnatural, a child housed in the living mausoleum of its mother, not a lodger but a permanent tenant, doubly preceding her to the meeting with death.

Jonathan sipped at his milk. *At least with my mother it wasn't the other way around; she didn't have to grieve for me.* That thought surprised. Past sixty now, he hadn't believed there was anything surprising left in the world for him to think about his mother's death.

And if the stone baby were a girl, all her eggs would be calcified too.

How did Geoffrey put it, that day, about the fish? "Stories that will never be told."

That was in 1914, when Jonathan and his brother sat on Locarno Beach and watched how, under the cooling September sun, the tidal flats glistened away into slate blue ruffled with white. Geoffrey picked up damp sand and squeezed it so hard his fingers quivered. He threw the grains away. They subsided, flat, into the wet sand.

"But Geoff, why are you so *cross* about Richard's enlisting?"

"Because I can't! I hate the way I look. Plenty of boys pretend they're eighteen, but no one would believe me."

"Maybe the war will last till you do turn eighteen."

"Two years? Don't be stupid. Everyone says it'll be over by Christmas. There's no hope for me."

Jonathan got up and walked away across the sand. Geoffrey watched his figure move against the shining. He closed his eyes.

The officer ran across the field of battle while his outpaced men panted ardently behind. Geoffrey overtook the fleeing Hun. He grabbed. He stabbed. A vermilion flower welled up on the grey Boche uniform, blooming in death. The German eyes trickled remorse for gallant little Belgium, and the soldier expired, no, drew his last breath. Shouldering his dripping bayonet, the officer urged on his heroic men.... All this happened on a green plain very like Brockton cricket oval, near bright water fringed with cedar, fir, and Sitka spruce.

Distant watery shouts from little brother Jonathan.

Hurrying back, the gangly boy carried something. A fish. The dead sockeye's hump was just developing. Its eyes bulged bright, and the reddish gills were sharp as devil's club. Jonathan got out his knife and began cutting.

"Where'd you learn to do that?"

"Hilda." As if it were a book, Jonathan opened the fish up, and translucent orange pearls cascaded on to the sand in a long shimmering pour. The boys gasped.

"So many!" With a fingertip, Geoffrey touched the mass.

Jonathan filled his hands and let the dripping globes slide through his fingers. "Slippy!" On his sandy palm he arranged eggs in graduated order. "Hundreds, there must be."

"And none will grow up to be fish." Geoffrey wiped his hands on his shorts. "None of these stories will be told."

"But why did the mother fish die?" Jonathan looked for a wound, found none. He smelled and felt her. "Why?"

Geoffrey got up.

"I'm not coming yet. I want to find out why." Jonathan turned the salmon over and pulled her jaw wide open.

When Geoffrey reached the path from the beach that led up through the woods to the Sasamat house, he glanced back at Jonathan, flat on his stomach with the fish. The incoming tide scrolled over the sand. Geoffrey looked then towards Vancouver. Glancing up, Jonathan followed his line of sight to the houses of the West End clustering on the periphery of Stanley Park's forest. From the brick-works and ironworks of False Creek, darkness curled up, oily brown. Slowly the wind wafted the precipitate eastwards. There lay Grandview.

Unseen, Jonathan had followed his brother there, twice. The brothers rode the long streetcar miles to the east side. First the older and then the younger, the latter careful to remain unnoticed, wandered the unfamiliar streets and drives—Clark, Commercial, Napier, Cotton, Kitchener. At the corner of Graveley and Woodland, Jonathan watched how Geoffrey looked west. He knew what his brother was looking at: the prospect their parents' bedroom window would have enjoyed if the Smyths' grand house there had been built. If their mother had not died. If that doctor had got there in time.

We never talked about our mother.

The cook Hilda had noticed that fact decades earlier, when Richard and Geoffrey and Jonathan were little boys together in the house at 1272 Davie. She did not quite say so directly to their father.

On a certain morning, Arthur Smyth as usual plastered his good bread with butter and began to trowel on the marmalade. "And Hilda. When I came home last night, Richard was playing with that Murphy boy again, cycling up and down the cinder path. I know they're neighbours, but don't encourage that friendship. They're Catholics." He crunched a large bite.

"It's really little Sally he plays with, sir. She's just three, and Richard likes pulling her in his wagon. She holds baby Jonathan in front of her and they all laugh."

"Girl and boy—even worse! Twenty years from now, who knows? All these people try to get inside our lives. Catholics. Jews. Chinks. Japs—they even steal their livelihood from the damned Siwashes, those people! All of them want what *we* have."

Hilda refilled his coffee cup.

"And another thing. The aunts are after me. Julie says Geoffrey disobeys, won't drink his milk. Flossie says he'll stunt his growth. Well?"

"He won't drink a glass of milk, sir. But I make lots of milk dishes for the boys. Soups, custards, rice pudding."

"Then why does he eat those?"

"Boys don't cook, sir. He doesn't know milk's in them."

Arthur Smyth smiled. "Good! We won't tell. But still— why? Don't all children drink milk?"

Hilda hesitated.

"Come on, girl. Spit it out."

"It started after Mrs. Smyth died, sir."

The marmalade spoon stopped halfway to the jar. Arthur Smyth's plump face lengthened so that Hilda winced. "Really."

"And Geoffrey keeps to himself a great deal now. Not like Richard, always playing with a friend or with baby Jonathan."

"But the two big boys used to play together. Always." He sighed. "She'd know what to do. Do you, Hilda?"

"Sir, before, you used to talk about moving. To a new house. That might be good for the boys, and the baby too."

Hilda waited while her employer drank. Finally he threw down his napkin and pushed back his chair. "There isn't a thing in this house that doesn't speak to me of her! I can't leave yet. And never to Grandview. But yes, Hilda. I'll think about another house." He stood at the head of his dining table and looked away from his cook. "Thank God the boy doesn't look like his mother. I couldn't have borne it."

To mark the move two years later to the beachfront property on Point Grey, Arthur Smyth searched through all his stock at Smyth, Stationer until he came upon exactly the right notebook, a big square one bound in good-quality black leatherette. Between finger and thumb he felt the paper and approved. He approved the rings, the index tabs.

"This is for you, Hilda. For your very best recipes."

Now, sixty years later, baby Jonathan was sitting in his office disguised as Jonathan Smyth, M.D., a more-than-middle-aged amputee and milksop.

He tilted the carton to his lips and then flicked through his long dense manuscript on extra-uterine pregnancy.

How much he'd learned, and what a story such a pregnancy made! What would Pliny have made of this riddle, this miracle? A baby still but not stillborn. A live body as a tomb, a tomb in a body. A living woman full of stony death. Yes, the Greek would have been amazed.

The closeness—Jonathan couldn't get over that. Only a film of tissue separated the main body cavity from the uterus. And after a while the female body, indifferent to any neighbouring reality, went calmly back to its monthly routine: egg and blood, egg and blood.

Such courage she's had!

As for the stone baby itself, to personify it tempted him. Jonathan wanted to imagine a conscious human's moment of realization that there was no exit, no access to the so-close birth canal, no hope of making passage to the open sea. *False Creek. Not even Capilano ever found the secret river where the seal went.*

But Gladys—she knew all that. Such courage! To know it all and to do nothing. To do nothing at all.

Jonathan took up his manuscript. *Look at these silly papers! What's paper?* He tore all the sheets into halves quarters eighths sixteenths and threw them into the toppling wastebasket. *And anyway—what I've written is too late.* King's article had come out a decade earlier. All sorts of men had published since—or so Jonathan supposed, not having kept up with the journals lately, having got so drawn into the busyness of an urban GP and into the great hospital's endless reconfigurations and reorganizations. Committees, meetings, minutes. *Rattlebrain!* He had nothing of value to say.

I don't need to say anything. She has survived. Jonathan finished his milk.

Looking out the window, he saw the early dark of February, clear now, with stars. *Never learned them. Never had children. I couldn't have borne the fear, so those stories never got told. I didn't choose to see the world.*

He checked his watch. By now, with luck, his cane would have come back with the bus to the Cambie Garage, across the street from his apartment; at Lost Property, Jonathan was so regular a visitor that the staff joked about its being his real address.

Time to go home.

Watching the signal above the elevator move along the arc of Roman numerals, Jonathan remembered *Caddy. That's it. Caddy, her little girl who died.*

Starting Again

1958—Owen, Collecting the Stones

At the Husky in Quesnel, Owen was leisurely about break-fast; being between jobs, he didn't need to gobble and go. Also, in the years since Mrs. Major's death there was no urgency about getting over to her place. A girl from the old days ran the cathouse now and Owen stopped by when in town, but that could wait.

Two eggs over easy, fat-crunchy hash browns, syrupy pancakes capped with cream, buttery toast, lots of ketchup and marmalade—Owen enjoyed this meal, each time, and the strong coffee after.

As the waitress poured his second cup, a bradawl of pain screwed through Owen just below his rib cage, burn-ing so he thought it must be Jerry's birthday. He twisted in his seat, trying to scream. His eyes bulged. Alarmed, the waitress touched his shoulder. Owen hit out at her torturing fingertips. His face poured sweat and he fainted.

Going off shift, Owen's nurse said to her replacement, "That old goat broke the record. So conceited! You'd think he'd done it on purpose. Take a look...pour 'em out." She nodded at an envelope lying on the counter. The new nurse tipped out a heap of small brown and grey tetrahedrons, stirred them, made a face.

"Forty-four of them Mr. Jones grew. And when he pinches you, tell him you'll throw his goddamned gallstones in the trash. Maybe he'll mind his manners then."

The gallstones had been inside him all those years. "*I never knew*," Owen said to anyone who'd listen. "*That's* the thing."

The stones went with him everywhere, stored in a pouch. By campfires and in bars Owen displayed them and told his story. He explained about bile and drew sketches of the stones' pathways within. In the galleys of fishboats he poured the little things out, *tap tip tap*, on greasy Formica tables.

"Guess what these are. Bet you can't."

"Guess how much they weigh. Bet you can't."

"Guess where I got 'em. Bet you can't."

In the late seventies when he was settling in the cabin by the river, Owen stole a small glass box from a store in Williams Lake. It was the first object he placed on his shelf; the morning light showed off the gallstones well. The second item was his bottle of aspirin.

In the eighties, the little girl Cheryl came with her parents sometimes to visit Uncle Owen and to bring him good food.

"Guess what these are."

"What river d'you think these little stones came out of?"

"How many? Eh? Cat got your tongue, girl?"

"How much d'you think they weigh? They're stones, right? Go ahead, guess."

In the nineties, "I *know*, Uncle Owen!" thirteen-year-old Cheryl shouted. "Forty-four. Less than an ounce. D'you think I'm stupid?"

"Cheryl! Don't be rude to Uncle Owen."

The old man looked appreciatively at the girl and pinched her bum. Cheryl refused for some time to go see Uncle Owen.

"Forty-four I got! Forty-four!"

"Those stones aren't nothing," Indian Tom exclaimed in exasperation. "I got better'n that. Shrapnel. Was in my uncle's leg from the war. The first. Remember I told you about him, in London there that time?"

"Back then? In our war?"

London. On leave.

Soon after passing a huge ugly pile someone said was the Imperial War Museum, Owen crossed a bridge. Filthy Thames. On the other side of the river was nothing, just more streets.

The roots of Owen's ears hurt, way inside his head. One ear did let in some sound now, but his smeller still didn't work. *Weak as a kitten.* Leaning up against a plane tree, he touched his wallet, wadded with cash. His pocket was still sticky. In an orchard near the Orne River he'd watched bees looping about the splintered trees, around the wreck of their hives; Owen chunked off some honeycomb, wrapped it in his handkerchief, ate the last of the fragrant stuff crossing the Channel, remembered Dora in the green room. Sweet. A sweet ache.

The London planes filed away down the street, and the damp road ran silver as a river in the new sun. On the other bank stood a Bella Coola Indian. Impossible, but the man was there. Owen wasn't just imagining because he was exhausted and deaf and nauseated. That solid shape, that warm skin—they were startling among the weedy English soldiers and the big Americans, beef-red or black. Shape and skin were familiar: Indian Tom.

Owen turned away. Too late. Seconds later Indian Tom crossed the street at a run and grabbed Owen's arm and shouted, purely by chance, in his better ear. "I'd know you anywhere, even without your beard, Owen Jones. Years, it is!" The big man glared down. "I been saving up something to tell you, boy. A long time. Your baby died, your boy you made with my sister Irene. You hear?"

Hours later, still in the pub they'd found nearby, Owen and Indian Tom began on the First World War.

"My father died in it," sighed Owen. "Cheap bastard. Never a penny for me or my mum. Always blithering about Mazatlan and the Aztecs. But to hear her go on about him when he died! November eleventh of 1914, see. In Montreal. Hadn't even got over there, yet. A crate fell on his head, at the train station. 'If only David had really been killed in the *war!*' On and on she'd go."

"My pa died too," said Tom. "Passchendaele. Ma never got no money. Pa's medal came, was all. A velvet box. My uncle wrote to Ottawa when he got back. The priest too. Lots of times."

The beer wasn't sitting well in Owen's stomach. When he couldn't take another swallow, he and Tom left the King's Arms and became wavelets in the tidewater of soldiers, sailors, fliers, and women filling up every traffic-bearing tributary that flowed towards Piccadilly and its centre, Eros.

Angry with nausea, Owen snapped at Indian Tom. "Your sister opened her legs for anyone. Could have been anyone's baby."

Chuckling, Tom shook his head. "Irene's fine. Got other babies, strong, healthy. But that one you made, he died, Owen."

Owen gestured at the sculptured boy above the fountain, aiming his bow and arrow. "Those things didn't do your people much good, did they, Tom? When we took over?" He turned and ducked and tried to slide away into the midnight jostling.

Tom came after him through the dark crowd. "If you wasn't such a bloody bastard, Owen Jones, you'd be a fine smart guy." Again he grabbed Owen by the arm.

Owen vomited and cried out in pain.

Nearby, a sarcastic English voice said, "Fucking Yank." Out of the dark came a Southern "Oh yeah?" and then, "Well we'll just see about that." Next came the meaty thud of bone on bone, the sharper sound of boots on bone, and soon the screamed curses of a full-scale brawl. A knee slammed into Owen's belly, just where he'd landed on the pump at the French farm. He doubled over. Strong arms clasped him from behind and someone big bore him away like a child from the fight's violent core. Owen crouched agonized and small, knees to chin, and with his hands shielded his ears from the angry feet jerking and kicking all round him.

The fight veered away. Owen looked about. No Tom. In his gut the pain diminished, until he tried to move.

Again he peered into the night. Someone started up a chorus of "Happy Days Are Here Again," but Tom was definitely gone.

Owen checked in his pocket for the braided trim of his wallet. That was gone too. Swearing, the little man limped out of Piccadilly.

Hours afterward, as the Dover train knuckled along the track, Owen stopped cursing and began to laugh. He'd had his nice quiet rest and was going back to the familiar drudgery of terror. Behind his seat, someone had left a square of treacle toffee, dark and sweet.

Now sitting on his camp cot in his riverside cabin, decades later, Owen glared at his old friend Tom. "I didn't hear you say nothing in all that about any uncle or any shrapnel."

"I got some anyways. You'd like it. Came out of his leg."

After long negotiations, the slivers of metal gave off a dull gleam on Owen's shelf.

An old girlfriend, Lillian, had a friend down at the clinic who got Owen fragments of glass from the forehead and thigh of a local motorcyclist who'd smashed into a car. Pressed deep into this man's wounds, the tiny particles sank in a backwater of his body's river and then mysteriously floated up. Owen used clear tape to fix the bits of glass on some bright blue cardboard where they glittered.

Cheryl scoffed. "That's nothing special, Uncle Owen. There's better stuff in the science lab at stupid old SAMSS."

Thus Owen entered a public school building, after more than sixty years.

After seeing the displays in the lab, though, Owen did not agree with Cheryl's judgement. *Ordinary. What you'd expect.* There were fetuses of this and that, tissue samples, sliced frog, some skeletons. *Nothing like what I got!* But the school library had books. Owen had not thought of books, or of magazines, journals, films. SAMSS also had the Internet, of which he knew nothing.

Writing home to Vancouver, the young teacher-librarian described Owen as *Such a character! Crusty, smart, intellectually curious—what could he have been, if he'd had the education?* Miss Gold showed him, led him. Although Owen never became a skilled Internet user, he got quite good at searching the library's catalogue.

Adipocere—although Owen did not find anyone who'd had more than forty-four gallstones, he read, amazed and delighted, about the formation of adipocere. From a museum in Boston there was a terrific photograph of a body that looked half-melted. To see that amazing picture, he made unwilling and uncomfortable Tom come in with him to the school. And Owen learned about bullets, pins, beans lodged for a lifetime in heads and arms and ears. He learned about *bezoar.* He learned about medical instruments left behind in the guts of surgical patients and retrieved only decades later at autopsy.

By this time the librarian termed Owen *that disgusting old pervert. He's shown me his gallstones about ten times,* she wrote.

He read of a woman who'd borne several children and later for some reason had X-rays that revealed her oldest child of all, an unborn twin, withered on the vine of an inadequate placenta and somehow lodged within her. "Unreal," admired Owen. He got this term from Cheryl. "Eh, Miss Gold?"

And he smells. Miss Gold underlined *smells.*

Owen learned about prostheses, although he could never get his tongue round the word and teased Miss Gold by pretending to mix it up with prostate. Every time, she rose to the bait; he couldn't believe anyone, even a woman, could be so dumb. However, his admiration of those ingenious wood, canvas, steel, and plastic contraptions was genuine. "Unreal." Also there were fine colour pictures of raw stumps with the ends of bones showing, like beef roasts, and then the same stumps all fixed up with skin folded over and the prosthesis attached.

Owen remembered the gimpy doctor in Vancouver. *Limping like that—show-off! Must have had that wound twenty years, by then.*

As for the phenomenon of the phantom limb, Owen talked and talked about that until Indian Tom banged the cabin door as he left and didn't come back for three weeks.

Then Owen came upon a lithopedion. To him, things inside were always more compelling; this seemed the ultimate. It took him a while to understand. He read and re-read, stared at the illustrations. His neck hairs prickled. He tried to steal the relevant volume of the encyclopedia but Miss Gold caught him, and she caught him again as he was about to rip out the pages. With much complaint, Owen paid for colour photocopying.

The horrible creature ought to be banned permanently from the school, Miss Gold wrote to her fiancé, *but the principal's such a wimp. He keeps going on about "community access."*

Owen went over and over the lithopedion material with Tom, in slow detail. "If I could get one on my shelf I'd die happy," he concluded, folding the papers carefully away in his drawer. Impatiently he waited for his fortnight's banishment from SAMSS to end.

"That's the most disgusting thing I've ever seen in my life," Cheryl declared, when shown the lithopedion photos. Laughing, Owen pulled up his shirt to reveal the scar from his gallbladder surgery. She screamed.

"Really, Cheryl!"

"Shut up, Mum! Just shut up!"

After that Cheryl refused to be anywhere near Owen again, until grade twelve when she had to, in order to get her Work Experience credits.

Owen savoured Elizabeth Preston's outrage. To Tom he chuckled, "It was great. She didn't know who to be madder at, her kid or me."

But even Tom complained as the months went by. "Owen—that damn stone baby—I'm pretty sick of it, see. Can't you talk about something else?"

"I want to *know*," obstinately. Owen reached down a bottle of massage oil and began to work his hands—always a sign that he was settling in for a full consideration of some subject. "What colour are they? Brown? Grey? And how big? And all shrivelled up, or not? Like a real baby? Do they *smell*, when the docs take them out? And what do they *do* with them? Bury? Baptize? Put 'em on the mantel? That's what I'd do!"

Sighing, Tom reached for his jacket. "I'll be back sometime. Try to talk about something else, will you?" The door closed.

Owen sat still, thinking, flexing his hands. Handling stone and wood and wire and fish for decades, getting knife cuts and misplaced hammer blows by the hundred, his skin had got roughed up into a coarse canvas. Bulges of muscle cupped the wrinkled palms. The thumbs were grossly spatulate and all the nails thick and brittle as old plastic siding; the fingers bore lumps of callus. The arthritis had deformed his knuckles till Owen's hands burst out from his wrists like twisted clubs.

His feet: the arches lay flat as pancakes, and his toenails bulged like lumps of ochre stone. All over, his knotted veins bulged and rippled in blue.

Eight decades of sun and rain and salt spray had tanned Owen's hair-tufted head to a tawny leather, stretched here, folded there, with ears nose eyes lips patched on anyhow, symmetry long gone. His right ear sat at an odd angle. His cracked tongue resembled weathered wood, fissured stone. His tongue was still pointy, though—"Devilish, upon my word," said Elizabeth Preston—and Owen could curl it both under and over, as he demonstrated often to Cheryl and Indian Tom and Miss Gold.

After thinking about the bezoar for a long time, Owen wrote to the *National Enquirer*. A long time after that, someone at the newspaper (at least that was the return address on the package) sent Owen a tangled ball of string. He had to collect it at the post office. The thing was about the weight and shape of a good-sized rutabaga, and stiff, as if marinated in starch.

For months, he and Indian Tom debated.

"It might be a miracle."

"Bullshit. Don't give me that Jesus crap, Tom. It's string was in that stupid cunt's belly."

"Or it might just be regular string. From the store, like."

From Williams Lake, Tom brought back various balls of twine; one looked identical to the alleged bezoar.

"Tom, first you say *miracle* and now you say *Home Hardware*. You bin drinkin again? This is booze talkin?"

"All I'm saying, the human body's a wonderful thing." Tom fell silent, gazing. In its clear alcohol bath, the string shimmered. "Wonderful."

Owen looked at him sharply, and his rare smile shifted every line on his face. "True enough. That lithopedion, now. *Fumin gloomin human loomin roomin wooman*, ha ha. *Wooman*." He pushed Ginger off his lap and reached for his photocopies and his peppermints. "Amazing, all right."

Tom sighed.

1958—Jonathan Deals with Prostheses and Nijinsky
Great ones hung on the walls of Dr. Lee's consulting room: Pavlova, Nijinsky, Fonteyn, Tallchief, and an amazing young Russian named Nureyev of whom people now spoke.

Young Dr. Lee himself was stocky and lacked physical grace. Nonetheless he was jumping successfully to reach the cord of the blind over his office window; it had snapped all the way up.

I couldn't do it, tall as I am. Even small jumps involved complicated manoeuvrings of Jonathan's good leg and prosthesis. *I'd have to hook that cord down with my cane.* He smiled at Dr. Lee.

Smiling back, the doctor held up Jonathan's new foot and stroked the plastic admiringly. "Look at this, Dr.

Smyth! A few adjustments and—perfection. You'll be much more mobile."

That day, I couldn't walk down stairs to find her. I could hardly get to the elevator and back. I nearly fell, I failed.

Over a quarter-century Jonathan had worn five prostheses, worn them out with his insistent walking, walking, walking. Each time he replaced the device, the medical men promised that because of its new angle or new fastening or new composition the thing would fit better. Circulation would improve. Range of movement would widen, limits of action expand. Pain—though they never said *pain*, only *discomfort*, a doctors' euphemism Jonathan tried hard to eschew in his own practice—would diminish. Always the new prosthesis was lighter. So he would limp less, tire less easily. So they said.

"I don't expect improvement in my new contraption," he told Dr. Lee cheerfully. "Not in anything, really. *To strive, to seek....* We don't ever really *find*." *I couldn't find her, then or ever. Who knows what happened to her?*

In serious startlement, Dr. Lee dropped his hands from Jonathan's stump. "But in your own lifetime, Dr. Smyth! Salk, Banting, penicillin. If you'd been wounded in any other war in history, think how easily you'd have died! Antibiotics, plastic surgery, old killers like TB almost gone.... We *have* found." Because the acne scars on his face made him appear even younger than he was, Dr. Lee's disagreement looked childish.

Jonathan tapped his stump. "This didn't come in any war. Only a foolish curiosity wounded me, right here at home."

Dr. Lee's hands hesitated for a moment and then returned to Jonathan's leg. "You puzzle me, sir. No improvements? But you have been a doctor for thirty years, so you yourself have made a great many people better."

"And killed some. Unwittingly, ignorantly. Two women anyway. Maybe three—the evidence was contradictory." Jonathan moved his leg as his colleague indicated he should. "You'll do more good than I ever have, Dr. Lee. You have focus, you concentrate. Already a specialist! I've dithered. Committeeing. I could tell you the history of every new toilet that's been installed in the General in three decades." He laughed.

Dr. Lee did not even smile. "Two dead, perhaps three, of many many thousands. What doctor could claim better?" He released Jonathan's leg and began making notes. "I declare for progress, Dr. Smyth. When your loss occurred, amputation was performed at what was then thought the best angle. Even as we judge today, your stump is not bad. A functional prosthesis was made. An improvement over early death, I say!" He indicated Jonathan's old prosthesis. "Back on, now."

"Now, not so many children get rickets. Maternal deaths are down." Jonathan picked up the leather and wood contraption. "Better dental health, here anyway. Anaesthesia. Cancer therapy."

"So you agree now? There has been improvement? What we have done has made things better?"

"Yes and no, Dr. Lee." Jonathan began on the buckles. "I always think of my brothers, you see. Unlike me, they were both soldiers in the First War. In the 72nd. Really they had the same war, except Richard had more of it. The Somme, Vimy, Amiens."

"Both lived? Your parents must have been deeply grateful."

"Geoffrey's shell shock we thought was temporary. *Rest, quiet*, the doctors said. *Good food.* Well, that he certainly got. And Hilda held him. But the nightmares! He couldn't be with people. He hid in his room. For years. A grown son who wept a dozen times a day...that wasn't what my father'd counted on."

"Did these symptoms continue?" Dr. Lee set his notes aside and gave Jonathan his full attention.

"But my brother Richard...he just picked up where he'd left off in 1915, jumped off the troop train as if it were a swing in a playground and got on with a stockbrokers' firm. All through the twenties Richard made piles. A week after Black Friday he married and began having daughters. Five!"

"A very different temperament."

Jonathan adjusted the laces. "That's part of what I mean. Chance. We can't do anything about chance."

"And Geoffrey? Children?"

"Not of his own. When the Second War started, all that same old geography was right back in the papers. Vimy, Amiens. The Hun, again. Belgium, again. Passchendaele." His prosthesis firmly attached once more, Jonathan tapped it on the floor. "By then I had this, so the Second wasn't a war for me either. Geoffrey woke up shrieking every night. Millicent held him, this time. But a librarian can't cry all day; he lost his job. The lists of dead, in the paper—he'd see boys he'd read stories to. His boys." Jonathan pulled his trouser leg down.

Eventually Dr. Lee asked, "What happened then?"

"On VE Day he attempted suicide. That time his wife found him. But after Hiroshima he succeeded. I couldn't save him."

Dr. Lee addressed his wall calendar, thick with appointments, conferences, consultations. "Your new prosthesis is, largely, made of a plastic whose pedigree is rooted in war, or at least in the work of the DVA. But your brother, like uncounted others, died at the end of the Second War essentially of injuries received in the First. A sad fact. Deeply sad, Dr. Smyth. In addition of course to all the millions killed in battle, and the civilians.... So you ask, 'How then can my new *contraption* be said to be *better?*'"

"You read my mind, Dr. Lee."

The young doctor grinned. He tilted his head so his hair hung off his scarred face like a blackbird's wing. "Yet you kept your appointment with me, Dr. Smyth. Am I to cancel the order for your new prosthesis? No? Then we agree. We can act, we must act, to make things better, even if only by a small margin. That is what doctors do. Not only doctors, either. My grandparents on my father's side...."

"Go on, Dr. Lee. Tell me about them."

"In my living room, a photograph. In 1902 they came, from their village in China. It is a stylized portrait, Dr. Smyth. Black and white. In some ways, charming. For the occasion they wore Western clothes, in a studio, by a painted palm tree with a sunset behind. Nonsensical! I never knew them. They had a hard time, after they left that studio. More sad facts, Dr. Smyth, sad and very hard. But I would rather have that paper facsimile than nothing. And I am a doctor. Better. They made things better."

The two doctors looked at the rough draft of the new prosthesis, all smooth pink plastic.

Jonathan sighed.

"In this, Dr. Smyth, you'll be jumping around like a cat." Dr. Lee waved at the photos of the leaping dancers. "Like them. Did you see Nijinsky? He came to Vancouver once, I'm told."

"Almost. I just missed him."

In 1917, hosting a family Sunday dinner, Aunt Julie gave her report on the Russian ballet.

"Mrs. Lowden was there, and Mrs. McCallum. Miss Forward. Mrs. Baillie. Mrs. Wilson. The Knoxes with a Mr. Finch from the States, so elegant! Sadie Addington's daughter wore such a dress as you never saw. If I were her mother I'd be ashamed. Not that Sadie spoke to me. I know she lost her boy at Vimy, but that doesn't excuse rudeness."

"But Aunt Julie, Nijinsky? Tell about him."

"Jonathan, anyone would think you were five, not fifteen. Yes, Nijinsky leaps. So does my neighbour's cat. Don't *dither*, boy. Gravy, or not?"

"But Aunt Julie..."

"And everything Russian may be fashionable now, but I thought his costume indecent. Altogether unsuitable for young persons, that performance." Aunt Julie drove the tines of her fork through spring lamb. "But my new coat—such a success! No one had anything like it. Miss Dearing was right about that satin lining. Ashes-of-roses. Very subtle! Everyone thought so."

Jonathan gave up and took gravy. Aunt Julie did not even deserve to know such a beautiful term as ashes-of-roses.

The first time Miss Pearl Dearing, the dressmaker, came to Aunt Julie's to deliver newly sewn garments, she saw that unlike many other houses Mrs. Crosse's had no small side gate on Haro Street marked *Tradesmen's Entrance*. She therefore rang the front doorbell.

Jonathan, hanging about upstairs (*Scatterbrain!*), heard his aunt's astonished angry exclamations. He went to the bathroom, which overlooked the back door, and waited to see the dressmaker's parasol come bobbing along the hedge in the back alley that ran between Haro and Barclay. Unexpectedly, two parasols appeared. Miss Dearing and a girl, who carried a large basket, walked into the garden and up the steps. Gently, the dressmaker knocked. In the few seconds before Aunt Julie yanked the door open to snap, "Well, I should think *so!*" and usher the two roughly in, the girl looked up at Jonathan. Her features were half-obscured by her sunshade and a soft mass of hair, but her expression was clear. Mutinous. Dour. Still. Her grey eyes did not blink.

For fifteen minutes Jonathan dithered about going downstairs in hopes of getting another look at that girl, but just as he reached the bottom step, jumping down three at a time (*three at a time! I could do that then!*), he heard the back door close. He'd missed her.

"*Admirable* work Miss Dearing does. Truly." His aunt, all smiles, showed him Wong's new uniforms, smock-like garments in fine white cotton. "I think I'll even order some shirts for you from Miss Dearing, Jonathan." Aunt Julie moved officiously towards the kitchen to introduce her cook to his new clothing.

Jonathan speared some more lamb from the platter. Definitely, Aunt Julie merited no connection with ashes-of-roses.

After dinner, though, Jonathan slipped up to her bedroom (*up the stairs, three at a time!*) and found the so-successful evening coat that Miss Dearing had made. Black velvet, satin-lined. Perhaps that girl might have tried it on? Certainly she would have handled his own shirts. Nijinsky's leaps, the coat's lushness, that girl fingering and stroking the smooth cotton meant to encase his own body: these combined in ecstasy.

Before rejoining the grown-ups, he eavesdropped as usual.

"I've never understood my sons." That was his father's voice, weary. "Except Richard."

"And Geoffrey's always been so sensitive." Aunt Flossie's.

"Those boys sensitive? Sometimes I wonder who on earth would choose to have children. *So* difficult. *Such* a burden."

I never will. Never. Never. Never.

He pushed open the drawing-room door.

"About time you turned up, Jonathan. Always late!"

Now a patient in nice young Dr. Lee's office, underneath the dancers, Jonathan looked down at his feet.

He flexed the right one and felt a twinge in the other, the phantom.

His two polished leather shoes were brown and supple and looked exactly alike. In the Vancouver Block, back on that day when he needed desperately to leap down those flights of stairs three at a time, four at a time, to catch her, find her, save her, his shoes had looked just so. They had shone just so uselessly.

Jonathan wondered what colours Dr. Lee's grandmother had chosen for her dress, for her Canadian wedding portrait. He got up to leave.

"My feet are like your grandparents' picture, Dr. Lee. Not real, but a good facsimile. Thank you for your fine work, and for reminding me that we do what we can."

On his way out, Jonathan remembered that he'd been thinking about suggesting to Dr. Lee the name of a really good dermatologist, a friend of his. Next time. Meanwhile he hoped that, by pretending to agree with the mantra *We do what we can*, he had reduced his young colleague's anxiety. *What I can do is never enough.*

1953—Dora, Making a Housedress

Hot needles punctured Dora's skin. She woke up into dazed pain. Heat squeezed out through her eyeballs and hair shafts, vibrating in its frenzy to escape. Her engorged cheeks hurt.

On the roof, rain sounded.

Dora stripped off her sweaty nightgown. She rolled off the mattress, the only thing left in the room, and went to the low window. Coolness came at her. Outside, airy darkness moulded the neighbourhood's grey flowering cherry trees, grey houses, yards, garden sheds. Saltchuck and wet June grass and the cannery wafted in the grey. She smelled herself too, her own body.

Round the street corner, the child Dora had lost her precious buttons and beads.

She lost her pearl ring and was whipped.

She and Marjo lost the blueing but found it but stained their clothes and hair dreadfully.

Dora lost everyone, and she lost almost everything all of them had possessed.

She lost Miss Pearl Dearing. After August 1918, the shunned girl lay awake listening to the *rum*-rum of the Singer, above. Then, losing her home, Dora had to move away. Months passed before she found Miss Dearing and her dummy again.

She lost her grandmother's pearls, too, or rather, she could not find that treasure, because of the kind of man her father had been and because of what her mother had done, to cope.

Earlier in her teens, Dora had lost the home of her body. Her flesh grew from being uneasy on her, as if ill-fitting, to being hideous—but she couldn't move away from her body.

When Alan was in high school and needed room, Dora lost her right to do her homework at the maple table.

Because her father with every year needed to concentrate more fully on his drinking, she lost his attention.

Her mother's, Dora never had. That was so great a loss she hardly noticed it but took the absence for granted.

Very small Dora lost a button in her bathwater.

Dora now in the spring of 1953 was slick all over. Hot flash. She leaned out of the window so rain would fall on her hair. Mist drifted over the inlet, smudging the lights along the docks and on Woodwards' and the grey-black downtown. Out in that mist were the shop where she'd been Mlle Annette, and the reservoir, and the sugar refinery, and somewhere Spencer's and the Vancouver Block and the women's workroom, where she'd been Gladys. Invisible, dark. Behind Dora were her own bedroom and three others, almost empty, and beyond them the rest of the near-empty house on Garden Drive.

Dora got to her feet stiffly and took her dressing gown over her arm. Naked, she went downstairs, the linoleum treads cool against her soles. As she passed through the kitchen she laid the flat of her hand to the fridge: *Kelvinator*. Near the bathroom, the tiny mother-of-pearl moon on the light switch glimmered.

The toilet was cold. Cold tile met her feet. Warm urine gushed into cold water. In darkness she sat quietly. Inside her in a great coil moved the beginnings of bowel action. She repressed the movement; the time was not right.

Dora brushed and tied back her sweaty hair, watching the motion in the dark mirror. She wet a washcloth and passed it dripping over her face, over her breasts and underneath, between her sticky legs, and then walked, air-drying, silently over the fir floors. Empty dining area. Empty living room. Empty back hall. Empty linen closet. Empty pantry. She was much cooler now. Through the kitchen door she peered out at the empty back porch where Caddy often sat on sunny days. Her fresh-washed hair smelled of its vinegar rinse.

On the rag rug in the dark front hall the colours were invisible. Where Mary's red velvet was tied to John's flannel, a lump bulged under Dora's arch. For years that had irritated her.

Here by the door was the Singer, and here was Flora the dummy on her metal feet, her hinges expanded fully to thicken her waist. At the bust, she was forty-four. Flora stood ready to collapse into her carrying case; the button jar already awaited her at the new house. Dora hugged Flora, her cloth cover, her metallic hardness. "Today," she whispered. "We're going, today." Except for being headless, the dummy's height was exactly Dora's.

Dora slipped into her dressing gown, strapped on her pin-holder, turned on the overhead light. She kicked the rug out of the way and on the floor unrolled pearl-grey cotton. The colour was the same as that of the blouse she'd worn that day with Owen.

First she worked with chalk. Then, slicing across the breadth—for a simple housedress she needed no pattern— Dora's shears shaped two large triangles, their apices blunted for a plain round neckline. One she slit, to carry the zipper. Then quickly she pinned sides and shoulders together and slid the fabric on to Flora, patting and tugging. Set-in cap sleeves she would do; her scissors curved through the cotton. Leaning her head on the dummy's shoulder as she pinned the sleeves in place, Dora smelled the stretchy black jersey that sheathed Flora's metal torso. "Today, I said, Flora." She took the cotton off the form and rough-basted, quickly. Then she opened her sewing chest and sorted through her zippers.

Upstairs in John's bedroom, Ned snored on a mattress. Nothing else was left in that room either—all gone, to the Island. No sign remained that a boy had lived twenty years of life there. John had even taken his dead uncle Alan's old copy of the *Boys' Own Annual*. Beside Ned's sleeping form lay his heap of clothes to be worn today for his move, to the suite in daughter Mary and Bill's house on the North Shore.

Dora measured, kneeling. The zipper she set in and basted was bright red. *Mine mine mine.* Red and pearl-grey went together well. The cottage on Eton Street was not in any part Ned's.

Dora shaped darts at bust and sleeve, folding and pinning the smooth grey, and got up from the hall floor. Again she fitted the dress on Flora, smoothing the fabric over the wire hips. She peeled it off, remembered peeling off the pearl-grey blouse in the green bower. Her shears sliced through interfacing. Her fingers layered the crisp stuff with the cotton, settled it, pinned, basted.

A blanket on the floor was the ironing board. Dora spat on the iron. "Ready, Flora!" She nosed it into every minute fold of the basted-in sleeves and ironed its whole front, smoothing and smoothing, smiling with pleasure.

The pale grey triangle now lay warm and creaseless. In the sewing bench Dora found rickrack. Kneeling, she tried the red strands all over, at the neckline, by the sleeve edges, neatly on the skirt in the shape of a patch pocket. "Flora, now watch this!" Dora stood and shook out the entire length of the rickrack, letting the twisty stuff float and fall so it scrawled big scarlet lollops and curves and symbols of infinity over all the grey, and then she picked it up again and made it a giant scarlet necklace round the dummy's absent neck. "Jewels for my jewel, Flora," Dora whispered in the front hall.

Then taking up a remnant of the grey fabric, she laid it under the bright needle to test tension. Bobbin and thread were in place, and Dora's right hand moved the wheel as her left guided the grey through. Her foot flexed on the treadle. Sound waves filled the hall, making Flora hum; that sound resounded through the whole house, but Ned now heard nothing that Dora was doing. "He won't even try to stop us, Flora." Dora made slight adjustments, and the machine eased readily into perfect tension.

Gathering up the grey dress itself, she slid it under the needle for the first long seam from armpit to hem. *Ah ah ah ah!* Triumphantly the Singer hummed. All down one side of the garment her pearl-grey stitches ran straight and even, precisely five-eighths of an inch from the edge. *Rum rum rum.* It slowed.

Dora snipped and tied off her thread. She ran the other side seam and the zipper seams. *Ah ah ah!* The slithery rumple became a dress. The Singer stopped. Flora ceased to resonate. Dora dropped her work over the dummy's shoulders, put an arm around her waist. "How d'you like it, Flora?"

Suddenly Dora pulled the zipper down all the way, to make a big red V. Within that scarlet angle, Flora's black torso deepened into a dark recess, as if her body were being opened up.

Dora peeled the dress off the dummy and held it out in front of herself. As if it were a dancing partner, its pearly grey bosom curved towards her and its skirts swayed, like Marjo's skirts and hers when they all danced together on the sprung floor, back when they were young. *I never danced with him. We never got into the same bed.*

With the coming of dawn, the fabric of the dress developed more sheen and seemed nacreous yet pliable, a soft metal. Through the front door's oval pane, the sky was now silver.

The set-in cap sleeves: although much shorter, those seams took longer to sew because of the perfectly ironed and pinned tucks. Carefully Dora worked the first sleeve into position. Flora waited, dark and solid, with her red necklace looped bright over the hill of her bosom.

Dora spat on the iron again. She took her water bottle and sprinkled the cap sleeve. At the shoulder things were complicated enough, where the seam met the cap, but in the armpit everything came together. The connection must be smooth. Any lump in the pearl-grey would make nasty welts. Dora pressed with the hottest iron possible; the damp cotton hissed.

Almost done. Smoothly the fabric slid over the dummy in a perfect fit. One sleeve stood marginally higher than its sister; Dora shrugged. "I'll fix that for you later on, Flora. In the new house." With her fingertips, she pouched out the offending cap to lower its profile.

On both sleeves she chalked hems and then knelt down again by Flora. She got her chalk marker out of the bench and right round the dummy Dora went, quick quick, squeezing and blowing at the hemline, and then all round again, pinning up the hem so fast the slits of nickel glinted, minnows in a river. Dora's dress barely reached the knee. "Too much leg. Ned and Mary won't like that!" Dora smiled and threaded her needle for hemming.

Almost almost done. Dawn almost here. To hem and iron those sleeves took no time at all; more time would be needed for the hem proper. Before Dora settled herself on the sewing bench, she opened the front door a crack. Fresh moist air rushed in. She could smell salt.

The hemming completed, Dora ironed the entire dress yet again and slid it on to Flora. She looped and swooped the rickrack so red ran right down pearl-grey, clear to the hem.

Gathering up strips and scraps of unused material, Dora set them away. She unplugged the iron and set it to cool, removed bobbin and spool. The Singer's lid went on.

Now she could take off her dressing gown to stand naked and on tiptoe, looking out at the grey morning light and stretching as long and tall as she could. The cherry trees on the street were flowering pink now; their wet trunks shone black.

Now she would have her last bath on Garden Drive.

Now Dora put the pearl-grey dress on a clothes hanger, rolled up the rickrack, collapsed the dummy. Flora disappeared. "Buttons," Dora said, closing the lid. "We'll brighten up your new dress with buttons."

As she tied the belt of her dressing gown, Ned came towards her through the kitchen.

"Doing a striptease for the neighbours? Why've you got the door open? It's wet out there." He closed the door and flicked at the dress. "Another bag?"

Dora went past him to the bathroom, bright now, and set hot water gushing into the tub. She sat down on the toilet.

"Can't you tell red from grey, Dora?" Ned spoke through the bathroom door. "That zipper! You'll be a perfect sight."

Dora smiled.

Pushing out her last bowel movement in this house, Dora heard Ned walking about the empty rooms.

All over her skin the sweat began to rise. At the roots of her hair, beads formed. Her body was going on.

The War

January 1946—Marjo, Speaking to God

"When I left you and the kids to go to the war, I lost every-thing," Mike says. "Now I've got it all again! Even better than when we were young."

No, worse! If our daughter Maureen married today, within a year I could be a grandmother and a mother both. Maureen, Mick, Murray, and...I was pregnant again, at forty-five.

"No M name," I said to Mike. "This baby's a new genera-tion." The boys are almost out of their teens, there's war brides everywhere...and here's *me*. "Forty-five!" I couldn't stop crying.

He hugged me. "And a bun in the oven—I'm proud of you!" And he *laughed*.

I slapped him, I said sorry, I cried more. Mike was plain bewildered. "I'm ashamed," I said finally. True, Lord knows. "A father at this age, that's fine. But a woman's seen differently. She's too old."

"Love you." A hug. "Forty-five, twenty-five. Bun, no bun." Another hug.

Who will this baby look like? Maureen doesn't look much like either of us. Mick is Mike all over again. Murray's a blend. Lord, please let it be a girl? She'd be likelier to look like me.

What must you think of me, God?

When I was seventeen I begged, I prayed, I pleaded to lose the baby.

Then, in my twenties, "Oh God, please let me keep this one. Just this one baby. Not another miscarriage!"

But here I am at forty-five, praying again for blood and cramps and loss.

When I was a teenager, though, I could let it all out to Dora. She saved me. This time the secret has to stay in me. Except the secret will be born, Lord, it'll come out of me— and what will happen then?

As for Dora's secret, I have no right to say anything to her about that ever again. I'd choke, I declare. She's done what she felt she could bear. What else can I do?

Three people know Dora's secret. She does, obviously. I do. Ned does. Four, really—that nice doctor Dora won't talk about, the one who tried to help her, John Smith, she *says* his name was. I declare, that's a joke I won't even try to laugh at.

I mustn't tell Dora.

God, I know that you know all about how this happened to me, but I have to talk, I swear. Dora was never a talker, but I simply can't be silent.

Since the men came back from the war, God, it's been a very sexy time. We're still Mr. and Mrs., but different. The men got through their war over there, and us girls got through, here. That's part of the sexiness—we're the same, yet we're not.

Ned was never handsome. Carrot-tops generally aren't. Why, when real redheads like me often are? *He's not a looker.* I told Dora that when I fixed them up to meet, but his sweet look said, *I could make you feel really good.* What a dancer! Such energy that man had. And his hand on your back was so firm. *I know what I'm doing—just let go and I'll get us there.* Oh, I was married, I was in love with Mike, I wanted Ned for Dora—but over the years there'd be a glance between me and Ned every now and then.

You've noticed that, Lord? I'll tell you what I think. Sometimes couples *stay* good friends just because of that little pull between what would be the *other* couples—if things turned round. I've seen that glance between Dora and Mike. He thought her skin was beautiful; he told me. Her skin still is, if we can say so at forty-five, God! And Mike liked her plumpness. How many times did I try to tell Dora men often *like* women so? Remember *utter udder*, God? That marked her, I declare, for the rest of her life. A day in school, a chance in a spelling bee, a mark forever.

Poor Dora. When those poison-pen letters came, Dora just couldn't *not* believe them.

Things work out oddly. Dora was never much for the union, hardly ever came picketing or on tag days though all the rest of us girls did. We'd bring our kids, have a fine time. But Dora never liked a crowd. Those awful letters made her feel even less like being with the rest of us. As if…if Ned hadn't been so strong for the union and got it in and made more money and been able to buy the house, well then, maybe those letters wouldn't have got written at all.

God, after the baby died in her, how things were was plain as plain: Dora never touched Ned. He never touched her. Not a hand on the arm, not a word in the ear. *Honey sugar sweetheart*—no more of that. No more dancing, with each other or anyone else. At parties they sat stiff as stones, the pair of them.

But still. But still. I'd bet any money you like, God, that Ned *believed* he'd come home from the war to find she'd had *it* taken out. Everything else had changed. Wouldn't that too?

So—last fall the men were all coming home, one by one. That day Mike and the kids went off with his folks, and I was preserving, using up windfalls to make chutney. Peaches, onions, cloves—the whole house smelled. I'd got juice and sugar and cinnamon all over me.

Steps came up to the back porch. A man's voice. "Marjo?"

That voice—I *knew* it—but who? I stopped stirring sugar down into the peaches and went to the kitchen door.

"Ned, wonderful! You're home! Come in! Does Dora—?"

That man somehow got himself into our back hall. He was so horny he could hardly stand up. Frantic. Desperate. He put his hands at my waist. "Dora doesn't." Again that strained voice. "She won't, Marjo." His face was hot and red, under that carroty hair. He stood panting in his khakis with the bits of red and metal on them: Ned Dow. He'd lived through the war and come home with a clutch of medals stuck on his chest. I couldn't not give it to him, God. I just couldn't not. Ned the laughing dancer.... He was so strong I could hardly breathe, but he held me so I didn't fall.

When I pulled down my apron and got back into my kitchen that pan of fruit still wasn't even near the boil, I declare.

Right away I was desperate.

Mike and me—together so long, he knows my cycles as well as I do, dear God. Later on, he'd calculate back and figure out my fertile time. There was only one thing to do. When Mike got home that night he was dog-tired, thought maybe he had a cold coming on, but I fed that man up on roast chicken and chutney and pulled him into bed. God forgive me, I got him to do it twice.

So the bun got baked. She was born. Mike was thrilled. And Hazel wasn't a year old when that ridge shaped up at the back of her head. I *knew* then, for sure and certain.

I love Mike, God. You know that. He's my husband, always. No hiding from you, but from everyone else the secret of Hazel's father has to be hidden. Always. Help me, God. Please help me.

1942–44—Dora, Sewing the War
Not long after Ned and Mike enlisted in December 1941, Marjo got on at Boeing.

From the first day she loved the camaraderie among the women, the noise, speed, purpose, laughter. "See my boiler suit, Dora! Don't I look cute? I *wish* you'd come too." But Boeing meant all those people. *To be surrounded*—after more than twenty years, Dora's stomach still turned at the thought.

Still, she too began job hunting. Though sullen, Ned could find no argument against her working, in the face of war. In any case he and Mike were now focused on Europe, the imminent journey.

Dora did not want to type. So often a typist must work closely with one or two others. Chatter, nosy questions. No. Also, many offices expected typists to be stylish, even in war. Instead she tried for sewing work. Although clothing factories like Dubbel-wear and Pacific Dress & Uniform were union, in full production, and hiring steadily, and although both supplied the loose work-wear that would be ideal for Dora, they were right downtown and so altogether too close to the Vancouver Block. When she went to enquire, Dora kept looking behind her. Also, those shops employed scores of workers. Out in Kits, the smaller Uneeda Towel & Linen had a lonely gossip of a manager; Dora'd have to watch every word, and the workers didn't wear boiler suits.

Then in the *Province* Dora saw "Wanted: experienced tailoress for a ladies' tailor." The ad ran repeatedly. When she reached a dim building on Broadway at Cambie and read the card on the door, she understood why. *Fine Ladies' Tailoring: Gerda Schmidt.*

This tall spare woman said at once, "I am German. If you do not wish, let us not waste our time, Mrs. ...?"

"Smith." Dora opened her bag. "I brought work to show you."

"Smith. I see. Yes. Do come in."

In the north-lit workroom a black-haired woman and a blonde, in smocks and sleeve protectors, smiled up from their machines and went back to their work.

"That is Miss Ko." Mrs. Schmidt glanced at Dora. "Jenny's mother is in the camp at Slocan. She herself hopes not to be taken. Her father—he is dead but was not Japanese, you see. And that is my daughter. She is—a little lacking, Monika." The blonde's second smile was over-broad, and she was not the young girl Dora had first supposed. "So. That is how we are, here."

Riding the streetcar to and from Mrs. Schmidt's workroom, Dora sat by the window with the air, the rain, the sun on her face. The bell sounded. The car clacked and sang down the track, swaying, sailing. Five days a week, Dora packed two school lunches and a lunch for herself (which Ned never noticed, so wrapped up he was in preparations) and rode. She buttoned on her smock. She strapped the pinholder to her wrist, strung scissors to her big patch pocket.

At lunch Dora ate her baloney sandwiches as Jenny tweaked a salted plum or a riceball from a lacquered box, while the tailor and her daughter munched dark rye layered with strong-smelling cheese. Soon, like the others, Dora drank tea from tiny flowered cups. Setting her treasures gently back on the shelf, Jenny said, "One less thing for them to smash, if someone tells and they search my room." Monika loved the porcelain cherry blossoms.

Many customers of the "ladies' tailor" were men, attracted by the European-styled garments Mrs. Schmidt made for their women. Dora learned to work with top-quality men's coatings whenever the tailor could get them, learned the hang of trousers, their cuffs and intricate silk pocketings. Dora watched the tailor hold a bolt in her arms, rub and fold and stretch it, peer and smell. When her shears finally made contact with the material, Mrs. Schmidt looked fierce.

That look was never turned on Monika, whose plain seaming was excellent. She did corners so well that even thick fabrics held a point like a mitred bedsheet. Buttonholes, though, and tricky piping or fine tucking were not permitted her, so sometimes there was trouble. Sometimes, even if Jenny brought down the flowered cups, Monika folded her arms and turned her back. Then Mrs. Schmidt sat by her daughter, held her and sang a bouncy German tune with *ha ha ha* and *ho ho ho* in the refrain. Monika smiled at last. Her small eyes squinted with giggling. A kiss landed on her cheek; she leaned into her mother's embrace and kissed her back, and happily returned to her machine.

In mid-1943 a day came when Jenny did not arrive at the tailor's until nearly noon. When Dora and Mrs. Schmidt and Monika saw her face, their machines whirred down into silence.

Mrs. Schmidt stood by her. "You will join your mother?"

"I could bear that! No. A beet farm. Alberta." Crying, Jenny collected her few things but left her teacups on the shelf.

Monika went to her. With her own embroidered handkerchief she dried Jenny's eyes, though at each touch more water welled up. Then Monika put her arm round Jenny's shoulder, sat her down, held her tight. She sang sweetly right through to *ha ha ha* and *ho ho ho*, till Jenny smiled at last.

As Dora and Mrs. Schmidt stood at the door and watched Jenny disappear down the long hallway, they heard behind them the flowered porcelain smashing. No more work got done that day.

With only the three of them left to sew, orders might pile up, Dora thought, but in fact as the war continued fewer and fewer clients came to the German tailor. Mrs. Schmidt worried.

Daily she wrote out a list of customers due for fittings. Early in 1944 Dora read *Doktor Jonathan Smyth, new, 2 p.m.* She sewed for an hour. Then she put her work down.

"You cannot meet this man, Mrs. Smith? Very well. But if you hide behind the clothes rack, Monika will laugh."

Trips to Woodward's and to Singer's to replenish the workroom's supplies got Dora away from Jonathan's consultation that day and away from the first fitting for his new overcoat. For his final appointment, she missed a day's work.

"A good man. I see you don't disagree, Mrs. Smith."

An ever rarer conversational comment from Mrs. Schmidt, this was. More and more, the tailor measured and cut, pinned and stitched in a heavy silence, or else sat with her work in her lap, gazing out the north window at the faraway shining Lions until Monika noticed and came to pat her mother's cheek.

One day, only Monika gave *Guten Morgen* to Dora when she arrived at work. Mrs. Schmidt's silence weighed down the workroom as if with piled heavy stones.

The day following, Monika was not there at all.

"Mrs. Smith, I cannot keep this to myself any longer." The sheet the tailor handed to Dora was stuck all over with newsprint letters: KRAUTS OUT OF VANCOUVER. WE KNOW WHERE YOU LIVE, KRAUT BITCH. "The fifth message. Always they are under the door, when I come in the morning. The landlord knows nothing. Of course not."

The two women sewed quietly for some time.

Uneven footsteps, one dull and one soft, came down the hall. No customer was due; Mrs. Schmidt opened the door only a slit.

"Dr. Smyth, such flowers! So beautiful. You are too kind."

"I came to thank you again for my handsome coat, Mrs. Schmidt. My receptionist approves, all the nurses approve, and envy consumes my colleagues. You may hear from some of them."

"Too kind!" A sob.

"What's this then? What's the trouble, Mrs. Schmidt?"

Behind the clothes rack, Dora heard the tailor tell it all— the ugly angry letters, Jenny Ko—and still more that she herself had not heard: telephone threats, daily now, apparently.

"We must do something about this."

Dora in her hiding place silently repeated the words.

When the limp limped away, the tailor put the red roses in water. "*Gott sei dank* for good people! He will try, nice kind man, but of course he cannot help. Not in this craziness." Mrs. Schmidt touched the petals. "Monika will love these. Well . . . I lasted quite a long time. I did not expect so long. Not in war."

The tailor gave a month's notice. Dora stayed on, to finish last orders and help with packing. Mrs. Schmidt brought her daughter back to the workroom, but when Monika saw the half-bare and disordered space she clung to her mother or else tried, sobbing, to empty boxes already packed up and labelled.

Mrs. Schmidt sighed. "Karen must look after her, then, while we finish here. In Kelowna, Monika will be happy again."

In three years of sewing in that workroom, five days a week for eight hours of collaboratively constructed suits and jackets and dresses and blouses and coats and capes, Dora had never once heard *Karen*.

She asked about Kelowna.

"Yes, my Karen has land, from her family. They are Canadian, here a long time. An orchard, they have. And we will grow grapes, my Karen says, and make wine. And will farmers in that part of the world—the Interior, they call it, so odd—will they wear a fine wool topcoat with a satin lining? I think not, Mrs. Smith. A different life I go to now."

On the last day Mrs. Schmidt gave Dora a jar of pot-pourri made from Jonathan's red roses.

Dora left the workroom and rode home on the streetcar. Cold sleet slashed at the windows, but she scarcely noticed. From time to time she opened the jar, to smell the crisp faded petals.

1942–1944—*Over There's Like Over Here*

The *fuckn English doc* was right in that after Owen's leave his left ear did work again. The other didn't. His smeller didn't either. Owen couldn't gauge the distance or direction of shells, gunfire, tanks; he got no signals from cordite, smoke, shit, gangrene; the war felt crazier than ever.

Lazybones was Owen's first army nickname. He was also *Taffy*, and *Frankie-boy* for his singing, and *Little Lucky* for surviving the cave-in.

After his leave he volunteered to go out with the padre to find the dying, so they could receive the last rites, for it had occurred to Owen that as an unbeliever he might be more, not less, likely than the faithful to receive divine protection…if such existed. Trailing after the muddy black skirts, Owen laughed.

Death clung close during the hours of fire he spent with Father Alphonse Bedard, S.J., of Val Marie, Saskatchewan. As they struggled back to their so-called lines—a spread of stony muddy fields among wrecked dairy farms—Owen laughed.

"Saved again, eh, padre?"

"Be quiet," snapped Father Bedard, crouched in the lee of a barn shelled to splinters, or else prone in a culvert with the stone-still dead.

The priest, once back in the bloodied filth of the dairy farm, inspected his robe's hem for barbed-wire tears. He looked down at Owen, and anger still edged his voice. "Did it never occur to you that the Almighty has more important personages to think of than yourself or me?"

Owen shrugged. He picked up the tabby cat that was the unit's unofficial mascot and cuddled her. She nosed into his armpit, purring and flexing her claws. The bombardment went on and on and on and on.

During the First Canadian's journey to the Somme, Major Redvers observed Owen Jones. His slight figure gave the same impression whether this soldier was jogging along, rifle in hand, or holding out his mess tin or sitting on a step: disengaged. Either the battle wasn't quite real, or he wasn't—so his stance said. Owen tilted his head. *As if he's talking to someone.* Sometimes, inside the surround of howl thud shriek batter crash howl, Redvers heard Owen's nasal chuckle. *He's like a kid, sitting on the steps reading a comic book.*

Having gained the other side of the river, Redvers, late at night in a greenhouse by another brutalized French farm, was writing notes for a report when he heard Owen's snicker outside. The soldier lurched towards the lamplight. Over his narrow shoulders was slung a big body. Down Owen's back, Bedard's skirts dripped blood. The young priest's blond hair shone like needles. The burden set down, Owen laughed harder. "He's got killed, not me! Crazy, eh? Who'll give *him* the rites?" And Owen pulled up his sleeves to show his loot: German wristwatches up to both elbows.

Much later, on his way to an hour's sleep, the Major contemplated recommending Bedard's bravery for recognition; that might carry some wan comfort to the hearts about to be broken in Val Marie. And there was Owen Jones's courage, too. That nasty funny man....

Next day, though, in a ridiculous accident involving a stolen Percheron and a ladder, Redvers broke his neck. A Major Halliday of Westmount took over. He and Owen soon met, about a goat. Behind the officers' mess, where he'd been caught stealing sugar, Owen was sleeping with his head on the animal's stomach. He was disinclined to move and claimed that Randy too was battle fatigued. *Brave*...that word was far from Halliday's mind. He didn't like Frenchies either, or priests.

With the new padre Owen continued to hunt for the dying, by day or night. His nickname now was "Crazy."

He dreamed sometimes of Dora in the green room. Awake, he sometimes thought about their schooldays together. When he got that terrible whipping, she was right there.

Autumn 1945—Throwing Away Treasure, I

Ned burst into the house.

His scrub-brush face scraped Dora's mouth and cheeks. Stomping in his big boots he went through the rooms and up the stairs with shouts of "John! Mary, sweetheart! Dad's home!" And down the stairs again, three steps at a time. "What the hell?"

"How was I supposed to know when you'd get here? Maybe they're over playing with Marjo's kids—I'll phone...."

"No, don't. Marjo, always bloody Marjo." The brush scoured again. Hands gripped her breasts and drove down at her belly. "Agh, is it still in you, that sin's still in you, you've kept it? Disgusting, Dora. My God." They shoved away from each other so Dora tripped over Ned's kit-bag. Its tough dun canvas, stained and lumpy, resembled Alan's exactly.

Ned slammed out of the house. The front hall reeked of sweat, dirty socks and khakis, tobacco.

Dora rubbed her ankle and shin. Then she went into the kitchen.

From the dresser she took down a porridge bowl. Unclasping her necklace, she slipped the pearls off their gold strand and poured them all out into the dish: twenty.

The biggest was 1929's and marked the birth of what was intended to be the last child.

The smallest: 1934, depth of the Depression.

The yellowest: 1940, John at thirteen. His blond hair began to darken then. To Dora he looked more than ever like Alan, but Ned could never see it, even when she got out the old photographs and showed him.

The pinkest: 1928, for Mary. "Born to be Daddy's sweetest little girl! See how the baby holds my finger."

The newest pearl had been on the strand barely a month, since August. All through Ned's absence in the army—1942, 1943, 1944, 1945—a few days before each of Dora's birthdays, Millar & Coe telephoned: "Mrs. Dow, we would be happy to deliver...."

The very whitest pearl meant Dora and Ned's wedding.

One pearl was dented. Early in 1942, just before Ned went off to war, in one of their fights he got the necklace off Dora's throat and threw it on the floor. Struggling with her husband, she heeled down hard on the little pearly wriggle. Ned went scarlet with anger. Next to that colour his hair didn't look carroty any more but sandy-grey. He never believed that Dora hadn't meant to damage the pearls.

Under the kitchen sink stood a white metal cylinder with a foot pedal. Dora depressed it to reveal milk-bottle caps, oats that the meal-moth had got into, a worn-out hairbrush of Mary's, shavings from John's pencil sharpener, a few stiff slices of Fray Bentos corned beef so dehydrated that they curled up hard at the edges, black as blood. Dora looked down at these things. She thought of her own mother going to the pawnbroker time after time, to get her treasure back. Riding the streetcar on the way to Abbott Street, Mrs. Cowan clutched the pawn ticket; on the way back she clutched the warm pearls, looped once again about her plump neck.

Dora let go.

Downward slid her pearls, silent or rustling. The gold chain rippled after.

Now that the husband was home, he would once more carry the garbage out to the tin that stood in the lane, for pickup. Ned himself would throw the pearls away.

1903—*Throwing Away Treasure, II*

Smiling tiny girl Dora slid herself down into the wash tub, full of deliciously hot water. She curled herself small. Under her bum rubbed the concentric ridges of the tub's bottom, hard ripples. The child slid down so she could rest her head on the tub's wall.

"Mum, why d'you make me keep an eye?"

"Now, Alan. She's your little sister. And I'm busy."

Hot water covered Dora's bent knees and her arms. It lapped over her chest, shoulders, ears, the back of her head, even her mouth. Only nose and forehead surfaced. Her eyelids closed.

"She's gone to sleep, Mum. I can't stay here forever!"

"Just you wait a while, Mr. Impatience."

Almost immersed, her limbs loose yet firmly supported, her body sensible of hot fluid lapping every crease and opening, Dora relaxed every part of herself except her right hand. In that curled palm lay a three-sided button, red as rage.

"She's sucking her thumb again, Mum."

"Oh, Alan, do let up!"

Gradually every cell let go of tension. At home in this medium the young body floated out of time. Boundaries dissolved. Only the screen of Dora's skin, a supple film, separated warm liquid from warm liquid. Immersed in pleasure, Dora lay entranced with her head lolling and the little smile still on her face.

"Dora's done it in the bath again, Mum! I can smell it, honestly I can. Pew pew!"

Mrs. Cowan rushed from the front room into the kitchen, hairbrush in hand. "Dirty girl! Bad girl! You're to do that in the morning, *not* at night!" She slapped through the water at Dora's thighs. "Look what you've done—water spilled everywhere." She yanked at Dora. "Out!"

Alan smiled, but his sister stiffened and braced herself against the sides of the tub and made herself so rigid that her mother could not pull her out. Alan had to help. Yells, splashes, slaps ended with the weeping child gripped on Mrs. Cowan's lap in a towel fragrant as toast from hanging on the stove rail.

"What's that then?" Alan bent to pick up a button.

Dora kicked and grabbed.

"Fatty fatty fat girl. Look at her legs. Piggy! Pink piggy!"

"You *are* a weight, Dora, I must say," Mrs. Cowan panted as she gave a final rub to the hot thighs and reached for the brush. "Throw that silly old button away, Alan. Now hush your noise, Dora! You don't want it! No, you don't. Your hair's in such a tangle as I never saw, and surely you've caused enough trouble for one night."

1943—Marjo Attempts Persuasion

Even as a kid, Dora held her cards close to her chest.

Her dad was a drunk and didn't care who knew it. He'd sit on the front porch, rocking away on that swing couch with his empties lined up beside him, and call out to the neighbours, "Six dead soldiers so far! Want to join me in the battle of the bottle?" In two shakes Dora's mum'd be out there shouting, "Charlie Cowan, will you *shut up?*" Dora never said a word. She buried all the shame inside. That's always been her way.

We hid under that porch. We hid things there, too, buried them and lost them. Pretty buttons, once—you'd think Dora'd lost her crown jewels.

Just last week when we were canning, I tried again to talk to Dora. Seems as though I never learn.

Of course I had to show Dora how to do everything. She's got no sense of food. None. Three dull meals a day— that's Dora. Even worse, in wartime. Her poor kids! But when the jars were in the oven and the brine on the stove and we were chunking up the salmon, I started in.

"Grieving's good, Dora," I said. "Think of Mrs. Hammond. At the cemetery *every day*, even though Jimmy's buried in France." So sad! Their only child, killed at Dieppe. They put up a headstone. Every time I meet them, I thank God my boys aren't quite old enough. Mrs. Hammond takes the bus, every day, to bring fresh flowers to the stone. In winter she *buys* them. Every day. "That's mother love. But what you're doing, Dora... it's not natural."

She was sawing away at the fish, getting a ragged edge, so I showed her how to angle the knife. We looked down into the canner.

"And think of Olive Burton, Dora."

The water was just beginning to lift and heave. We watched it for a bit, but Dora didn't say anything.

Dora and me and Olive went to school together. When Olive's Timmy was coming home from Notre Dame for lunch, he got hit by a car right at Hastings and Slocan. Just thirteen, he was. Olive's got a silver brooch with his baby photo in it. She wears it *all the time*. She rakes leaves with that brooch pinned to her overalls. "I bet Olive pins that brooch on her nightie, but it's a *photo*, Dora. Not a dead body."

Not a word. The more I say, the less she listens, I declare.

My timer jangled. The brine was boiling, so I lifted the jars out of the oven and we began fitting in the chunks of fish.

Or maybe it's like this: the more I say, the less chance Dora'll say anything at all. My words cancel out hers. I can't stop, though. I keep thinking *something* I say will reach inside her where she won't let anyone see.

"I declare, Dora, you're even worse than old Mrs. Williams." The old woman lives way east on Wall Street, in a cottage she and her husband built when he got on steady with the CPR, back before the war—the first one. In 1910 he was working on the line by New Brighton, and—they call it a runaway train. Somehow, trying to stop it, Mr. Williams got his head caught in the coupling. Ever since, she's kept his ashes on the mantel. Thirty-three years. No children. Whenever Sears delivers or the man comes to clean the windows, Mrs. Williams carries the urn to the front door, to show. Poor postie! He's heard the story a hundred times. "She's a good housekeeper. She dusts her husband, and she talks to him. That I can understand, yes.

But she doesn't keep him *inside* her. Dora, don't fill the jars so full. Here's the tongs."

She got them round a chunk and just stopped, silent.

"Take it *out!* You should take it out. You're a walking talking coffin, and that's not *normal*." I took the tongs and got the piece of salmon and plopped it into another jar.

Splat. Salty water from above, down into the salmon. *Splat splat.* Dora, crying! I wouldn't say she never cries, but I'd only need a few fingers to count the times, and we've been friends since we were tinies.

The last time was a year ago. A drizzly day. We were walking home with groceries, and on Triumph a family was setting out goods to sell in the yard. Pathetic, really, odds and ends, stewpots and toast racks and bowling shoes and fireplace sets with the poker gone, all on tables. I was checking decks of cards to see did they have fifty-two when Dora gasped.

She was down on her knees on the wet grass, peering under a table. Then up she got. From her look, it could have been her birthday and Christmas and Dominion Day all in one. "Marjo, it's Mum's table! Look, there's my initials, and Alan's." Tears. Yes, then there were tears. Of course when I hugged her, Dora pulled away. Not really hard, but I could tell she wanted me to stop. I'd have held her tight for hours, seeing her so.

But this time, with the fish, when I hugged her, Dora said something into my shoulder that I couldn't hear. Her mouth moved against the bone. I couldn't think what to say to get her to repeat, so I didn't say anything. That worked. "It's all I have," she said, clearly, because now she was pulling away. And then if Dora didn't keep right on going, out my kitchen door!

Jarring that salmon—I hadn't the heart, but it had to be done. I cried all the while. Oh, so many things I wished, I wish I'd said to her! *Dora Dow, you're so close to a good life. So close! Happiness is right there. Reach out, touch it. Ned's a good sweet man. He loves you. He's worked steady and he'll do it again when this war's over. You know that's no small thing. And yes, Caddy died—but John and Mary are growing. Healthy wonderful kids, Dora. Other people lose children and go on. You can, too. You have a nice house. You're a good dressmaker. Ladies all over the city love your work. Isn't that enough for happiness? Dora, there's ten thousand women in Vancouver would change places with you in a minute. Can't you get that dead baby out of you? Can't you take hold of your good life?*

But Dora was gone.

After the canning was done and the kitchen clean and the table set for supper, I walked over to Dora's with her share of the jars. She took the salmon, but she wouldn't meet my eyes or ask me in for a cup of tea.

Lord knows who'd eaten what off that maple table! Some rough times it'd been through, all right. Scarred with black from cooking pots, hacked about like a workbench. Dora stripped the whole thing down, except for all the initials. Not only hers and Alan's were there; since 1918, everyone who'd owned that table had got their initials in. One set we tried to read but never could, for sure. Black old-fashioned lettering, the kind legal papers use. "S" was the second initial, but the first—was it "T" or "S" or "J" or "I"? Afterwards came "MCMXXXV." Roman. Dora and me, we'd seen that in school, but it was young John figured it out. 1935.

Dora sanded and sanded. For hours, for days, I declare. Smooth as satin that wood got to be. To run your fingers over the grain felt sweet. Then she found a cabinet maker who helped her to fill the splits and hack marks, and when she laid on the wax—well! The colours of that maple came right up. So pretty. To see her table like that would have made Mrs. Cowan happy. She loved pretty things, did Dora's mum.

But still—I can't get over what Dora said to me that day we canned the fish. "It's all I have."

Diagnosis and Prognosis

1935—The Sequence

Scene 1: Leaving the doctor, amputating herself from his kindness, Dora rode down in the waiting elevator to the lobby. A woman there shook rain off a yellow umbrella. Through the revolving doors, Dora glimpsed Granville Street. She found the stairs down to the basement of the Vancouver Block.

Scene 2: In the front hall of 202 Garden Drive North, Dora knelt by Caddy. The child huddled up against her and whispered warmly on her cheek, "Mummy, I don't feel good."

Scene 3: The dressmaker's dummy stood in the angle under the stairs, Dora's sewing corner; here Ned had built shelves for Dora's notions, a tabletop that swung to the wall, a fold-up ironing board. Dora leaned on Flora's hard breast and felt the stretchy jersey covering against her forehead. She hugged the dress form and cried.

1: Leaving the doctor, amputating herself, Dora rode down. Water drops spiralled off yellow. 2: Caddy's mouth softly touched her cheek. 3: Like a mother's skin, the jersey covering of the dress form moved against Dora's forehead.

The sequence could begin anywhere, with a detail from any scene: the worn lips of the stairs in the Vancouver block, Caddy's whisper, the elevator's hum, hard metal under jersey, the elevator's juddering stop, the smell of Caddy's hair.

The images, like a button turning in Miss Dearing's fingers as the dressmaker considered its appropriateness for a garment under construction, rotated continually.

No one but Dora ever saw or knew about the sequence. Over time, it acquired for her a hard material reality. Like an odd three-sided stone, polished and burnished by her human touch, the sequence became an object Dora secretly examined and re-examined all her life.

November 1935—Diagnosis and Prognosis

In her heavy body the woman stood sideways so she could listen close to the frosted glass door of Office 636. In its waiting room, shadows waited. "Isn't that awful? Did you ever?" the receptionist said to the phone, squelching a caramel juicily in her mouth.

Down the hall the woman went to the second glass door, the one that opened directly into the doctor's consulting room. The light was on. A tall man with a big head bent over the desk. She tapped. He turned.

Within a minute, the examination began.

"The head's way over here." The doctor's own head, strung with its stethoscope, moved over the woman's belly and stopped. "An abnormal presentation. No activity at all, since dawn?"

"No."

"But you say it's moved regularly, late mornings and early afternoons." He snatched a pen and made notes.

Silence.

"The pains?"

"Not like labour. By lunchtime it still hadn't stopped. When the kids went back to school I thought I'd better come."

"Describe."

Her face screwed up. "Bad. Hard. Not stopping. All over." From breast to thigh, she drew her hands down and across.

Who did that? Who moved just like that?

"Not Braxton-Hicks." He scribbled. "The stirrups—there by your foot? Knees well up."

Alarm pounded in Jonathan's brain and heart. The diagnosis itemized itself, as if he were at school with Miss Lawrence reciting *nominative genitive accusative dative ablative,* or with Mr. Yeatman, *kingdom phylum class order family genus species.*

One, absolutely no dilation of the cervix. Stenosed. Hasn't a clue anything's happening. All that life, inches away—but as far as that cervix is concerned, nothing's doing. Wonderful.

Two. Abnormal presentation: transverse. Not significant, alone, but....

Three, pains unlike labour. Similar pains at the first trimester's end, if she's right about that? Why shouldn't she be?

Four, rigidity. I've never felt anything like it. Her torso's stone. Rock. Granite. Precambrian Shield. Scatterbrain!

And, fool Jonathan, five. Five. Five. She said so herself weeks ago. "It doesn't feel like the others." What the patient says. What Mrs. Hawrylko said. Listen listen listen. One one one.

Jonathan took the woman's hands and pressed their small warmth, bending over till his eyes were close to hers. "You need surgery. Get dressed. Here, I'll draw it for you."

The woman searched vaguely along her dress's seams to find the opening for her head. Roughly Jonathan shook open the folds, held her underpants so she could step in. With dreamlike care she fingered and fingered and at last did up her buttons while he grabbed a pencil and slashed at paper.

"The pregnancy's gone through the tube. Here." Jonathan scrawled organs, a birth canal, a placental attachment site. "Hurry! Look. No place for the baby to go. Nature has to act. It can't stay there.... No, not quite true. It *can*. But rarely. Are you ready? We have to go right away. We can't risk it. What happens..." Under a fierce Roman I, Jonathan listed *Rup Hem Dth*, a stabbing asterisk by each. Stroke stroke, Roman II. *Inf Perf*, asterisked. "Massive infection. Into the other organs, all jammed together." Jonathan spiralled his pencil, darkening the body cavity. "Fecal contamination. Poisoning. Against that we can do nothing. Now look, quick quick," but Jonathan put his hand over his eyes. "The surgery. Dangerous. If the attachment's broad, see, here, the bleeding.... Torrential, it can be." His hand went back to the sketch. "But it's the only way. We have to act."

"To save the baby?"

The doctor groaned, stretching his bad leg. "*You.*"

From the office window she saw a shining stream of umbrellas move down Granville Street, black, grey, navy, one bright yellow.

"Mrs. Whatsername will find your husband. He must give written consent, meet us at VGH. I'll phone the surgeon. But first..." Jonathan limped to the reception room, flung the door open and cried, "Fairmont three, ambulance! Emergency!"

The receptionist, chewing and chatting, did not hear the doctor. Jonathan had to limp over to her and repeat, repeat. The waiting room hushed as Mrs. Angell's forefinger touched the phone at last.

Re-entering his consulting room, Jonathan found no one.

On the interface between the surface of his stump and that of the wooden prosthesis, a frisson tingled. As Jonathan went out into the hallway, sweat broke out. His glasses slid down his nose. He hobbled towards the elevator; its signal arrow was angling to the left, from VI to V to IV to III to II to I. Jonathan looked at the stairs, turned back with a sob, leaned on the call button. A woman with a yellow umbrella got off at his floor.

Down in the lobby the air rushing in from Granville Street was cool, refreshed by rain.

"Did you see a pregnant woman come out of the elevator? Out of this building? It's urgent, did you? Yes, run to the corner, run, try that shop, there, try there, there...."

Eventually he stood before the elevator again. The signal moved. Jonathan's stump now hurt so much he wished for his hated crutches. His waiting room simmered with curiosity, but the doctor, as if in one of those dreams in which spirit-forms press urgently about a traveller who nonetheless continues, ignored everyone.

"Get me Miss Smith's personal file. And remake all these appointments." He slammed the door of his consulting room.

Instead of saving her I scared her.

Her file was thin. A typing test. An application form.

Smith, Gladys. Address: 2222 North Garden Drive. Highland 3456. Shapely numbers, but from the operator Jonathan learned that no such address or phone existed. She had no listing for a Smith anywhere on Garden Drive. No Smithe or Smythe or Smyth.

He checked the directory. Including all spelling variants, he found six hundred and fifty-odd Smiths. He began. After each answer, Jonathan took his ruler and pencilled through the number. The lines were neatly parallel, but after ruling six he stopped.

False name. She's run away, won't let me help her. He broke his pencil and threw the bits at the window where the rain pearled down. *I've lost her.*

Back to the file. A reference letter from Spencer's for a Miss Gladys Smith, more than ten years old, offered routinely admiring phrases. *So even then she was hiding, under another name.* Jonathan noted the department store's phone number. *But what could Spencer's do to save her?*

So obvious an improbability, that quadruple two! He ripped his sketch of the extra-uterine pregnancy from the pad and on a fresh sheet began to list the telephone numbers for emergency rooms in all the city's hospitals—but broke off, to head the list *Morgue.*

Jonathan's stump crawled with pain. His phantom foot burned as if just severed.

Rather than running out to Granville Street or to the lane behind the Vancouver Block, Dora found the basement stairs.

A door: *Storage.* A stool. She sat. In the dark her lungs and heart decelerated. The elevator, moving in its shaft, resonated against the hollow hum of ducts and pipes. Often, somewhere, water flowed down invisibly. Dora smelled floor-cleaning compound. She set her purse down by her feet on the cold painted concrete. Under her belly, by the dead head, she clasped her hands, and she leaned back gratefully against the concrete wall. Her breathing, now quite regular, grew slower still. The hum, the flow of water, the darkness.... Dora's jaw and shoulders and thighs eased until she slept, still as a stone in a river.

When she woke her cheeks were wet, her chin slippery. Wiping with her handkerchief, Dora listened. *There's no place for the baby to go, but it can't stay there. No, not quite true—it can. Rarely. But Nature has to act. We have to act. Hemorrhage. Torrential. Dangerous.*

Down the hall Dora found a ladies' room. Her urine gushed out; she must have slept for some time. The soft sounds of other women reached Dora, their trickling, skirts rumpled up and smoothed down, *hssh* of stockings, *tiktak* of high heels on lino.

Dora ran her hands down her strong solid body. She splashed water on her face and pulled out lengths of roller-towel to fill her nostrils with the clean smell.

Dangerous.

In a 1935 hospital just as in 1918, there would be whispers looks gasps glances exclamations shudders grimaces—and far more telephones. Three dead in a family of four: that had been notable, newsworthy. A dead child not leaving a living mother: what would they make of that?

Dora took out all her hairpins and shook her head so the fawn-coloured crinkle sheeted her shoulders and upper back. Her hair formed a triangle, with her head as the apex, and overlapped another, her body, of which her dress hem was the base. In the mirror, the woman next to Dora smiled sympathetically at her pregnancy. Dora coiled, twisted, pinned.

The Block's basement exited directly on to the alley between Granville and Seymour. Dora headed north, with the dead weight housed inside her. The winter light was fading. She was exhausted.

At Dunsmuir Dora glanced east, to the Labour Temple. Where was Owen? In November, the grass in their bower would be ragged and brown and flattened out by sleeping deer.

As for that other boy, the tall serious one riding the bicycle that Owen stole, Dora knew exactly where he was but turned from the fact, even though, she knew, he would offer to carry, help, hide, keep safe. She saw herself, instead of Marjo, as the burden. *No.* Instead, Dora hurried to catch the Number Twenty. She must get home before Ned.

Nature has to do something. It can't stay there. Hemorrhage dangerous torrential. No, it can. Do something.

Heavily pregnant, she easily got a seat on the crowded streetcar. Her legs shook from fatigue. *But I'm never ill.*

Dora had gone through the 1918 epidemic, spent days in a hospital filled with the dying and survived. She never got holes in her teeth or headaches or a boil, hardly ever caught a cold.

At home, John would be perched at the kitchen table, one foot dangling and the other tucked under, doing homework. As soon as she came in the door he'd head for his room, with a quick smile.

Mary would be hanging about the front hall, schoolbook in hand, kicking the door. The child had scuffed clear through the paint to the wood till even Ned scolded her.

"Mum, I can't find my ruler."

"Teacher didn't show us! I can't! I don't know how!"

"She's so mean to me."

"That's not how teacher said to do it."

"If she marks me wrong it's your fault, Mum."

"Mum, you never help me enough."

In the icebox there was leftover cheese pudding. In Dora, a dead baby. John must go to the butcher on Hastings for meat, or Ned would rage.

He'd rage anyway, on hearing what a state she was in. He might even cry. Rage and tears would be brief, though. Then, Dora knew, Ned would drag her by force, by her long hair, into the car and off to hospital.

But Dora was strong. Her eyes were perfect, not like Alan's. She never got bad cramps when her visitor came, not like Marjo. Dora had had three easy labours. This morning's pains had stopped; the last terrible one had announced itself as just that, *the last*. Dora's front was still rigid. Exhausted, yes, bone-tired, bone-breaking tired, but the due date was a month off. Ned wouldn't be concerned until after that. Babies could be weeks late. Even husbands knew that.

Do something? I will do nothing. That's what I will do.

Sitting on the streetcar, Dora looked down at her little feet. Her shoestraps indented her flesh.

I will. I will. I will do nothing.

April 1935—A Trip to Vancouver

In early April Owen stumbled out of the bush and came into town with the first relief-camp strikers, sixty hungry men from Squamish.

As the freight neared North Van he wished more and more that he knew for sure. Was that girl dead?

Loudly, the strikers sang the "Internationale."

Long ago there was a stupid girl who got herself knocked up, not by him, no, not by damn by him, and she had something done about it and maybe probably likely possibly she died, and because of that girl Owen never got to hold the other one, not even hold, never never never.

Owen admired the strikers' gall, their fury against the camps, but socialism and revolutionary mass action he thought stupid. Because many of these big boys were so eager to brawl, he didn't say so. To one older longshoreman, more melancholy than militant, Owen did observe, "Life's always rotten for the guy at the bottom, and some guy's always there." He got no response. Owen also loved singing with the strikers. Such pleasure, to blend his voice with sixty others in "Solidarity Forever" and "Are You From Bevan?" and "Hold the Fort, For We Are Coming!"

When Owen reached the hospital he found his mother worse off than expected.

Word of her illness had taken months to reach him. In November 1934, Patricia, Ellen's co-worker for years in cafés up and down Hastings and Abbott and Carrall, wrote to Owen. He'd sent an occasional card to his mother, but the only address she had was General Delivery, Bella Coola. There Lillian, a woman who occasionally sorted mail, remembered him well. Her affair with Owen was still in the future; she'd only met him a few times, but the thrill of dancing with that deft quick man on New Year's Eve in 1918 remained starlit in her memories of girlhood.

At Christmas, Patricia's letter went from Lillian to her brother-in-law visiting from Williams Lake. To please his wife, he put some effort into tracking down this Owen Jones. *Lazy lump*, he'd heard, *Damn careless, feckless, useless bastard* and *Skirt chaser* and *Can that man sing!* and *Wouldn't trust him as far as I could throw him and that'd be a long ways, the skinny little runt.* Fired repeatedly for talking back or screwing up or simply not showing up, in Quesnel, then Fraser Lake, back to Williams Lake or Bella Coola.... Oddly, he wasn't on relief. As a sour-voiced telephone operator from Burns Lake opined, *Owen Jones'd sooner take a chance at getting some fool woman to buy his grub for him.*

By February a likely Poste Restante was identified, back in Quesnel. At Mrs. Major's brothel there, the letter lay for six weeks amid other forlorn correspondence. *When he's randy enough, he'll be back*, Lady said. Duly, in late March Owen appeared, having been fired, or quit, or walked off without troubling to quit, in Prince George, Fort St. James,

Smithers, somewhere, anywhere. At last he read what Patricia had to say.

In the cancer ward at the General, mother and son looked at each other without great interest. Ellen's disease was far advanced. Her once-springy auburn hair straggled yellow-grey over the pillow. Morning and evening Owen sat with the small dying woman, mostly in silence. Ellen napped and woke, napped and woke. Owen read the *Daily Province*, or the bulletins put out by the Relief Camp Workers' Union and the Single Unemployed Men. When his mother coughed bloodily, Owen got the nurse.

Ellen's doctor was a tall man called Smyth. *Phony spelling. Stuck-up. What's wrong with Smith?* The doc had a gammy leg, looked about Owen's age. *S'pose he lied and enlisted. Our brave boys. That crap.* With Dr. Smyth, Ellen's face softened into her old flirtatious look. Owen rolled his eyes as the doctor patted her hand. "Ah, Mrs. Jones! We should've met when I was still whole," and he knocked his prosthesis on the bedframe so the metal rang. Owen went into the hall to smoke. Following him, the phony said phonily, "Her pain. You see her most—tell me if you think she needs a higher dose." Owen said nothing. Dr. Smyth limped away.

At other times Owen went about the city. The swimming pool at Kits Beach amazed him, and the Dunsmuir Tunnel. At the arched entrance of the Marine Building, he stared. *Bloody fuckn lobsters they've carved for God's sake. Lobsters!* Owen spat. Down at Snauq under the fancy new bridge there were hardly any Indians, none Owen knew anyway. Just young whites, jobless, drunk. South and west, new houses rose all over; all over, men on relief smoothed scrub and bush into sheets of green, for golf.

Everywhere downtown appeared the tin-canning strikers in their khaki sweaters, in twos and threes or mass-marching in snake parades. *Fools!* Right *there* stood the horses with those red-jacketed riders, Sergeant Scanlon's squad: the Cossacks, everyone called them. Owen shook his head.

Ragged families holding gunny sacks huddled in the rain behind the *Daily Province* building, in line for beans and soup bones. *No one ever gave Mum and me any fuckn bones.* Everywhere children ran about, thin as Owen had been and was, their rickety legs like sticks. To earn pennies, boys guided cars through the smoke enveloping the bridges over False Creek. Yet the strikers' illegal Tag Day raised an amazing five thousand dollars. When he learned that, Owen thought maybe he'd made a mistake not falling in with the rebels; Ellen had hardly any money, he had less. Everywhere nailed-shut shopfronts were stuck with signs, *Abolish the Slave Camps, Work and Wages.* At the Powell and Cambie Grounds, the strikers spoke and spoke and spoke. *Shut up!* The socialists did their *damn speechifying* at the Royal Theatre too and on street corners and even in Woodward's; Owen was there, looking at doeskin gloves. Exasperated, he went back to the hospital early.

When Owen saw how many police—Vancouver, Dominion, Royal Canadian Mounted—attended the first of the really big rallies at the Vancouver Arena, he concluded that anyone with half the sense the Good Lord gave him would stay well away. Therefore, in mid-April when another big "do" was planned at the Cambie Grounds,

Owen for the first time since his return to Vancouver went to the East End.

That girl. Dead, maybe—he wanted no encounter with anyone who knew that story, but today half the population was downtown anyway. *Ready to have its damn fool head beat in.*

Owen worked his way towards Cedar Cove, looking sharp; he was glad of his beard. The sporting houses—now they were along Union and Prior. *Not half as smart as old Alexander Street.* On the sagging porches, scrawny girls lounged. Their marcelled hair lay flat against their skulls; in the spring sun, the blond dye looked green and the black looked harsh purple. Indolently, women waved at the spry little man. Squatters were reclaiming the jungles on the False Creek Flats, Owen saw; the cops had only recently cleared them out, but again men were pushing barrels and packing crates down the slope, and the same by the old Hastings sawmill. The low shacks crouched on the waterfront. Fingers of smoke twitched in the air.

Some householders along Owen's way, desperate to stave off foreclosure or eviction, had piled porches and grass patches with anything that might be saleable: dressers, jackets, platters, bedsprings, rakes, baby carriages, tin jugs. On a once-handsome table, crockery was stacked by a bootjack, a broken meat grinder, an album. Black circles from cooking pots scarred the bird's-eye maple. Owen scowled at children who tried to draw him towards the goods, moved on.

In the alley off Victoria Drive, his and Ellen's old stable no longer smelled even faintly of horse. Those who lodged here now—the filthy, the starved, the drugged, the desperate—drank cheap booze and pissed and ate...raccoon? Dog meat from Chinatown? The place stank of burned fur, of alcohol and shit. Grey dry bones lay about. The loft itself was unusable, its floorboards stove in. Owen went away.

He walked southwards up the hill, around Grandview planted with its young trees, back towards Highlands. Spare and shabby and twice-repaired these neighbourhoods looked, but not wretched. In a Jap corner store Owen thought about stealing but finally bought some toffee. It filled his mouth with watery sugar.

Coming towards Owen on Hastings Street was Dora, after seventeen years, walking along with a boy and a whiny girl and a carrot-top fellow with a face like raw sourdough.

Moving slowly, holding her son by the hand, Dora gazed at nothing at all, not the air or the afternoon. Honey. The pale waxy bloom on the surface of clover honey... Dora's skin was that colour, and as smooth. Owen's palms itched. His pecker moved. He remembered her feathery hair as no-colour-in-particular, but with the sun behind her those high-piled coils glowed platinum. And her breasts.... *Utter udder Cow-Cow*, how they'd all laughed at school. He winced, remembering. Now under her grey blouse two beautiful shapes rose with Dora's surprised breath on seeing him.

"I didn't recognize you, with the beard!"

As she introduced him to her family, Owen saw, above Dora's first blouse-button, how her breasts squeezed lightly together. Not slim, never, never would be.... *I want her.* Those soft heavy thighs. That hair sheeting her shoulders and breasts, how it would smell, how those big nipples would tickle his palms.... He got harder. Owen hoped sourface saw the bulge.

Moments after parting from Dora, Owen identified that odd look on her face. Sad, yes—*and why not, if that ass-hole is who she's ended up with?*—but that was not all held in her vague unfocused gaze. *The hots. Out in broad daylight, she was horny as hell.*

While Owen was wondering where he could go to jerk off, he heard "Owen!" Dora ran up to him, panting. "I'll tell Marjo I saw you. She married Mike Morgan, remember him? They've got a girl and a boy." The sun touched her face now. By Dora's eyes, faint wrinkles showed. Silver filaments curled at her temples. She smiled down at him. The tip of Owen's tongue slipped out. Blushing blushing blushing, Dora ran back to hubby and kids.

Owen took a deep breath and headed for the Princeton.

There he drank one beer standing up, instantly ordered a second and sat by the window looking towards the water. *That damn girl didn't die. All this time. Married. Kids. Fine!* Silently Owen cursed her. As he relaxed, Dora's image grew more vivid. Honey and cream, plump and soft.... He'd never held her, even. The water of the inlet shimmered.

As soon as the first few men who'd been at the rally came in, loudly boasting, Owen left and headed for Garden Drive, where Dora'd said she lived. Maybe Vinegar Mug wouldn't be around?

At Wall Street the slope of blackberry, salmonberry, salal, morning glory, and wild grasses rose to twice the height Owen remembered, a towering mass. Pathways into it were apparent; he needed to take a leak, and entered.

Almost hidden under the arching brambles, the door of the green room opened. Dora knelt there on the raw grass. The colours of her bruised upper arms and her rasped neck were caught in the April light. By her eyes, tear tracks glinted. As she turned to Owen, some of the dry berry leaves from last year fluttered down into her hair, while others clung. She raised her arm to push back a branch, and the gesture made her breasts move under her blouse. Her hands, returning to her lap, lay palm up. She smiled at him. He knew what was going to happen.

When a fuck makes a baby—Owen prided himself on being able to tell. With Irene it was the way she cried out, and also she herself was sure. Two days later when Owen went by her place for more of the same, Irene wasn't interested. "I've started one," she said, as if she'd done it all herself and had no more use for him. A particular juiciness that meant *connection*—Owen's penis nosed it delightedly in Marian (Williams Lake) and Marlene (Vanderhoof) and Carol (Terrace). All three, Owen found out through inquiries circuitously made much later, visited local abortionists. *Not the first time or the last, I'll bet.* Lillian—no. Even though Owen's fucks with her were among his best ever, none ever *took. Her fault,* he knew, because years afterward Lillian and the dumb ox she married couldn't have any kids of their own. They fostered. Later, they even adopted. *Idiots.*

Around Dora sprang this year's grass, shooting up through clumps of last year's, long and brown-grey, that lay flat from the sleeping weight of the deer that still wandered about Cedar Cove and into the gardens of Highlands to nibble rosebuds and early lettuce. In this green room, she and he were invisible. Owen knew that inside this woman was a baby just waiting for him to light the match.

First Owen tenderly kissed all Dora's bruises. He licked her rasped neck, hurting from those other, those rough hands. She cried. He kissed her tears so the salty pearls fell into his mouth. "There there," Owen muttered into her wet cheek, "there there. S'all right. Won't let the bastard hurt you any more." Owen loved kissing women's eyes; they moved under the lids, under his lips. Then up went his fingers into her hair. He felt all over for the pins and put them into her waiting palm, and Owen combed her hair down with his hands. The warm filaments ran, floated, over his skin. He touched his face to the strands and breathed their odour. "Honey." On the waving grass, the two lay down. "Honey, I want you." Breasts, mouth, the big thighs, so much, over-whelming almost. "Honey, I have to go piss or I can't fuck you."

When Owen came back through the brambly green, Dora was still laughing. Sitting up, she had unbuttoned her blouse and was looking up at the blackberry branches; the new leaves, bright green, were loosening their pleats. She looked younger even than when he'd stepped into this green wilderness, far younger than when they'd met on Hastings only hours ago. Dora looked as she looked in August 1918.

"When I was a kid...." Giggling, she turned to accept his kisses. "Marjo and I thought the man peed inside the woman. Guess I wasn't far wrong!" She relaxed downwards on to the grass, drew Owen to her and drove her tongue into his mouth. Laughter still vibrated in her throat.

❧ ☙

A few days later, attending the strikers' picnic at Lumberman's Arch, Owen still couldn't believe what a sap he'd been as a teenager, what a sucker. *Left Vancouver. Never had Dora. Never even had a chance with Dora! And all the time that bloody Marjo was fine.*

He wandered about the grass. *Talk about saps...looky here.* Hundreds of hungry striker-boys sat with families who themselves hadn't enough to eat but who unbuckled hampers stuffed with ham sandwiches, soup, hard-boiled eggs, bananas, bread-and-butter pickles, lemon pie, jam-jams and thimbles and matrimonial cake and beer. *Are they blind?*

Those two bitches. Big fuss for nothing. I could have stayed. Owen's anger at Dora rose because now he'd have to leave, again.

The family feeding Owen were not even Communists, just soft-headed mutts who thought the city was "sure to grant relief to the men, sure to." *I could have stayed.* Owen finished up the family's cake, smothered in pink boiled icing. "Been at the Lillooet camp," he told them. They believed him. "Was it awful there?" asked the kids. *I'll have to go.* When Owen sharply suggested they read the *Relief Camp Worker* to get the details, the mother actually apologized for their pressing him to tell about his "bad times."

At least today there was no speechifying, no stuck-ups like Slim Evans savouring their own voices. Owen got a fag off the father of the family and lay silent, blowing rings.

When Mum goes, I'll go. Because of a baby, again, he'd have to save himself. Again. He wouldn't see Dora, perhaps never, certainly not for a long time. And the boy? Never. Well, not for years. He'd have to be grown up first. A man, not a boy who needed him. *Shit.* Singing began. Owen smoked. *Yes. When Mum goes, I'll go.* Abruptly and without thanking those who had fed him, he left Stanley Park and went back to the General.

Owen's mother came to her end as the May Day parade shouted through the city. To her hospital room, the roars and songs of thousands choking Vancouver's downtown came as faint cries.

Patricia wiped her eyes. "Your poor old mother."

Owen walked away from the women and looked north, where the demonstration was in progress.

"You've a heart of stone, Owen. Can't you even cry for her?"

He calculated Ellen's age: fifty-one. From his own thirty-three that seemed not far at all. His mother looked much older than half a century, though, not only because of the cancer's wasting. Her hands, from years of dirty sinks and floors, walls and stewpots, plates and toilets, were coarse as army canvas, and her skin was deeply fissured, like wood long exposed to weather, in spite of the months at rest in a hospital bed. All her joints were grossly misshapen.

That tall skinny gimpy doctor came in then. On Ellen's breast, the hands lay folded; he patted them. *Who's he, to touch my mother?* Turning to Owen, Gimpy looked down all preachy and sad. "Mr. Jones, you'll have the same, you know," he said, and actually took Owen's hands in his, felt the joints. "Yes. Arthritis. See the thickening." He nattered on about soaking, massage, warmed oils.

"I got no time for this," Owen snapped.

Gimpy shrugged. "I'll be going then. A strong woman, your mother. It wasn't easy for her, you know, raising a child alone."

"Who asked you?" Owen shouted. Already as the doctor limped down the hall, white-winged nurses clustered about him. Chatter chatter, fuss fuss fuss. Owen turned away.

Only Patricia was left in the room, sobbing quietly.

For decades, Ellen had waitressed with Patricia. And with Grace Ruth Annie Mabel Bella Tilda Thelma Verna Velma Vera Lois Alice Elsie Ellinor Edie. For decades, she'd been one among that chorus of hard-working women's voices.

"Ellen, I'm ever so sorry but I can't mind Owen this afternoon."

"Ellen, I've been waiting and waiting! I'll lose my job if I'm late one more time! I swear, that baby didn't stop screaming for ten minutes together the whole three hours he was here."

"No. I could mind him Tuesday night or Thursday night but not Monday."

"Can't you take Owen with you?'

"Can't someone else help you?"

"Can't you leave him on his own for a few hours? He'd just be sleeping."

"Doesn't David ever give you money?"

"Ellen, there's no call to get so angry, I'm sure."

"Well, if you're going to fly off the handle like that...."

"Of course, Ellen. All men are like that. Every waitress in Vancouver'll tell the same tale. You're nothing special, Ellen."

"One hand on his fork and the other...."

"Round your waist."

"On your titty."

"Up your stocking."

"Under your skirt."

"Into your muff, right in! Yes, that's happened to me."

"They only want one thing."

"Willy in the honeypot."

"No, I can't look in on Owen for you this afternoon."

"Owen won't mind what I tell him, Ellen! That boy won't mind anyone. He needs a good slap."

"He needs whipping. If it was me I'd do it regular."

"He needs a man around the house."

"Doesn't his father give you anything for him?"

"He doesn't even seem like a child."

"Can't you put him in some kind of a Home?"

"Tantrums! Angry! I've never seen such a carry-on. That boy needs leathering now, or what'll he be like when he gets big?"

"Honeypot's a moneypot."

"Honeypot's a moneypot."

"Standing up, standing, standing. Fallen arches. Bad back. Heavy plates and trays, till your arms hurt. Greasy scum all over you. For seven hours! Or you can let a man do it to you for three minutes. It's the same pay."

"At *least* the same. Lots more if you're pretty."

"You *are* pretty, Ellen. If only you'd get that frown off your face! You've a wonderful figure."

"And men love hair like yours, all bouncy and rippling… but you've such a rough tongue!"

"Can't you make David give you some money?"

"Just leave Owen by himself. He's big enough. The language he knows—it's shocking!"

"Oh, Ellen, can't you find someone else?"

"No, I won't take him overnight! It's not as if Owen's a nice child to be with, Ellen. He's not even *like* a child."

"He won't mind."

"He won't wash his hands."

"He won't blow his nose."

"He won't eat."

"He did his business on my floor! Disgusting."

"What he did to that wretched dog—I never saw such a thing in my life. He has a heart of stone, that boy. Stone."

"Honeypot's a moneypot."

"Remember—the same pay for a lot less work."

"You could bring them home, Ellen. Your place is private, down the alley there, and Owen would just be sleeping."

"You could buy food."

"Shoes for him."

"An umbrella."

"A coat for winter."

"Eggs, meat...."

"Don't be silly, Ellen. The men wouldn't even know he was there. And what would Owen care? He doesn't care about anything."

(That was exactly Jonathan's judgement, thirty years later; of course, those women's voices could not reach him.)

So in 1935 came the end of red-haired beautiful Ellen Jones, whose tongue cut sharp.

Leaving Vancouver this time, her son Owen had an angry fancy to retrace the route he'd taken in 1918, although, since no one was after him this time, he rode the ferry over to the North Shore. He didn't meet any deer, either.

In late May, Owen reached Bella Coola and lucked into a couple of weeks' work rebuilding a cannery that winter storms had left tilting dangerously. He met Lillian again. She slid away from whatever her home situation was (as with Dora, it never occurred to Owen to inquire about any of that) and slid into Owen's unmade bed. Since his last encounters with her, she had certainly learned some stuff, but Owen couldn't stop feeling Dora, holding Dora, kissing Dora. Lillian was too skinny. Owen got angry. The grace that made her such a good dancer kept her thin. Even her cunt felt skimpy.

Angry, angry all the time.

Newspapers from the Lower Mainland finally got up the Coast.

In the room he'd rented in Bella Coola, a lean-to tacked on to a house near the docks, Owen lay by Lillian and read about the strikers. She'd cooked a big breakfast fry-up, potatoes and eggs and buttered bread with lots of jam, and afterwards they went back to bed.

"What a goddamn stupid thing to do. Occupy a museum!"

"But McGeer gave them six days' relief," Lillian said, reading further. "They got what they wanted. And look, everyone outside helped them. Brought food. And chocolate. Money. The White Lunch sent in coffee! Wasn't that nice?"

Owen threw down the *Province*. "What the hell good does that do? Sit on your arse with mummies and skeletons, drinking coffee and singing 'Hold the Fort'? Can't you see nothing's changed?"

"But don't people have to fight for what they want?"

He shook his head. "Dumb, Lillian. Don't you understand it won't do any good? Look who's on the other side."

Lillian opened her mouth to argue and then closed it. She slipped her hand gently under the blankets. Owen pushed her away. He thought he might hit her.

When he held his pay in his hand, Owen considered. The grease trail inland lay choked with spring mud. To do that trek again—a sickening thought. Already the flies were terrible. He caught the next boat north for Rupert.

Scrounging for work on the docks there, he met a Haida woman from Skidegate, big-breasted and short. His beard attracted her.

After a long rainy summer on the Charlottes, Owen got back to the Mainland feeling as though he'd been in another world, been out of time. In the *Daily News* appeared a day-by-day recapitulation of the On to Ottawa Trek.

"I said it'd be that way. I told those damn fool strikers, down in Vancouver," Owen insisted in the bars of Prince Rupert and Terrace and Smithers. "Of course the cops got them. Of course they got shot and beaten and jailed. If it wasn't Regina it'd be someplace else. Assholes! *That's what happens.*"

Several months later, in Quesnel, after an excellent Merry Christmas fuck with Mrs. Major, Owen lay beside Lady angrily thinking about his son, now nearing the end of his time inside the house of his mother. *One month to go....*

Before they got into bed, Lady had brought a plate of fruitcake up to her room. Now Owen peeled the almond paste off all the slices and began to eat the sweet sticky strips, one by one. Lady protested. Owen let his thoughts go. Giggling, the two daubed their bodies and mouths with marzipan and then fell to sucking and licking and kissing it off each other.

Afterwards, Owen went back to thinking. *Tim, Jim. Ed, Eddie, Ted, Ned—no, definitely not Ned. Jack, Mac, Nick, Chuck, Mike.* Half-asleep, he reviewed the possibilities. *Pat and Mike. Frank, Hank. Al, Mel. Bob, Rob, Robby. Bill, Phil.*

The holiday over, Owen got back to work. He went on thinking about names. Sometimes men with less common monikers turned up at the job sites. *Alastair. Sounds like a Scotch lawyer. Elmer—and Daisy, no. Paul—that's sissy. Adam—and Eve, no. Ben. Sam. Dave, David—not him, no. Gus. John—a dime a dozen.*

On the due date, the name "Jerry" occurred to Owen. *Very merry Jerry.* Right away he liked it. Jerry Jones.

Of course the boy could never be that. He'd be Something Dow; who knew what name that sour-faced man would stick on his son? Realizing this for the umpteenth time put Owen far down in the angry dumps. *Sick of it, sick of it.*

At week's end Owen's foreman handed over his pay. "Get your grouch out of here, Jones, and don't come back. There's plenty of cheerful men need work."

Owen drank heavily Saturday night, Sunday night.

Berry derry ferry fairy. He made a face. *Not bloody likely.*

Hairy kerry merry perry...a drink, that was.

Terry very wary. That's funny.

The name repeated itself, repeated. *Jerry. Jerry. Jerry Jones.*

The Great Divide: forever after, so Owen thought of that trip to the Big Smoke in 1935. Yet in many ways not much changed in his life.

He still drifted, place to place, woman to woman, job to job. Everywhere he worked, the same abuse got thrown at him: *sloppy unreliable late dreaming half the time sitting on his backside won't take orders won't take orders won't take orders.* He still looked boyish, childish even, with wet workclothes stuck to his little body and bandy legs. Still he lit fires whenever one of his snarling swearing rages erupted at some man—boss, union organizer, workmate—who wanted *to make him do something.* The union men especially enraged him, with their do-goodery. Owen hated to see them take people in, those men so frantic for any straw of hope. In his sudden furies, Owen felt his entire casing of skin so scratchy and tight and crisp with anger that if he didn't light the match and set it all burning off him he'd go mad, he knew.

But there were differences, after 1935. Smaller things got burnt: a sheepskin coat, a canoe. Once he partly melted down a typewriter (it belonged to the Wobbly organizer). Still Owen never got nailed. When people called, "Hey, Firebug!" he didn't answer. Other terms his bosses and mates used were *mouthy little man, full of himself, answering-back bastard.*

Also, after 1935 Owen found Mrs. Major. *She's not Dora.* But they got on, were companionable. Lady made him laugh. Owen began to spend months at a time, whole winters even, at the house in Quesnel. He liked staying someplace regular because then he could have a cat around. *For the mice and that. Has to earn its keep.* And in the Bella Coola springs and summers he found that although fishboats were bloody goddamn hell-hard jeezly killing work, when a trip was done, it was *done.* He signed off, at some shack on the dock, and then walked away free and clear.

Owen learned, too, that if he did what that fuckface gimpy doctor in Vancouver said, rubbed his hands with warm oil or soaked them, they felt a lot better. *For a while, anyway, Jerry.*

Most important of all: after the Great Divide, nine months afterwards, there was Jerry. In 1936 the birthday celebrations began: inescapable.

April 1935—Jonathan, Giving and Receiving Advice
As the Depression wore on and Aunt Julie aged, her truculence heightened. Neither the postman nor Eaton's nor the paperboy could ring the doorbell of the house on Sasamat without the old woman raging out to the porch to blame them for *everything bad that's happening.* She scoured the daily papers for sinister photographs of neighbourhood prowlers and of mobsters like R.B. Bennett and Mayor McGeer. *Bad men, they are,* she insisted to Jonathan.

For once he agreed with his aunt. More and more, his patients' presenting symptom was hunger, their disease poverty. Fear, forced idleness, and forced hard labour transformed their once well-muscled bodies. Rail-thin boys coughed horribly, while apathetic girls lined up for hours to get a cup of beans, a bag of bread. Every day people knocked at his apartment door. *Anything. Sir, I'll do anything.* A chalk squiggle marked Hilda's kitchen: *Food and kindness here.* Tramps found their way to Point Grey, trailing furtively along the beach.

Jonathan felt inadequate, useless; he worked himself to exhaustion and still felt useless. Yet what task could he do each day but this—first hospital rounds and then the family?

Daily, he or one of the brothers dropped in to see how Hilda was coping with Aunt Julie and Uncle George, her children in their dotage.

Hilda managed to hold the household together through Christmas and into the New Year of 1935, but finally Aunt Julie's incontinence defeated her.

On a bright summer morning, therefore, hardly able to believe that he—*littlest, youngest, scatterbrain*—was the agent for this deed, Jonathan bundled Uncle George and Aunt Julie and himself into a taxi. He held their hands. He rode with them to the nursing home and left them, puzzled, there.

Back at his own apartment for a quick lunch, Jonathan contemplated the childhood treasures heaped about his rooms: *Legends of Vancouver, Stalky & Co.*, the Hardy Boys, *At the Back of the North Wind*; shells of clam and crab and sea anemone and chambered nautilus; the hollow bones of seagull and flicker and bush tit, sanderling and wren and ruby-crowned kinglet; the solid bones of the dear pet rat Angelica. *I need a bigger place. Room to move. Time to move.* Piled high on his fine bird's-eye maple table were minutes of the hospital's renovation committee and Jonathan's sketches of rearranged rooms, wards, wings. *I need a real desk. A roll-top. Get rid of this old thing.*

Jonathan ran downstairs, heading for a consultation at St. Paul's, and turned south at Richards for his daily pleasure of collecting streetcar numbers. About to cross at Helmcken, he looked west to the rosy brick of the hospital. White coats flickered in the sun. His eyes were full of light as he walked right into the car singing north.

Jonathan believed he would go insane if one more person said to him, *You don't know how lucky you are to be alive.* Richard's wife, Louise, stressed this point. "You should be grateful," she said. "You have been spared. Doubtless there is a reason why."

During his weeks of pain and forced inactivity, Jonathan carved his initials on the underside of the maple table, in Gothic lettering. He inked them in, blackly. How he'd struggled to form those strange shapes, back in Miss Lawrence's classroom! The dates and initials elsewhere on the underside mostly varied from scratched to hacked. Only one set was neatly incised: "DC & AC, 1910." That ampersand had given trouble. His own "JS, MCMXXXV" was the tallest signature of all.

"You're lucky to be alive, young man," Dr. Campbell said, unwrapping Jonathan's stump. "Though you're not really so young, are you now? At your age, Dr. Smyth, the tissues don't repair themselves so quickly. But you know that. Probably you know everything I'm going to tell you." The gauze spiralled off Jonathan's left leg, amputated six inches below the knee. Dr. Campbell took off his glasses and put his nose to the stump. "In the war, though...." Jonathan rolled his eyes. "In France, probably you *don't* know this, all those young soldiers on our hands, lads really, boys, children even you could say—how fast their stumps healed! Startling, upon my word." The doctor's thumbs pressed firmly. "Sensitive, eh? But clean. A good healer, you are." He took up fresh gauze. "And soon we'll have your nice new prosthesis."

Jonathan spoke through his teeth. "Dr. Campbell—the phantom foot. How long does that phenomenon last?"

Unreeling the white strip, the doctor's hands turned palm up, palm down, palm up. "The pain that isn't there? Ah. There's many a lad tries to find the answer to that one, Dr. Smyth."

To strive, to seek, to find, and not to yield. Miss Lawrence got them all to memorize that bit.

On May Day 1935 Jonathan arrived, limping at VGH to learn that one of his patients had moments ago died of her cancer. He was glad, for she had told him her story. He stood by her bed. *How pretty she must have been. How sore her hands look.* Her son was there, a small sullen man of about Jonathan's age who got up and went over to the window, turning his back. Jonathan joined him. Standing together, they heard the parade.

Jonathan offered condolences. The son shrugged. On impulse Jonathan took Owen's hands in his. "Mr. Jones, you've arthritis too, you know." The digits were leathery, calloused, lumpy-knuckled. "See the thickening?" The son yanked his hands away. Jonathan spoke of massage, soaking, warmed oils.

"I got no time for this."

In his turn, Jonathan shrugged. Hunger, anger, death— *Maybe he'll think of it, later.* "I'll be off then. A strong woman, your mother. It can't have been easy for her, raising a child alone."

The doctor left the bereaved son waif-like in the hospital room. His expression too was common in men on relief. Dislocated, they looked, as if unable to imagine how they'd got to wherever they were. *And how did I get here?* Jonathan hobbled up the stairs to the next floor, to a living patient.

Downtown today was the greatest demonstration in his

city's history, during a crisis paralyzing not only Vancouver, not only Canada, but the globe. *And here I am, mooning over a woman past any help I can give. Fussing about the future of a man who isn't even my patient and doesn't care anyway. Milksop!* Jonathan remembered August 1918. *Ineffectual as ever—but at least this time I did no harm.* The achievement seemed inexcusably small.

1935—Dora's Six Weeks of Work

In the early fall of 1935 when Dora's pregnancy by either Owen or Ned was well established, John's stutter took the boy and his mother to a speech specialist.

Ned insisted. "If John was going to grow out of this, he would have by now. At school they laugh at him. The thing's got to be dealt with, Dora. Take him."

To Dora's surprise and Ned's later dismay, the doctor was a woman. She made it clear that John must be alone with her, so Dora went wandering from floor to floor about the Vancouver Block. Behind the office doors sounded busy talk, phones, the clack and *ting!* of typewriters. As if typing herself, Dora flexed her fingers and smiled at their speed. If only she could do that, here. Gladys Smith could come back, as a typist this time; she could breathe this strange, exhilarating air. Something medicinal hung in it, plus the women's perfumes and men's hair oils.

Dora went down one staircase beside a tall lanky man with a crutch and an artificial foot. Awkwardly he laboured, but managed an uneven grin. "Practicing. There's to be a fire drill this week, so I must find my way on my own two feet." By the time they reached the sixth floor, though, he trembled as he took Dora's offered arm. At

Office 636 he fumbled for keys and gave them to her, and when Dora opened his door Dr. Jonathan Smyth, G.P., almost collapsed on to a chair. He had a big head. His face was deeply carved with sadness, and Dora knew him. August 1918.

His office was empty. "Mrs. Angell's gone, for six weeks," Dr. Smyth panted. "I need someone."

For John, Dr. Howard prescribed word exercises and games. Riding home on the streetcar, mother and son practiced, seriously at first and then laughing together.

Listening to his son repeat *shadow, chard, sheet, chin* and *thorn, these, thick, thousand,* Ned cried, "What's this rubbish? Where's his medicine? What silliness have you women got him doing?"

That first day working for Dr. Smyth, Dora was so tired by the time the last patient left the office that she fitted the leatherette cover over the Remington and laid down her head on the machine.

"You must get a good rest tonight, Miss Smith."

His kindness opened Dora's mouth. "I'm *Mrs.* Smith." She sat up and faced him. "And not a widow." Dora gestured to the door. "Do you want me to go?"

"Where? What would I do without you? As I said, get some rest. We've a full day tomorrow." Dr. Smyth patted the leatherette and went into his consulting room, leaving Dora to poke about in her change purse for her wedding ring so she could put it on before she left the building. She was afraid of forgetting to do so.

Next day, Office 636 was empty when Dora arrived. She pulled up the blinds; birds drifted by. Soon, not more than a quarter of an hour later, Caddy joined her mother. She came to play.

Telephoning from the General, Dr. Smyth assured her that he would arrive in time for his first patient. "And I wanted to say, Mrs. Smith"—the doctor's voice sounded as if that was truly her name, as if he knew the two of them had known each other for years—"we all have things we'd rather not talk about. And reasons for what we do."

If Dr. Jonathan Smyth had spoken those words to her face to face, Dora would have said, "I remember you. You know me."

During the six weeks that she worked for him, her fingers played over the Remington's keyboard as smoothly and rhythmically as on the Singer. The rubber pad beneath the machine absorbed her fingerstrokes. In long swift runs she stitched words on to the engraved letterhead, seaming paragraphs that always formed the same patterns on the page: short, then long, then very long, for when Dr. Smyth dictated, his first thoughts and phrasings hesitated, but as he entered more and more deeply into accounts of births or estimates, consultations or floor plans or agendas, there emerged longer and longer units of speech. Quickly Dora filled the columns of her shorthand pad, turning her pages as sentences ended. In her typing, a cadence developed that comprised the steady *ting!* of the carriage-return and the *flap* of each turning page and the shapes of Dr. Smyth's sentences as they lengthened from simple to compound-complex. All the words were formed with even impress and perfect spacing.

Because no patients came in the mornings, when Dora took her hands off the keys the silence flowed into that

high office while outside the gulls flew in a white squawk-
ing flurry past the window. Right now, no one in her world
knew where Dora was. Only Marjo knew she was being
Gladys again. Not even Marjo knew that Dora still sometimes woke up out of Annette-dreams, from long before
Caddy, Mary, John, Ned.

Often Caddy sat by her mother in the reception room,
watching and giggling, admiring Mummy's clever fingers.
The little girl smiled at Dr. Smyth. She liked his funny
brush cut and the way the deep lines by his mouth curled
up when he smiled. Flipping the pleats of her plaid skirt,
Caddy jumped about. Sometimes she hid in the consulting
room and scared the doctor. "*Boo!*" Dora heard her, clearly.
Caddy knew about the new baby, too. She liked to lean on
Dora's belly and laugh when she felt her little brother or sister move. On Caddy's hair, Dora smelled sunlight, even
when the windows from the sixth floor sheeted with rain.

Once a patient arrived with her own little girl of five or
so, who wore new Mary Janes. Caddy didn't like her at all.
She went away. When Dora got herself under control, she
went to the ladies' room and gripped the square-edged
rim of the sink. *Twyford*, the porcelain basin said in black
letters. *Twyford*. A bar of Pears' soap lay in the china dish.
Caddy wouldn't come back to Dr. Smyth's office for days.
Always after that she lived for Dora in the smell of Pears', in
its soft underside.

Caddy didn't like Mrs. Roper, either. This young woman
with a long straggle of hair muttered to herself as she
waited to see Dr. Smyth. Coming suddenly over to Dora,
this patient gripped the Remington. "Don't stare at me! Is it

funny ha ha I look, or funny peculiar? What's your name? Smith? I don't believe you." She grabbed at the letterhead and carbons and flimsy all curled together over the platen. "Don't make fun of me!"

By then Caddy was gone, run right away, and just as well, because Mrs. Roper wasn't in Dr. Smyth's consulting room five minutes before she began to scream, "You killed my baby! You killed him!" She wept and kicked and twisted about as if trapped in an airless bag.

Together, Dora and Jonathan forced her down into a chair and held her till she went limp. Dora found the flask of ammonium carbonate. She telephoned. When the husband appeared, he and Dora helped Mrs. Roper, still sobbing, out to the elevator. Jonathan limped clumsily alongside, with nothing to do.

"There was nothing to be done," he said as they sat in his office, recovering. His leg obviously hurt. "Poor little chap, right at the last the cord got wound tight round his neck. A minute. That's all it took. Death is so random."

Dora felt faint. She bent over, as well as she could at five months, to get blood back to her brain. The smelling salts came out again. At first she managed only three words. "My girl died."

Caddy didn't appear, even while her mother cried and cried on nice Dr. Smyth.

Caddy didn't come back even when Mummy got the last two words out of the house of her body, where they had been stored, buried, unspoken for eighteen months: "Of polio."

1934—Dora, Gaining

Ned asked, "Haven't you put on a bit of weight, Dora?" This was three months or so after Caddy died.

Later, "Why don't you watch how much you eat? It's not good for you to be that heavy."

Then, "Haven't you got any willpower?"

"What kind of example for the kids d'you suppose this is?"

"Do you realize you're turning into a blimp?"

"Do you think you're the only one grieving?"

"Can't you sew yourself some pretty clothes? You used to."

"The children are shamed, Dora. A fat mother—the other kids laugh at them. Mary's fat enough herself already. John stutters. Haven't they got enough on their plates?"

Dora slept on the chesterfield. If the children woke with a tummy upset or a bad dream (for John these were frequent), they went to their father, alone in the big bed.

Before sleeping, Dora fingered the piping she'd used, re-upholstering the chesterfield. On the left arm, it didn't run quite smooth. Dora ran her hands along it again and again.

Dora ate bread between meals, a loaf a day, thick with butter and jam. Her menus for family meals, always narrow, rigidified: porridge, baloney sandwiches, stew. Porridge, baloney sandwiches, stew. Dora ate seconds, thirds. She had two bowel movements a day and sat on the toilet twitching, shivering.

Only if Ned raged and raged at the sour-smelling icebox and the black mould growing by the sink would Dora clean.

When John pointed out that May 24 had come and gone, Dora planted the vegetable garden but did not water or thin the seedlings unless Ned nagged. Often she didn't think to check the gate, so the deer got in and ate the infant plants.

On weekends, Ned continued the family outings customary before Caddy's death. Dora sat by English Bay and watched the water: in or out, out or in. Ned and the children went off to swim and splash, poke at starfish and hunt for oysters with pearls inside. Shown these discoveries, Dora had nothing to say.

When Mary picked blackberries in Stanley Park, Ned helped. He insisted that Dora make jam with her daughter. "No, *not* at Marjo's, not this time. *You're* her mother. You show her."

Mary read the Vancouver *Sun* and made a blackberry cobbler, crusty and tender with purple syrup richly veining the dough.

Once the four took a day trip on a paddlewheeler up Indian Arm. Viewing East Vancouver from this novel angle fascinated John. "Look, Mum! You can almost see our house!"

Dora went below decks. In the lounge, someone had left an instruction manual: *Teach Yourself Typing*. Dora fingered the printed keyboard, did some exercises before the boat's whistle blew at the dock in Coal Harbour. The manual went home with her.

Now, each night before she slept, Dora flexed her fingers in these new patterns. Each morning around four she woke for her nightly bout with grief; when her tears exhausted themselves she practiced further, sometimes tapping the blanket keyboard until dawn. The first word of her own that she chose to type was "Caddy."

One night when Dora put on her nightgown and left the big bedroom upstairs, Ned barred the way. "March, April, May, June, July, August. It's six months now. I want you here."

"Six months *and eleven days.*" Dora pushed past him.

"Did you hear me? I want you in our bed."

His wife, descending the stairs on her way to the chesterfield, looked up at him, plainly bewildered.

He waved his arms. "We're married, remember?"

Dora shook her head and went on down. With each step, her haunches stretched the nightgown's thin cotton. Ned slammed the bedroom door. Then he opened it again, for the children.

In the kitchen next morning, Ned found Dora rhythmically tapping on the table while she read the *Province* want ads.

He snatched the paper from her and slapped the table with it. "You don't do the job you have now, Dora!" *Slap.* "Aren't you ashamed, the wash not done and no dusting and Mary cooking half our meals? A child! Not eight years old!" *Slap.*

"She likes cooking. I don't."

"I'll check every want ad in that paper, Dora. I'll phone." *Slap.* "I'll go." *Slap.* "I'll ask, 'Has a Dora Dow applied here? Well, I'm her husband. And I say she. Can't. Take. The job.'"

Dora tapped and tapped.

Summer 1934—Marjo Sews a Seam

Six months after Caddy's funeral, Dora hadn't so much as touched her thimble.

Ned came to me. "She's worn the same navy-blue *bag* for a month now." So harsh, his voice. "The ladies call.

They drop by, they want their clothes, but Dora just says *I'm not sewing.* The machine needs maintenance, too. It can't stand unused."

How Ned managed it I don't know, but next Sunday he got the whole family out to Stanley Park, to pick blackberries.

To be in their house without them; to sit in Dora's sewing corner without her beside me....

Tall Flora stood there of course. She was wound out to full size, and I felt as if she was cross. I didn't dare collapse the dummy and pack her into her case. Only Dora could do that. Flora's big dust cover I found, though, and pulled it over her top to bottom, and set her in the corner with her front to the wall. She still looked big and angry.

I'd brought a suitcase, for the clothes Dora was working on when Caddy died. Dresses, blouses, skirts—I folded them all away in tissue paper, to take back to her ladies; if they wanted to get their summer wardrobes finished, they'd have to find other dressmakers. Such puffy short sleeves we all wore that year! Peaked, like wings on our dresses. A lovely blue cordelaine crepe there was, with wide white revers. I see it still.

All round the machine and on that folding table Ned built for Dora lay needle-papers bobbins smocking-dot papers spools silks patterns scraps. I cleared and sorted and dusted them all off, set them on those special shelves he'd built for Dora. And her great button jar. How many of those jars has Dora filled, over the years? First a pillbox, when we were little kids, and then a Marmite jar—her dad loved that stuff—but by the time we were in high school she'd got a row of pint sealers. She'd pour the buttons out on her bed; we'd scoop them up and let them fall, as if we were at the beach. Such bright shapes!

By the time Caddy died Dora had a jar eighteen inches tall, from an Italian grocery on Hastings. Olives it might have held, or artichokes. So heavy! Ned had a niche for the button jar, on the shelves, and I managed to heave it up there.

Then I had to tidy away Caddy's bits of sewing, her doll clothes and the patchwork she'd started. For those I'd brought a nightdress holder, such a pretty thing, a quilted satin envelope with a silk frog closing, all in pearly white. And perfumed—I put a sachet of pot-pourri inside to give it to Dora, later.

Oiling the machine wasn't hard, though Dora could do it with less mess, I'm sure.

Then I went through the pink fabric to find the largest scrap and set to, working the treadle and seaming with an empty needle. Flora stood near me. *Ah ah ah!* cried the Singer. From Caddy's birthday dress, those scraps were. Salmonberry colour. Dora'd smocked it in shades of pink.

I sewed until the stuff ran clean. Such a big sound in that empty house—*ah ah ah ah ah!*

No one can smock as beautifully as Dora. *No one.*

All the oily scraps went into a bag, and I took them away from Dora's house.

February 1, 1934—Caddy Gets New Shoes

Ned stared at his wife. "A storefront on Hastings for your dressmaking? And sell notions? Are you crazy?"

Caddy ran into the kitchen and scrambled up on a chair. Eagerly she stuck out her gleaming black patent leather feet. "See my new Mary Janes, Daddy! Is your 'flection in them? Mummy's is. And see my gold buckles!"

Ned hugged her. "So pretty, sweetheart!" When Caddy ran off again to her toys, he said to Dora, "And how much were those?"

She rummaged in her purse and showed him the bill.

"Using your pin-money for a treat—yes, that's fine. But Caddy doesn't *need* those shoes. What she *needs*, I pay for. What John *needs*, I pay for. What Mary—don't interrupt! I pay for what's *needed*. That's my job. Why can't you do yours?"

Dora said nothing.

Ned threw up his hands. "The house is a mess, nothing's ever clean, but you just sew. Do I rent a storefront on Hastings for my model trains?" He got up. "*I* make the money. *I* work. *I* pay. John's stuck upstairs, reading that old *Boys' Own Annual* again. Don't you worry? He should be out in the fresh air. And where's Mary? At Marjo's. Sure. You'd think she wasn't our daughter."

The front door opened. Moments later Mary burst wailing into the kitchen. "Why can't I have new Mary Janes? Why does Caddy always get what she wants and I *never* do?"

For her birthday party, Caddy wanted favours to give to all the girls from her dancing class. Each would choose a button from Dora's button jar—that was one. The other Dora found at Woolworth's on Commercial. Perfect! A celluloid doll, three inches high, clasped a tiny painted paper fan—but in that hole where the fan stuck into her body could go a dandelion, a grass stem, a feather, a pipe cleaner, a straw … anything, everything! The fan itself bore cherry blossoms. A minute bluebird perched on the twig to open its wings.

After Caddy died (one of eighty-three polio fatalities in British Columbia that year) but before she was dressed for burial, Mary crept into her sister's room.

First she found the dolls. Then under Caddy's bed she found the new shoes. Mary let out the shining gold-buckled straps to their last hole, curled up her toes and scraped sores on her heels, trying, but she could not fit her feet into those shoes. She could not.

Dora heard her daughter crying and came upstairs. With a hairbrush, she hit Mary's legs till they bled.

Dolls tumbled from the child's hands. Dora took all the celluloid favours down to the kitchen and stuffed them into the stove. Wild flame blew up. She barely got the lid on in time.

Damage

Owen Moves Around

When Owen ran away from the Bella Coola Valley the first time in 1924—this was after the fire at the Norsk lumber mill and all the trouble with Indian Tom's sister Irene but long before Jerry was conceived, eleven years before—he first shaved off his beard. Then he crossed the river.

For days he trudged up dark steep rainy forested trails that stank of fish oil. Finally hauling himself up into sunshine on the windy plateau of the Chilcotin, Owen Jones thought he'd never go back down. *At Tatla Lake I've drunk to you, Jerry. At Nimpo. Alexis Creek. Where'd I go then, that first time? Oh, Quesnel I spose. Hundred Mile. Williams Lake.* There the annual rainfall was eleven inches, to Bella Coola's sixty. Owen preened like a cat.

But, also catlike, he was uncomfortable anywhere exposed. The broad sweeps of the Cariboo trapped him. No quick way out. *And then? Damned if I remember. North to Fort St. John, maybe, that first time. South, far as Coalmont.* Here, after spitting at the mine manager, a tall heavy man with a rough tongue, Owen was let go. Soon fire ravaged the shack where all the mine's records and accounts were kept. Also, a terrified Coalmont girl and a woman from Tulameen—*Jeez, Jerry, was she a juicy armful!*—had to find their way to that nasty doctor in Princeton. *Spent some time in the Kootenays. Not so much up in Terrace and Rupert and that. Too rainy.* Owen drifted south again, to the sun.

At an orchard near Peachland where he was picking one August, Owen found *good cash money lying right there on the windowsill. Asking for it, bloody fool owner.* The big beefy man didn't see it that way. Literally, he kicked Owen off the property. Although that night's fire was quickly doused and the trees lived through it, the smoky apricots were unsaleable. Furious, the owner put out the word. Many people sought Owen. He had to run much harder than he liked and so persuaded a pretty girl to row him across the Lake in the dark. He giggled noiselessly all the way over while the waves went *lap-lap-lap.*

Landing, he headed first north and then west. For far longer than he preferred, Owen went without sleep, but he got clear away and then veered and tacked and wandered back to the Coast he'd left four years before. *Back to the liquid sunshine. That's another laugh, eh Jerry? Hell on the arthritis too, this weather. The thing is, though—at Bella Coola the river's right on hand. There's always a boat to steal. Remember "Three Sailors Went*

Sailing" I taught you when you were little? Because Owen was still beardless, many in the town did not at first recognize him.

Singing and word-chaining and fighting, for twenty years Owen earned his living by casual labour wherever the province was opening up. He cracked stones for roads, bruised his back, through weeks on end lived white with dust. He drove trucks for logging crews; jouncing on corduroy roads made his back worse while the greasy food played hell with his guts. On one broken-down fishboat after another, Owen cleaned gear and fixed it, sort of, wired things together for one more run, made enough of a hash of his work to annoy but not quite enough to get fired, though some owners didn't hire "that asshole" ever again after just one season.

Unless he could see immediate benefit to himself, such as getting on shore sooner, Owen never worked hard or well. *It'll do. It'll pass. S'okay like that.* He was never the first chosen for any crew, nor the second or third. This didn't bother him. Why should a boss care about him? He cared for no boss. Work had to be done. All right. He put out the minimum effort. Then he got paid, ate, slept dry and warm, with a woman sometimes, a cat whenever he could, and when he was young he swallowed as much beer as he was able without falling down unconscious.

In the bars, he'd amuse a woman by word-chaining. *Gimme a letter, I'd say. C? Right you are, copper. Here I go. Copper dipper flapper gripper hopper leper, ha ha, that's good eh? and nipper pepper ripper supper topper wrapper yipper yay! Everyone'd laugh, Jerry. The whole room.* The little man's eyes gleamed. With luck, someone would have a guitar or an accordion. The singing lasted for hours. *Jerry, you'd have such a good time!* Up through the forties the songs went on like that, dozens in an evening with none repeating. Till TV came.

Owen himself never owned an instrument. *Just something to be stolen, Jerry, same as a steady job's just something to lose. And as for those fires, they never proved anything. Not a damn thing.*

This was Owen's pattern of life until 1935 when the letter came from Vancouver.

After 1935, Owen considered that if those bloody assholes in Ottawa could move Thanksgiving around like fuckn Tiddlywinks—and they did for years, now October, now November, just to suit those federal big-bellies without a fuckn functioning pair of balls among the whole goddamned bunch, R.B. Bennett included—then he didn't see why Owen Jones couldn't fiddle his son's birthday around to please himself. So from the beginning he did. *Tiddly, fiddly....Fiddle, fiddle....Sure, addle coddle diddle fiddle guddle huddle middle noddle paddle riddle toddle waddle yodel, ha ha, so there!* And Owen laughed at his word-chain.

As a birthday, January 15 satisfied Owen because it was, close as could be, the middle of that month. Another kind of precision was offered by January 20, exactly nine months from conception. January 17 was good, too, because of Owen's own birthdate in September. So, come January, whether Owen was cold and damp on the Coast or all iced up in the Interior—*You've got a jeezly month for your birthday, Jerry, either way, but at the time your mum and me weren't exactly thinking about weather*—Owen picked his day and raised his glass to his son.

Jerry Jones. All over B.C. I've drunk to you, son.

1922–1934—*Prairie Boy and Sonsy Girl*

Mary snuggled up to her mother. Her pudgy fingers and thighs repelled Dora, but at least the child didn't mouth-breathe. Throughout the funeral, John's wheezing held its note. His ears stuck out like Ned's. In the white box lay Caddy, who resembled only herself and wore her new "best" shoes.

"In my Father's house are many mansions; if it were not so, I would have told you. I go to prepare a place for you." *This is the same pew I sat in before, in 1918.*

Down the street was the room where once Miss Clara Forbes offered tea to her younger work-mate; Dora had then been at Spencer's three years. At the department store, Dora used, bore, wore the name of Gladys Smith. It made a layer of protection for her against an invasive, disapproving world that sought to expose and judge her.

When Gladys started at Spencer's in 1922, ultra-short skirts and deep-dropped waists filled the display windows. The woman who interviewed her and the man who hired her both wagged jocular fingers. "No running off to Hollywood for you! *One* Mary Pickford is enough." A smile was the only answer.

Hearing this anecdote, Marjo rolled her eyes; she had never liked the name-costumes Dora wore. Dora therefore did not tell her best girlfriend the pleasurable details of how she'd closed out Annette LeClerc's old account at the Royal on Commercial and opened Gladys Smith's new one in the Dominion Building.

At Spencer's, Dora's eye drew the attention of the assistant buyer of ladies' wear, Mr. Heseltine, because she could pick out high-style garments wearable by more than the minority of women who were naturally small-breasted and hipless. Dora became his assistant and stayed so for several seasons, though other people moved, or seemed to. Gradually she saw the pattern: men up, girls sideways. Then came Mr. Heseltine's heart attack.

"A man to replace him! Newer than you! Younger! Less experienced!" Miss Forbes's tone blended shock with the savour of *I could have told you, if you'd asked.* No one had. Miss Forbes was imprisoned at the old-lady counter in Lingerie, stacking wool undervests and corsets with the coercive power of steel. Her grovelling to customers made young noses wrinkle, like her looks—grey spitcurls, huge spectacled moth-eyes, stick-limbs. "You *trained* this young man, Gladys! And now you are cast aside."

"We brought nothing into this world, and it is certain we can carry nothing out." *Caddy had her new shoes on.*

Riding home on the Number Twenty, the two women sat side by side. Miss Forbes's hands fidgeted; her nails were hard from hitting the cash register yet perfectly almond-shaped.

"Be it ever so humble!" giggled the older woman, at her door, her welcoming gesture suggesting a space more than tiny. Dora's own apartment on Commercial Drive was no larger...but she was only twenty-four. Anxiously Miss Forbes made tea, fiddled and fiddled with sugar scoop and teaspoons till they fell noisily. Dora was reminded of Miss Hector at Macdonald Elementary, whose hands trembled so when she got angry at Owen Jones for shouting out the right answer that she dropped the chalk.

"The days of our age are threescore years and ten, or, if men be strong they may come to fourscore years." *Without Caddy, I can't reach any more score.* "Yet is their pride but labour and sorrow; so soon passeth it away, and we are gone."

Marjo *tsk!*ed, hearing of Miss Forbes's high-pitched apologies. "Dora, it's high time you *really* changed your name. You don't want to end up like Miss F, do you?" She kissed her baby. "Don't make faces, Dora! Come in the boat this weekend? There'll be some nice fellows along."

Marjo and Mike and Mick—still their lone child, after repeated miscarriages—often went up the Inlet to Port Moody, to picnic and then to dance till all hours on the sprung floor at the Tourist Hotel, while Mick with other toddlers and babies slept on a high pile of coats in a corner. When finally all the young Vancouver people went back to the dark salty dock and set off in their boats together, everyone sang Gershwin and Hammerstein and Kern in the watery moonlight, as they floated home on the tide to the city.

Who, who, who stole my heart away?
Who made me dream all day?

That weekend, Ned Dow and Ed Rowe came along. Neddy and Eddie. Curly Ed, Carroty Ned, both in smart straw boaters. Eddie fisherman from Ontario or Neddy sugarman from Saskatchewan—which was who? Everyone laughed. Both boys danced with all the girls. First Ed, then Ned walked towards Dora, hands held out to meet hers. So Owen walked once, smiling, no, grinning—that full-lipped grin of his. In another few seconds, he would have held her tight tight.

Next week Dora went with Eddie Rowe to sigh over *Romola* with the Gish girls *and* Ronald Colman, but with Ned Dow and some other fellows from B.C. Sugar and their girls, all dressed up—Owen would never do such a thing, Dora knew—she went to the Pantages for the Charleston contest finals, and just like everyone else she cheered and laughed and danced in the aisles.

With Eddie, Dora gasped at Zane Grey's *Wild Horse Mesa* and sighed with Gloria Swanson in *Coast of Folly*; with Ned at the Orpheum, she laughed at *My China Doll* with Barbara Bronell.

Who, who, who stole my heart away?
Who makes me dream all day?
Dreams I know can never be true
Seems as though I'll ever be blue

"Don't you want to hold Mick?" Marjo dandled her baby boy. "Now, Dora, isn't Ned more fun than Spencer's? You wouldn't have to work! I *know* you say you like it—but honestly, on your feet for hours, those snobby girls, and those awful travellers and floorwalkers. Ogling and pinching! And no one even knows your real name. I declare, at Spencer's you're not even you!"

Dora smiled but made no answer.

"Now. Mike found out everything I told him to." Marjo began feeding Mick his cornmeal mush. "Ned hardly takes a drink, so no worries there. He's a good worker—they all say so—*and* all for the union. He's trusted, Dora. *And* frugal. Just like you!"

The spoon went in and out of the small wet mouth.

"And about Saskatchewan. Why Ned left, I mean. His mum died long ago, his dad just last year—a ploughing accident. Terrible! The land wasn't even theirs. Ned thought if he struck out for the Coast, things'd be better." Marjo wiped Mick's face. She dug dried cereal out of his neck creases. "Hold him, Dora, while I do these dishes. Not so stiff! You're like a wooden doll, I declare. Just sit easy. Mick'll lean on you."

Dora sat.

Can I ever look at a baby again? "O whence cometh my help? Even from the Lord, who hath made heaven and earth. He will not suffer thy foot to be moved." *Then why did Caddy die?*

Ned was lean. Ned was energetic. Unlike Owen, Ned was *here*. Who knew where Owen was? Ned wasn't like Dora's handsome brother Alan, all wistful and fretful, nor like Dora's father, soft-bellied Charlie who slathered spuds with butter and endlessly swayed on the porch swing. "Tomorrow," he repeated as his wife wrung her hands. "Betty, I'll do it tomorrow." Ned Dow worked, cycled, hiked, climbed, danced, laughed, swore, kissed. "Let's go," he urged. "Dora, now." He was handy, good at contriving. Sturdy and plain, he called Dora his *sonsy girl*.

To tease, Marjo called Ned *prairie boy*.

"His looks will wear well," she insisted. "Dora, we'd have so much fun, us four! Mike likes him too. *Mrs. Dow*—isn't that better than a name that's a movie star's, not even yours?"

Who means my happiness, who?

Who would I answer "Yes" to?

Well, you ought to guess who!

No one but you!

"Dora—no, I won't stop! You're not getting any younger. Think of Miss Forbes. You don't want to be Sonsy Old Maid."

Ned Dow's body was muscular. When he felt Dora's abundance through the second skin of her clothes he did not suddenly withdraw his hand, unlike the few others who'd got so far with her. (Owen's hands had never even reached Dora's, when they stood so close together in the dawn.) Now Ned's rough cheek warmed her smooth skin. She felt the bony ridge at the back of his skull, under the warm hair, and she laughed. He laughed.

"Foolish man, that which thou sowest is not made to live, except it die." *Then, please, when can I die?*

Ned planted kisses all up her throat to her open mouth. "Dora, with all my worldly goods I'll thee endow, Mrs. Dow."

At the wedding on 23 June 1926, Mike Morgan stood up for Ned and Marjo for Dora.

Miss Dearing made Dora's silk gown. The buttoned front, with each pearl looped in lace, drew a strong vertical line downwards; at the back, the hem dipped to flutter about Dora's slender legs.

"So small!" Ned poked at a pearl with a large finger. "How'm I ever going to undo those, Mrs. Dow?"

Who, who, who stole my heart away?
Who makes me dream all day?
Dreams I know can never be true
Seems as though I'll ever be blue

Telling no one at Spencer's of her marriage, Dora continued to work. Prairie Boy put his arms around Sonsy Girl and sighed. "I'll sure be glad when you've got something better to do."

Marjo *tsk!*ed in exasperation. Dora's silence answered, but Marjo would not leave it alone. "But *why* can't you just enjoy being Mrs. Ned Dow? Why pretend to be single?"

More silence. "I thought it was crazy when you liked being Annette, or whatever Mrs. S. made you call yourself at Martine's. But this!" Marjo gestured *I-wash-my-hands-of-it*. "How does a false name keep you safe?" Silence.

Then Ned burrowed at Dora's breasts, nuzzling, biting, sucking. "You, and a baby too! I left the prairies with nothing, and now I'll have everything. Give notice at Spencer's!" His voice was angry, happy. "No more excuses, Dora. You're not *Miss* any more."

Soon Miss Gladys Smith was no longer employed at the department store, though her bank account remained active.

Soon after learning she was pregnant Dora received a letter.

The pink envelope, scalloped and scented, held handwriting that sloped from the salutation *To the Bride*—all the way down the page to *Ned's thing is turning up! in places where it shouldn't.* The words sloped all down the next page too. *In the bushes out back of the refinery, that's where Ned gives his sugar to her. Why can't your husband keep his pants buttoned? Maybe he's got too much fat to fry at home. From a Well-Wisher.*

Dora folded the pink paper into a wad, unfolded it, replaced it in the envelope, refolded both to a minute pink cube.

To doubt the letter did not occur to her. Nothing in her two and a half decades had led Dora to expect constancy or to believe herself worthy of or entitled to constancy. Rather, every loss, negation, and absence of those years told her and taught her that nothing was her due.

She clutched the tiny lump of letter in her fist, deep in the pocket of her housedress where no one could see. Again and again her fingertips rotated that small hardness.

Leaving the rented house on Frances, cosily kittycorner from Marjo and Mike's, she headed for Wall Street. Where the bank fell steeply to the water, Dora dragged apart the hurting tangle of berry thorns, bindweed, hissing sharp-edged grasses; she found one of the wild tunnels through the foliage and hunched over to walk in some way. Then she dropped the pink cube down into earthy prickled darkness. Surely Owen's bicycle was still down there, too, from a hundred years ago or whenever all that happened? Dora's hands bled.

She took a roundabout route home, walking up Owen's lane. Evidently his mother wasn't living in the loft any more, because the windows were smashed. Right here Owen and Dora stood that morning, so close she could see the specks of dirt caught in the pores of his nose and see the lift of his eyelashes. She smelled him. She'd cried. And that rich boy with the shoes, the soft white shirt—so kind he was, that day. His big gentle hands touched that wounded man's head, tenderly rolled and tucked the jacket under to make a pillow.

Dora went home to be alone with the man she'd married.

Now she refused sex. She refused. Silently, she refused.

His face close enough to kiss her, Ned snarled, "Frigid! frigid!" Dora counted: one night he said that fifty times. He looked nothing at all like the boy in the straw boater of two summers before. His head looked like stone. She said nothing.

Sometimes his words ground Dora down into sexual response. Worst was when, after giving in, she came. "So you didn't want it, Dora? That's what you *said*. Liar. Cockteaser."

271

By day, Ned brought Dora candy, tarts, a Valentine card; would not let her carry anything heavier than a glass of water; in the house, scrubbed, waxed, washed, and built baby furniture. "Prairie Boy loves Sonsy Girl," he crooned on her swelling belly. The movements of the child enchanted him.

Dora learned to suppress arousal. She would not feel. She would not feel. She would *not*. Her nipples flattened, the ache in her thighs faded, her labia shrivelled.

To Dora's three, Marjo was five months pregnant; she and Mike began to hope she might carry to term. "Oh, Dora, remember playing with our dolls? And hiding our secret things? But this'll be *real!*"

To experience yet conceal arousal—this Dora learned too. She practised. Alone, she stood by the kitchen counter as if preparing food and meanwhile slipped a hand through slits cut in the pockets of her housedress. She studied being still. Breathing was hardest. To move air in, out, quietly and gently, while one iridescent outburst fired desire for the next—Dora learned.

"O God, whose days are without end, and whose mercies cannot be numbered: Make us, we beseech thee, deeply sensible of the shortness and uncertainty of human life." *Caddy wasn't yet five.*

And Gladys Smith did not stop working. For Miss Dearing, Dora did hand-hemming, repaired buttonholes, let out seams. She turned collars on shirts made of that exquisite Egyptian cotton, replaced frayed lace with fresh on ladies' dresses. Her button collection grew. On an old machine that the dressmaker sold her, Dora did plain seaming: curtains, sheets, spreads, tablecloths. Sewing orgasms were her most intense. Dora sat so that operating the treadle stimulated her. The humming needle raced in crescendo along the seam.... When alone Dora at first cried out—but a shut mouth intensified the final burst, she found, and so kept silent.

Because she sewed at home and kept her work neat and out of sight, Ned had no idea of her hours or her skills, no idea that Gladys Smith still had her own solid bank account and made small regular deposits.

On 5 June 1927, a son was born, easily, at home.

A week later, the returning midwife was pleased. "A natural, you are." Her hands took up handfuls of Dora's flesh. "Tighten yourself inside how I said, Mrs. Dow, so this flab'll go. A tight inside'll make hubby happy too! The sucking helps. My goodness, Baby's latched right on! Another natural. What's his name?"

Ned had stated, "He's my son. John, for my father. Alan can be his second name if you like."

Ned gazed, held, murmured, stroked the new limbs as though the boy and he lived alone in the room, the house, the world.

Dora did not tighten her muscles.

Ned brought her his body.

"The midwife says it's not time yet."

"I'm not healed."

"Not yet! It'll hurt me."

"No, it isn't time."

"I'm not ready."

"*I don't want to!*"

When John was three months old, Prairie Boy forced Sonsy Girl.

"Look, we beseech thee, with compassion upon those who are now in sorrow and affliction; comfort them, O Lord, with thy gracious consolations; make them to know that all things work together for good to them that love thee."

The day after the rape, Dora took her son across the street to Marjo's. Lying on blankets, the babies John and Maureen waved their limbs about and made small sounds: *tseep-tsip, cla-cla*. When John cried, Dora got him up off the floor, opened her stained blouse, held him to her.

"Let *down*, Dora! You're stiff as stone. Your milk can't get out if you're that way. You'll dry up. What's wrong?"

Dreams I know can never be true
Seems as though I'll always be blue

"But Dora, whoever wrote that letter—she's lying. You *know* B.C. Sugar's out to get the fellows, because of the union. They lie and trick, trying to split them up. Of *course* lots of women would write a letter like that for money! Why do you believe it so easy, Dora? Ned wouldn't do that to you, ever."

Silence.

Marjo put her arms round her rigid friend. "Oh, Dora, I want you to be safe! Not alone! With a husband and a home and a baby! And you *are*. That letter can't touch you, Dora. It's gone. As if it's buried a long ways off, in a box with the lid on."

Silence.

"Something else has happened to you, Dora, I know. I've known you all your life, Dora Dow. I love you. What's wrong?"

Silence.

"Please tell?"

"Forasmuch as it hath pleased Almighty God of his great mercy to receive unto himself the soul of our dear child here departed...." *It pleased Him. Pleased Him!*

Dora took John off her breast and went home. While the baby napped, she took off her clothes and looked in the mirror at her raped flesh.

Big vague nipples—not pert, not perky. Brown moons. Fat stomach, fat thighs. Like blancmange when she walked. No, waddled. The thigh flesh rubbed till sores appeared. Under the arms, flesh hung. Under drooping breasts—not delicious palmfuls but bags hanging to the short waist—a rash came if Dora didn't towel herself carefully after a bath. Underpants gouged red lines round the waist. Corselettes did the same to the rib cage. She had haunches, not thighs.

Dora's eyes told her that men with slim wives, when they looked at Ned's wife, looked down on Ned.

Those wives too saw Dora. They pitied Ned. Sex with *us*, with *me*, those slim women thought smugly—how much more that poor man'd enjoy himself! And without even a thought those women, like Marjo, walked and leaned and gestured so as to show off their sleekness. These women pitied Dora too, the way strong healthy people feel sorry for the disabled and the sane for the crazy.

But...Dora's skin, her hair, her legs. Ned went on and on and on about them. ("Surprisingly shapely," Marjo's mother once said of Dora's legs.) Ned covered his head with Dora's long dun hair, wrapped it about his neck. He kissed her scalp. He held her small feet, admiring the arch and the perfect pink nails.

Before the mirror Dora stretched her legs wider and wider until even at the top they were visibly parted.

Once Marjo and Mike, Dora and Ned all went overnight to Bowen Island, camping. As the sun sank, Marjo stood in her trim bathing suit on the beach, looking west, while the others sat on the sand. Gold and bright pink flamed in the sky and in the small triangle between Marjo's legs, just where her graceful thighs curved in under her pussy. Mike and Ned and Dora all three looked up and saw that fiery hole. Dora couldn't look away. That evening Mike drew Marjo into their tent even before the bonfire died down, and during the night Dora heard them going at it again.

Ned—at first, so awkward. *Farm* all over him still, despite his smart city clothes and straw boater. And the way he stepped into Mike and Marjo's boat! *Prairie boy*, terrified on tidewater.

"We therefore commit her body to the ground."

Dora's breasts—Ned groaned on about them too. "They fill me, they fill me." His fingers splayed out over the big bags.

Nursing, baby John cried and dropped Dora's nipple and seized it and didn't get what he wanted, dropped it and cried.

Ned learned to sterilize bottles. At two a.m. he lit the stove and hummed to the hungry baby in the fold of his arm, warmed milk and tested it on his wrist. Lying in the dark marriage bed, Dora heard father and son in the kitchen. Ned murmured. John cried and then gurgled at his bottle. Months later, Dora still sometimes felt phantom milk let down.

Rape made a new baby.

Dora threw up when she smelled scallions in the neighbour's yard. Onions, milk, beer, cheese, yeast—for months these revolted her, and well into the second trimester Dora was still too exhausted to sew much. The Dominion account scarcely grew. For hours each day she lay on the chesterfield, with John inert beside her or crawling slowly but unchecked about the rooms.

"Dirt, dirt, dirt. Filthy, Dora."

Once, after Dora managed to sew a set of bed linen for Miss Dearing, she rode downtown to make a deposit for Gladys Smith. Miss Forbes boarded the Number Twenty. Right then, at Carrall, Dora got off and walked the miles home, carrying John. She told Miss Dearing someone else must help her, and lay still even more.

Again Marjo miscarried.

Holding her friend, stroking her hair, Dora cried as never for herself.

"He shall feed his flock like a shepherd: he shall gather the lambs with his arm, and carry them in his bosom."

When the new baby arrived, Dora recognized her at once.

In Dora's own babyhood, the Cowans had managed to afford some visits to Theo Gates's photography studio on Hastings. Alan, locked in oval sepia all gilded and moulded and pasted on black cardboard, gazed in slender childhood beauty. He grasped a drum or a book or a toy train; even in his christening robes, Alan held a rattle. Baby Dora just sat. Her baby chin doubled. Her knuckles dimpled. Fat creased her wrists and neck.

"Take heed that ye despise not one of these little ones." *Ugly as me, Mary was, right from the start. Ugly as me.* "For I say unto you, that in heaven their angels do always behold the face of my Father which is in heaven." *Caddy was always beautiful.*

John was the first baby, the good baby. As prescribed in *The Normal Child: Its Care and Feeding*, regularly he slept and hungered, but the colicky second-born cried and cried and cried, cried until Dora slapped her, cried more.

The baby was not named deliberately. Ned had no ideas about what to call a girl. *Mary* was simply the first and most ordinary name that entered Dora's head. For her Granny Cowan and for Mademoiselle Annette LeClerc, she added Anne as a middle name.

The colic lasted for months.

"Mary Mary quite contrary!" Ned smiled at the baby, played with her and cuddled her, but when she cried at night he rolled over and pulled the covers up. "You're her mother, Dora. I need my sleep. Canvassing to do for the union, tomorrow after work."

Baby Mary shook away the rubber nipple, grizzling. Then she bit bit bit at the thing. She had to be held in half a dozen positions before she would burp and let go of trapped air. Not for a year did Mary sleep through the night, nor did Dora make a single deposit in Gladys Smith's account.

When Mary was just beginning on solid foods, Dora received another letter on the scalloped notepaper. A third came before the little girl's first birthday. Toddler- and baby-bound, Dora lacked the will for the journey to Wall Street. She memorized the words and threw the pink papers in the stove.

Who, who, who stole my heart away?

Because of John's jealousy, Dora could not leave brother and sister alone for a minute. The two scrapped and snarled. Once John let the baby at the button jar and small Mary nearly choked.

"In heaven their angels do always behold the face of my Father which is in heaven."

In the cramped house on Frances Street the rooms accumulated torn toys, dirty clothes, smeared dishes; they exuded the smells of ammonia, foodstuffs, and soured bottles.

Ned went to Marjo. "Filthy! If she keeps up like this we'll have rats. Can't you speak to her? Aren't you her friend?"

"Dora never drops by, Ned. I'm at three months. That's when I lose them. I've got to be still. No upsets, no running around."

"It's not fair, Marjo! I'm working overtime whenever I can, *for us*, to buy a house. At meetings till all hours, trying to get the union in. I do my part. Why can't Dora do hers? Just cleaning and cooking. It's not as if she had anything else to do."

In bed, Dora lay like the granite bed of a river while Ned exhausted himself on her. As her rock melted, he ran dry and collapsed on the hard shores of her thighs. His teeth scraped and gritted on her flesh.

Dreams I know can never be true
Seems as though I'll ever be blue

Marjo was still pregnant when Ned found the house at 202 Garden Drive North. The two women walked slowly over to see it.

Raw lumber—the smell filled the street. Everywhere, sawdust sifted down. Skiffs of new green grass patched the slope down to Wall, and all over Highlands the city was planting oak trees. The Dows' present house faced a larger one that blocked the light, but here the spring sun shone right into the front room. By its bay window stood a radiator; its familiar handle imprinted warm petals on Dora's palm.

"Dora," Marjo said as they wandered through the rooms, "Mum says Miss Dearing's retiring. You could set up as a dressmaker. You could buy her good Singer, Dora. Her notions. Her fabric."

"O God whose ways are hidden and thy works most wonderful, who makest nothing in vain and lovest all that thou hast made, comfort thou thy servants, whose hearts are sore smitten and oppressed."

In front of Dora, Ned got down on his knees. "For whatever I've done, I'm sorry. I love you. Please. We're moving to a new house. Can't we start again—Sonsy Girl and Prairie Boy? *Please.*"

Dora cooked a proper supper and served it on time in a clean kitchen. John sat up nicely at table. Mary, sullen but quiet, watched from her high chair.

Dora said to her husband, "I have some money saved up. For the house."

On the first night at Garden Drive, Dora leaned out of the window of the big bedroom. The ornamental cherries planted by the city, little saplings, were in bloom. Lumber, saltchuck, wet grass, and fish wafted in the summer air. She'd sewn flowered curtains for this window; now Dora drew them closed. Going up to Ned, she stood so her body touched his.

Ned's birthday present to Dora in August 1928 was an add-a-pearl necklace with three pearls already strung—one for John, one for Mary, the largest and most lustrous for

Dora in remembrance of their wedding day. Soon Ned knew that next February he'd need another pearl. He'd move all Dora's sewing stuff and nonsense out of the tiny fourth bedroom and down to the angle under the staircase.

"Open thou our eyes, we beseech thee...." *Caddy opened her eyes and looked right at me.*

Carol, the new baby started out. Ned added the *e*. "It looks classy like that." Then, Marjo's mother had an old friend in England with twin granddaughters, Miranda and Amanda. Mrs. McEwan had forgotten what Miranda meant but knew Amanda was *to be loved*. Soon, Carole Amanda Dow became Caddy.

Who, who, who stole my heart away?
Who makes me dream all day?
Who means my happiness? Who
Would I answer "Yes" to?

For Caddy's first birthday party, Marjo baked the cake, as she had done each year for John and for Mary. She studded the cake with pink sugar roses and draped pink swags on the pearl-white icing. Mike, Marjo, Mick, Maureen, and the new baby, Murray, all came over to the Dows' house to celebrate.

Mary wouldn't leave the cake alone. "I want to eat a rosebud! Now!" She pulled at the tablecloth.

"Oh oh, who's my big girl? Who's my grown-up girl?" After a few minutes' private time with Ned, Mary was smiling.

To Marjo, Ned praised the cake warmly. A look passed between Dora's husband and Dora's friend. Dora saw. She stood rigid.

Mary let Caddy at the button jar. The toddler nearly choked.

Until Caddy died, the Dora-Marjo friendship went into ice-cold storage.

"Thou hast now taken this child into the arms of thy love."

At Mountain View Cemetery in 1934, however, Marjo stood right by Dora's side as she had done in 1918. As then, Marjo placed her warm firm hand on her friend's shoulder when the gravedigger's shovel bit into the gravelly soil and threw its first load down. Dora's body received the fall. Marjo felt the shock in her own flesh. Small stones chattered on the polished wood. Deafening. Then more and more darkness thudded down on Dora until there was no light left at all and the young mother disappeared.

The 1920s—Jonathan Tries to Help

In the garden at the Sasamat house, Arthur Smyth sat by marble Amelia and talked soundlessly to her. His settled pose suggested he'd been consulting with his wife for some time.

During his childhood, this scene upset Jonathan deeply each time he witnessed it. He ran away, hid, never told, not even Hilda. Now Jonathan Smyth, just arrived from Montreal as a freshly baked McGill M.D., wiped his eyes as he stood watching under the flowering trees. He was home, for good.

In fact he stayed only till he found a suite at the Homer Apartments. "You'll have the place to yourself at last, Dad!"

Arthur Smyth snorted. "You young people don't see what's plain as a pikestaff, do you?"

After his father explained, Jonathan went to Hilda. "Uncle George living here—fine, he and Dad have always got on well. And Flossie, if she were still here, she was always so sweet, but Aunt Julie? If she weren't Mother's older sister, he'd never...."

"But she is." Hilda's hands moved on pastry dough.

For the first time Jonathan put out his own garbage, changed his own washers, chose furniture for his own apartment and for his new office in the Vancouver Block. Second-hand, he bought a bird's-eye maple table, battered but well-proportioned, with a handsome grain, to be the central feature of his living room.

Arranging his new goods and chattels, he thought of ages. Aunt Julie was seventy-eight. Uncle George, seventy-three. Dad, sixty-five. Hilda, forty-three. Now Hilda would have children to look after all over again: old ones. Had Hilda ever wanted her own babies? Wanted a non-Smyth life?

Shame at these questions' novelty drove Jonathan to Aunt Julie's dark fusty house on Haro Street, soon to be sold. A lavatory now occupied the front hall's closet. The upper floor was no longer in use. Cardigans and combs and Church papers lay about the drawing room.

Immediately his aunt warned, "Now, Jonathan, don't you get too big for your britches just because you're a doctor. You're not important in the world, you know."

The homemade caraway biscuits Wong brought in with the tea were also the same as ever.

When Jonathan raised the matter of Hilda, Aunt Julie's gaze grew melancholy and compassionate. Her mouth worked; the hairs along her upper lip twitched. Then she fiddled with a starched doily, slapped it on her chair's arm. "Nonsense. Hilda's been very lucky. They beat her, out at that farm in Eburne."

When Jonathan left, he went to the hospital, for an evening meeting about Ward X, and then home to 208 Homer Street, Suite Eight. Home, homer, homest. Eight divided into both 1272 and 208. *The residence of Dr. Jonathan Smyth, well-known in Vancouver medical circles as a....* Already he saw that, compared to the Royal Victoria in Montreal, the General was a disgrace. Ward X! Jonathan imagined McGill's Dean McCurdy bellowing outrage in that airless cellar among addicts, psychopaths, cancer patients, a woman struggling with an abortion gone septic....

He lay sleepless, Hilda and Aunt Julie and his father filling his mind. *Rattlebrain! What good does this do?* But his eyes wouldn't close. And what had happened to the man he'd wheeled into St. Paul's, the day of that riot? *Did I do any good, then? And that girl. She wouldn't even let me try to help her.*

A caraway seed emerged from between two of Jonathan's teeth, trailing its acrid taste.

The first time his uncle and aunt sat at table as residents of Sasamat, Jonathan helped prepare dinner. "Hilda, I can't imagine me and my brothers living together when we're old."

"D'you suppose these three ever dreamed they'd have to do this?" Hilda tipped sauce into a pitcher. "Your dad's putting in a ground-floor lavatory. Under the stairs."

Jonathan stopped licking butterscotch off the spoon. That angular space had always, always held schoolbooks, rugby boots, racquets, coathooks that once seemed for ever out of reach.

Hilda nodded at the potatoes. "Slice, please. Not too thin."

As he peeled, Jonathan's fingers got wrinkled and gritty. *How many times have I done this?*

Hilda opened her own recipe book, pushed her thumb along the gutter to flatten the page. Her chin formed puffy folds as she looked down to read. Setting the volume aside, she reached for a mixing bowl. The cook's stance seemed statuesque, fixed. Her big hands had always been mixing that stuffing for the salmon; they always lifted and let fall those buttery crumbs, tarragon, celery. Husband? Children? He couldn't ask. Hilda rinsed her fingers and began slicing lemons.

At dinner, Aunt Julie ate butterscotch sauce greedily. *Did she ever want children?*

At his boarding house where he stayed during his time at medical school at McGill, in Montreal's student quarter, Jonathan once found Madame's calico cat asleep on his bed. He admired her harlequin coat. Movement inside her startled him. Arlette opened one citron eye, closed it. He laid his hand on her, to feel life.

When the kittens were born a month later, Jonathan was flat on his back with flu, but Madame insisted that he come downstairs to see. Gripping Jonathan's arm, she pulled him through the kitchen—dazed, he saw her stove was a Western Treasure, like Hilda's—and into a storeroom reeking of blood and birth.

Arlette emitted a long rippling multi-toned call of delight. Then she screeched. By her back legs lay a black wriggle veiled in membrane. With impossible grace the cat flexed her spine and washed the newborn, purring top-volume purrs rounded off by upcurled squeaks of joy.

"*Elle est heureuse,*" Jonathan managed in his fractured British Columbia French, through tears.

"Of course!" Madame Dancette did not even bother to speak her own language to him. She frowned. "A normal birth. Joy, and pain. Always both. Remember that, Mr. Doctor." Invariably, Jonathan thought first of pain.

Two more kittens were born. Arlette's tongue rasped away the membrane; she ate the ropy stuff, licked her vulva clean. The kittens found the fat white nipples poking through her motley fur, mewed and sucked, flexed their minute claws.

"No." Madame stopped Jonathan's reaching hand. "Your smell will be on the kittens. She might kill them."

The cat purred on her bloody bed; her body circled these beings who, to live, must smell right. Then a fifth kitten emerged but lay limp under Arlette's licking. Had it died days before the labour? Or, only minutes ago as it waited its turn for the birth canal, had some jostling sib snapped the lifeline? Only a moment: everything changed. So with his mother's death. As much as if she'd lived, her death shaped and defined her children's futures. *Why didn't that doctor take better care?*

Arlette stretched her back legs; the placenta slid out. Crouching, she sniffed and ate.

Madame gestured—*So it goes.* "She is happy with her babies. As you will be a happy father, one day," she added, didactically.

"I don't plan to take that chance, Madame."

Her eyebrows went up. "Plans and life differ." She took the dead kitten by the tail and raised the lid on the waste bucket. Then she gave Jonathan camomile tea to take upstairs.

Back in bed, Jonathan felt fever take hold. Flannelette and wool sheathed him in soreness. He spilled his tea. When he tried to read, his head throbbed. He turned out the light and saw how, beyond the dormer window, the night sky curved dark blue. Flakes of snow drifted past. *If that streetlight weren't there, I could see the stars.* How many times had he thought that? His brain forgot how to multiply and divide. Stars and days and kittens criss-crossed.

Jonathan dreamed of holding his dear newborn cat, a tabby with two heads like a Pushme-Pullyou, that purred doubly and stropped its noses on his hands. Then in a hospital lab he found himself holding a pan of sliced cat, its eyes clouded, dull fur bloody. *But I didn't mean to kill you!* He woke up sobbing.

In the morning, feverless Jonathan found Arlette lapping cream; he remembered the bottles at home, from the Avalon ranch, with their scrolled tops, standing by the kitchen door. Illicit, his finger dipped into inches of cream.... Arlette's whiskers bore beads of white. Weakly, he cried to hear the kittens mewing in bewilderment at the great warmth's absence. Milksop!

෴

"To the idiocy of patients, gentlemen," intoned Dean McCurdy of McGill's medical school, "there is no end." He swept up a black-gowned arm and ticked off on his fingers. "A man complained bitterly of deafness, bitterly I say, when his personal hygiene was so deficient that his ears were full of wax as an egg of meat. Another declared beef pernicious to health, yet, falling victim to anaemia, he wondered why." Here the Dean sipped water.

Sighing, Jonathan and his friends laid down their pens.

"And as for the ladies.... One told me not six months ago she'd cured herself of tuberculosis by dosing with peppermint tea. Straightfaced, I say. Stone dead now, stone. And another got it through her poor muddled head she should start her bairn on vegetables at three months of age. Worse dehydration caused by diarrhea I never saw, gentlemen. And then the little lady at home for hours in agony. Appendicitis. Why did she not visit our fine hospital? Why, I say? Her menses, gentlemen. In that distasteful condition she did not wish to cast aside her nether garments before the inquiring eyes of men. And what came of maiden modesty? Peritonitis." Crashingly the Dean cleared his throat.

Jonathan went into his head. Aunt Julie said at once, *He's too big for his britches!* Then Arthur Smyth's weary tone came. *Your brother Geoffrey doesn't mend. What's to become of him?*

McCurdy's answer was easily imagined. *These moral weaklings...Wilfrid Owen....Fiddling about with brains like our young Dr. Penfield! Buck up. Chin up. Bear it. This so-called war poetry!* The acid explosion of that *p* would curdle cream.

"Gentlemen, a policeman doesn't chat with criminals, a banker doesn't gossip with depositors, and a McGill-trained medical man doesn't palaver with patients. Tell them the minimum! More...Pandora's box. Muddles. Mishearings. *Disagreements!* No no, alone we bear our great responsibility. Alone, I say."

Too big! Jonathan laughed out loud.

"Mr. Smyth, I'll see you in my office."

After the apology, McCurdy critiqued Jonathan's plans for specializing. "Chop and change, young man? First you thought of epidemiology because of the Spanish flu, and now you're thinking of obstetrics because of a death on the prairies? Unsteady."

Jonathan thought about an obstetrical death on the West Coast. Every day of his life he thought about it. Sometimes he thought he'd never be able to think of anything else but the tiny time, the handful of seconds in which *something might have been done*, that invisible inaudible clock of the body ticking *Help me, help me.* "I'm quite certain."

The longshoreman who collapsed before him at the riot in Vancouver: had he lived, or died, because of Jonathan's intervention? The girl, that same day, stood dirty-faced and dirty-skirted, her legs bruised, her hair a wild feathery mess about her head. Clearly her errand was as desperate as she. That girl hunched over the bike as if pursued, but all Jonathan did was call after her, *Can I help you?* Did she get *there*, wherever it was, inside that tiny time?

"Quite certain, Dean McCurdy." He didn't mention that before obstetrics and before epidemiology there'd been linguistics. That had lasted nearly two years.

"*Quite*? A qualifier? A year from now will you be *quite certain* about something else?"

❧

In April of 1927, at the Sisters of Mercy Hospital in Saskatoon, a frozen newborn was found on the stone steps just by Shipping & Receiving. The night watchman believed he'd heard a cat yowling. That was on the first day of Jonathan's practicum with Dr. Albert.

A fortnight later, prairie spring arrived in a rush. With delight everyone sloughed off parka, boots, scarf, mitts, fur hat; Jonathan was at his coastal weight again, but, even as he looked with pleasure at the huge skies alive with birds and the bright green sheeting the rich soil, he longed for cedar and dark Douglas fir, for sandstone caves on wide misty beaches. Remembering that girl with the luminous hair, he set her, with him, on such a beach. While they talked, tidewater filmed the sand so it shone under thick grey cloud cover.... However, since UBC had as yet no medical school, here on the wide prairie Jonathan must finish out his first two years.

He slumped in his chair. "I'm so tired."

Dr. Albert snorted. "Take the crop off, make a baby. It's the same, every May and June. Who's next, Sir Medical Student?"

Mrs. Hawrylko was short, thin except for her pregnancy. Her fair hair, bundled up at her nape, curled delicately. Jonathan asked her all the questions appropriate for the third trimester. On examination, all looked and felt normal.

Dr. Albert double-checked quickly, eyes and hands everywhere at once, fingers light yet firm and confident. "Good!" But he frowned. "So why're you here? Nothing's wrong with you."

"This baby"—and Jonathan saw Mrs. Hawrylko arranging the English syntax in her head—"feels not like my other children."

Mentally glancing at a language-map, Jonathan saw Ukrainian with her Slavic sisters near Indo-Iranian and Italic. "Not like? How?" He composed his features lest she think him cross too.

Gracefully Mrs. Hawrylko raised her hands and placed them low, beneath her child. "It feels more tighter. Here."

Jonathan laid his hand by hers. Dr. Albert did the same and shrugged. "It feels fine, Mrs. H."

"Different...." Then Mrs. Hawrylko giggled at Jonathan's worried face. "But I don't know how to say, English."

"Tough as boots, these Ukies," Dr. Albert advised later. "Don't waste your time with questions, son. People *enjoy* talking to the doctor. Fine, but we've got better things to do."

A few weeks later, a three a.m. call roused Jonathan. Mrs. Hawrylko lay on the operating table. By now Jonathan knew blood well—but not like this. Surgery produced a dead boy, whom a nurse set aside to watch the hemorrhaging mother die from shock.

"Nature!" shouted Dr. Albert. His shoes were scarlet.

Jonathan picked up the perfect baby.

"Nature," said Dr. Albert again, at dawn in the cafeteria with Jonathan, speaking low as if in contempt.

The floor had been washed, the bodies removed, the lights turned out in the operating room, the husband told. Morning chores awaited him at the farm; he was heading back.

The coffee poured fresh and strong.

"Jonathan, Nature's a bloody fool female who doesn't know when to kill. Remember that, Sir Medical Student."

"I don't understand."

"One in a million, Mrs. H. You'll never see it again in all your career, I guarantee. Ectopic pregnancy.... Remember that little farm girl a while back? That's what *should* happen.

There's only one place babies should grow. When they don't, Nature's supposed to throw them out. But she's a bad housekeeper. Dust under the beds, mould on the cheese, a nasty outhouse. Like that." Dr. Albert moved his coffee cup off the paper placemat and took out a pencil. He drew. "Amazing, isn't it?" He admired his sketch. "Mrs. H. took an extra-uterine pregnancy almost to full term, bless her. That boy could have made sixty and seen Halley's Comet come again. Or eighty, and seen the new millennium."

"But couldn't we have told, if we knew what to look for?"

"You examined Mrs. H. Was there anything of note?"

Jonathan saw pale skin, silvery stretchmarks. Her nails were cut short. When she giggled, how her pointed features changed!

"She said it felt *different*. We should have listened."

"Mrs. H. couldn't say how, though, could she? Not her fault. And we couldn't teach her English. Not ours."

"But...her children," Jonathan remonstrated, thinking of Richard and Geoffrey and himself. "She has little children."

"Now now now," Dr. Albert remonstrated in turn. "You don't want to head down that trail any further, my boy. Too sad."

⎯⎯⎯ ✿ ⎯⎯⎯

While he was attending the University of British Columbia, Jonathan's favourite route home was down the timbered hillside to Spanish Banks and so along the beach.

One pale spring day, when his linguistics professor had lost his temper over a silly student joke about the Great Bowel Shift, Jonathan as he walked over the smooth sand looked across to the toy-town of West End rooftops.

Somewhere amid them stood Aunt Julie's house (Uncle George's too, but no one ever called it so) where she once barked so shockingly at that dressmaker. Shame: Jonathan felt it burn still. *I couldn't do anything.* That silent girl who'd come to Haro Street with Miss Dearing wore an expression that Jonathan still struggled to name—resistance? endurance? refusal? On the front porch beside the dressmaker she stood, stood unmoving before Aunt Julie's shouts.

Jonathan turned his gaze to sad Grandview.

He was almost home when there came towards him, through the hedge that bordered the beach side of the Smyths' property on Sasamat, a thin old man. He moved furtively, his face half-concealed by a hat, and rammed his hands deep in his pockets. Because he glanced about at the riotous salal and Oregon grape as if at enemies, he did not see Jonathan until they almost touched.

"Geoffrey! Are you going for a walk?"

"What the hell does it look like?" Abruptly he changed tone. "Little brother—come with me?"

Once on the sands, Geoffrey went east at a slow trot. "This morning I went seventeen minutes. Longest yet. Trying again."

"Where?" Jonathan trotted alongside his older brother.

Geoffrey laughed. "Away from the house. To a far country where I don't have hysterics. Or sweat till my clothes drip. Or curl up like a salted slug." He took Jonathan's hand. "Sorry. *There.*" He pointed. Smoke held low over False Creek, sails flickered and smokestacks breathed out on English Bay. "To Granville, Burrard, Pender. Any busy street. Any!" The brothers moved in companionable silence. "Don't know what to say, little brother? Me neither." Geoffrey let go Jonathan's hand but stayed close. "Talk. Tell me about UBC, out there on the Point. On the point indeed... dammit. The sarcasm just comes. Sorry. Please?"

Hesitant at first, Jonathan described linguistics with Eberts, Anglo-Saxon with Livermore. His voice sounded hollow in the salt air, but Geoffrey's gait stayed steady, so Jonathan went on for some time about Halkomelem, Squamish, Straits, and his professor's conviction that these were *real* languages. "Like French or German. Systems. They're not written, though. Don't you think a real *language* has to be on paper, Geoffrey?"

But Jonathan was alone by the grey-green water.

When he reached the fallen figure on the sand, Jonathan wound his arms tight round Geoffrey and sat so till the trembling lessened and the breathing normalized.

Geoffrey checked his watch. "Twenty-two minutes out of the house! With you, little brother, I've gone five more. It's the longest time yet."

Together they struggled back to the garden. Wordless, they passed their marble mother Amelia and entered Hilda's kitchen.

That night, Jonathan flipped through his text on linguistic theory while the tide pulled out from the beach.

Because I was there, that attack wasn't so bad. Better than if he'd been alone. The wounded man, the desperate girl... their images came to him. *At least this time I was of use.*

Jonathan wiped his eyes and began to study the tables and lists for the Great Vowel Shift.

1919—Dora, Working Retail

Mrs. Sinclair, a thin spry woman, owned Martine's Dress Shop (large letters) & Dry Goods (small) in the fourteen-hundred block on Commercial. Because her ambitions reached beyond the East End, she made her salesgirls refer to women's underwear as *lingerie*, not *lonjeray*, and she required them to assume French work-names.

"Helene, Annette, Chantal, Marie, Josette.... Take your pick." Mrs. Sinclair pursed her lips. "Perhaps not Chantal, there's nothing like that in English."

Dora's grandmother was Annie Cowan, the never-met and hardworking seamstress back in England who saved her money and sent pearls, out of love, so Dora picked Annette. Mrs. Sinclair added LeClerc.

Early in 1919, still stunned by death, Dora came to Martine's. The shop catered to matrons, but young Dora's figure did not intimidate the customers. She worked capably and without enthusiasm. The nearby shops—tinsmith, baker, bicycle shop, printer—offered goods at first no less interesting to her than the hang of a gored skirt or the quality of serge. But Dora learned to say, "That's got good wear in it, ma'am," as if it mattered to her. Soon enough it did.

Unlike the other girls, Dora never attempted a French accent. Nor did she giggle when during the February sale Miss Acorn of Domestic Science entered Martine's and Mrs. Sinclair, smiling her limited smile, said, "Mademoiselle Annette will be happy to attend you, Madame."

When her customer selected a coat in brown Melton, Dora got her to try the same model in a garnet red. She turned up the collar by Miss Acorn's pale cheek. The teacher smiled into the long mirror. Standing by her, Dora on impulse untied the self-belt, a thick strip knotted in front. Miss Acorn ceased to be a belted sausage as the coat's line ran straight and slim.

"Thank you, Miss LeClerc," said Miss Acorn as she paid.

"That," said Mrs. Sinclair to her assembled girls at the close of business, "is *selling*."

Dora took the compliment home to her housekeeping room, where she kept only herself. She counted her earnings to date; they were stuffed into the Toby jug. (On Cambridge Street she'd kept her money in a jar buried under the front porch.)

That night she awoke, breaking a dream in half, when a voice like Miss Acorn's sounded. "Your friend's all done." Camphor, violets filled the air. Marjo sobbed by her bed. Dora saw Owen's dirty scabbed face, felt the strong pull of his hand. The tall boy's shirt was white, so white....

To calm herself, Dora remembered her working day. She had received praise. A small energy stirred in her.

Next day at the Royal Bank, the girl at the wicket had recently shopped with her mother at Martine's. "Good morning, Miss LeClerc," this teller said. Opening the account in that name was thus simple. Now truly Dora's money was well hidden.

In late June when Mrs. Sinclair was ordering autumn stock, she and Dora paged through the travellers' design books.

"At least skirts are no higher this year," Mrs. Sinclair said. "But these styles don't allow for hips. And see this." Her finger stabbed at a typical dress. A georgette collar, fringed, met a broad crushed-velvet belt that gathered a messaline tunic in folds over the garment itself. "Such fullness! Who can wear it? A broom-handle like me, but you? Our customers?"

"Girls will love these styles, though. My friend Marjo...."

"Martine sells to Mrs., not Miss. Years I've spent, building up this clientele." Wearily Mrs. Sinclair took off her glasses, rubbed her brow. "My head hurts. Let's finish tomorrow."

That evening Dora took the design books... home.

After her solitary supper she walked over to Cambridge Street and up the steps of the Cowans' old house, where she took a deep breath and knocked on the door to the upstairs suite. Since the triple funeral, she and Miss Dearing had not met. Slow footsteps came down, and the door opened.

The dressmaker saw the young round face, so solemn. "Come in, dear, do."

They looked at the design books, and then Miss Dearing cranked out her dummy, Liza, into her most rotund form. She and Dora arranged lengths over Liza's shoulders, like stoles; they crimped fabric into vertical tucks running from neck to waist.

"Now, Liza," said Miss Dearing, "we'll just see how this'll drape across your tum-tum here. My, that's a sweet line. Lovely in a fine wool, eh Liza? Or in silk."

The two folded cloth on the bias and fixed it diagonally to Liza's hips. The steel-headed pins ticked on her metal. In the books, Dora marked the styles best for Martine's.

Next day Dora reported all to Mrs. Sinclair. "And in *dull* fabrics." She consulted her notes. "Vertical lines. Good drape. And at the shoulders, lace or ruching. Frogs. Knots."

"*And* hems," said her employer. "Fringe, scalloping, anything to draw the eye down, especially if a girl's got nice legs, like you. A row of good buttons does wonders. Never forget buttons!"

Mrs. Sinclair then gave Dora a discount on a dress she'd seen the girl fingering on the rack. In striped artificial silk, pale green on dark, its bias-cut skirt fluttered becomingly just below the knee. Not since the deaths had Dora worn new clothing. The stuff slid cool over her skin.

"I hope you have someplace nice to wear that?"

"The Victory celebration at English Bay. I'm going with Monique and Josette."

Later, the two other salesgirls told Mrs. Sinclair about their outing. "We had such fun! But Annette got all shaky. She said there were too many people and wanted to be alone. So she went *home!* She missed the dancing on the beach."

In the autumn, stock moved out of Martine's as fast as the girls could arrange the window displays and the dress racks. Mrs. Sinclair thanked Dora. To her customers, she said, "A wonder for alterations to ladies' dresses, Miss Dearing is, and really most reasonable." She also raised Dora's wages.

Resentful, two other girls began to pilfer. Dora sensed something wrong; Mrs. Sinclair kept the accounts strictly to herself, but Dora knew what usually appeared in Martine's till during a rainy midweek or on a bright payday. She told Mrs. Sinclair, though she named no names. The girls were fired. For Mademoiselle Annette LeClerc's bank account, a fine Christmas bonus resulted. The following spring, Dora on her own went through the travellers' design books and made out the fall order.

Dora received two more wage increases, two more Christmas bonuses. Mrs. Sinclair began hinting at a partnership.

Late in 1922, Dora moved to an apartment in a brand-new building on Commercial just south of Hastings. She was just settling herself there, in a way quite different from her bewildered frantic flight to Templeton Drive, when Mrs. Sinclair visited her doctor because of a vague unbalanced feeling.

"It's all over," said Dora's employer next day. Looking frail, Mrs. Sinclair sat by the cash register—unheard of! She was always on her feet in the shop. "I'm going home to Ontario. My sister's. In St. Thomas." Uneasily she touched her head and then gestured at the bright dress racks, the camisoles layered on the counters, the cotton batting and holly in the windows. "All this has to be ... done."

Because Mrs. Sinclair could think only of her brain tumour, Dora organized the closing-out sale. She interviewed prospective buyers, advised on their offers. Eventually Martine's went to a man with a wife and daughters all ready to work in the shop, so Dora paid out the last wages to Helene, Jeannette, and herself.

Less than a month later, Dora in her new sitting room sorted needles and embroidery silks into the set of sewing drawers she'd bought. Close by stood Miss Dearing's old Singer. Curtains, slipcovers, bedspread—Dora had sewn them all for herself, set them in place. Through the north-facing window of her kitchen, snowy light poured in. Plenty of money lay in Annette LeClerc's bank account, and Mrs. Sinclair had written an excellent letter of reference, but another future had been torn away.

The War Before

Armistice

Neurasthenia. More and more frequently as the end of the war came nearer, Jonathan saw this bizarre word in the newspapers, along with *shell shock, nervous prostration, breakdown.*

When Geoffrey came home to Vancouver, he fainted on the granite floor of the CPR station. Hilda supported his head. Arthur Smyth chafed his son's hands. At the continent's edge, the empty troop train sighed. Jonathan didn't recognize this fallen man with the grey skin. What to do? He noted the engine's number in his diary.

A fortnight later a grinning Richard jumped off his train into his family's arms. Now at last would Jonathan hear tales of bloody gallantry he could carry to school?

Because of the flu, Arthur didn't drive his beautiful McLaughlin Touring through downtown on the way home. "Stay away from people, boys," the father warned. "Stay away."

Richard changed into civvies at once. Neither he nor Geoffrey ever wore uniform again, ignoring pleas for photographs.

As the flu invaded the city, Hilda kept Jonathan from school. Arthur ran Smyth, Stationer by phone and messenger boy. Geoffrey went nowhere, but Richard flung out to see all his friends. "I didn't go to war to stay shut up at home. Cheerio!"

December. Geoffrey stepped into the garden. Wet bronze foliage coated paths, raspberry canes, Amelia's marble curls. He went down to the cold quiet sands and watched how the rain netted the ocean's surface.

Hilda and Jonathan regularly visited the fruitcakes in the pantry. They peeled away cheesecloth, stabbed with skewers, poured in brandy. This pleasant work done, Hilda made tea. She pointed to a photo in the *Province*. "Look at her. This flu!"

Three coffins. A church. A girl, plump like a black pear, or like a seal. Her wind-blown hair waved. She held her coat close.

"What will happen to her?" Imagine if everyone were gone! Father, Richard, Geoffrey, Aunt Flossie, Uncle George, even Aunt Julie (but Jonathan wouldn't miss her). "What will she do?"

"Be poor. Alone. That's All Saints, way out east. No crumblies or shortbread for that girl. Scrape the bowl now."

After tea came word from the farm (Hilda's brother Jim now ran it—not well). Sister Emily, only eighteen, had typhoid.

Near midnight Jonathan realized what his imagination had assumed: that he and Hilda would, must survive any disaster. He got out of bed then and at his desk wrote out a cake-feeding schedule. If he did everything right, Hilda would return from the farm, to her attic room now so peculiarly empty.

The Smyths attended young Emily's funeral. In the car coming home, Geoffrey's shiver made his teeth click like stacked plates.

Christmas was imminent. Aunt Julie found the preparations demanding. "Arthur, you should tell that girl of yours to get back here where she belongs."

"Don't talk as if Hilda were a Chink or a Jap! She's one of *us*. And *my* servant. She'll stay out at Eburne with her family as long as she likes."

At the festive but somewhat disorganized meal, Aunt Julie complained. "Boys, you never speak of what you did in the war. So selfish! You were part of Britain's victory. Why can't your family hear?"

Geoffrey pushed back his chair and rose gabbling, "Lice and rats, Aunt Julie. Crumps. Rat bites. Mud. Blood. Shit. Roar. No, I won't stop, Dad, yes we'd shit ourselves, step on dead heads. Live men are squashy too, Aunt Julie, except if bayonet hits bone. Then they flap like gaffed fish, but the French rivers were mud. Amiens lasted five days. I held back. True, Dad. Your son! Another Vancouver boy stepped ahead. Have you ever held an eye in your hand? I held his. Bigger than you'd expect. He had curly blond hair. Then I ran bravely forward—forward, Aunt Julie! To get killed. I tried. I tried."

Geoffrey left. The kitchen's swing door went back and forth, each time scribing a shorter arc. Sixteen swings. Jonathan's age.

Aunt Julie broke the silence. "Jonathan, for goodness' sake get your wits together and bring in the pudding."

Geoffrey now kept to the house, to his own room.

In the New Year, wards and clinics released fewer dead and more living. Jonathan returned to school, Arthur Smyth to work. Hilda mourned. Briskly, Richard canvassed banks and brokers' offices for jobs. To be a millionaire by thirty, married, the father of a son: these were his ambitions.

Spring came, summer came.

For Jonathan's seventeenth birthday, his father gave him a telescope, early. Before going to English Bay for the Victory celebrations on Dominion Day, he sat in his bedroom's window seat to watch the crowds gather. For months, the epidemic had inhibited civic revel. For this one day, death was to be ignored. Geoffrey would not go, though, and Richard, with army friends, headed in the other direction; they would take the ferry to the North Shore to climb Seymour and camp out.

Through the magic lens Jonathan identified, first, 1272 Davie Street. On Beach, he saw, new houses were a-building; he could pick out individual planks and even knotholes in the stacked lumber. Already people were thick on the sands. He counted feathers in one lady's boa and then watched a plump girl, plump as a pear, re-pin her hat. Her striped dress fluttered, green on green. She couldn't see him, but he saw her pretty legs. He felt himself rise, fumbled at his trousers.

Downstairs, he saw that Hilda was making chicken sandwiches. He heard her sobs, the slow deep kind that endure through solitary duties.

Back in his room, Jonathan remade his bed, doing proper mitred corners. He rearranged his natural history collection—stones, shells, skeletons. After half an hour he went down again.

"Yes, I put lots of salt. Don't squash those berries! And Chelsea buns. No, I'm not up to going. You'll meet your father."

As Jonathan walked along the beach to the last streetcar stop on the line, he kicked and kicked at the sand. Once on board, he heard the wheels clack *Hilda's not here, not here, not here.* The worst was that he knew it was only pretence to think he might go back to comfort her.

Clickety-clack past 1272 Davie. Jonathan glared. A paper-weight snowstorm, a calico kitten—these images of his childhood were not his, he knew. He'd been told about them.

"You liked your ducky coverlet," Richard told him.

"Mallards? Scoters? Don't laugh!"

"Red and blue duckies! In threes. With curly tails."

Straining for memory, Jonathan squeezed his head. *There my mother died. I hate Aunt Julie.* He ate his strawberries.

At Denman Jonathan stepped, scowling, off into the roaring crowd, into brass bands thumping "Say a Prayer for the Boys Out There," photographers, speeches, ice cream, cheers, patriotic waves splashing madly blue, fried fish, "When Your Boy Comes Back to You," sweat, egg salad, pork pies, beer, hurdy-gurdies and screaming children and clowns, "The Anchor's Weighed," sobbing parents and lovers, "Tom Bowling," banners billowing from the Sylvia

Hotel, flags, balloons, uniforms, Panamas, and so many pretty dresses a-flutter. Where was that green-striped girl?

Nowhere.

No one.

Just as on the August day of the strike and the riot, Jonathan felt utterly forlorn among the crowd. There but not there. Not engaged, not involved. A milksop, always dreaming of a mother who never was and a world that never happened.

I'll run away. Jonathan sat on the sand, facing the ocean, and ran, which mean that he went into his big head.

Across the city, past Grandview where his mother and father once planned to live, before Jonathan came and his mother left, lay three small lakes. He loved to think of them. Silent among fir and swaying cedar, sipped by elk and wolf and beaver, by deer and vole, these lakes made links with streams that flowed through cranberry swamps and among huge timbers down to the salt marshes where Burrard Inlet narrowed for the second time.

(In fact, when the railway ran from New Westminster those lakes had been filled in, as Jonathan well knew. Now earth from the Grandview Cut filled in False Creek . . . but he shook his head.)

Jonathan saw the king seal, pursued by Chief Capilano, still heading for those lakes. He still swam underground, far under, through the secret waterway that started at False Creek and led to those three pools. *To strive, to seek, to find, and not to yield!* The pain of the spear embedded in his back—that great animal endured it. Peer of Ulysses, he exerted his full self, escaped all the Chief's wiles and skills, and triumphantly swam along the chain of those three pearls that shimmered under the moon.

Capilano never got his spear back, either. Only the frayed rope.

A band marched and crunched over the beach, right behind Jonathan, and whined into "Just a Baby's Prayer at Twilight." He came back to English Bay, sighing. For some minutes he sat aimlessly throwing sand at the sea. The grains sank, dispersed.

When Jonathan got up to brush off his trousers, the fluttering green dress was there.

The girl was almost tearful. She was walking as fast as she could in her strappy shoes but not straight, because she kept looking over her shoulder at a trio of photographers who strolled not far behind, casual yet alert for any striking image in the crowded colour swirling over the beach. The girl tripped and almost fell against Jonathan. He put a steadying hand on her shoulder and blushed horribly at the memory of what he'd done with her, to her, earlier in the morning, from afar.

"I must get away from them." She blurted some such— Jonathan could never remember exactly—with a catch in her voice—but he'd heard that sound before. Where? Without meeting his eyes she headed up the beach towards the car stop at Denman and Davie. He followed. In the loose sand, she almost went over on her slender ankle. Jonathan took her arm, aided her over tussocks and drift-wood to the sidewalk. The green dress fluttered against his own legs. Milk-white her skin was, her cheeks flushed, damp with agitation. Under her shady hat, her abundant short-cropped hair shone with health, its filaments a radi-ant aureole; sweat glittered at her nape (where had he seen that?) and on her arms; her green dress gleamed in the sun.

When they reached the boardwalk, the girl did not stop and turn and look up at Jonathan and say, *Thank you so much for helping me* and smile politely. She just boarded the wait-ing streetcar and walked right to the end, where the seats were shaded by street trees. She sat down. She faced for-ward, her body stiff, urgent, but for some time the smiling motorman went on looking at the crowd before at last he checked his watch and set down his paper and took hold of the controls. The girl sat still. Where had Jonathan met her? Her hat moved away.

When he turned back to the beach, the photographers stood clustered by the blue frilly waves with a young mother and her infant. "Look, baby! The whole world's there, across the water!"

Arthur Smyth came towards his son, carrying two chocolate ice creams and smiling fondly.

November 1918—Dora, Riding the Cars Back and Forth
The Number Twenty car was about to start when Dora arrived.

So she did not have to wait.

So she could just go.

So she would not need to stand waiting.

"Are you with us or not, Dora?" Motorman Merry. Since childhood, she'd ridden with him on the Number Twenty.

Dora boarded.

The car would move now.

Right away, it did. That was good. The noise was good to hear, clackety-sing along the rails.

The car carried her along. She herself didn't move but the car moved her. Good, because Dora could not be still, nor had she strength to move. *I pulled all of Marjo's weight, though.*

Cordova, already. Too fast. Crossing Columbia now, clackety-hum. Dora would be home before she wanted to be. When would she ever want to be at home again?

She would never want to go back where she had just come from, that hospital ward.

Main, already. In no time at all the car would cross Heatley Gore Jackson Clark Commercial and reach Wall. There she must get off the Number Twenty and in the rain walk all alone to Cambridge Street, one foot after another, and up its wooden sidewalk and over the muddy pebbles to the Cowans' front stairs and across the porch. She must glance at Miss Dearing's door, glance away. She must turn her key, open her own door and step inside, all alone, in the silence, and set her purse on the hall table that wobbled. Take off her hat. Shake off raindrops. Set her umbrella on the pink chenille mat. Breathe in camphor. How the stuff stayed in the air! All this must be done; it could not be helped.

Dora put forward one foot after another and did what must be done.

To delete all evidence that four particular humans had lived for over a decade in a certain rented house—how surprisingly quick and simple! Soon those familiar spaces stood empty. They shrank, in that paradoxical way of rooms when their furniture and people are withdrawn.

Dora could have worked even faster if the Cowans' landlady, next door, hadn't fussed and fussed and called the neighbours in.

"And you only eighteen, Dora!"

"What's to become of a wild girl like you?"

"This terrible terrible flu."

"Oh, it's awful. Young Mr. Evans from the corner store. Old Mrs. Mackenzie." Mrs. Findlay savoured the telling. "To St. Paul's in the morning and dead before dinner, she was."

"At the Chinese hospital the man nurse died and no decent white girl'll go *there*. Dying like flies, they are."

"Awful. They say it's a judgement on us."

"They say...."

Dora closed the door. Alone she scrubbed and stacked. Her mother, her father, her brother surrounded her in a thousand poses. Their lips moved. Behind these shades trembled Marjo; Owen grinned and winked. The tall sad boy stopped running.

She washed, sorted, packed in boxes, going on, one foot forward after another.

Her mother's pearl necklace from Granny Cowan was in pawn, but Dora could not find the ticket anywhere.

Mrs. Findlay advised selling the family's furniture. "It'll only be a burden, Dora. You'll be in a little rented room and have no use for that heavy lot." Again came the neighbours. They bought vigorously. Mrs. Findlay herself took the bird's-eye maple table for her Triumph Street house and told the tenants, "In all of Highlands you won't find another landlady who provides such quality furnishings."

To her neighbours, Mrs. Findlay reported never seeing a bereaved person cry as little as Dora. "Something unnatural about that girl. Of course, when you remember what she...." Nid-nod, all the heads. Nid-nod, nid-nod.

Dora pulled out her brother's Army kit bag from under his bed. Inside lay his dirty socks, pairs and pairs, stiff with French dirt and Alan's sweat. Dora couldn't stop crying. When after a long time she still could not stop, she got off the floor and found a jacket and crossed the rainy street to Marjo's house.

Since August, Marjo's mum had shunned Dora, her daughter's best friend; now her hands comforted. Marjo and Mrs. McEwan stroked Dora's long hair and held her until the tears gave out.

Back in hot August Marjo's dad had shouted, "Our door is closed to you, miss, from this day forward." But now Mr. McEwan went with Dora, to help her talk to the minister at All Saints, Mr. Nurse, and to the man at the Union Steamship office. He dealt with Mrs. Findlay, who even before the funerals was fussing about December's rent and about a torn screen on the meatsafe in the Cowans' kitchen.

Constantly, as if back at Macdonald Elementary doing memory work for a history test, Dora reviewed the dates.

On the first of November 1918, Alan's filthy clothes came back from France with most of him. His left eye stayed *over there*, having departed its socket at Amiens on the eighth of August. ("But he was always so *handsome!*" sighed his mother, yet secretly she thought the black eye-patch Byronic and becoming.) His blond curls were so dirty and greasy that she cried.

The war ended on the eleventh.

On the seventeenth, the Cowans gave a welcome-home "do" for Alan, with friends and neighbours. Exhausted, the returned soldier fell asleep before the party ended and so upset his mother. She feared her son would be thought rude.

On the twenty-first Mr. Cowan accompanied Alan to the doctor to discuss his son's injured remaining eye, his asthma, his headaches and insomnia and eczema, and an oddity: once-loved foods like cream, liver, and eggs now smelled loathsome to him.

Father and son had to wait a long time to see the medical man, and then Dr. Marlow was abrupt, as if his thoughts were elsewhere. Mr. Cowan was quite put out.

Alan and Mrs. Cowan felt poorly next day, but Mr. Cowan jollied them along. "Buck up!" The soldier's father proposed taking Alan around among the neighbours. He wanted another celebratory beer, another, another. He wanted to exhibit his living son.

On the twenty-fourth Charlie Cowan himself felt poorly, very poorly, far worse than his wife and son. Dr. Marlow made a house call on the twenty-fifth. Then Dora lost control of the dates.

Confusion, panic

The parents bewildered, collapsing, pitiable

Kettles boiling

White enamel basins full of vomit

Stench of uncontrolled bowels and bladders

Alan whispering, as Dora wiped his buttocks clean for the third time in an hour, "Could be back in the field hospital!"

Alan's breath horribly sour

Reek of camphor camphor camphor

The heaving of tears: Betty Cowan wept far less than her husband, stared barefaced, dry-eyed at death

By day and night, the treadle sounding overhead: Miss Dearing sewing, sewing

Hospital

At all hours, Dora riding back and forth on the Number Twenty, alone

Reading the headlines alone, reading the statistics

In Vancouver, two hundred dead of the Spanish flu

Three hundred dead

Four hundred

Church services cancelled, theatres closed

Five hundred

Dora walking from ward to ward, bed to bed, one foot forward after another

Holding hands

Washing, wiping, listening, sponging, covering, soothing, holding, crying, staring

Staring along the rows of beds at the dying

So many many young people! This flu loved the young

Kissing the cold foreheads

Kissing

The treadle running, overhead

Laundry? In all that, there had been no time for Dora to open Alan's dunnage bag and do his laundry. Eventually a man from the Army took away Private Cowan's kit, French dirt and all.

To life in a housekeeping room on Templeton, Dora brought some knives and forks and blankets and plates and towels and the coffeepot and her own bed and her clothes and her tall jar of buttons and her mother's bureau and bits of jewellery and the tablecloth from Niagara Falls that her parents had picked out on their honeymoon and a photo album and Alan's 1916 *Boys' Own Annual* and the bathroom scales and the Toby jug that came with her father from England. And that was about it. She stared at her small possessions, piled on bed and bureau, and remembered Owen's fat burlap bag—his "collection."

As the coffins were carried into All Saints—the pall-bearers putting one foot forward after another—Dora watched from the sidewalk. She could only think of the rector's name. Less than a month before, she and Alan had snickered at it, during the service of thanksgiving for the war's end. "Nursey, Nursey!" the sister and brother whispered to each other, giggling.

Mrs. Cowan *ssshhd* her grown-up children. "Really!"

Now a sleety Arctic outflow blew off the Inlet and up the hill to All Saints, disarranging Dora's fascinator. She pulled her coat tight about her body but still her eyes teared in the cold. With her hanky, she blotted her face.

Standing thus, she caught the eye of the *Province* man, sent by an editor who'd read the triple obit and thought there might be something worth snapping. This photographer's morning assignment had been at Granville and Hastings, where for the very first time in Vancouver a policeman directed traffic. That big white-gloved man with his magisterial gestures of control, and now this young girl's floating hair, the coffins, the way she hugged her plump body as if she owned nothing else in the world....

Readers all over the city sighed for the girl with the wind-blown tresses and prayed for deliverance. The wire services took Dora's image to the Island, the North, the Interior, the prairies, even Toronto, though the *Globe* did not use it. Vancouver's reporters took the Number Twenty to Cambridge Street, to get more, more.

The *World* found the dressmaker. Back in August, Miss Pearl Dearing had literally spat at Dora. "Wicked, sinful girl! Shame, Dora, to break God's word." Now she denied knowing Miss Cowan's whereabouts.

The *Province* found Mrs. Findlay. Sadly, the landlady had nothing new to tell except that December's rent was paid. (She'd got double, from Dora *and* the new tenants, but did not say so.)

Mr. and Mrs. McEwan took Dora in and closed their door. Dora stayed away from windows. If a knock sounded, she ran upstairs (one foot forward after another).

In Marjo's bedroom, the girls spent hours talking of their schooldays, playing with clothes, not talking of August, not talking of the deaths.

They cut each other's hair. In high school, Marjo's fly-away strawberry blond had produced a desirable Gibson Girl look, but this was now passé. Dora, scissors in hand, did not hesitate, but even so her friend insisted, "Shorter, shorter!" Then Marjo looked in the mirror, giggling. "You'd think I'd put my fingers in a light socket!" Her parents were not pleased but because of Dora's bereavement said little.

Trimmed to chin-length, Dora's hair waved agreeably. Grief had thinned her cheeks. Marjo's mum loaned her a coat that hung heavily on her, waistless, double-breasted, a garment for a middle-aged woman. Dora smiled in the mirror. Her facial muscles bent stiffly.

Thus the girls were transformed.

Finally, after days and days inside, Dora ventured out of the house with Marjo, on a rainy afternoon just as the winter light was failing, to take the Number Twenty downtown and see the shop windows all decorated for Christmas. To ride the streetcar, the death-car, was a difficult prospect: Dora said nothing but put one foot forward after another as she walked with Marjo to the stop and waited. Several men watched with the girls as the streetcar turned off Garden Drive and shone down the watery slope. Dora breathed deeply and boarded.

"Very sorry, very sorry, Dora," said Motorman Merry.

Dora got her hanky out to blot her face.

"That's her all right," said one of the men.

"Miss Cowan? Miss Cowan, just a few questions for you...."

In the shouting scramble, hands grabbed Dora's arm, Marjo cried out, and the two girls struggled for the door, barking their shins on metal seats and steps. August...this was just like August. Only this time Dora was trapped doubly, inside the streetcar, and this time no Owen was there to reach out his strong hand for hers.

"Miss Cowan!" Motorman Merry blocked the reporters while the girls stumbled into the rainy street, soldiers struggling to get back to their own lines. Raging and weeping they ran to Cambridge Street (one foot forward after another). The rain fell on the exposed nape of Dora's neck—a new sensation.

A few days after this came the earthquake. Instantly the Vancouver press forgot Dora Cowan, motherless and fatherless and brotherless, alone at eighteen, possessed only of herself and a few dollars folded in a Toby jug.

In her housekeeping room, Dora pictured home. Fir floors gleamed in the winter sunshine. The radiator knob filled Dora's hand but did not warm it; the furnace was out of sawdust. Unaccountably, Mrs. Findlay hadn't noticed the chip on the bathroom tiles where Charlie Cowan had smashed the cough syrup he used to mask the alcohol on his breath.

In January 1919 when the epidemic's crisis was well past, Mrs. Findlay got the Spanish flu and died, intestate. All her houses were sold at public auction. Her tenants on Triumph Street skipped out, taking with them the bird's-eye maple table.

2 August 1918—Struggle

Dora, Owen, and Jonathan stood together in the same place and touched each other, all three, only once in their lives, on the north side of Dunsmuir Street in Vancouver on 2 August 1918.

Young adults, they were. Dora and Owen had more than seven decades of life ahead of them, Jonathan fewer.

They were still very near to their beginnings.

Jonathan, 2 July 1902

His mother Amelia woke at midnight because her milk was coming in. Happily, she felt her firm heavy breasts. Soon her sleeping child would nurse. She loved Jonathan. Amazing, how with every baby a new room opened in the house of the heart! Meanwhile the summer night was warm. The moon would be shining on the crinkles of English Bay.

"Let's go see the world, baby." With effort, Amelia got herself out of bed and went barefoot to the window, turned Jonathan to see, kissed his fuzzy head. "Look, sweetheart! You'll never in all your life have a grander view. See the ocean? See the stars? When you grow up, you'll learn them all." The infant's gaze veered about the heavens as he grasped his mother's finger.

Humming, Amelia gazed at the glittering sky till her feet grew very cold. Her legs wobbled, getting back to the bassinet and the bed; she collapsed there.

Weak. Chilly. Very chilly, but pulling up the bedclothes was too hard. She lay still and longed for the warmth of her baby. She wished not to feel the inner loosening she felt. She wished someone would help. The nurse heard nothing, for hours.

What awakened all in the house, except unconscious and hemorrhaging Amelia, was Jonathan's wail. He'd discovered hunger.

Owen, 17 September 1902

By the stable door, asters and goldenrod and sharp-smelling tansy bloomed, and a few late blackberries gleamed among the dry leaves. David Jones picked the fruit. Ellen had made no breakfast for him, let alone any noon meal. This thing was interminable, it seemed, and now the afternoon was getting the amber-glazed look of summer's slide into autumn on the Coast.

Welcoming the distancing warmth of the sun, David Jones rolled up his jacket for a pillow. The old worn tweed was soft. He bent his legs and tucked his hands between his thighs. A few ants, he saw, bustled about nearby. Their thoraxes shone black as the berries. On the hard-packed earth, they heaved themselves over twigs and grass tufts. David smiled at their toil and closed his eyes. *Owen* was a fine name. It meant *well-born*, and he went to sleep while his son arrived in the world.

Dora, autumn 1900

At two months, baby Dora's eyes focused on the sparkling brooch Mrs. Findlay wore at her lapel.

"There's a pretty girl, there," cooed the boarding-house keeper as the infant lay stiffly on her arm. *Of all the plain poor mites I ever saw!*

Then Mrs. Findlay jabbed in her hat pin and set off to take another hard look at those meat safes, for her new houses.

On the humming streetcar, she fell to thinking about all those years ago when the CPR train had snorted out of Toronto's Union Station with herself aboard, alone, having abandoned shiftless Findlay unwitting in his hungover sleep. She'd headed out the long way west, alone, across those oceanic provinces and endless territories, alone, herself still young and thin and dreaming along with all the other passengers of how, at the end of the weary journey to Terminal City, they would make a fresh start out here on the Coast.

2 August 1918

Dora sat. She smoothed the green cotton folds of her skirt and stared at the willow-ware platter on the dresser.

Marjo would need support. Girl chums walking arm in arm were common—but how to boost Marjo up on the streetcar without people noticing her weakness? With luck they'd get a seat at the front, not have to stand as the car jolted and turned. But if Motorman Merry sat at the Number Twenty's wheel and wanted a chat? If he noticed Marjo looked off? Merry's lantern-jawed face rose before Dora, as if she could touch the dry brown wen on his temple.

"Your friend. Her packing's in," that voice whispered. A rustling white bulk settled by Dora, a female rampart of carbolic and Yardley's Violet between her and the others nearby.

All that china on the dresser—did people eat here? In this ante-room for girls having things done to them for which no words existed? This was just an ordinary house, plain boxcar-red among its sisters here on West Fourth in Kitsilano. A vine drooped over the front porch. In this ordinary dining room, the Welsh dresser held flowery plates and tureens in blue, green, rose. Dora's mother had a willow-ware platter just like that.

"I said, *her packing's in*," the woman breathed, peering at Dora. Treacle-brown, those eyes resembled Miss Acorn's, of Domestic Science—but that austere classroom never smelled so.

"What does that mean?" Dora whispered back.

Seven girls and two women in their thirties, all trying to overhear, gazed down at the shabby Brussels carpet.

"Gauze," replied the nurse, if she was one, in exactly Miss Acorn's didactic tone. "Surgical gauze. Yards, all packed in, righty-tight-o. Sterile, of course. Sometimes there's a bit of a bleed from the you-know-what."

"Can my friend go soon?"

"An hour." Across the room ticked a grandfather clock. The bulk heaved up and left the room.

Dora smoothed the green cotton and let the pattern of the Brussels fill her own vision. If the streetcars came right, she and Marjo could get home by four. Their fathers would still be at work; Mrs. Cowan at All Saints, rolling bandages or packing food for the war effort; Mrs. McEwan at home with her younger children. She would assume Marjo-not-home meant Marjo-at-Dora's. *A bit of a bleed....*But Marjo could rest before the supper deadline of six. Then both girls must sit, fresh and lively, at either the McEwan or the Cowan table.

Time went on. Pale Marjo appeared.

Passing under the faded vine and down the steps, Marjo leaned hard on Dora. Delightedly they saw the streetcar coming.

"But why's it going so fast, Dora? He's not stopping!"

The destination sign in the car window read CAR BARNS.

"Never mind. Look, there's another."

But this too clacked past, and a third.

"Why won't they stop for us?" Marjo was crying already.

"Sit down on the grass. Rest." Dora stepped on to the track and waved at the coming car. The motorman raised his fist at her but braked. The girl below, the man above talked, gestured. The car moved on. Frowning, Dora came back and sank down by Marjo.

"It's a strike. Some man's been shot. Someone called Godson."

"Oh, Dora, how will we ever get home?"

"He says three men died."

Suddenly the door of the house behind them framed the nurse's bulging figure. "No, no, girls! Not on our lawn. You'll draw attention. Away with you now." The slam fluttered the vine.

At a café near the corner of Granville Dora put a fork in Marjo's cold fingers, made her nibble pie and sip sugary coffee. Meanwhile Dora rubbed her friend's other hand. Gradually Marjo began taking real mouthfuls. Dora watched, hungry. She had only carfare left now—no money for a jitney. Marjo had emptied her purse in that house. Certainly she could not walk home. In this neighbourhood, no familiar door would swing open to the girls. Downtown, though—that cross motorman had spoken of a mass meeting, a rally. Surely there Dora could find someone she knew who could help? But what to say or ask? Putting her hand to her mouth, she smelled carbolic and violet.

"I know who he meant!" Marjo exclaimed as they left the café. "Goodwin. Why didn't you have pie, Dora? Last night Daddy was yelling at Mummy, *He should be shot again. Once isn't enough!* Oh, he'll be angry! He just raged when the motormen went out in June, and now this. Where are you taking me?"

"We'll find a safe resting place for you. I'll get help."

The girls walked slowly north, away from houses and among garages, auto shops, dyers and cleaners. The air was thick with chemicals. Down a wooden roadway between lumber sheds they passed through great halls of stacked resinous timbers. Silent.

"Where is everybody? Why aren't they working, Dora?"

Near the entrance of Rat Portage Lumber, sheds and lean-tos were clustered. Shouts and angry calls came faintly from the Creek, but no one was nearby. Dora picked a shed half-concealed by another. In the girls crept. Tramps had slept and drunk and pissed there; with distaste the girls sniffed, yet when Marjo lay down—fell down, more accurately—on the piled rags and newsprint in the corner, her whole body eased in relief.

"I'll be back for you, Marjo, soon as ever I can."

By the time Dora was halfway over Granville Bridge, running, pairs and trios and groups of men were moving past her, many in uniform. Limping. One-eyed. Bandaged. Coming off the span the men took over the street, shoving and spreading so as to slow the traffic.

Near Dora, a soldier on crutches lost his balance and knocked down a boy on a bicycle with a cart attached behind. Other soldiers boosted their crippled comrade up on to a willing running board—he waved his crutch and cheered—and then they set the boy back on his bike and ran before him, north on Granville, clearing his way among cars, jitneys, carts, trucks. With glee the boy looked back. His face brightened, seeing Dora. The bike veered.

"Owen! Owen!"

"Catch me! Catch me if you can!" He turned away and pedalled madly. Tears burned in Dora's eyes as the crowds shoved past her, gaining speed now, trotting past Drake to

Davie and thence east to Richards and Homer, their anger a hum, a buzz, a growl.

"To the Labour Temple!"

"Get the German traitors!"

"Bolsheviks! String 'em up!"

Trying to stay on the horde's edge yet keep Owen in view, Dora ran hard, east by north and beside the Cambie Street Grounds. About the Armouries, the khaki uniforms were thick. She held her purse close. Then at Dunsmuir all movement stopped. Struggle as she might, Dora could make no way across the noisy crush of men. Until the crowd's tilting sway suddenly took her right off her feet as if she were wading up a river in spate, so her body was pressed against one unknown soldier after another; she saw their angry faces, inflamed or blanched, saw the bristles and the pores, felt their limbs jerking. Then the veterans began to push west on Dunsmuir towards the Labour Temple. Dora glimpsed Owen, ahead. Moving with the current, she strove diagonally across the shouting column—"Kill the Hun-lovers! String up Midgeley!"—until on reaching the other side of the street she barked her shin on the high wooden sidewalk. Pain shot through her leg.

Owen grinned down at her. He straddled the bicycle, reached out a hand for her, and pulled. Up Dora came to face him, and his arm went round and held her tight. All round, the noise was tremendous.

In his other hand Owen held a big paper bag of boiled sweets, bright pink and green and yellow.

"Want a candy, sweet Dora Cow-Cow?" he shouted.

Dora slapped his face so hard that he dropped the bag and candies showered among the shuffling smashing feet.

"Bitch! I'm selling them! They'll all get broken!" screamed Owen. He jumped down to scrabble on the street as the cursing veterans tripped and kicked past him.

Dora bent over and shrieked, "Help me. Marjo could die."

A roar rose from the men. Movement rolled through the column, and the crowd surged towards the Temple in a ragged formation that solidified into a thunderingly matched pace, a massed slow run that made the boardwalk shudder. Candies lay bright in Owen's dirty hands. Saliva filled Dora's mouth.

"It wasn't me poked Marjo," Owen shouted, sorting through the sweets. "*And* I told her where she could get it taken care of. Don't forget that, Dora Cow-Cow."

The human river beside them roared louder than ever as the men chanted, "Throw them out! String them up!" But the sound, being more regulated, allowed the two to hear each other.

"Don't call me that! You know Marjo. She's a friend."

"Not of mine. I haven't got any *friends*." Owen dropped filthy candies between the planks. "Other people's business."

"Rule Britannia!" The column of men thudding alongside them broke into song.

Dora snatched a candy wrapper. "You stole these from Snelgrove's on Powell, didn't you? Started a fire in the rubbish, so he'd run out back and you could grab them?"

Owen grinned. "Mrs. Snelgrove ran outside too. She's so fat she looks funny running, Dora. Waddles like a duck-duck."

The last round ended: "Never, never shall be slaves."

Across Dunsmuir, a single voice cried, "Don't do it, boys! We're not Americans—we don't lynch—we're British!"

The crowd heaved and buckled and boiled. Stones arced through the air and fell, unheard. Veterans, long-shoremen, motormen shouted and punched, bit and kicked, thrashed at each other with crutches and canes.

Owen dropped the bag of candy into the cart behind his bicycle. Dora took hold of his strong shoulders and spoke into his dirty ear. "Why are they fighting?"

His tongue flickered on her earlobe. "Ginger Goodwin. The longshoremen are all out for him. They say he had TB. That the police shot him in the back. But the soldiers are glad he's dead. They'd like to kill some more people too." Owen's arms tightened round Dora, his hands slid on her sides. Then he pulled away. "I'm off, Dora. Their throats aren't sore enough yet. I'll wait at the Empress, for the rally."

At this moment half a dozen fighting men burst out of the ranks and crashed on to the sidewalk so that Owen fell over hard in a jangle of bicycle while Dora sank under ponderous male flesh grunting out of control, writhing, blundering. Muscle and buckle imprinted her skin. Angry sweat filled her nostrils.

A longshoreman tripped over a soldier's boot. As he fell towards Dora, a moving stone met his head. The quality of this longshoreman's dropping changed. His arm was out-stretched to break his fall, he was all grimace and force—then in an instant he lolled limp. His skull struck the sidewalk's sharp corner.

"Midgeley!" came a scream. "They've got Midgeley out the second-floor window!" Everyone ran on again.

Dora still held her purse. Her left shin had taken a kick, so the skin was split and turning blue, and her left thigh another. The pocket was almost torn off her skirt. She sat on the street beside the wounded longshoreman, touching her scraped cheek and checking her palm for blood. Her ribs hurt. Roars and snarls came from the Labour Temple, and crashes as of machinery thrown about, and window-smashing, and the wrenching sound of timbers torn from their places and battered against stone.

On the grey dirt of the street there stood before Dora a man wearing shoes. Not boots—beautiful leather shoes. Dark brown, not new, yet so richly polished and supple that all she could think was *Better than new.* The shoelaces had fringed toggles at their ends that hung like tiny brooms.

Now facing these shoes came Owen's old boots, scuffed and half-broken and knotted up with string.

Dora looked up to see a tall boy with a big head. He hunkered down now to inspect the too-calm face of the longshoreman, on whose forehead blood beaded in a neat line towards his hair. Dust floated on to that beautiful leather of his shoes. This boy's trousers were of fine wool, his shirt of best-quality Egyptian cotton. His face and hands were clean and his expression uncertain, even sad.

"Get the skunk!"

"Make Midgeley kiss the flag!"

"For king and country, make him! Make him!"

Dora and Owen glanced at each other. What would this West Side creature do?

He said to them earnestly, "We must help this poor man. Get him to St. Paul's." He saw Owen's bike. "We'll use that cart."

"No. It's mine."

"Make Midgeley kiss it!"

Furious cheers filled the air, snatches of "Britannia."

"Please," Dora begged. "Please, Owen?" She still felt the pressure of his hand, its slide up her body towards her breast.

Owen glared.

The boy reached into his pocket. "How much?"

"Now Thomas! Make Thomas kiss it! Make the traitor do it!"

"Men, we'll show these Germans how Vancouver deals with traitors! Keep 'em down on the ground there! Let us at 'em!"

Jonathan's long fingers placed coins in Owen's small square hand. He counted them.

Then three young people lifted the fallen man and got him more or less on to the cart, though he was a big fellow and his limbs flopped over. The tall boy rolled up his jacket, gently slid it under the unknowing head. That tender movement: Dora could not imagine her father or her brother or indeed any man she knew making it.

Owen saw her reaction and his face hardened.

The longshoreman's head was bleeding now, all the beads broken and spilling.

Owen turned away.

Dora grabbed his arm. Electrifying. "Please come with me?"

Owen stamped. "*I* told her the place! *I* stole the bicycle! That's *enough!*" He squeezed into the crowd and disappeared.

The tall boy gestured courteously towards the bicycle, and Dora got up on to the handlebars.

With the cart tilting and clunking over the roadbed, Jonathan pedalled south on Cambie, the maiden before him on his noble steed. To the rescue! The nape of her neck shone with fat drops of sweat. Slowly the riot's clamour sank, becoming a strange aural background for streets already strange without the metallic song of the streetcars. Georgia and Robson and Smithe lay bare, except for random clusters of shouting men.

"Have you to help someone else?" asked the boy. The bicycle jounced through the afternoon heat. Dora did not respond, thinking of Marjo in that smelly shed. "Could I help you?" he asked. No answer to this, either. Was Marjo bleeding?

At Helmcken he turned towards the hospital and the sun.

A boy like this would have a watch. "What is the time?"

"Almost four," said the tall boy sadly.

At St. Paul's more tumult met them, for their cargo was only one of many arriving pell-mell, by ambulance and jitney and in the arms of friends or comrades, at what was essentially a construction site. A new wing was underway, the courtyard a maze of stacked building materials. None of the medical staff rushing about in the confusion approached the trio.

"Look at him," said the boy. The longshoreman was much paler now. The moaning Dora heard was his. She waited. Her chance, Marjo's chance, was imminent.

"I'll carry him inside—you keep an eye on the bike."

When the boy lifted the limp body, the injured man cried out. This finally brought a young agitated doctor. "A head wound, and you've been banging his skull like a drum in that wretched cart? Stupid boy, stupid! Oh, God, well, there's a stretcher, here, help carry him in. No, this way, careful, the door. Perhaps there'll still be…perhaps we can still…." Obediently the boy carried his burden.

The helpless maiden scrambled on to the bicycle and rode away, full tilt, and as she swerved out of the hospital's courtyard, Dora heard the tall boy cry out to her, "Wait, wait! I'll help you!" She pedalled as hard as she could.

When Marjo saw Dora and the bike and cart, she laughed, a high titter reminiscent of schooldays. The shed stank of vomited apple pie. "Why were you so long, Dora? I feel awful. Down there—I'm all stuffed. I've nothing left to throw up but I still want to." Marjo began to cry, but no blood stained her skirt or the rags and papers in the shed, to Dora's deep relief.

"Get in," she said. "We have to hurry." Marjo resisted the cart, tried to sit on the handlebars; after only a few turns she slid helplessly off and wept more as she squeezed herself down into the box. "It's like a coffin." Dora rummaged through the ragpile and found an old raincoat. It concealed Marjo's head and shoulders. Then Dora got on the bike and figure-eighted about the mill yard, testing the weight to be pulled, bracing herself.

"Which way? I'm dizzy. It smells awful in here!"

"Broadway."

"But Dora, the hills…I can't bear it."

"Keep your head down, Marjo! There's a riot on Dunsmuir. We can't go through downtown."

Dora began to wheel, past the iron works and stables and coal yards, the fish packers and the City Pound, heading east, and as she pedalled she considered her route. Eventually she could turn north on Main to reach Powell, but that would take her by two busy train stations and right through Chinatown. Too many people would see a fat girl in a dirty torn green skirt, her cheek and ankle scraped, her hair a mess, an ugly fat girl riding a man's bicycle with a delivery cart full of—what? Something heavy, something covered up that shouldn't be.

A boy could do it, of course. Owen could do it easily, and from all his riding about the city he'd have no trouble with any hill. No. Dora would ride the alleys parallel to Broadway: no shops, few people. Further east she'd make her turn north, maybe near Laura Secord School. And she must pedal fast, fast! Because the melted-gold look of the sun on False Creek said the time must now be nearer five than four.

All the way, Dora's ankle and thigh and ribs and face hurt. Because the bicycle was too big for her, riding strained her whole body, while the pull of the cart made steering difficult. Marjo several times cried, "Stop!" so she could retch up more pie and coffee and at last a thin bile. Dora rode and pushed and pulled the bicycle and its freight up and down the raw roads that scored the hills. She rode over streetcar tracks and train tracks and mud, and along stretches of alley so potholed she did not dare ride but walked the bike, while Marjo groaned at every jolt.

The gears streaked Dora's green skirt with oil, and somehow the smears found their way on to her waist too. Sighing, she thought of that tall boy's clean white shirt. A year or so before, she'd worked with Miss Dearing on cotton like that; the dressmaker got Dora to peer closely at the fine weave and even to smell the cloth, so she would learn its character.

The dressmaker's sketch showed a loose smock. "A

dozen of these, for Mrs. Crosse's Chinese cook," the dressmaker explained. "She's in the West End."

"All this cloth?" Dora fingered the fat white roll.

"Oh no." Miss Dearing sniffed. "When I'm done with the cook's duds, a real shirtmaker, a *man*, will make up the rest for the *gentlemen* of the house. That Mrs. Crosse wouldn't let a mere dressmaker make a shirt, I'll be bound."

Now Dora smelled her own pungent sweat, felt it rolling down her body.

At Woodland Park she almost stopped because she was so thirsty and the blackberries shone ripe, and again almost at the water fountain in the schoolyard at Macdonald . . . but instead Dora went on and on and on.

She passed the lane where Owen lived. Where was he? Perhaps at that rally now, selling candy to soothe the gritty throats of men who'd screamed and marched and fought for hours? Owen's lips were full. When he grinned, they stretched wide. Dora rode on till she turned the corner of Powell on to Wall Street.

Awkwardly, because her left leg had gone to sleep, Marjo got herself out of the cart. She cried as feeling pierced her limb.

Dora wheeled Owen's bicycle and cart down deep, invisibly deep, into the tunnels of salal and blackberry and bindweed that sprawled and tangled along the Wall Street slope. Emerging, with trembling fingers she picked berries and ate greedily in spite of the thorns scarifying her arms and legs. That sad boy with the big head—Dora would bet he'd never in his life eaten so. In her dry mouth the glistening black nodules burst, painfully sweet.

"Blackberries, Marjo?"

"I don't want to be sick again."

The western sky over the city was deeper blue now. Curls of pearly cloud rippled over the colour. Because of the strike, the smoke above False Creek hung sparse; the summer evening's light gilded the stained air, and nearer to the girls the light gilded some sawdust and a few planing curls that drifted in the breeze off Cedar Cove.

"Your house first, or mine?"

They considered. Mrs. Cowan's annoyance at Dora's lateness would quickly turn to anxiety for Marjo's—what would they say? *Her terrible tummy upset.* Mr. Cowan in his evening stupor was no threat, either. Mr. McEwan, though, would be alert with anger at his tardy daughter, the more so because of the strike and Ginger Goodwin.

"And while I rest at your house, your mum can go tell mine I'm all right," Marjo summed up. "Then she won't be so mad."

The girls licked their hankies and dabbed at each other's cheeks, smoothed and shook out their skirts. Dora hoped desperately she could get to her room and change before her mother saw her.

She looked closely at Marjo's skirt. "I can't see any blood."

"I feel dreadful."

Starting up Cambridge Street, Dora took Marjo's arm; her friend's elbow trembled by her ribs. Had that vision of the girl-chums arm in arm come to her only hours before? Was this still Friday? Willow-ware, the running men, candies and snarling screams, stones, kicks, that tall boy's sad face and his rich-people's shoes, the water bright under Granville Bridge as she pedalled back to the sawmill and Marjo....

In his shirt sleeves, his belly bulging over his trouser band, Mr. Cowan stood with Mr. McEwan in the middle of Cambridge Street. Before the two fathers cringed Dora's mother. Mrs. McEwan stood near. From their doorsteps, neighbours watched.

"You stupid woman!" shouted Mr. Cowan. "You might as well be a traitor and be done with it! This Goodwin's a disgrace to this country. D'you hear me, Betty? The man's a Bolshevik."

His wife sobbed. "I won't say what you want me to, Charlie Cowan. You don't know a mother's love."

"Oh, God." He flung up his arms. Beer splurted from the bottle in his right hand. "Now look what you've made me do!"

"I didn't! Not any more than today when you dropped that cough syrup. You broke that bathroom tile, Charlie, and you'll have to deal with Mrs. Findlay. You never—"

"Mrs. Cowan," broke in Marjo's father, all earnest patience, "your boy's in *France*, perhaps in that battle shaping up towards Amiens. How can you speak for a draft evader? A man with so little patriotism that he *ran away* into the woods? Aimed his rifle at the Dominion Police? Your good Alan would never do such a thing. Surely you don't think...."

"She doesn't think, McEwan." Dora's father gestured repudiation. "No arguing with women. They're not capable of it, really they're not." He took a pull on his beer.

Mrs. Cowan's face was flushed and wet. "Goodwin had TB. They shouldn't have made him go, nor my Alan neither.

Don't you laugh, Charlie. You didn't care and Alan was angry, but I tried. His eyes are weak, I told that army doctor, weak ever since he was a tiny." Mrs. Cowan took a deep breath and faced the men. "Mr. McEwan, my boy could be meeting his Maker right now—but he shouldn't even *be* in France! No more should a man with TB. And I don't care where he hid or who he shot. I don't care." Mrs. Cowan wept.

As the girls halted by the adults, Marjo's bearing changed. Still clasping Dora's arm, she leaned sideways and opened her mouth to vomit bile. She fell then. A red twisted line trailed from underneath Marjo's skirt and down her leg, turned at her ankle, and dripped on to the packed dirt of the street.

Before dawn, Dora got up. She'd hardly slept; she couldn't lie on her back or side because of the weals where her father had thrashed her, and lying on her front hurt her breasts. Her body stung, ached, twinged. She slipped out of the kitchen door. *Find Owen. Warn him.*

There'd been rain in the night, and the back steps still shone wet when she sat down to put on her shoes and tie them.

Dora walked downhill. The Inlet shone. Light from the east radiated in the mist rising off the water. After the riot and the rally, the city lay in worn-out quiet.

Would he be home? Would he be awake? Would Ellen shout curses and throw things out the loft window?

Turning off Semlin, Dora saw Owen coming up the alley towards her. He carried a big burlap bag and grinned at her in happy surprise.

August 1918—Owen, Leaving the City

Though his burlap bag was heavy, Owen found it pleasant to walk eastward through the city so early in the morning. After the riot and the rally, motormen and soldiers and longshoremen had roamed till all hours, fighting and singing drunkenly through the downtown streets and along the waterfront and under the bridges. Everywhere, broken glass crunched underfoot. Solitary in the crowds, sober Owen looked sharp and found easy pickings in all that confusion. He did well.

All those rioting roaming white men were mad, completely mad, the Indians said when Owen dropped in at Snauq for a rest before heading home. Tom was there. He was a regular visitor from up the Coast, Bella something; a big man, tonight he laughed till tears filled the creases on his cheeks and overflowed. Owen was glad. He and Tom had met at Snauq before, and Owen liked this big joky fellow who taught him a bit of Chinook and didn't use his size to make small men feel small. They sat companionably by a bonfire, eating candy.

Now Owen's body buzzed with the false energies of sleeplessness and hunger; his step was light, his eyes wide open. The last bright candy melted in his mouth as he strode along Cordova. Soon, at home, he would drop down on the chesterfield and be asleep in a minute. In half a minute. In fifteen seconds.

The Inlet shone silver, brown, sleek as a seal. Owen turned south on Victoria and then east into his own alley.

Hurrying to him down the slope was a long-haired girl in green, running, lips parted and skirt a-flutter, holding out her two hands to him. Fresh sunlight shone behind and around her so she was outlined in radiance, yet her face was indistinct. The strands of her gilt hair lifted and waved in the light breeze to make a floating aureole. "Owen!" the girl called. He stopped. He smiled. He put down his collection bag and held out his arms.

Faster she came, closer. How sweetly her breasts moved under her blouse! But now he saw Dora's face, all screwed up in tears.

Police. After that one word pushed out of Dora's mouth to hang heavy between those two in the clean morning air, Owen scarcely heard the others: *doctor, mother, hemorrhage, father....*

"That's enough."

"Your bike's on Wall, the cart too. In the blackberries."

"I said *enough*, Cow-Cow!" Abruptly Owen grabbed up his scavenging sack and brushed past Dora. "I'll have to leave."

At the stable he pulled off his boots and ran lightly up the steps to the loft.

In the breadbox lay a single Chelsea bun, rather stale. Chewing quietly, Owen looked at the old brass bed where his mother snored. At the roots, her red hair showed yellowish-grey.

The strip of lino across the floor, Owen saw, had nearly lost its pattern, once geometric—in his childhood, a great source of interest. The exposed jute was worn to strings.

Owen stuffed his burlap bag into hiding behind the beaten-down chesterfield. A blanket lay folded on its back; he lifted a woolly corner to his nose. Horse, still, faintly.

Ten minutes later, Owen used the outhouse one last time, a small bent figure, anxious because his shit wasn't coming quickly. Often he'd tested himself, seeing how many days he could go without a shit, squeezed his sphincter muscles till the pain backed up inside him like a snake and his appetite disappeared and a dreadful heavy feeling suffused his flesh. Now, though, the sunstripes coming through the rough boards began to warm and calm him. Owen sighed and opened his bowels.

That sun felt sweet as honey. Deep in the warm woods on Grouse, Owen calculated, he could sleep an hour or two on the slithery pine needles before moving on. Maybe he'd even spend the night on Hollyburn, find some forgotten moss-sheathed cabin and curl up there to think of Dora. In the morning, the resin smell in the woods would be strong. Then somehow he'd get himself to Gibson's and catch the *Cassiar* for Texada or Port Neville or.... Somewhere, anywhere up the Coast. But first he must reach the North Shore, and not by ferry either. *Full of Nosy Parkers.*

Owen stepped into the alley and looked both ways. Empty. Of course she was gone. Dora's floating honey-hair, her full blouse, the girl running to him with her hands open.... His body trembled. He slung his small rucksack over his shoulder. Above, Ellen snorted in the way that meant she would wake soon. Owen hurried.

Along the waterfront, keeping as much under cover as he could—though the few people out early on the Inlet took him for a child—Owen laboured eastward. Rocks and bull-kelp and driftwood. Towering arches of salmonberry, blackberry, salal. A heron that thrashed screeching out of reeds six feet off and startled Owen so he lost his balance and scraped his shin all bloody, which made him think angrily for a moment of that snob with his fancy leather shoes.

Snags, scrub, battered logs ... on and on Owen struggled, till he was past New Brighton and just east of the Narrows, where he found a boat to steal.

Still close to shore, Owen rowed on to a screen of overhanging shrubs; the oarlocks squeaked in the dawn quiet. He tied up and waited, drowsing. Owen rubbed at his bristly chin and decided to do just nothing about that. He would grow a beard, be unrecognizable. He watched the water. At the slack, when the Inlet got that ample brimming look, he'd cross.

Doing so some hours later, Owen met two deer swimming the other way, with their antlered heads sticking up high out of the saltchuck. They looked surprised to see him in the little rowboat.

Acknowledgements

For guiding me to many valuable sources relating to Vancouver's past and to matters medical, my thanks are due to the Vancouver Public Library (particularly Special Collections, Newspapers and Periodicals, History); to Special Collections at the University of British Columbia; and to the librarians of the Langara College Library.

Bruce Macdonald, author of *Vancouver: A Visual History*, was generous in his assistance. Researcher George Bain was most helpful. I learned a great deal from books and articles by Jean Barman, Robert K. Burkinshaw, John A. Cherrington, Chuck Davis, Henry Ewert, Daniel Francis, R.F. Hume, Pauline Johnson, Michael Kluckner, Rolf Knight, Ronald

Liversedge, Henry T. Logan, H.E. McDermot, Daphne Marlatt and Carole Itter, Susan Mayse, Robert McDonald, James V. Ricci, Veronica Strong-Boag and Kathryn McPherson, William Henry Walsh, Robin Ward, and The Working Lives Collective, among others...but any mistakes are my responsibility.

Conversations about older Vancouver with Ross Johnson and, long ago, with Ruth Bullock and Sally Creighton played a part in making this story.

At the Banff Writers' Studio in 1996, consultations with Audrey Thomas and Edna Alford were of great assistance.

For the excellent work done by my editor, Susan Renouf, and by my agent, Helen Heller, I am most grateful.

To Dean Sinnett, *sine quo non*, my thanks for making the computer behave. And thanks to Valence and Rhoda, for keeping the chair in the study warm.